W. H. Elliott

Block and Interlocking Signals

W. H. Elliott

Block and Interlocking Signals

ISBN/EAN: 9783337363543

Printed in Europe, USA, Canada, Australia, Japan

Cover: Foto ©Andreas Hilbeck / pixelio.de

More available books at **www.hansebooks.com**

Block and Interlocking Signals.

By W. H. ELLIOTT, Sig. Eng.,
C., M. & ST. P. R.R.

WHAT THEY ARE FOR.
WHAT THEY DO.
HOW THEY DO IT.

———•———

LOCOMOTIVE ENGINEERING,

NEW YORK.

1896.

CONTENTS.

BLOCK SIGNALING.

WHAT IT IS FOR. WHAT IT DOES.
HOW IT DOES IT.

By W. H. ELLIOTT,
Signal Engineer, C., M. & St. P. R.R.

CHAPTER I.

"What are we stopping for, conductor, out here in the woods? This is a limited train. What! stopped by a signal, a block signal, you say? Why, what is that? Oh, I see! You have a red blade projecting from the top of a pole to indicate to the engineer when the blade is moved up or down whether he may enter the block or not, the block being the piece of track extending to the next signal. So, then, when we are stopped by such a signal it means that another train is in the block, and we will have to wait until it has passed out."

And thus it is that to-day trains are being run through towns and cities, over mountains and prairie, through bridges and tunnels, in cuts and around curves with absolute safety, a fact not fully appreciated by the traveling public, but which becomes to the engineer, whose responsibility is lightened and from whom anxiety is removed, a guiding star, telling him that the track is his and that there will be no one to dispute it with him, for such little arguments, you know, are sometimes disastrous.

Block signaling, though limited in extent in this country, in proportion to the miles of track operated, is so rapidly being extended, not only from the natural increase of business and conse-

quent demands for a safe method of operation, but from the general knowledge being acquired of the advantages to be gained from such a system, that I believe an article on the subject would be both interesting and instructive. To the man well posted on signal matters, little that is new will be found, as this article is written more for those who are constantly guided by a signal, but have little idea of its construction.

The commencement of signaling may be said to begin with the use of the locomotive, for it soon became manifest that something would have to be devised, not only to prevent collisions between trains, but to give information to engineers regarding the position of switches and the right to go ahead. Many forms and devices were used in these early days, few of them being seen to-day, but which, as in the development of the locomotive, became stepping stones to things much better.

As each engineer pre-

1. Home Block Signal—" All Clear."
2. Home Block Signal—" Danger, Stop."
3. Distant Signal —" All Clear."
4. Home Block Signal—" Danger."

ferred his own devices to those of others, it followed, as a matter of course, that the practice was very varied, so much so in some cases that the safety signal on one road became the danger signal of another. Naturally enough, this state of things brought about many serious accidents, and finally resulted in a meeting being held by those interested, for the adoption of a standard form of fixed signal to be used by all the roads. The choice fell upon the "semaphore," a signal designed by Mr. Gregory in 1841, which indicates—by position and not by its form—whether the track is clear and the train has a right to proceed.

It was decided that a horizontal position of the blade should indicate "danger" or "stop;" a vertical position, "all clear" or "go ahead," and a position midway between these two, making an angle of forty-five degrees with the horizontal, "caution" or "proceed carefully."

Its construction was very much the same as that used to-day, consisting of a blade pivoted at the top of a pole and capable of being turned through about a quarter of a circle. The colored glasses for giving the night indications were carried in a separate frame pivoted lower down on the pole, instead of being held, as in modern practice, by the casting to which the blade is fastened. The blades for governing train movements in one direction were always put on the same side of the pole. In this country, the blade projecting on the right-hand side of the signal pole, as looked at from an approaching train, is the one that governs. In England, where all trains run on the left-hand track, signal blades projecting to the left side govern.

The signals were operated under what is called the "time interval system;" that is, not allowing one train to follow another into the block until the lapse of a certain period of time. When a train entered the block the signal was put at danger and kept there for five minutes, when it was pulled to a cautionary position, and after the lapse of five minutes more the signal was "cleared," giving the right to the next train to proceed.

Experience with this method of operation soon demonstrated that the principle was not correct. For while a train may have passed, a certain length of time, the signal gave no indication of how far it had gone. The many accidents occurring under this system stimulated the invention and adoption of electric indicators and telegraph instruments as a means of communication between signalmen, making it possible to keep a space interval between trains, and not allowing a second train to enter a block while it was occupied by the first. This method of blocking, keeping a space interval between trains, is the end to which all the modern systems of signaling are designed, although the methods by which this result is obtained vary considerably.

The next important principle to be developed was that the normal position of a signal should be at *danger*, not at safety; or, in other words, to assume that danger existed unless known to the contrary. For with a signal constructed as were those first used, on an accident happening to the apparatus, or in case of any of its parts becoming disconnected, it would at once fall to the "all clear" position, and no protection would be afforded a train in the block. An engineer, of course, not knowing that the signal was out of order, would take the indication as one intended for him and proceed accordingly, a result very likely to cause trouble, but for which he could not be blamed.

With the signal always remaining in the danger position, and being so constructed that any accident or breakage of the apparatus would cause it to assume the danger position, no accidents from this cause can happen, as trains would be stopped instead of being allowed to proceed.

In the most approved systems, the signal automatically returns to the danger position immediately upon a train entering the block, thus making it impossible for a second train to enter, as might easily occur—under the old system—should the signalman fail to return the signal to the danger position.

As showing the commencement of block signaling in this country, the exhibit of the Pennsylvania Railroad at the World's Fair, of a pole and ball signal used on the Newcastle & Frenchtown Railroad in 1832, is very interesting, the following information being obtained from a letter written by Mr. A. Feldpauche, principal assistant engineer of the P., W. & B. Ry., in regard to its use. The road was about 20 miles long, and the signals seem rather to have been used for conveying information from one end of the line to the other than for that of a block.

"When the train was just starting from Newcastle, the man

in charge of the signal at that point raised the ball to the top of the pole. The man at the next station, seeing the white ball raised by the first man, raised his ball to half the height of his pole. The men at the other stations, each on the lookout with his telescope, which, you will see in the cut, were placed in the guides provided for the purpose on the side of the pole, also raised their balls to half mast, thus conveying the information throughout the line that the train had started.

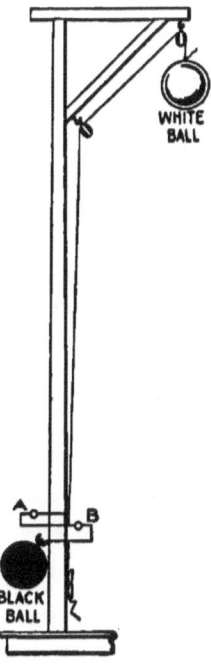

"When the train reached the first station, the man would immediately raise his ball to the top of the pole, as a signal both ways that the train had reached him, lowering his ball when the the train reached the next man ahead, this being repeated successively at each of the four stations.

"When a train, having passed one station, did not arrive at the next, or was seen to be in trouble in any way, the man at the station next nearer Newcastle would lower his white ball and substitute therefor a black ball, kept at hand for the purpose, and would raise it to the top of his pole as a signal to be successively transmitted to Newcastle, whence a relief train would be dispatched to the assistance of the regular train."

Block signaling may be said to be practiced in this country in two ways—that of "absolute" blocking, in which one train only is allowed to occupy a given block, and "permissive" blocking, where, under certain regulations, more than one train is allowed to enter.

From the definition of a block—"a section of a track between two signal stations, the use of which is controlled by fixed signals"—it is seen that where absolute blocking is maintained, both head and rear-end collisions are impossible, and were it not for the expense and occasional delay to traffic, such would be more generally practiced. It is a fact, which experience is demonstrating every day, that more trains can be run over a given piece of track and with greater safety by a properly arranged block system than by any code of rules that can be devised, and although one cannot show in figures how much can be saved to a road by immunity from accidents, it will certainly repay any investments made in apparatus and operators' wages.

More particularly is the problem of block signaling increasing in importance as the traffic on many roads is becoming too dense to be handled without such a system. Managers who thought that the results obtained by the English with absolute blocking could be ignored on account of the different conditions of operation in this country, are gradually finding it to be the only safe way to operate their roads.

In point of fact the means are already at hand, and any road having a telegraph wire and operators can, at a moment's notice, put the absolute blocking of all trains into effect, should conditions arise under which it would be desirable to do so. That many roads do not take advantage of this and train their operators is much to be regretted, and it is to be hoped that with the spread of information regarding the working of block systems and the safety to be gained by their use, managers will come to a full appreciation of their merits.

With roads using a block system, where, from considerations of expense, the blocks are of a greater length than is advisable, "permissive" blocking has, with certain restrictions, come very much into use. Although it is an abandonment of the "space" for that of a time interval, the results obtained are such as to make its use in many cases a matter of good business judgment.

Before describing the different methods of operating block

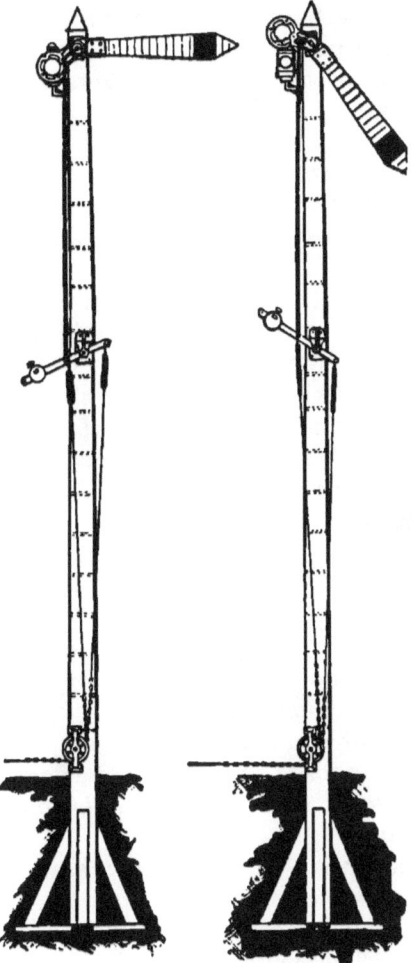

FIG. 5.

signals, it will be well to describe the construction of a semaphore signal and to discuss the interesting questions connected therewith.

As will be seen in Fig. 5, a casting is pivoted at the top of a pole which holds the blade and colored glass; this casting is called the arm plate. The blade is a thin board 5 feet long, tapering from 7 inches in width where bolted to the casting to 10 inches at its outer end. The end of the blade is often pointed, to more easily distinguish the block signal from other semaphore signals. The height of the pole, ordinarily, is about 25 feet above the ground, and a ladder bolted to its side allows of easy access to all the parts.

About midway of the pole is an iron lever called the balance lever, to which are attached the wires for operating the signal. An up-and-down rod connects this lever with the arm plate casting, being attached to the casting on the opposite end from the blade.

By putting a weight on the balance lever, it is seen that the blade will be greatly overbalanced, and will, of course, be held in the horizontal position until a force is exerted on the lever sufficient to lift this weight and lower the blade. This constructon fulfills the requirement that the "normal position of the signal should be at danger," as it calls for a direct effort on the part of the signalman to change the signal to the "all clear" position.

To give the different indications at night, a lamp is so placed that the light, when the signal is at danger, will show through a colored glass held in the arm plate casting, and will show an unobscured white light when at "all clear." While the signals for use in the day-time were going through the various changes from one of "form" to that of "position," those for use at night simply became a question of color, as nothing has as yet been found which compares with it in distinctness and simplicity. This question of the proper color to be used for the different night signals is one of great interest to all railroad men, and one which is being widely discussed.

What engineer has not had to pass an examination for color blindness, or has not felt somewhat "wrathy" when a sleepy operator has allowed his signal lamp to get low or go out?

Who has not felt his pulse quicken when, on some dark night, a red light has suddenly appeared on the track ahead, even though it should prove to be only a "wide-awake" drummer anxious to get out of town, and who has stopped the train by putting a match inside of a red bottle?

Red is used for the danger or stop signal everywhere, as it makes the greatest impression·on the sense of sight. White is used for the "all clear" and green for the "caution" signal on most roads in this country, although a few follow the English practice of using green for the "all clear," white not being used for any signal. The use of white to indicate "all clear" and green for "caution," at first sight appears to answer all the requirements; but so strong are the arguments against this arrangement, that if a more satisfactory color could be found for the cautionary signal, green would be universally used for the "all clear" signal and the use of white abandoned.

These arguments are, first, that the glass fastened in the arm plate casting may break and show a white light when the signal stands at danger.

Second, engineers may mistake a light in some street or dwelling for the signal light and run by it.

Few accidents have happened from the glasses breaking, but the possibilities of a serious collision are always present. For this reason stationmen should always "keep an eye" on the signal to see that the glass is in its place, and engineers should, whenever possible, see that the position of the blade corresponds with the indication given by the lamp.

The use of green for the all clear signal overcomes both objections against white, but leaves no available color for a cautionary signal. The practice on one road using green for the "all clear" is to show both a red and a green light for the caution signal, blotting out the red for "all clear." On another road three lights are used, two showing in a horizontal line to indicate "caution," and two in a vertical line for "all clear."

The color the blade is painted has nothing to do with the indications given, for while the blade may change its position the color does not, and consequently only one indication could be made. The blade is painted red for distinctness, that being the most easily discernible color; but on this point opinions differ, as one very prominent road paints them yellow. It may be well to note here that there is one system of blocking, "an automatic electric," in which the different indications are made by a change of color, or rather the appearance of a red disc for "danger" and its absence, thereby showing a white background, safety.

The next to be considered (having seen how a signal is constructed) are the different signals to be found at a block station, with the meaning each is intended to convey; not that all are to be found at every station, but that it may be better understood how a good block signal system is operated.

At first the only signals used were those at the entrance of a block, these, for economical reasons, being put at stations or at points where switch tenders were already stationed. As traffic increased and the speed of trains became greater, it often happened when the signal was at danger that trains would run by, owing to the location of signal, or to the conditon of the weather being such as to prevent engineers from seeing the signal soon enough to stop. The result of this was that engineers were forced to slacken speed and approach the signal very carefully, so that if found at danger they could stop before passing it.

To make this unnecessary, a second signal was erected which would give the same indication as the first signal gave, being placed some distance down the track from which the train was approaching; the engineer, by this arrangement, being informed of the position the controlling signal would be found in, some time before reaching it.

For the sake of distinction, the more important signal—the one controlling the block—is called the "home" signal, and the other, or caution signal, the "distant" signal, these being the names by which they are known to-day.

The possibility of operating the distant signal from the same place as the home signal, strange as it may seem to us now, was not thought of for some time; the distant signal being placed only so far down the track as it was possible for a man to run, after first putting the home signal in the clear position, before the arrival of the train.

A bright switchman, anxious to save himself the trouble of so much running, was the first to think of connecting this distant signal by means of a wire to a lever in the tower in which he was stationed. That this should have escaped the engineers and have been thought of by a switchman, recalls the invention of the valve motion by the lad who, getting tired of working by hand the steam engine valve, attached it to the end of the engine shaft by a stick.

Both signals were originally of the same form, but owing to the necessity of making a distinction of some kind between them, a notch was cut in the end of the distant signal. To make a still further difference, the distant signal blade was painted green—a color which expresses the character of the indication given by the signal.

A very amusing anecdote is told by Mr. W. J. Williams, traffic superintendent of the Brighton Railway, England, of the origin of the notch. Thinking that a distant or caution signal should be different from a home or stop signal, he sent a workman to a station on the main line between London and Brighton to cut a notch out of the end of the distant signal blade. The Brighton tracks are at this point used by the Southeastern Railway Co., and two or three days after the notch had been cut he received an indignant letter from that company, asking why he allowed his signals to get into such a state of disrepair that large pieces were actually chipped out of the end of them.

Soon after the distant signal came into use, the cautionary indication, as given by the home signal blade, became, to a great extent, discontinued, owing to engineers not properly observing it. For a "cautionary indication" is really permissive blocking, a time interval between trains, and, unless great care is used by the engineer, accidents are very likely to happen.

Another fact that made its use objectionable was the difficulty of keeping the signal properly adjusted, for, unless it was always lowered to the same position, engineers would be in doubt as to the exact meaning intended. And if the safe side were not taken, serious consequences were likely to follow.

Where permissive blocking is used the best systems do away with the inclined position, and either stop the train to give a "permissive card" or else use two signals on the same pole, the upper one being used for the "danger" or stop signal and the lower for the permissive or cautionary indication. This arrangement consists in placing a permissive arm, painted green and notched on the end, or a green light at night on the pole below the block arm and to work in connection with it, as shown in Fig. 6.

The indications as given by these two blades on one pole are plain and unmistakable, and are as follows:

Block and permissive arms *horizontal*, or upper light *red* and lower light *green*, signifies "Danger, stop!"

Block arm *vertical* and permissive arm *horizontal*, or upper light *white* and lower light *green*, signifies "Caution, proceed slowly!"

Block and permissive arms *vertical*, or upper and lower light *white*, signifies "All clear, go ahead!"

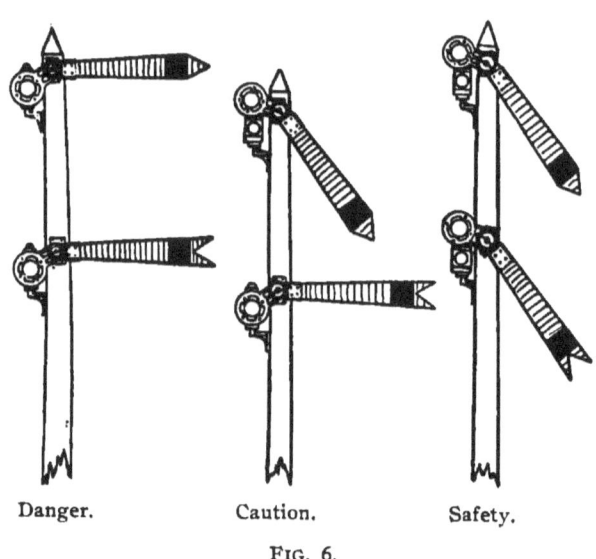

Danger.   Caution.   Safety.

Fig. 6.

It is here that attention should be called to the two ways in which caution signals may be read, for unless clearly understood, the indications as given by each signal will not be correctly interpreted. Not that the indication for "caution" does not mean to exercise due vigilance and care in either case, but that the extent to which caution is to be observed varies greatly.

One indication for caution is given by the signal blade in the inclined position, or when the lower arm of a two-blade signal is in the horizontal position, the upper one being vertical; the other as that given by a distant signal when at danger, indicating the position in which the home signal will be found. The one is permission blocking, pure and simple; the other a warning to the engineer to use caution in approaching the home signal, expecting to find it at danger.

The two signals at a block station, the home and the distant, were for a long time all that were necessary to properly handle trains without causing serious delays. But with the congestion of traffic as found on many roads, these have proved deficient, and a third signal has been added in many instances, thereby increasing the number of trains it is possible to run over a division in a given time.

The third signal is aptly named the "advance" signal, from the position in which it is placed, being put far enough in advance of the home signal to allow a train to clear the latter at least 300 feet before being brought to a stop.

The indications of the *advance* signal are positive, the same as those of the *home* signal—the *horizontal* position of the blade meaning "Danger, stop!" a *vertical* or inclined position, "All clear, go ahead!"

Without this signal it was often found that trains working at stations delayed following trains, from the fact that not having passed the home signal the block was not clear, and until it was the other train had to wait. With the use of the advance signal it was possible to so locate the home signal as to make a short block of the track between these two signals. By making this short block include the station and side tracks where switching was done, a train standing at the station would have cleared the block just behind it and at the same time remain under the control of the signalman.

The location of the home and advance signals at any station is pretty well defined by the character and amount of the business transacted. That of the distant signal, however, is one that will vary with each locality, and calls for the exercise of care and good judgment, for on the position in which it is placed, more than with any other signal, will its usefulness depend. As the signal is intended to repeat the indications of the home signal, it is necessary that the signal be placed at such a distance as to enable a train after passing it to stop before reaching the home signal, no matter what the conditions are.

Common practice in this respect is to put the distant signal

1,200 feet from the home signal, unless the conditions are such as, from the speed of the trains, or on account of grades and curves, it cannot be seen. There is a limitation to the distance it is possible to operate such a signal mechanically, owing to the difficulty of properly caring for the expansion of the wire and also the power required to "clear" the signal. The lever for this signal must also be interlocked with those of the home and advance signals, so that the signal cannot be pulled to "all clear" until they have both been cleared, thereby making it impossible for the signalman to make a mistake. Being placed at a distance from the home signal and the first seen by the engineer, it has become, in practice, the governing signal, allowing trains to keep a uniform speed under all conditions of operation. The number of signal poles in use at any station or tower varies, of course, with the system used, from that where the two signals for trains running in opposite directions are carried on one pole, to where six poles are used, each signal being placed in the best position with reference to the track which it governs.

Before taking up the different methods of operating block signals, it is perhaps advisable to call attention to the principal points which have just been considered, and which it would be well to bear in mind.

"Absolute blocking," or the maintenance of a "space" interval between all trains, is the only sure method of preventing collisions.

The indications of a semaphore signal are made by the position of the arm, and not by its form or color.

The normal position of all signals must be at *danger*.

A semaphore arm displayed to the right of the signal pole, as seen from an approaching train, is the one that governs.

A *horizontal* position of the semaphore arm, or a red light at night, means "Danger, stop!"

A *horizontal* position of a semaphore arm that is notched in the end, or a green light at night, means "Caution, go slow!"

A *vertical* position, or one nearly so, of a semaphore arm, or a white light at night, means "All clear, go ahead!"

A *block* is a section of track between two signal stations, the use of which is controlled by fixed signals.

A *home block signal* is a fixed signal at the entrance of a block to control trains entering said block.

A *distant block signal* is a fixed signal of special form used in connection with the home block signal, and placed at such a distance as will enable all trains to stop between the distant signal and the home signal.

An *advance block signal* is an auxiliary fixed signal, placed in advance of a home block signal to control trains that have entered the block.

CHAPTER II

METHODS OF OPERATION AND RULES.

There are three general methods of operating block signals, under which all the different systems may be classed. These are respectively called the "Telegraphic," the "Controlled Manual" and the "Automatic," the last-named including the "Automatic Mechanical," as well as the "Automatic Electric."

Of these let us first consider the telegraphic method, as, from its simplicity and cheapness, it is in use on more miles of road than any other; its name being derived from the means by which communication is had between the different block stations for the purpose of ascertaining whether or not the block is "clear."

The equipment of a station consists, primarily, of a signal for controlling trains, which, although preferably of the semaphore type, very often is not; of a lever for working the signal, placed in a position most convenient to the operator; of a wire used in connection with the ordinary telegraph instruments, or an electric bell for conveying the information necessary to properly work the block. The telegraph instruments of a division may all be put on the same wire, in which case it can only be used by one operator at a time, and every other operator can hear what is being said; or else the wire may run from one station only to the next, and thus be a local wire and ready for use at all times.

That there is an essential difference in the manner in which these two arrangements arc operated can be seen at once, although the result desired is the same in both. With the first arrangement the train dispatcher is expected to keep track of the operators and see that they properly report to the stations on either side of them the arrival and departure of trains. The dispatcher may be expected, in some cases, to give an order for the "clearing" of each signal, thus making him entirely responsible for the blocking of trains and allowing the operators no discretion in the matter. With the second arrangement, where the block wire extends only from one station to the next, the operator alone is responsible for the proper blocking of trains, reporting their arrival and departure to the stations on either side of him and clearing the signal only when the block is clear. There is, of course, with this latter arrangement the usual train dispatcher's wire in each office, but it has nothing to do with the block system and is only used by the operator to notify the dispatcher of the movement of trains. Of the two the latter is much the better plan, the advantages to be gained by using a separate block wire between each two stations being that it places the responsibility upon each operator and that fewer men will be needed, as the dispatcher will be relieved from the routine work of blocking trains and can devote his time to fixing meeting-points.

Each operator is provided with a train register sheet, on which he records the arrival and departure of trains as reported to him and as he reports to others. The sheet is divided into two columns by a vertical line, the record of all trains in a given direction being placed on the same side. These sheets are kept on file at each station, but should any question arise as to the acts of an operator, they can be sent for and compared with the sheets from other stations.

To prevent operators from making mistakes and giving the wrong signal, there is quite a difference in the means adopted on the various roads.

On some roads, where the signals are normally kept at danger, the operator is required, before clearing his signal for an approaching train, to ask the operator at the next station ahead if he can do so, although his train sheet may show that the last train admitted has passed out of the block. He is not allowed to hook or fasten the signal lever in the position corresponding with the "all clear" of the signal, but is required to hold it there so long as it is necessary to keep the signal at "all clear," a method very certain to insure the signal being returned to "danger" as soon as possible.

Others depend entirely on the train sheet, assuming that in case of doubt the operator will ask the next operator and find out if the block is clear.

Others, again, keep the signal at "danger" only so long as a train is in the block, clearing it as soon as the train has passed the next station.

Form 124. CHICAGO, MILWAUKEE & ST. PAUL RAILWAY CO.

TRAIN REGISTER SHEET.

RECORD OF TRAINS PASSING MERRILL PARK, NOVEMBER 3, 1894.

WEST BOUND.

Train No.	Conductor.	Block Clear or Permission Given.	Passed O. S.	Passed M. S. Arr.	Passed M. S. Dep.	Passed J. N.
		P. M.	P. M.	P. M.	P. M.	P. M.
33		1:42	1:34	1:40	1:44	1:52
Ex.	Smith.	3:07	3:02	3:07	3:07	3:14

EAST BOUND.

Train No.	Conductor.	Time 58 Given.	Block Clear or Permission Given.	Passed J. N.	Passed M. S. Arr.	Passed M. S. Dep.	Passed O. S.
		P. M.	P. M.	P. M.	P. M.	P. M.	P. M.
26		2:01	2:25	2:08	2:18	2:25	2:34
42		4:13	4:27	4:15	4:27	4:27	4:40

NOTE.—Operators will call for 58, and will insert time response is given in proper column, and will fill all blank spaces as called for. 58 meaning to block West Bound trains,

The first is the best method, as two men, one at the beginning and the other at the other end of the block, have to agree before a train is allowed to enter. Besides, keeping the signal normally at danger is an additional safeguard, as it requires the operator to be certain of what he is doing and to put himself on record that the block is clear.

In regard to the use of permissive blocking with a telegraphic block system, the method most generally adopted is to put the entire control in the hands of the train dispatcher and allow the operator to give a "caution" or permissive signal only when authorized by him. If the conditions as to weather and track are favorable, permissive blocking is frequently made use of for freight trains. But, between passenger trains, the absolute block is maintained unless exceptionally good reasons present themselves for doing otherwise. The permissive signal can be given in several ways, as has been said before; but the best plan, I believe, is to require the operator to give a permissive card to the engineer, the same as with a train order stating for what train caution is to be observed. With this card there can be no mistaking the information given, as might occur with a caution signal, more particularly the three-position signal when such is made by the inclined position of the blade.

That a system of signals operated through the means of communication afforded by the telegraph instrument is cheap and in every way advantageous, is clearly proved from the fact of its having been so widely adopted by roads that apparently could not afford to spend money on anything not absolutely necessary. But one wreck will very often pay for a good many signals and the few extra operators required to work a block system; so that by drawing on one's imagination as to the size of the wreck, it is very easy to figure out a great saving to any road. A system of block signals is certainly a much better arrangement than is any practice of flagging trains, but the trainmen must be properly educated as to the extent of the protection afforded by the system and not look for it to do more than it is intended to do. Not that flagging has as yet been abandoned where any system of signaling is in operation, but it is used merely as a check on operator and enginemen in case they should make a mistake.

The benefits to be derived from any system of block signals

depend in a great measure on the rules governing their use and also on the extent to which they are observed. A set of rules for operating a telegraphic block signal system gives, first of all, the definition of a block, defines a signal and then states how the different signals are to be read. As these have already been given —as have, also, several important points which are usually covered in the rules—I will give in a somewhat condensed form only those which have not been previously mentioned and which are essential to the proper working of a telegraphic system of signals:

Trains between A and X will be governed in their movements by a block system which is designed to protect trains running in an opposite direction as well as in the same direction. This system will be independent of the general rules governing train movement and the movements directed by special telegraphic orders, and must not be confused with them.

The block signal must never be fastened at the "clear" position, except when the office is closed, but must always be held at that position, when it is desired to clear a train, until the rear car of the train has passed.

When there are no train orders, and the block ahead is clear for an approaching train, the signal should be changed to "clear" as soon as and not before the engineer is in sight of it, that the train may enter without reducing speed.

At stations where the block signal is used, a red flag by day and a red lantern by night will be attached to the block signal mast to notify trainmen to call for orders, the block signal in addition being kept at danger until the orders are delivered.

CHICAGO, MILWAUKEE & ST. PAUL RAILWAY COMPANY.

River Division.

. . . . .189..

C. & E. . . . .

USE PERMISSIVE BLOCK.

From . . . .*to*. . . . .

Train . . . ., *entered at* . . . .*M.*

. . . .*Operator.*

Engineers and conductors receiving permissive block card will run with great caution. Where view is obscured they must reduce speed to insure against collision with a train that may be running ahead of them.

The responsibility for colliding with trains when permissive signal is given will rest with train receiving and moving under such signal. This will in no way relieve conductor and engineer of train stopping within block from flagging.

If no markers are displayed on the rear of the train, the operator at the next block station ahead must be notified to give the approaching train a signal that train is broken apart. The block station in the rear must be also notified that the track is blocked until information is received from the conductor that he has all the cars in his train.

When a train is on a siding clear of the main line and the markers have been seen, the block may be cleared.

In case of failure of the wires, or if, for any reason, the operator cannot get orders for a train, he must give it written notice of the reason the proper signal is not given.

A train intending to use a cross-over between block stations must notify the signalman at nearest block station. Train shall not use cross-over until a flagman has been sent out.

Signalmen should closely watch each train as it passes, and if anything is noticed that is wrong, must report it to the next station and have train stopped.

The rules governing the use of block signals do not relieve trainmen from observing all other rules relating to the protection of trains.

The rules for use where communication is had by telegraph, generally contain a code of signals by which information regarding the condition of the block can be quickly transmitted. Where a bell is used the code has to be much more complete, and the number of taps required is often large, as one cannot talk with it as is possible with a telegraph instrument. For this reason a great deal of care should be exercised in the arrangement of the code, so that no serious consequences could result from a mistake in counting the number of taps. The best arrangement of taps is that where a combination of numbers, as, for instance, 2-3-2, is used rather than a consecutive number.

While, undoubtedly, there are dangerous situations which may arise with the use of a telegraphic block system from lack of a more complete equipment, it is certainly a great help to the train dispatchers and a protection against collisions. That engineers have run by signals when they were at danger, that operators have allowed trains to enter blocks when they were not clear, accidents being caused thereby, has only resulted in a closer adherence to the rules on the part of the men and stricter discipline on that of the officers. But the fact still remains, that where a human agent is used he is liable at times to fail, and the greater the precautions taken by mechanical means, and by using two men in place of one, the less likely is it that mistakes will occur and accidents happen.

Work in this direction has resulted in the development of a system in which the labor of two men working in conjunction with each other is required to clear a signal and admit a train to the block. This method is called the "Controlled Manual," of which the Sykes system was the first brought into extensive use, and Patenall's improvement of the Sykes, a later development. Other systems have been invented, but, as yet, have only had a limited introduction. The two systems mentioned have only been applied to roads having double tracks, but another system has been invented, which, although not yet in extended service, accomplishes practically the same results on single track.

The equipment of a station consists principally of a machine having separate levers for each signal, those for the distant signal, if such are used, being interlocked with the corresponding home signal. Distant signals are shown in the cut, as they are to be found at nearly all stations where this method of operation is used, but it is not to be understood that they are a necessary part of any system.

To each of the home signal levers a locking bar and latch are so connected that when the signal is placed in the danger position the latch will fall into a notch cut in the bar and hold the lever in this position. To work the latch, electro-magnets are arranged, with the several parts that comprise the instrument, in a suitable box placed on the machine in a position most convenient to the leverman. There are two indicators in the side of the box, one of which, working in connection with the latch, shows whether the instrument is locked or free. As there are two of these cases, one for each track, and as the equipment for each track is separate and exactly alike, that for one track only will be spoken of.

Wires are run from the machine at one station to the machine at the next station, and so connected with the electro-magnets working the latch that when the circuit is completed by pressing on a contact piece on one machine the latch of the other is lifted and the lever unlocked. This contact piece, which is lettered P in the cut, is known as a "plunger," and the operation of closing the circuit, thereby unlocking the lever at the next station, is called "plunging." The plunger is constructed mechanically, so that if the operator has once plunged he will not be able to do so again until the signal has been cleared and returned to the danger position. The object of this is to prevent him from letting a second train in the block before the one admitted by him when he plunged has passed his station. To prevent him from clearing his signal and putting it back to danger again, and thus release the plunger, as might easily happen through mistake, a certain portion of the track is made part of an electrical circuit, and arranged so that the circuit between the two instruments made by "plunging" will be broken until a train has passed over the track circuit. If, now, this track circuit be placed at a certain distance beyond the home signal, it is seen at once that the block will be clear before the operator can plunge and again unlock the signal at the next station.

Working in connection with the plunger and placed just above it, is an indicator which shows the words "clear" or "blocked," for the purpose of indicating whether the operator has or has not plunged. If the operator *has* plunged, then the instrument at the next station is unlocked and a train can be admitted to the block, so that from his standpoint the track is blocked. If he has *not* plunged, then no train can be in the block, and, consequently, it must be clear. It must not be forgotten that the indicator is changed from "blocked" to "clear" when the home signal is returned to the danger position, but that unless the train has actually passed out of the block and over the track circuit the operator cannot unlock the signal circuit at the next station by plunging. A separate wire is strung between each two stations, and used in connection with an electric bell for transmitting the information necessary for the proper working of the signals. Telegraph instruments can be used, if preferred, but as a bell does not require such close attention and can be understood by anyone, it is the one most generally adopted.

In the cut, the levers and signals for a train moving in one direction only are shown. Three block sections with the stations A, B and C are represented, the signals being shown in the proper position for governing the trains which are supposed to be approaching. To make it easier to follow the indications as given by each machine, three positions of the train are shown. The method of operating the signals is as follows: Supposing a train to be in block 1, approaching block signal station A, the lever and signals being in the position shown in the cut. A asks B, by ringing the bell, to unlock his lever if block 2 is clear. B, looking at his indicator, sees the word "clear" and plunges, thereby unlocking A's instrument and changing the indicator on his (B's) machine from "clear" to "blocked." The instruments are shown in Fig. 1 after this action is supposed to have taken place, A's lever being unlocked but with the signals still at danger. A pulls his lever as soon as it is unlocked and lowers the signal admitting the train to block 2. The movement of the lever changes the indicator to again show locked, although the lever is not actually locked until the signal has been returned to the danger position. As soon as the train has passed the home signal, A returns the lever to the danger position and the latch drops into the notch in locking bar, and A is mechanically prevented from again clearing the signal.

As the train approaches, B asks C to unlock him, which C does, provided the block is clear. On B's indicator changing from locked to free, he lowers the signal admitting the train to block 3; the indicator changes back to locked, and we have the condition of things shown in Fig. 2. When the train has passed, B returns the home signal to danger, unlocking the plunger and making the indicator show "clear" again. He could now plunge and unlock A if the circuit was restored; but this circuit is only restored after the train has passed the track circuit, which, as it is 300 feet beyond the home signal, insures that the block will be clear before another train can be admitted.

26

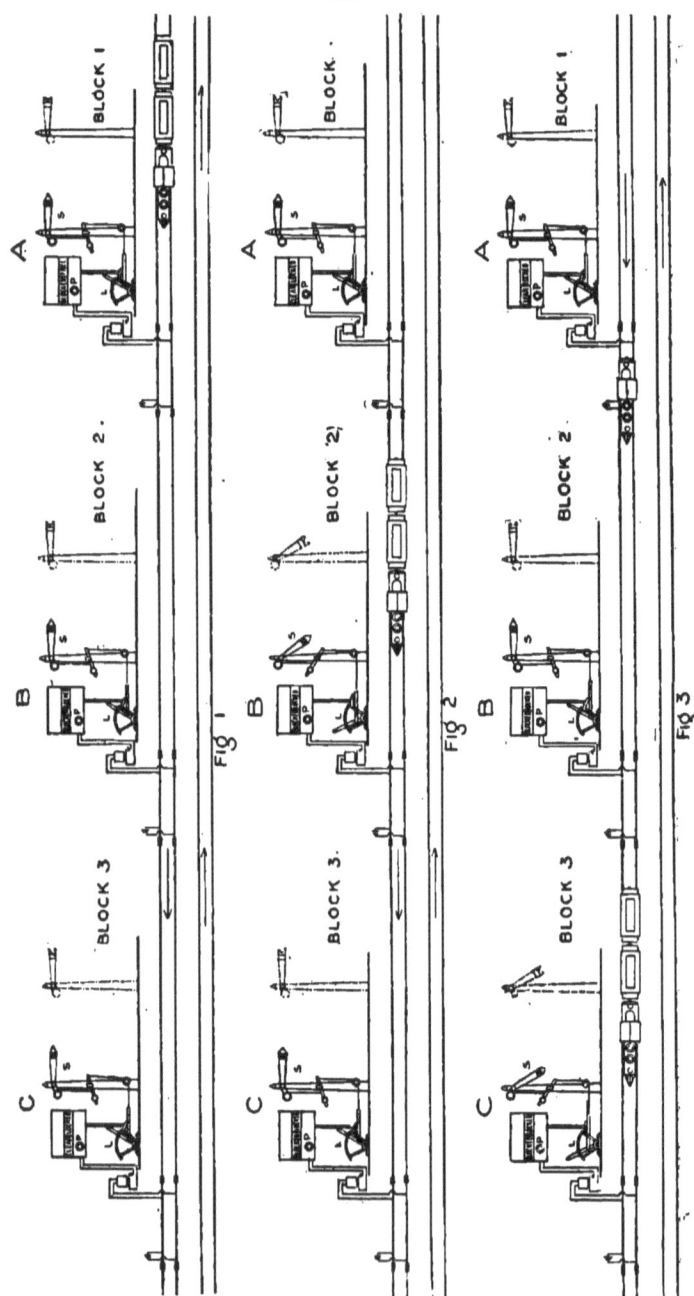

BLOCK 1
A
BLOCK 2.
B
Fig 1
BLOCK 3
C

BLOCK.
A
BLOCK '2'
B
Fig 2
BLOCK 3.
C

BLOCK 1
A
BLOCK 2
B
Fig 3
BLOCK 3
C

When the train approaches, C asks D to release him, and we have the condition of things shown in Fig. 3, the operations as above described being again repeated. In Fig. 3 the action of a train on the track circuit is shown. The wheels short-circuit the current, so that the magnet of the relay is demagnetized; the armature dropping makes an electrical contact, which restores the unlocking circuit in the instrument.

From this description it is seen that only through the efforts of two men, one at the beginning and the other at the end of the block, can a clear signal be given, and that not until the last train admitted to the block has passed the track circuit can this result be secured.

The rules for operating any of the different "Controlled Manual" systems are practically those for a telegraph system, with only such rules added as are made necessary from the construction of the machine. One, that is perhaps the most important in this respect, is—"In case of failure to get unlocked after operator has plunged, a clearance card must be given for the train to proceed to the next station." Or, the operator, if the rules allow permissive signaling, may signal the train to proceed, using a green flag by day and a green light by night. The bell code of signals is made very large, in order to cover any conditions that may arise.

The blocking of trains by this method of operation has proved it to be much better and safer than one where no check is put upon the operator; so much so, that many prominent men believe it to be the best system of those in use to-day. But, with all this, the fact remains that the personal factor is a necessary part in the operation of the plant, and just so long as this is the case will mistakes occur. While men may have the best intentions and strive faithfully to perform their duties, error is an essential part of human action, and, sooner or later, the time will come when some mistake will be made. Any system that will do away with the personal factor and, at the same time, give as reliable indications, must certainly be in the line of progress toward that perfection and absolute security which all systems strive to attain. The objection to an automatic signal that because no man is on watch the signal may be disregarded, is not valid, for all that any of the systems that have been mentioned are designed to do is simply to indicate the condition of the block controlled by the signal. In any case, faith must be placed in the engineer that he will obey such signals. "The warrant for that faith," to quote the words of Mr. Sullivan, general superintendent of the Illinois Central R. R., "is the fact that no engineman of sound mind will knowingly run into danger. A man will give all he hath for his life—the pledge of the engineman is the highest that can be given."

Many automatic signal systems have been invented, some of which are in use and giving good satisfaction; others, again, have been tried, and, it is hoped, forever relegated to the scrap pile. The automatic mechanical systems have, as yet, had only a limited introduction. The staff system, while extensively used abroad, has been put in service on but one road in this country, and that for the operation of only one block.

The most successful systems, and those generally alluded to when an automatic system is spoken of, are those which depend upon electricity for the controlling agent, whether or not it is the force actually used to work the signal. Of these, two systems may be taken as representing more clearly than any others the different lines on which automatic signals have been developed. One is the Westinghouse electro-pneumatic, where compressed air is made to work the signal, its action being controlled by electricity; the other is the Hall, where electricity is the only force used. The equipment of the electro-pneumatic system more nearly resembles that of a telegraphic or a controlled manual system than any of the others, as it gives the indications by means of the ordinary sema-phore blade. To the engineer the two systems are alike, except he knows that the electro-pneumatic is automatic, and therefore shows exactly the state of the block and not what the operator represents it to be.

A current of electricity run through the rails and energizing a magnet, which is short-circuited by a train, or even a pair of wheels, in the block, is the agent depended upon for the proper working of the system. This magnet, by means of a second and more powerful current of electricity and the action of compressed air, changes the signal to indicate the condition of the block. If the current passes from one rail to the other without going through the magnet, as it will do when the rails are connected by a pair of wheels, the signal is made to indicate danger; if the current of electricity goes through the magnet, the track must be clear and the signal is held in the "all clear" position.

It is seen that if such a system is made reliable and does not get out of order easily, it is an ideal one, having the double advantage of being automatic and using the position signal. The testimony of the superintendent of a road where sixteen miles of track have been equipped and successfully operated for some length of time, shows that the apparatus is reliable and practicable. He says that "there is a failure to give a correct indication only once in 250,000 times, and that the error then is always on the side of safety;" that "without this system the traffic could not be handled on the same number of tracks, owing to the time it would take operators to go through the necessary motions with either a telegraphic or controlled manual system;" that "no dispatchers are needed, as the trains follow each other irrespective of orders, being governed entirely by the signals."

The Hall automatic electric signal has come into more general use than the one just spoken of, and is no doubt familiar to most railroad men. This signal differs considerably from those of the semaphore type, in that its indications are given by color and not by position. The mechanism of the signal is placed in a large box having a circular glass center. Behind this glass a red disc is shown for danger; raising the disc out of sight and showing a white background is the means employed to indicate "all clear." The signal is operated by a current of electricity controlled by a track circuit. As long as the current is flowing through the magnet, the disc is held up and all is clear; when the circuit is broken, by a train entering the block, the disc falls and indicates danger.

It is thus seen that there is practically no difference in the way the two systems are operated, so far as results are concerned, if the difference in the way the indications are given is ignored. Of course, every man is entitled to his own opinion, and while many think there are great objections to giving up the semaphore type and relying entirely on a color signal, others think that the advantages of a position signal are offset by the increased cost of installation and maintenance, that of the electro-pneumatic being greater than that of the Hall. Certain it is that both of these systems are coming more into use every day, as the prejudice against an automatic signal is gradually being done away with. They are also making a record, both in the matter of expense and the expeditious handling of trains, that other systems cannot approach.

The method pursued in the operation of an automatic electric signal is very simple; the indication of the signal being positive, a train finding one at danger, stops; when the signal clears, it proceeds. As the blocks are generally short and trains can be run as close together as it is safe to run them, the blocking of trains is absolute and no permissive blocking is provided for. Apparently, the only rule necessary is "to obey the signal," but in practice it is found that they, like everything else about a railroad, occasionally get out of order and give a false indication; that is, they indicate danger when the block is clear. If some provision was not made in the rules to cover such cases, it would result in tying up the road until the signal was repaired. Practice on the different roads varies, in the rule adopted for the guidance of trainmen when a signal is found at danger. A reason for this difference is found in the character of the country through which the road runs, the grades and curves, as well as the general difficulties of operation. If the road is easily operated, the grades light and the country open, the general practice is for a train to stop, when the signal is found at danger, from two to three minutes, and then to proceed as under a caution signal. If the next signal is found at "clear," the train proceeds under the clear signal, reporting the block that was out of order.

The practice where a road passes through numerous tunnels, over high trestles and heavy grades, is for the train to stop at the signal for five minutes, at the same time sending on a flagman who precedes the train all the way to the next signal.

The writer recently rode on an engine over a division that was equipped with an automatic electrical signal, and had a good opportunity for watching its performance. There were twenty-four tunnels in the 100 miles of road, and it was certainly a great satisfaction to pass a signal showing "all clear" before the train entered any one of them. The trainmen on that division say they "do not see how they ever got along without the signals, and if the company were to do away with them, a good many of 'the boys' would want to 'quit the business.'"

From my experience with the automatic electrical signal, I think it is the system of all others for a road to adopt, for it will show at all times if there is a train or a part of a train in the block, it has no operators to make mistakes, it will always indicate danger when anything goes wrong with the apparatus, and it will fulfill all the requirements that a signal alone can be expected to fulfill.

A railroad superintendent, speaking of the benefits to be derived from an automatic signal, thus aptly describes the difference between a telegraphic and an automatic electric system. He says that "the telegraphic block sometimes goes to sleep, sometimes gets drunk, sometimes becomes insane, and almost always lies when in trouble. The automatic block is a mechanism that has neither the ability to go to sleep, get drunk, become insane, nor to lie. It speaks for itself."

The automatic mechanical systems go a step further than do either of the electric systems mentioned, in that they attempt to stop the train by opening a valve and setting the air brakes, if the engineer disregards the signal and runs by it. It is, perhaps, needless to say that nothing better could be desired in the way of a signal system than one that will give correct indications and stop a train if the signal is disregarded, provided the apparatus is made practicable and durable. But the facts are, that to make the apparatus work successfully the blocks have to be very short, too short for a road running fifty-car trains, and that where trains are run at high speed the life of the apparatus is limited. The mechanical systems, however, have been very successfully applied to elevated roads, where the speed is low and the blocks as well as the trains short.

The staff system, of which, I suppose, nearly everyone has heard, is quite a new thing in this country, and, so far, is giving a very satisfactory performance. Two machines are provided, one being placed in the station at each end of the block. There are twenty-one staffs in the two machines, removing one of which from either machine locks both, so that no more staffs can be taken out. Put the staff back in either machine, again making a total of twenty-one staffs, and both of the machines will be unlocked and a staff can be removed from either. Permissive blocking is accomplished by providing six tablets or tickets, which tablets are unlocked and removed from the machine by using one of the staffs, called a "permissive staff," as a key. Each one of these tablets can be given to an engineer in place of the regular staff, so that it is possible to let seven trains follow each other into the block.

The staff system is, ordinarily, worked as an absolute block, the tablets, or permissive blocking, being used for freight trains, and then only when conditions are favorable. There is only one rule to be observed in the operation of this system, and that is that "no engineer must enter the block unless he has a tablet or staff with him." If the engineer is given a tablet, or the permissive staff, caution must be observed, as there may be other trains in the block that are running in the same direction.

Before giving the details of construction of the various systems, let me call attention to the three methods of operating block signal systems, about which this article has been written, and which it is well to bear in mind:

1st. The telegraphic method, where operators can at will clear the signal, a telegraph line being used as the means of communication between the two stations.

2d. The controlled manual, where the work of two men, one at the beginning and the other at the end of the block, is necessary to clear the signal, and where a train having been admitted to the block, the signal cannot again be cleared until the block is clear.

3d. The automatic, where the signals, either by position or by color, indicate the actual condition of the block. Where the signals are entirely automatic, and in case of failure will assume the danger position.

CHAPTER III.

CONSTRUCTION—THE TELEGRAPHIC SYSTEMS.

The telegraphic systems derive the name from the method used in conveying information from one station to the next regarding the position of trains and the state of the block.

The equipment of a station consists of:

First—A wire and the necessary telegraph instruments, or if so desired, bells may be provided, if a suitable code is arranged that will cover all the conditions likely to present themselves in the blocking of trains.

Second—Of a signal by which information can be conveyed to engineers and trainmen of the condition of the block, and whether or not they have the right to proceed.

Third—Of a lever, if such is used, and the necessary connections for the proper working of the signal.

The construction of a semaphore signal has already been explained, but as a road may block trains by using any one of several different designs, it is necessary that a description be given of the ones most generally used. While most of the fixed signals are used for the blocking of trains, they are often used solely as a train order signal (commonly called by trainmen "order boards"), so that while there may be a difference in the information conveyed, there is no difference in the construction of the signals used for the two purposes.

The simplest form of a signal is a flag stuck in the edge of the platform, or placed in some more conspicuous position, where trainmen will be most likely to see it.

A very good arrangement, as shown in Fig. 1, is to bolt a simple bracket, in which the flag staff may be placed, to the outside of the station building. Trainmen will soon learn its location and will then know just where to look for a signal in case one should be put out for them. A little hook on top of the casting near the end serves as a catch to hold the lantern, when, at night, one is used.

The "Swift Train Order Signal," as shown in Fig. 2, is something of an advance from a simple flag, and is really a much better arrangement, as it is placed in a more conspicuous position, and, from its being made of sheet iron, cannot be blown about by every wind, but is always seen to the best advantage. Its construction

is very simple, consisting of an oval-shaped piece of sheet iron, riveted at its center to a shaft. The turning of this shaft, and with it the sheet, through a quarter of a circle, by means of a bell crank and a lever placed at the operator's office, is the method used in giving the different indications. The night indications are made by a lamp placed on the top of the shaft, which is made to extend up through the framework supporting the signal. The lamp is the same as an ordinary switch lamp, having two of the lenses red and the other two white. These are arranged so that the light, as seen from an approaching train, from either direction, will show red or white, and give the same indication as is given by the board.

If the board is set parallel with the track, it will not be visible to an approaching train, and is, therefore, understood to mean that there are "no orders," or that the line is "clear." If the board

SWIFT'S TRAIN ORDER SIGNAL.

is set at right angles with the track, it will be plainly visible, and the indication is made to "call for orders," or "danger, track blocked." Hooks are provided in the operator's office to hold the lever in the position in which it is placed. These hooks are painted red and white, corresponding with the indications made by the signal, to always remind the operator of the position in which the signal has been placed.

The signal shown in Fig. 3 is one used extensively on the

E. T., V. & Ga., and other roads, and although of a semaphore type, the indications being made by the position of the blade, it is of a radically different construction. A cast-iron framework

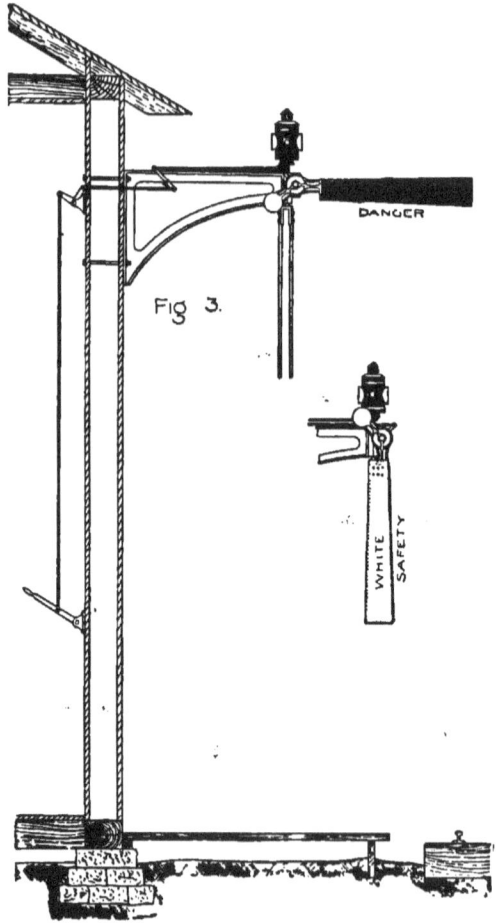

SIGNAL USED ON E. T., VA. & GA. R. R.

or bracket bolted to the outside of the station building, carries at its outer end two shafts, which are set at right angles with each other, and are provided with the necessary levers and cranks to turn them through a quarter of a circle. A blade bolted to the horizontal shaft and painted red, serves, when in a horizontal position, to give the danger indication; a counterbalance weight being provided on the opposite side of this shaft to make the blade assume the danger position, should any of the parts become disconnected.

The lower end of the vertical shaft is provided with a casting, to which are bolted two blades, in the manner shown in the cut. These blades are painted white and are spaced a sufficient distance apart to allow the red blade to pass between them, when it is lowered from the horizontal position. This blade, if at right angles with the track, will, of course, be seen by an approaching train, and being in the vertical position would indicate "all clear." If parallel with the track, only the narrow edge of each would be presented, and no indication would be given, as they could not be seen.

To indicate "danger," the arrangement of the cranks attached to the two shafts is such, that if the red blade is in the horizontal position, the white blades are parallel with the track, and the red blade only will be seen. The "all clear" signal is given by pulling the lever and turning the white blades through a quarter of a circle, bringing them at right angles to the track, and on both sides of the red blade, which is lowered from the horizontal position, thus leaving only the white blades visible, and consequently giving the "all clear" signal or "safety" indication. The lamp, supported by the vertical shaft, is the same as that used for the Swift signal, and gives the indications by color that correspond with the indications made by the blades.

This signal, it will be seen, is one in which the indications are given by color, as well as position, and beyond the fact that it is impossible to designate with the arrangement, as shown, the particular direction in which it is desired to hold trains, the indications as made are clear and unmistakable. The great objection, however, to a construction of this kind—one that is of great force in a northern climate—is that in bad weather the blades are very apt to become clogged with snow, or else frozen together, in which case there is a possibility of a wrong indication being given, and a certainty that the signal could not be worked.

With all the signals that have so far been described, it is impossible to designate by the signal the direction in which it is

38

desired to block trains, so that to prevent mistakes, every train which is at a station where the danger signal is displayed must assume that it is intended for it and be governed accordingly. Taking up those signals which are designed to give separate indications for trains running in opposite directions, that of Gravit's Railway Signal, sometimes nicknamed "the bootjack," may be said to represent the first step in this direction.

This signal is shown in Fig. 4, and is of very peculiar construction. It is in general use on the Lake Shore & Michigan

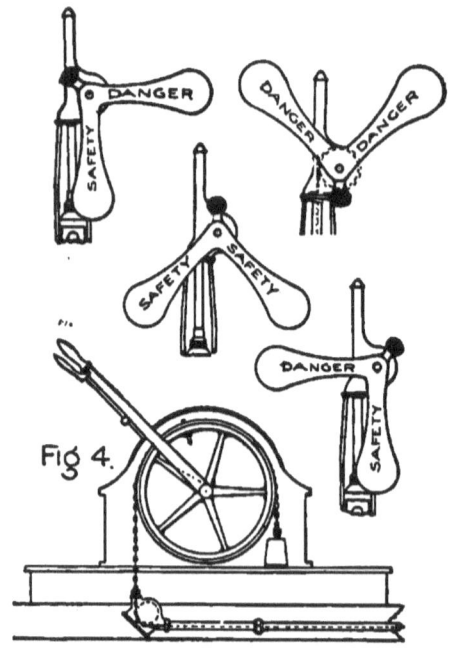

Fig 4.

GRAVIT'S RAILWAY SIGNAL.

Southern road. The two blades, which are fixed at an angle of 90 deg. with each other, are so mounted on a shaft that they can be turned through a complete circle. A lever placed in the operator's office serves, by means of a chain, and up and down rod which also acts as a weight, and a rack and pinion, to turn the shaft and with it the blades to any of the four positions it is necessary for them to take. On the lever stand there are four notches or positions for the lever, with lettered plates at each, indicating to the operator the position of the signal blades, as "All blocked," "Clear for west-bound trains." The lamp case seen in the cut below the signal blades, is fitted with the necessary colored lenses, a lamp being raised or lowered behind them, so that the light will show through the lenses, giving a color indication in each direction that will correspond with the indications made by the blades. Openings in the case on the station side are also provided with colored glasses, so that the operator can at all times see that the correct indication is given by the lamp. With this signal it is impossible to indicate either "danger" or "safety" in both directions and have the blades occupy the usual positions. This is certainly a great objection, as it becomes necessary to have the blades at different times occupy different positions when indicating the same thing; danger being indicated by a horizontal position of the blade in one case and an inclined position above the center in another; safety, likewise, being indicated by a vertical position and also an inclined position below the center.

The Mozier three-position semaphore signal, shown in Fig. 5, is a signal that is somewhat of a departure from the ordinary semaphore signal, not only in its construction, but in the manner in which the several indications are given. It is in general use on the Erie road, and is reported as giving very great satisfaction. It is designed to give the three indications—danger, caution and safety—with a single blade, but instead of making the cautionary indication by the usual position *below* the center, it is made by raising the blade to an inclined position *above* the center. This position, as well as the general arrangement of levers, etc., is clearly shown in the cut.

In the construction of the signal, two chains or wires are run from a lever placed in the operator's office to a pulley fastened on the pole, and from there to the signal casting, one being used to pull the blade to "safety" and the other to pull it to the "danger" position; a very good arrangement, for as both motions are positive, it can be depended upon that the signals will occupy positions corresponding with the positions of the levers. A weight sliding in a vertical plane on two roller bearings is suspended by means of a chain from two pins on opposite sides of the center of the arm-plate casting, for the purpose of making the signal assume the danger position if any of the parts should break or become disconnected—a very necessary thing, as has already been pointed out.

The arm-plate casting is made to hold two glasses, one red

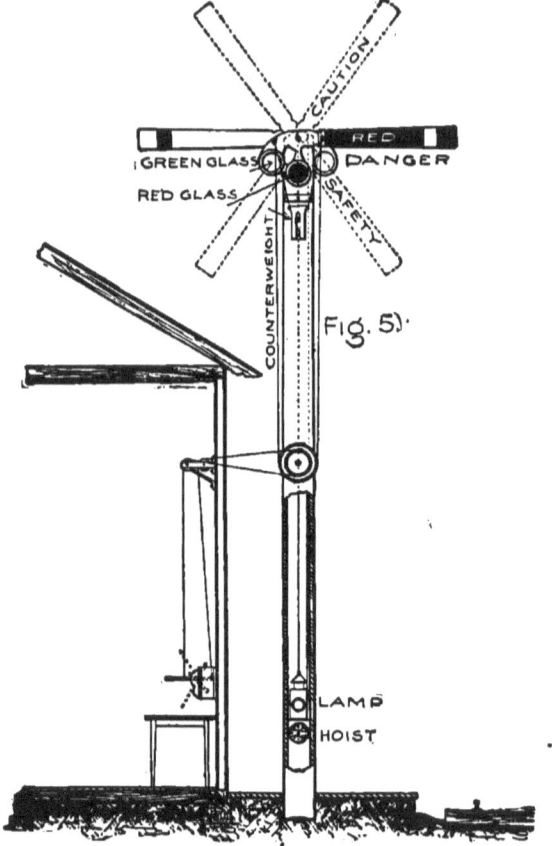

MOZIER THREE-POSITION SEMAPHORE SIGNAL, AS USED ON
N. Y., L. E. & W. R. R.

and the other green, that one being brought in front of the lamp which, by its color, will give an indication corresponding with the indication made by the blade. With the arrangement, as shown in the cut, the lamp is raised by a windlass and chain to the top of the mast, which is represented as being made of iron pipe, but any form of pole will answer just as well, if some means be provided by which the lamp can be put in place.

The construction of the signal is a good one, although I believe that solid connections to the arm-plate casting give better results, and are certainly safer than any chain or wire as is used in the present case. The objections to giving a cautionary indication by any signal have already been noted, but as the operation of

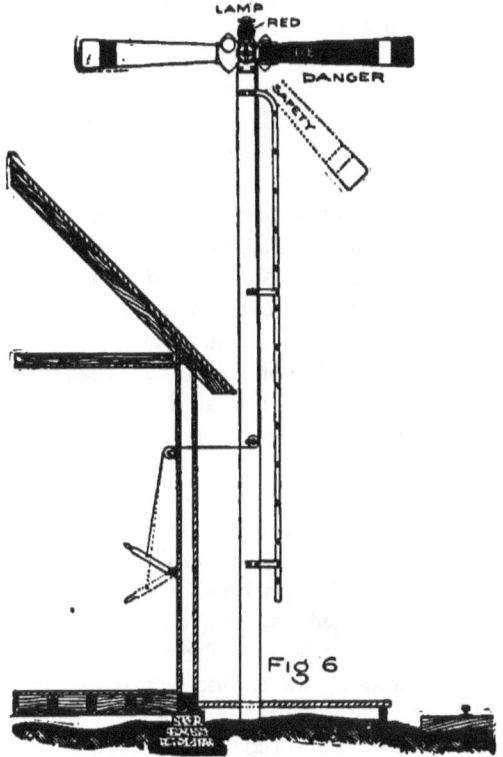

SIGNAL USED ON CENT. R. R. OF GA.

each road is a problem in itself, to be dealt with by men holding very different opinions on such matters, it is not to be wondered at that the practice should be very different on the different roads in such an important branch of railroad operation as signaling.

A semaphore signal that is very extensively used in the South is shown in Fig. 6. It is of a somewhat cheaper form than the ordinary semaphore, and is operated by means of a cable passed around a circular rim cast on the arm plate. The arm-plate casting is made heavier than the blade, so as to carry the signal back to the danger position when the lever is released. It will be noticed that the red lens is carried in an arm projecting above the center and not in the counterbalance part of the arm-plate casting; a lens being used instead of an ordinary red glass so as to concentrate the rays of light, as the lamp used is an ordinary hand lantern. The construction of this signal is very light, and for severe climates is not a good one, as snow or ice is very apt to make it stick in the "all clear" position.

The signal shown in Fig. 7 is that of the three-position signal used on the Pennsylvania road. A very noticeable feature in the design of this signal is that the blade, when in a truly vertical position, projects from the side of the pole so as to be plainly visible and give a positive indication that a clear signal is intended.

The arm-plate casting is made to hold two glasses, a red and a green, as the usual practice on this road is to allow the operator to give a cautionary signal (the inclined position of the blade) whenever it is desired to block trains permissively.

The arrangement as used on the St. Paul road is shown in Fig. 8, and is one, I believe, that fulfills all the requirements of a good signal, and at the same time is simple in construction and of low cost.

It will be noticed that the ends of the blades are pointed, a practice that the St. Paul road has been the first to adopt; the reason for doing this being the desirability of making some distinction between a block signal and a signal used at an interlocking plant. Undoubtedly some such distinction must be considered advisable, when it is remembered that with a signal used at an interlocked crossing the engineer must stop his train at the signal if at danger, the derail not allowing him to run by it. When, with a block signal, he is allowed to pass it, if it is necessary to do so, and have the train stop in front of the station. Certainly it is not consistent practice to allow him to run by a signal in one instance and require him to stop at the signal in another, if there is no way in which he can distinguish one from the other. What objection can there be to pointing a block signal blade, if in any way such pointing helps to denote the character of the indication given?

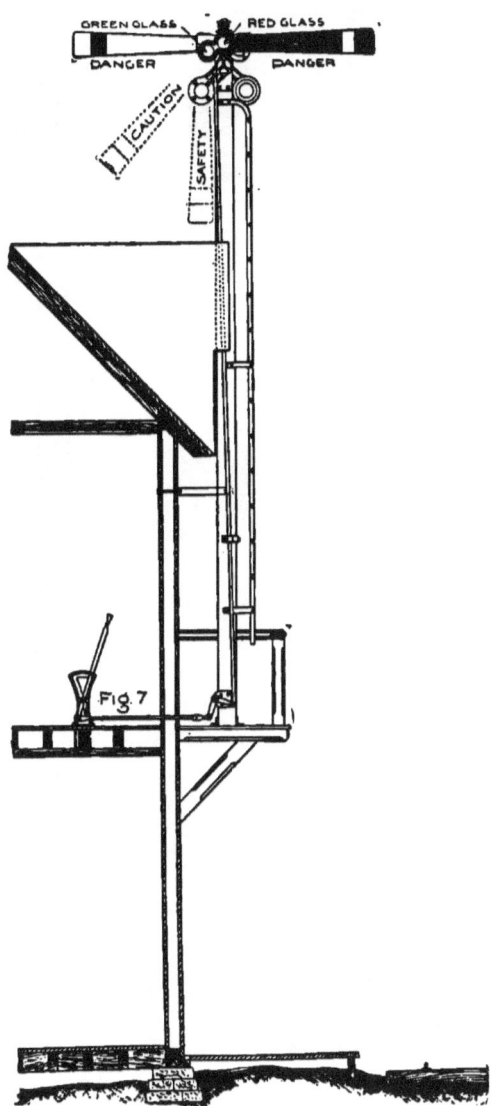

GREEN GLASS   RED GLASS

DANGER   DANGER

CAUTION

SAFETY

Fig. 7

BLOCK SIGNAL USED ON PENN. R. R.

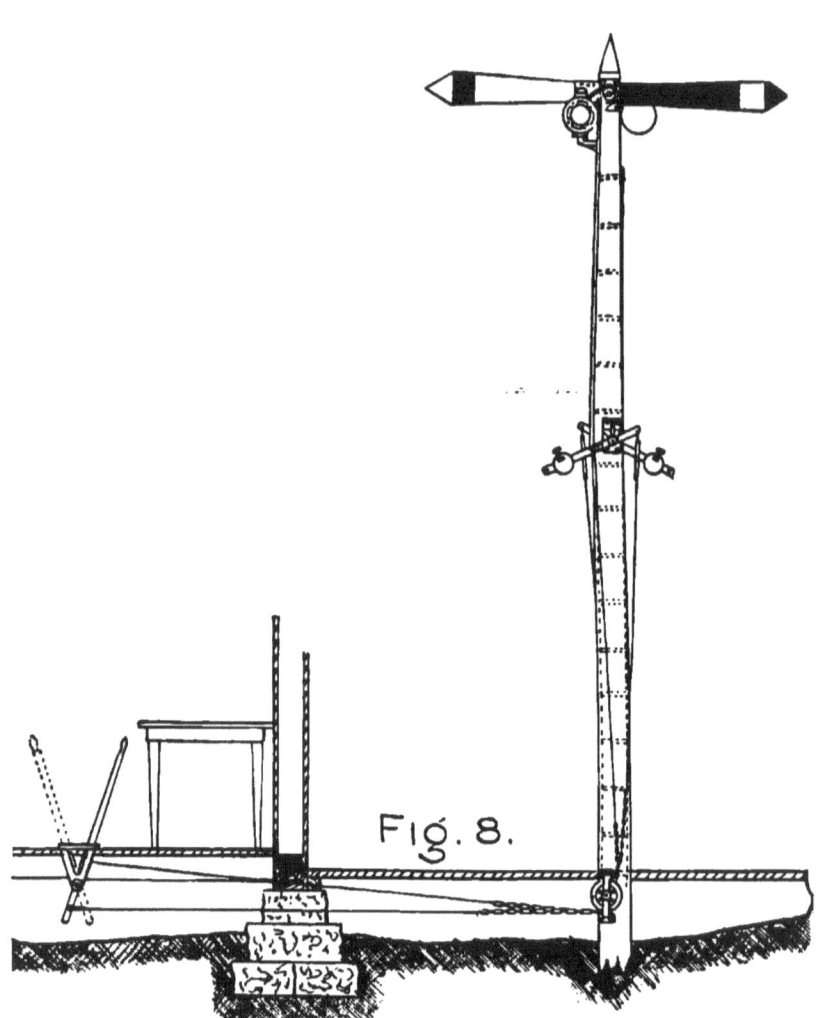

Fig. 8.

BLOCK SIGNAL USED ON C., M. & ST. P.

In the equipment of a station, only those parts have been
shown in the drawings which are necessary to work a signal
placed in front of or near the station. When a distant signal is
used in connection with the home block signal, it is necessary
to use a lever stand of much heavier construction than any that
have been shown, as it requires about all the strength the average
man possesses to clear a signal placed a distance of 1,500 feet or
over. The levers also must be so interlocked that the distant

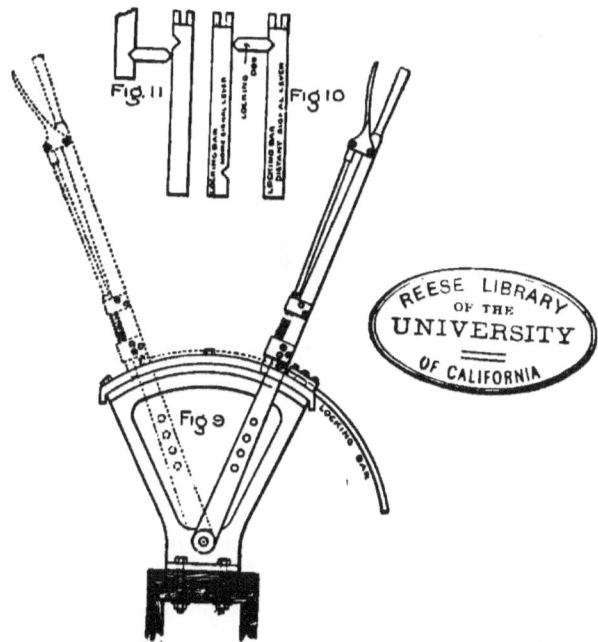

signal cannot be cleared until after the home signal, and in
returning the signals to the danger position, that of the distant
signal must be moved first. A lever stand provided with the
necessary locking and which is of simple construction, is shown
in Fig. 9, the parts by which the locking is accomplished being
shown in plan view in Figs. 10 and 11. The long bars, having
a notch in one side, are called "locking bars," one being provided for each lever. The cross piece having its end tapered
to fit in the notches cut in the bar, is called a "locking dog,"
and is made of such a length as will allow it to fit in between the two locking bars, provided one end be placed in

one of the notches, as shown in Fig. 10. It will be seen in this figure, where both levers are supposed to be in the normal position—that is, with both signals at danger—that from the position of the locking dog, the home signal lever is the only one that can be moved. If this lever be pulled over and the signal cleared, the bar will be drawn back, bringing the notch in that bar opposite the one in the other bar. This now makes it possible to pull over the distant signal lever, as the locking dog is forced into the notch in the other bar, as shown in Fig. 11, locking the home signal lever in the reversed position, until the distant signal lever is once more returned to the normal position.

In locating the signals at any station, several things have to be taken into consideration, which are regulated to a great extent by the system and the number of signals used. Where the two signals are placed on one pole, the location of the pole does not fix the exact spot at which trains must stop, as it frequently happens that trains have to pass the signal when at danger, in making a stop in front of the station. An arrangement of this kind has but one thing to recommend it, and that is its cheapness, while there are several grave objections. As has already been stated, a train must often run by the signal when at danger, to make a stop or to do any switching at the station. At night, if they have so run by the signal, the engineer and trainmen cannot see if it has been cleared, and the conductor has to walk to the other side of the signal to make sure that it has been cleared for his train to enter the block. That the operator from his office can see the light showing through the red glass of but one signal, and would not be likely to detect it should the glass of the other signal get broken.

The best practice in locating such a signal at any station, is to put the signal on the same side of the track as the station, and at either end of the station building, where the operator can see the signal lamp from his office window. The object of such a location is to have the signal where it can be seen by a conductor without his having to look through or over a train to see it, and also where the operator can see that the light is burning properly, and that at least one glass is in its place. Of course, if the view is such that on account of a curve, buildings, or what is more likely, a water-tank, the signal—so located—would not be seen, it would have to be placed on the opposite side of the track. Where this will not overcome the difficulty, the best plan is to put the signal on a bracket pole, as is shown in Fig. 12, bringing the blade very nearly over the center of the track.

A better arrangement, if a road can go to the necessary expense, is to have each of the two signals on a separate pole, placed

A BRACKET POLE.

on the right-hand side of the track as viewed from an approaching train, and at a sufficient distance past the station to allow the train to make the stop in front of the station without having to pass the signal. The operator would then be able to see each signal light, and would be likely to notice it were either glass broken. This is a very important point, when it is borne in mind that a signal is changed from "danger" to one indicating "safety," whenever this happens; and that it happens very often is not to be wondered at when it is seen that a glass may be broken by the jarring occasioned by letting the blade return to a horizontal position with too much force, from strains due to improper setting of the glass in the arm-plate casting, or by someone throwing a stone or shooting the glass out, as will often happen near large cities.

In regard to the location of the distant signal, no stated distance can be said to answer for all situations, as the grades and the speed at which trains are run have to be considered before deciding at what distance from the home signal such a signal should be placed. Ordinarily the distance is 1,200 feet, but as the distant signal is the governing one, as regards the speed of the train, it would seem that a greater distance than this is to be preferred, as in so short a distance a heavy freight or fast passenger train cannot be brought to a stop, should they pass the distant signal at schedule speed. While it is possible to work a signal a distance of 3,000 feet from the home signal, it is not advisable to go beyond 2,500 feet, owing to the difficulty of keeping the wires properly adjusted and the labor required to clear the signal. The change in the length of such a wire, due to expansion and contraction, is considerable; so that unless very carefully looked after and adjusted, the blade will not be brought to the proper position, and the engineer will be in doubt as to what the signal indicates.

Of course, the objection to such long wires would, to a great extent, be done away with if a good compensator might be had to automatically take up the changes in the length of the wire, so that the proper working of the signal would not be affected. At the present time, only one wire compensator, that invented by Mitchell & Stevens, can be said to be a practical success, and were it not for its cost, it would certainly come into more general use. Its construction is very plainly shown in Fig. 13. The expansion and contraction of the wires are taken up by a sliding frame, the wires being kept taut under constant tension, by means of a weight. The objection to the use of a weight is that if the wire that pulls the signal back to the danger position were to break, the weight would pull the signal to the "clear" position, and thus give a wrong indication. To overcome this objection, the two wires are attached to a loose lever, as shown in the cut, which would be pulled away from the cranks if either wire were to break, thus leaving the signal free to return to the danger position by the force of gravity.

There is one question in connection with a telegraphic system of signals, regarding which very different views are held by different superintendents, but about which I think there should be no doubt as to which is the best practice. It is this: Shall the block signal be also used as an order signal, or shall there be two signals at a station for trainmen to observe—one the block signal and the other the train order signal? The argument in favor of using the two signals is that an operator, on receiving a train

MITCHELL'S & STEVENS' COMPENSATOR—NORMAL POSITION.

order, has to put the train order signal at danger before the "O. K." is given by the train dispatcher, and is therefore certain to stop a train for which he has an order; that with only the block signal, which is kept at danger unless cleared for a train, there is nothing to depend upon for the delivery of the order, except the operator's memory, and that on hearing the whistle for the signal, he may forget that he has an order to deliver and give the train a clear signal, particularly if he had fallen asleep and had just waked up.

The argument in favor of making the block signal answer for both purposes, and which I believe to be the stronger of the two, is that the engineer is more likely to take the indication of the more conspicuous signal and forget to look at the other one, than is the operator to forget that he has an order for a train. That this is true, and that an engineer will sometimes fail to look at the order signal while taking the indication of the block signal, the writer is convinced of, from the fact that two such instances have come within his knowledge.

CHAPTER IV

CONSTRUCTION—THE CONTROLLED MANUAL SYSTEMS.

With these systems, as their name implies, the labor of two men, one controlling that of the other, is required to clear the signal for a train to enter the block. The work of "clearing" the signal is done by the man at the entrance of the block, the same as with a telegraphic system, but the controlling power, or the actual permission to so clear the signal, is given only by the man at the end of the block.

The arguments used in favor of this method of operation are, that where two men are required to work in this way in connection with each other, they are less likely to make mistakes, each acting as a check on the other; that placing the control of the signal in the hands of the man at the end of the block is a much more reliable and certain plan of operation, as he will know whether a train admitted had actually passed out of the block; that by making it impossible, by means of the track circuit, for the signal to be again cleared until after the train admitted has passed out of the block, all chance of a mistake being made by either operator is eliminated, and the indications given by the signal can be relied upon as showing the actual condition of the block.

The arrangement of the several parts of a Controlled Manual system is somewhat more complicated than are those of the telegraphic systems, and while a description of the instruments sufficient to explain the operation of such a system has already been given in a previous article, the special parts peculiar to each system have yet to be described.

Of the three systems using this method of operation, that known as the Sykes system will be the first considered, not only as it was the first to be invented, but because it has come into more general use than either of the other two. This system may be said to consist of a machine having the necessary levers for operating the signals, of the Sykes lock instrument, and of an interlocking relay, the latter being used in connection with the track circuit to prevent an operator from again releasing a signal until the train for which the signal had been released has passed out of the block.

A machine having the two levers for operating the signals governing trains moving in opposite directions, and the corresponding lock instruments, is shown in Figs. 1 and 2. The principal parts of the instrument, the lock bolt, the lock bar, the lock rod and the plunger rod, are also shown in the figures, the levers being in the normal position with the signals at danger.

To explain the operation of the instrument, the operator, when he plunges, releases, by means of an electric circuit, the lock rod of the instrument in the next station, allowing it to fall by its own weight and lift the lock bolt from the lock bar, releasing the lever and allowing the signal to be cleared. As the indicator is attached to the lock rod, the indication would be changed to show the word "free" as soon as the lock rod dropped, showing to the operator that the lever had been unlocked. Clearing the signal, forces the lock bar forward, which, by means of the inclined plane and roller, raises the lock rod to its normal position, where it is held until again released by the operator at the next station. Raising the lock rod, changes the indicator back to show the word "locked," although the lock bolt does not fall into the hole in the lock bar until the lever is returned to the normal position.

The construction of the instrument whereby the lock rod is released and allowed to drop when the operator at the next station plunges, is shown in Fig. 3. The magnet M attracts the armature A, thereby raising it and slightly turning balance lever L on its center C; this releases trip T, which is then free to turn on its center, allowing the lock rod to drop by its own weight, unlocking the signal lever, as has already been explained. .

Fig. 4 shows the construction of the instrument, whereby an electric circuit is completed when an operator plunges. Pressing in the plunger P raises the cross-bar X, which, by means of the contact springs D and E, completes two circuits—one through contact D, Fig. 3, to the magnet of the next instrument, releasing

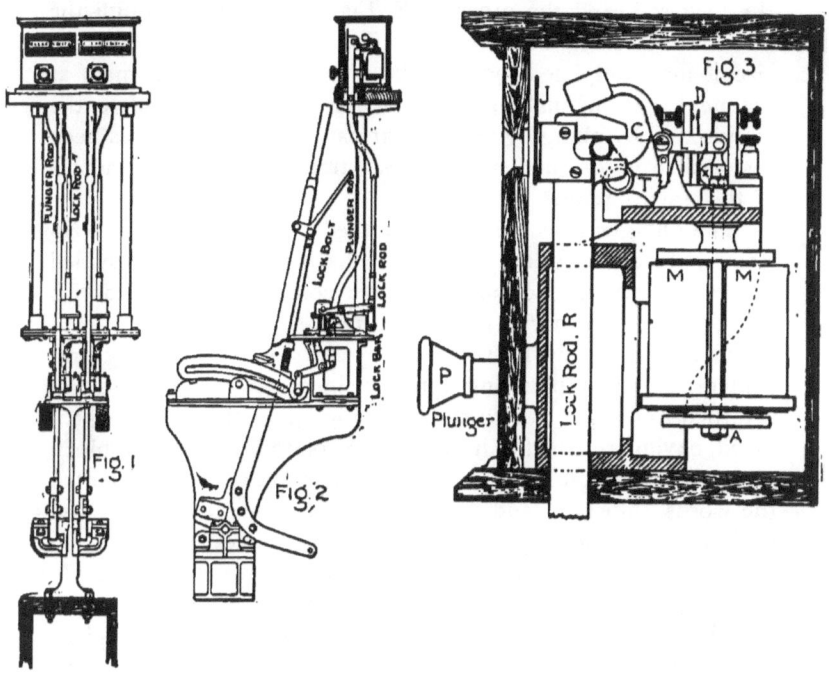

Fig. 1

Fig. 2

Fig. 3

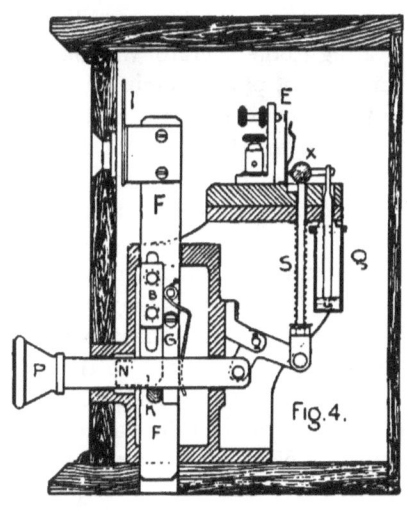

Fig. 4.

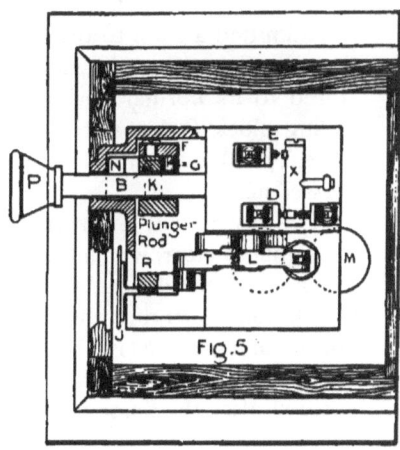

Fig. 5

the lock rod, and the other at E, Fig. 4, a circuit through the interlocking relay. This contact at E causes the relay to break the circuit just completed through the magnet of the instrument at the next station, making it impossible to again complete the circuit at D by plunging until the armature of the relay has been restored to its original position by a train passing onto and off of the track circuit.

The plunger when released is forced out of its original position by the action of the spring S, a dash pot Q being provided to retard this action, so that the electric contacts made at D and E will not be of too short a period of time.

The arrangement by which an operator is mechanically prevented from again plunging until the signal has been cleared and returned to danger, is also shown in Fig. 4. A trip rod F is provided, having attached to its side a pawl piece G and sliding block B, and carrying on its upper end a plate I, on which are painted the words "blocked" and "clear." Attached to the plunger rod (not shown in the cut) is a pin K, which, by means of the pawl piece G, supports the trip rod in the position shown in the cut.

The plunger is provided with a side piece N on the side next the trip rod, so that when the plunger is pressed in, this side piece will strike the pawl piece G, pushing it off the pin K and allowing the trip rod to drop, the sliding block B striking on the top of the side piece N, which is then underneath it. When the trip rod falls, and with it the indicator, it brings the word "blocked" in front of the opening in the case, indicating to the operator that he has admitted a train to the block, and cannot plunge again until the train has passed the station and the instrument has been restored to its normal position. On releasing the plunger, the sliding block B drops still further on the projection of the side piece N, and mechanically prevents the plunger from again being pressed in.

The instrument is restored to its normal position by pulling the signal to clear, which the operator will do as soon as the train which had been admitted to the block by his plunging, approaches the station. Clearing the signal, draws the plunger rod to the bottom of its stroke (Fig. 2), catching the pin K (Fig. 4) under the pawl piece G, so that when the signal is returned to the danger position after the passage of the train, the plunger rod is raised with it and the plunger unlocked. When the trip rod is raised, the sliding block B is raised with it out of the way of the side piece N, being held in the same relative position by the pressure of the pawl piece G. The raising of the trip rod changes the indicator to again show "clear," indicating to the operator that it is possible for him to plunge once more.

A plan view of the instrument, the parts by which the locking of the plunger is accomplished being shown in section, is shown in Fig. 5.

To explain how the locking circuit is broken and restored through the combined action of the plunger, the interlocking relay and the track circuit, reference must be had to Fig. 6, in which

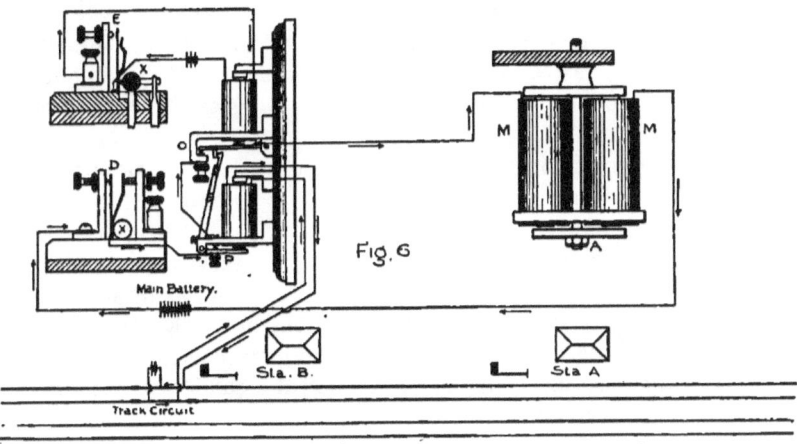

Fig. 6

all the parts made use of in this operation are shown. The relay and track circuit shown are those belonging to station B at the end of the block, the releasing magnet being the one belonging to the instrument of station A at the entrance of the block. Separate views of the contact points D and E are shown to make it easier to follow the action that takes place when the plunger is pressed in and crossbar X raised.

The construction of the bar X is such that the contact at D is made on the up stroke and that at E is made on the down stroke, the projecting point that engages with the spring E being arranged to turn on the bar as a center and press against the spring only on the down stroke of the bar. The relay points being shown in the normal position, it is seen that the lower magnet is energized by the current which passes through the two rails forming part of the track circuit, and the armature is held up. The circuit of the upper magnet being broken at E, its armature is down and makes a contact at O.

When the plunger is pressed in and the crossbar raised, a contact is made between the points at D, completing the electric circuit through the main battery, the magnet M and the points O and P, energizing the releasing magnet M, and unlocking the signal lever at station A. On the crossbar X being forced down by the action of the spring S (Fig. 4), contact is made, as already explained, at the point E, momentarily completing the circuit, energizing the upper magnet, and thereby raising the armature and breaking the releasing circuit at O. On the circuit being broken at E, the armature falls, but now strikes on the hook on the upper end of the armature belonging to the lower magnet, and is held up instead of making a contact at O, and it is impossible to complete the releasing circuit as long as it is in this position.

On a train passing out of the block and on the track circuit, the current passes from one rail through the wheels of the train to the other rail, and the lower magnet of the relay is demagnetized and the armature drops, breaking the releasing circuit at P, and letting the armature of the upper relay fall, again making a contact at O. When the train passes off the track circuit, the current again flows through the lower magnet, energizing it and raising the armature, making a contact at P and restoring the relay to its normal position.

From this it is seen that the interlocking relay in connection with a track circuit, makes it impossible for an operator to plunge and again release the instrument at the next station, until the train for which he had previously plunged had passed on and entirely off the track circuit, and therefore out of the block.

To prevent an operator from leaving his signal in the clear position, and not returning it to danger after the passage of a train, as he should do, an instrument has been designed called an "electric slot," which automatically sets the signal at danger and compels the operator to return the lever to the normal position before he can again gain control of the signal. On his restoring the lever to the normal position, it is, of course, locked until released by the operator at the next station, and thus the purpose for which the slot was designed is accomplished. The action of the electric slot is obtained through the use of an electromagnet, energized by a current from a battery passing through the two rails of an insulated section of track. The armature of this magnet acts as a latch, and makes the connection between the signal and the lever whenever the magnet is energized. When the armature falls, as it will do when the magnet is short-circuited by a pair of wheels on the insulated section of track, the connection between the lever and signal is broken; and the latter goes to danger by the force of gravity.

The Sykes system is in use on the New York Central & Hudson River Railroad, between Poughkeepsie and Buffalo; on the New York, Lake Erie & Western, between Jersey City and Turner's, and on a portion of the New York, New Haven & Hartford Railroad.

In the practical working of the Sykes instrument, several defects were discovered, which, in the endeavor to perfect the system, resulted in a set of requirements being drawn up by Mr. C. H. Platt, of the N. Y. C. & H. R. R. R., which a properly designed controlled manual system should fulfill. These requirements were met in the machine designed by Mr. Patenall, electrician of the Johnson Railroad Signal Co., and which is now known as Patenall's block signal instrument.

The requirements of the new machine, and the objections to the Sykes instrument which it was designed to overcome, are:

First—That gravity must be overcome by the action of the electric current in unlocking the signal levers, instead of allowing it to assist, as it now does, in withdrawing the lock rod from the locked position. This means nothing more than that a failure of the apparatus should lock the signal lever at danger, and not unlock it, as now happens with the Sykes lock, if the latch holding the lock rod in place should slip or be jarred loose, allowing the operator to clear the signal whether the block was occupied or not.

Second—That the magnets for unlocking the signal levers must not be in the electric circuit except at the moment of actual use, to prevent an accidental release by the crossing of wires, lightning or other causes. This requiring an intentional setting of the instrument before it can be plunged to and released by the next succeeding station.

Third—That no interlocking relay must be used, the contacts all to be made in the instrument, where it is impossible for them to be tampered with or changed.

Fourth—That the signal levers be perfectly free after having been once unlocked, so that the operator can change the indication of the signal as often as he desires, and not to have the lever locked whenever the signal is returned to the danger position, as is the case with the Sykes.

The construction of the instrument is shown in Fig. 7, in which P is the plunger and D and E the contact points by which the releasing circuit is completed, when the plunger is pressed in. M is the releasing magnet, which locks the sliding bar S whenever the latch A is dropped into either of the two notches in the bar S. This sliding bar, when it is drawn out by the hand latch H to its full extent, engages, by means of the pin K, with the rocker C, lifting the lock rod R and unlocking the signal lever by freeing the locking bar or tappet T, as is shown in dotted lines in Fig. 10.

This sliding bar S, by means of a second crank J (shown in dotted lines in Fig. 7), lowers, when pulled out, the vertical bar B, which, in turn, moves the lever L, bringing the inner end into contact with the plate N. This inner end is made in the form of a jaw and presses on both sides of the plate N, making a metallic connection between the plates fastened to each side. The plate N is made of insulating material having three metal strips, two on one side and one on the other, to which are attached the wires from the two circuits used in operating the instrument. The wire from the releasing magnet is attached to the one strip, the line wire from the instrument at the next station being attached to the lower and the wire from the track circuit to the upper strip on the other side. There are two indicators, one working in connection with the plunger P and showing the words "train on" whenever the operator has plunged; the other working in connection with the slide S by means of the lug G, the rod I and the indicator plate O, and showing the word "locked" or "free," according to the actual state of the signal lever.

The operation of the instrument may be explained as follows: Supposing a train to have entered block 1 and to be approaching station B. B asks C to release him, at the same time drawing out the hand latch H and pressing it down between the two lugs on

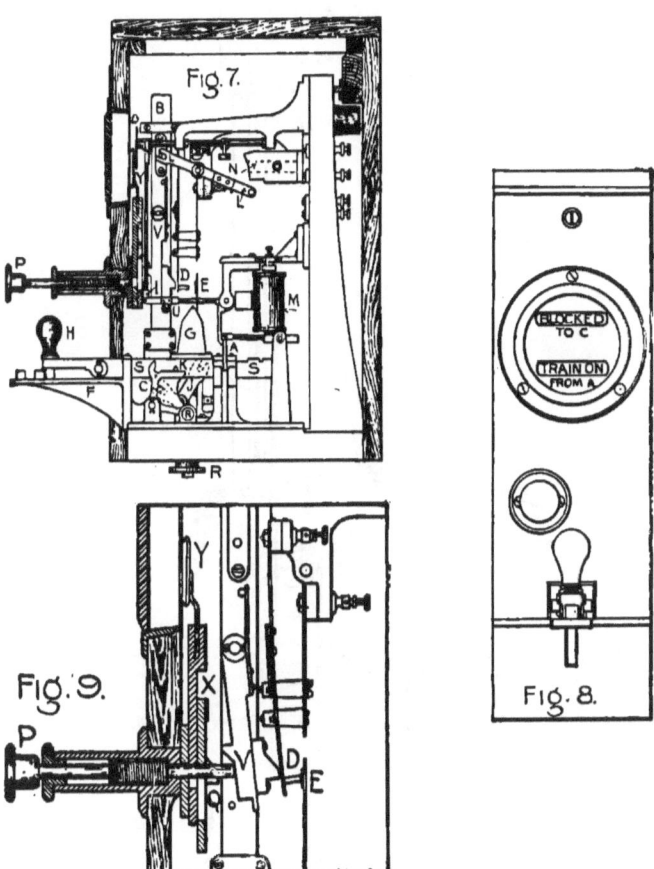

the bracket F, to hold it in that position. This pulls out the slide S and raises the inner end of the lever L, so that a metallic connection is made between the strip on one side of the plate N and the lower strip on the other, putting the releasing magnet in the circuit with the line wire and the instrument at the next station.

When C plunges, a contact is made between the points of his instrument at $D E$, as is shown in Fig. 9, sending a current of elec-

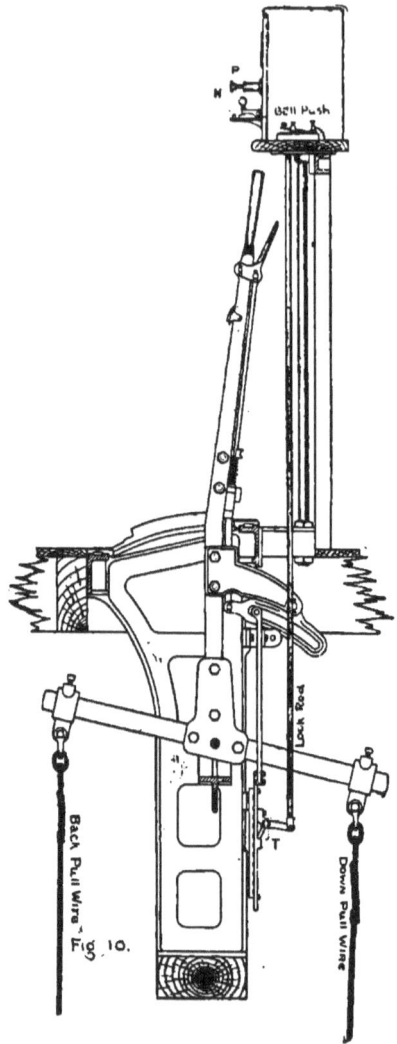

Fig. 10.

tricity through the magnet M of B's instrument, raising the armature and with it the latch A, unlocking the slide S, which B now draws out, raising the lock rod R and unlocking the signal lever, as is shown in dotted lines in Fig. 10.

When the plunger is pressed in, the pawl V is forced off from the lug Q and the slide X drops, carrying with it the indicator Y. On releasing the plunger, the slide drops still further, making it impossible to again plunge until the slide has been raised to its former position. The words "train on" have now been brought in front of the opening in the case, indicating to the operator that the track is blocked.

When the slide S was pulled out to its extreme position, and the bar B dropped, the inner end of the lever L was raised, breaking the connection with the line wire, and connecting the magnet M with the track circuit relay. The breaking of the circuit demagnetized the magnet M and the armature falls, dropping the latch A into the slot in the slide S, locking it in this position until it is again raised by the magnet M.

When the slide S is pulled out, the lug G engages with the roller U, raising the rod and changing the indicator O to show "free," as the lever is now unlocked.

When the train passes out of the block and over the track circuit, it demagnetizes the track circuit relay, the armature of which falls and completes a circuit through the magnet M, raising the latch and allowing the operator to shove in the slide S. This lowers the lock rod R, locking the signal lever at T, Fig. 10, breaks the connection at the plate N, raises the bar B and with it the slide X, unlocking the plunger and making it possible for the operator to plunge once again. The indicators are changed back to their normal position, showing to the operator that the machine is locked and that no train is in the block. An electric slot on the signal pole is provided, which restores the signal to danger on the passage of a train, to make it impossible for the operator to hold the signal in the "all clear" position, and admit a second train to the block.

This system is in use on the N. Y. C. & H. R. R. R., between New York and Poughkeepsie; on the N. Y., N. H. & H. R. R., between New Haven and Providence, and on the Long Island Railroad.

The equipment on the N. Y. C. & H. R. R. R., through the tunnels in New York city, is, perhaps, the most complete of its kind in the world, and one that, considering the business that is handled, can hardly be equaled in the amount of protection afforded by any other system.

As has been previously stated, neither of these systems—the Sykes nor the Patenall—are applicable to single-track roads, from the fact that a train on passing over the releasing section would release the instruments at the station in front as well as in the rear, and thus make it possible to admit a train to the block and bring about a head-end collision.

A controlled manual system that is applicable to single as well as double-track roads, and one that has been in service for about two years and has given good results, has just been patented by Messrs. Fry & Basford. As it is of low cost, thus bringing it within the reach of many roads not able to afford the more costly apparatus of either of the other two systems, a short description of the system would be advisable.

The apparatus made use of may be briefly stated to be: An electro-magnet for controlling the signal lever; a polarized relay and pole-changing switch to energize the electro-magnet at the next station and unlock the signal lever; a track circuit, and a track instrument with the necessary relays to restore the releasing circuit when a train passes out of the block; an electric slot for putting the signal at danger immediately a train has passed by the signal.

As the drawing showing the several relays and the different circuits is somewhat difficult to read, I will not give it here, but will say that the apparatus is inclosed in a neat box with the handles of the two switches that are worked by the operator projecting from one side.

But one wire is used in this system, the telegraph instruments being cut out whenever it is desired to unlock the signal. The line wire is also grounded whenever the signal lever is pulled over and the signal cleared, so that the operator is cut off from communicating with the next station and is forced to keep the lever in the normal position as much of the time as possible.

The lock for controlling the signal lever is shown in Fig. 11, it being made to work with the ordinary levers used in operating the signals by the telegraphic method. L is the signal lever; S a sliding bar, with notches cut in it as shown and attached to the

lever L; A is the armature of the magnet M, the end being made
to fit in the notches cut in the bar S, to prevent the lever from
being pulled over unless the armature is raised; M is the magnet
for raising the armature and releasing the lever when the proper
connections are made and the electric circuit completed between
the two stations.

The operation of this system is as follows: Supposing a train
to be approaching station A, and that A has asked B to release
his signal, the block being clear, B shifts his pole-changing
switch and reverses the current sent out from his battery to the

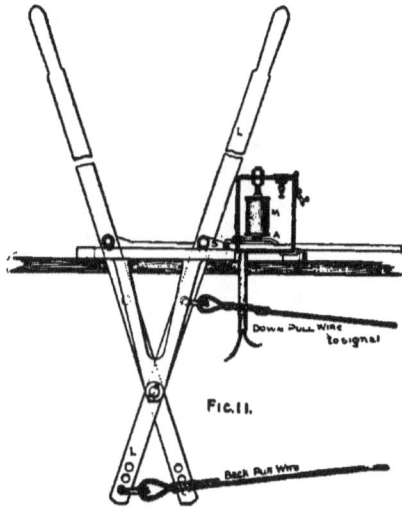

Down Pull Wire
to signal

Fig. 11.

Back Pull Wire

main line. At the same time, A shifts his switch connecting the
polarized relay with the main line, thus closing a local circuit
through the releasing magnet M and unlocking the signal lever.
Pulling the signal lever to "clear," breaks the main-line circuit,
dropping the armature of a magnet in the instrument and making
it impossible for the signal to be released a second time should
the operator at B leave his pole-changing switch in the reversed
position. On shifting the pole-changing switch back to its normal position, the circuit is broken between the battery and the
ground, and positively held open until the train which has entered
the block at A clears the track circuit and, consequently, the block

at B. In this way the admission of a second train at A is prevented while the block is occupied. To prevent a train on passing out of the block from restoring the circuit to stations on either side, and make it possible to unlock the lever at the next station ahead, as well as the station in the rear, two circuits are made use of, by which, unless they are passed over and completed in a certain succession, the releasing circuit is not restored and, in consequence, it is impossible to clear the signal. One of these circuits is completed by the track instrument, the other by a track circuit which is placed on the station siding, as well as on the main line, so that a train pulling into the siding would restore the circuits the same as if it had passed out of the block on the main line. The two circuits completed by this means are so arranged that the circuit made through the rails works a relay which closes the circuit completed by the track instrument, so that unless a train passes over the track instrument before it passes over the track circuit, no action is produced on the relay of the second circuit, and the releasing circuit to the next station is not restored. From this it is seen that the system affords the same protection to trains on a single track that is given by the other systems, which are applicable only to double-track roads.

Where roads have been equipped with a controlled manual system, the matter of expense has not cut such a figure as with the more simple apparatus, and the equipment has usually been more complete and all that good practice would require. As a rule, the instruments are placed in station buildings, but where these are too far apart, special cabins or towers are erected for the purpose.

If placed at a station, it is usual to put the signals for each track on the right-hand side, and at such a distance beyond the station as will allow the trains to stop at the platform without having to pass the signal. Where there is no station and a tower is used, it is usual to put the two blades on a pole placed immediately in front of it, as shown in Fig. 12, as the connections are shorter and the cost is less. If there are several tracks to be governed and there is no room to put the pole next the track which the signal controls, it is necessary to make use of a bracket pole having separate masts for each track, or else a bridge may be erected spanning all the tracks, the signal being put immediately over the track which it controls. The use of distant signals is, of course, optional, but the general practice is to put them in wherever the view is obscured, or the conditions such that the home signal cannot be seen until the train is quite near to it.

With a controlled manual system, it is possible to lock electrically all the switches and the levers of any interlocked crossing

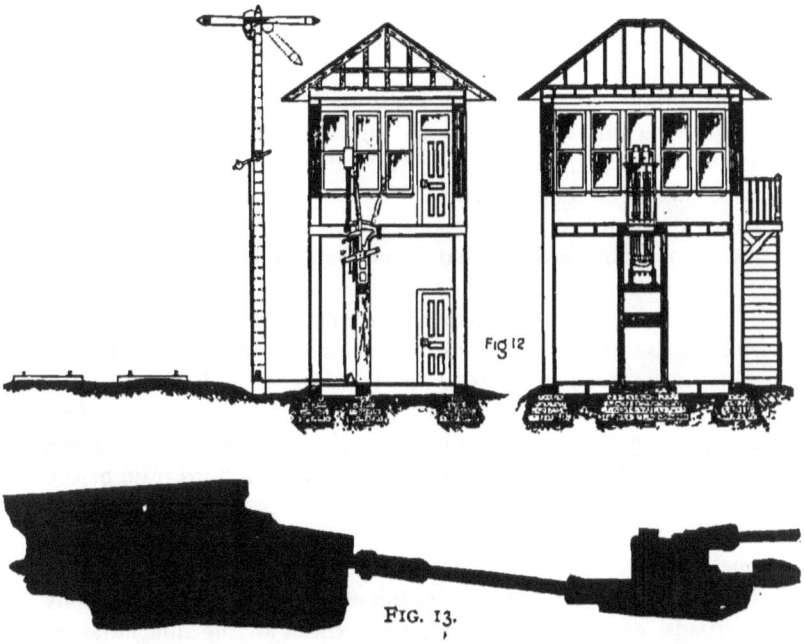

Fig 12

FIG. 13.

machine that may be in the block, so that when a clear signal is given it not only means that the block is clear, but that all the switches are set for the main line, and the derails and signals of any interlocked crossing are set for the train to proceed. This locking electrically is performed by fixing an electro-magnet on each switch and lever, so that it is impossible to open them unless the magnet is energized. This is done from the tower where the block signal machine is placed, and is so arranged that when the electric switch is set to release a switch in the block, the releasing circuit between the two stations is broken, and the operator at one station cannot plunge and release the signal at the next station.

The automatic torpedo signal—an auxiliary signal that works in connection with the home signal—has of late come very much into use with the controlled manual systems. The machine is bolted to the rails, and is so arranged that when the semaphore signal is put in the danger position, a torpedo is moved forward from the magazine and placed where it will be exploded by the first wheel that passes over it. When the signal is cleared the torpedo is withdrawn from the rail and a train passes by without exploding it.

It is thus seen that such an instrument is of great value in such places as a tunnel, or where the signal lights are apt to be obscured by smoke, or are in any way difficult to see, as it furnishes an audible signal about which there can be no mistake, and one which compels the engineer's attention. If exploded, it furnishes incontrovertible evidence that the engineer did not obey the signal but ran by it.

With the controlled manual systems, it is, of course, impossible to use permissive blocking, as such use does away entirely with the protection afforded by the automatic features of the system. For, if two trains are admitted to the block, the first one passing out would release the signal at the entrance of the block, and allow a careless operator to admit a third train before the second train had cleared the block.

This is undoubtedly a great objection to such a system, and one that will stand very much in the way of its general adoption by many roads. Its field of usefulness is thus limited to sections of roads, or divisions, where, on account of the difficulties of operation, or the number of trains run, it is not safe to make use of permissive blocking.

CHAPTER V

CONSTRUCTION—THE AUTOMATIC ELECTRIC SYSTEMS.

The automatic systems may be divided into two classes, the automatic electric and the automatic mechanical, the distinction being made in the power used to operate the several systems.

It is the purpose of this article to consider the automatic electric systems only; but before doing so, it would be well to say a few words about the electric battery and the relays that are used with these systems, for it is upon the arrangement and construction of these two things, more than anything else, that an electric system depends for its proper working. The battery used is the one commonly used for telegraphing, and is what is known as the gravity battery, being made by placing a piece of copper and a piece of zinc in a glass jar and surrounding them with a solution of sulphate of copper. Chemical action takes place between the sulphate of copper and the zinc, resulting in the formation of an electric current flowing from the copper to the zinc, if the two are connected by a wire to complete the circuit.

If the wire in which the current of electricity is flowing is wound around a piece of iron, it will cause the iron to become magnetized in proportion to the amount of current and the number of turns of the wire. If the iron is soft or annealed, it will lose its magnetism when the circuit is broken. A piece of steel or hard iron will retain a part of its magnetism and become a permanent magnet. It is this property of a piece of soft iron to become magnetized by a current of electricity and then to lose its magnetism when the circuit is broken, that is made use of in the construction of the relay to transform the energy of the electric current flowing through the wire into the motion of the relay armature. For, by arranging a piece of soft iron in front of the poles of the magnet, it will be attracted when the magnet is energized and pulled away, either by a spring or gravity, when the circuit is broken and the iron loses its magnetism, a certain motion being thus imparted to the piece of iron each time the circuit is completed or broken. The piece of iron is called an armature, and the motion imparted to it is the one made use of in doing any mechanical work by electricity, whether it be to make or break electric circuits, to move valves, to turn a pulley, or any of the thousand and one instances that we find in every-day use.

Electricity is susceptible of measurement, the same as if it was a piece of solid matter having size and weight, and while science is yet unable to say that it is anything more than a force, its laws and properties are well understood. The electrical units of measurement are the "ampere," the "volt" and the "ohm"—the ampere measuring the amount of current that is flowing in a given circuit, the volt being the tension or pressure existing between the two poles of the battery, and the ohm the resistance offered by the wire, or other parts of the circuit, to the passage of the current. The amount of electricity flowing through a given resistance is directly proportional to the pressure; the lower the resistance, the greater will be the amount of electricity flowing with a given pressure; the greater the resistance, the greater must the pressure be to send a given current of electricity through that resistance. If there are two channels through which a current of electricity can flow, the amount flowing through each will be inversely proportional to their resistance. A gravity cell, such as is used to work the different relays, gives a current of one-quarter of an ampere, at a pressure or electro-motive force of .9 or about one volt, and has an internal resistance of four ohms to the passage of a current of electricity. If the cells are arranged in series—that is, with the copper of one attached to the zinc of the next—the electro-motive force or voltage is increased one volt for each cell, and the amount of current remains at ¼ ampere; if the cells are in parallel, with all the coppers connected to one wire and all the zincs to the other wire, the electro-motive force remains the same, while the amperes are increased ¼ ampere for each cell.

Having these facts and figures, we are now in a position to take up and consider the arrangement of a track circuit, the relay, and the action which takes place when a train runs on the track circuit; for, as the track circuit is the controlling agent of the best of the automatic electric systems, it is necessary that a thorough understanding be had of the part that it plays in the successful working of such a system.

In equipping a road with an automatic electric system, the track is divided up into blocks of any desired length, a signal of the pattern adopted being placed at the entrance of each block. The rails of each block are made into a track circuit by insulating the rails of one from those of the next block, by means of a fiber end piece of the same size as the rail, and by using wooden splices in place of the iron ones, as shown in Fig. 3.

It has been found impossible, in practice, to make the length of any one circuit longer than 3,000 feet, owing to the increase of the resistance of the circuit, causing in wet weather such a loss of electricity, by leakage across the track from one rail to the other, that enough electricity does not flow through the relay to magnetize it, producing the same result that a pair of wheels would if it were in the block. In consequence of this there may be

several track circuits or sections in a block, each one being insulated and separate from the next, but so arranged, by means of relays, that the same results are obtained as with a single-track circuit the length of the block.

Each rail in the section is joined with the one next it by a bond wire, as is shown in Fig. 2, for the purpose of making a continuous circuit from one end of the section to the other, the contacts made by the angle bars being imperfect on account of wear, rust or the loosening of bolts. There are two bond wires to each joint, being usually placed on opposite sides of the rail; so that if, from any cause, one should get broken, the circuit would be maintained through the other one. At the end of each section furthest away from the signal, a battery of two cells is located, the two poles of which are respectively joined by wire to the two lines of rail; the manner of attaching a wire to a rail being shown in Fig. 1, the connection between the two wires being soldered.

The cells, for protection, as well as to prevent their freezing in cold weather, are placed in a box or battery well, shown in Fig. 4, and buried in the ground. At the signal end of the section a relay is placed, being connected by wires to the two lines of rails, and in this way establishing a complete circuit from the battery to one rail, from the rail to the relay, from the relay to the other rail, and from that rail back to the battery. Owing to the fact that water makes the earth a fairly good conductor, it is necessary that the resistance of the circuit be kept as low as possible, so that

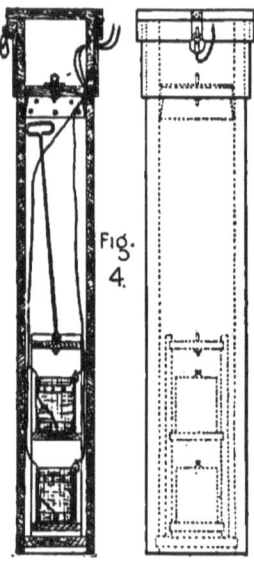

Fig. 4.

even under adverse conditions there will be less resistance through the relay than across the track, and the electricity will follow the rails and energize the relay, making it work properly in all kinds of weather. To keep the amount of electricity that leaks across from one rail to the other as small as possible, the two cells are arranged in parallel, the amount of electricity being increased thereby, while the voltage or pressure remains the same as with one cell. This reducing of the pressure reduces the power of the current to flow through a certain resistance, so that where there would be a large leakage of electricity across from one rail to the other, if the cells were in series, there would be but very little 'if they were in parallel, the current flowing through the relay instead and energizing it. In practice it has been found that the resistance of the relay should very nearly equal that of the external resistance of a circuit; but as the resistance of a track circuit is only half an ohm, it is practically nothing, and so the relays are made of the same resistance as a cell, or four ohms.

The relay used in connection with a track circuit, from the nature of the work, must be a very sensitive one and able to work with the least possible current. The magnets should be comparatively large, the armature light and well proportioned, and the parts well fitted without lost motion, so that a maximum of pressure for a given current will be exerted on the platinum points and a good contact made. The working parts of the relay should be enclosed in a dust-proof box or case, so that no foreign substance can get between the points and thus prevent a contact.

Assuming that everything has been properly arranged, and that a current of electricity is flowing through the relay, energizing the magnet and attracting the armature; if now a train, or even a pair of wheels, should enter the section, a short circuit would be formed from one rail to the other, cutting out the relay, as there is practically no resistance through the wheels and axles—the current from the battery flowing to the rail, from that rail through the wheels to the other rail, and back to the battery.

When the current is cut out in this way, the relay loses its magnetism and the armature drops, separating the contact points on the end of the armature, and thereby breaking the current passing through them.

This other or second circuit flowing through the contact points is a more powerful one than that used for the track circuit, and is the one made use of to operate the signal, whether this is done by the application of electro-magnetism to the parts of the signal, or by controlling the action of compressed air, or the force of gravity, any one of which may be the power actually used to work the signal. The battery cells in the second, or signal circuit, are arranged in series, as the resistance of the relays and the wires connecting the signals is much greater than it is with a track circuit. The number of cells varies with the number of signals to be operated by the current and the length of the wire connecting the signals, or, in other words, according to the resistance. If the resistance is low, few cells will be required; if high, it means that there is more work to be done, and a greater number will have to be used. The number used varies all the way from four to twelve cells for each circuit, eight being about the average number required for blocks one-half mile long. The cells are either placed in battery wells or in small houses built especially for the purpose. These are generally sunk in the ground to prevent the cells freezing in cold weather.

The length of the blocks varies on almost every road; but as the expense of maintenance of an electric signal is small, the blocks are usually made much shorter than where operators have to be employed to work the signals. Then, again, as the length of the block regulates the distance apart which it is necessary to keep trains—the shorter the blocks, the greater being the number of trains that can be run in a given time—there is every advantage to be had in making them as short as the amount of money the road can afford to spend in this direction will allow.

An excellent feature of the track-circuit system is the ease with which switches and side tracks can be connected with the signal, and, by setting the signal at danger, stop a train if the main line is not clear.

A switch is protected by running either the track or the secondary circuits through a circuit breaker, worked from the points of the switch. If the switch is set for the main line, the circuit is not interrupted, and the signal shows "All Clear." If, however, the switch is open, the circuit is broken, and the signal will indicate danger.

By wiring up the ends of the side track and making it form a part of the track circuit, any train standing on that portion of the track will keep the signal at danger the same as if it were on the main line; so that whenever a train enters a side track in the block, the signal remains at danger until the train has entered the siding and cleared the main line.

A track circuit also affords protection against a broken rail, for if this should happen, the circuit through the rail would be broken, from a separation of the ends of the rail, and the signal would be set at danger.

Everything that has so far been considered is common to all

the automatic track-circuit systems, and may be said to be the ground work upon which they depend for their proper working, so that it is from this point that they diverge to the several devices which constitute the different systems.

Taking up the Westinghouse pneumatic system, it will be remembered that this system makes use of the ordinary semaphore to give the different indications of the state of the block, the work of moving the signal being performed by means of compressed air controlled by a valve, operated by an electro-magnet; the compressed air being supplied from a central pumping station, at a pressure of sixty pounds, and in as dry a state as possible, to prevent clogging the apparatus from the condensation of water.

The general arrangement of the apparatus showing the connections to the signal blade are shown in Fig. 5, the photograph being made of a signal on a road where green is used for the all-clear signal. It will be noticed that the signal casting is made to hold two glasses, one red and the other green, that one being brought in front of the lamp which will give an indication corresponding with the position of the blade. As is customary where this system is in use, there are two blades on the pole—the upper a home signal, painted red, and governing the block immediately ahead; the lower, a cautionary signal, painted green, and working in connection with the home signal of the next succeeding block. Each signal is operated by a piston working in a cylinder which is three inches in diameter, the piston rod being so connected to the balance lever as to move the signal to the safety position, when air is admitted from the supply pipe to the cylinder; the weight of the signal casting and that on the balance lever, if such is necessary, causing the signal to return to the danger position when the air is released. From this it is seen that although the normal position of the signal is at safety, not at danger, the fact of its being at safety is a sure indication that everything is all right; for if anything should happen to the air supply, or any of the parts become disconnected, or either of the circuits get broken, the signal would immediately assume the danger position, and remain there until the defect was remedied. The details of the cylinder, the valve and the electro-magnet are clearly shown in Fig 6, the parts being shown in a position corresponding with the danger position of the signal. M is the magnet, A the armature, and V a valve worked by the armature. P is a piston working in the cylinder C, S the pipe by which the air is supplied; E, F passages for admitting air to the cylinder; X a valve worked by the spring Z, to shut off the supply of air whenever the current passing through the magnet M is broken; and Y the exhaust opening into the atmosphere by which the compressed air is allowed to escape.

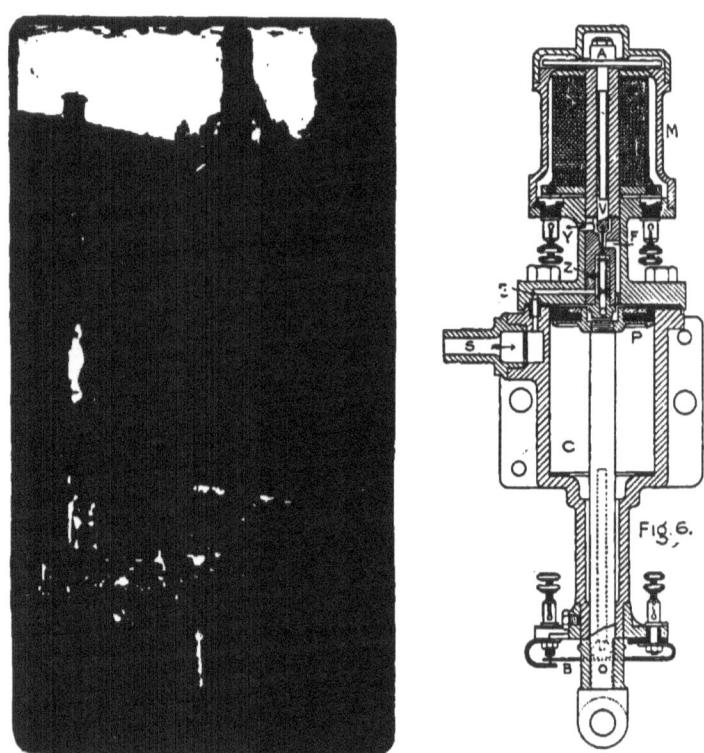

THE ELECTRO-PNEUMATIC SIGNAL.

B is a circuit breaker, worked by a pin on the side of the piston rod, being so arranged as to break the circuit operating the precautionary signal whenever the home signal assumes the danger position.

The operation of the signal may be explained as follows: Supposing the signal to be in the danger position, and that the signal circuit, or the one energizing the magnet, had just been closed by the track-circuit relay. The current would then flow through the magnet M, causing the armature A to be attracted. This presses the valve X from its seat, at the same time seating the valve V, closing the exhaust and allowing air from the supply pipe S to flow along the passages E and F into the cylinder behind the piston P, forcing it through the cylinder the length of its stroke and clearing the signal. As the piston was pressed down, the spring of the circuit breaker would be released, the circuit closed, and, if the next succeeding block was clear, the cautionary signal would assume the "All Clear" or "Safety" position.

A diagram representing a piece of track, divided into several block sections, with the necessary signals and the several electric circuits, is shown in Fig. 7. The upper signal, with the pointed end, on each pole, is the home signal; the lower one, with the end notched, is the cautionary signal, showing the condition of the next succeeding block ahead. An engine is supposed to be in Block 2, the signals of the several blocks being shown in the position they would assume in consequence of this block being occupied. In Block 1 we find that, as there is no train or part of a train in this block, the current from the battery is flowing through the rails of the block and energizing the relay, the armature being held up and the signal circuit closed. This energizes the magnet of the home-signal cylinder, and, by attracting the armature, opens the valve and admits air to the cylinder, clearing the signal.

As the lower, or cautionary signal, must indicate the condition of the next succeeding block the signal circuit operating the magnet must be controlled by the track-circuit relay of that block, and, as the relay is short-circuited by the engine in that block, the signal circuit is broken and the signal is shown at danger. This is clearly shown by tracing out the two circuits of Block 2. The armature of the relay is down, breaking the signal circuit at the point E, the current from the main battery being cut off from the magnets operating the home signal of Block 2 and the cautionary signal at the entrance of Block 1—the signals, in consequence, indicating danger.

It will be noticed that the circuit operating the cautionary signal is made to pass through the circuit breaker worked by the home signal placed on the same pole, so that if the home signal

76

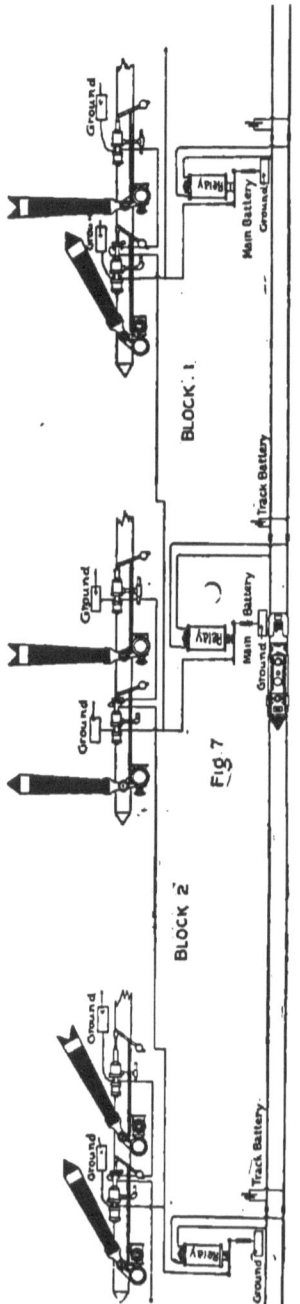

Fig 7

BLOCK 1

BLOCK 2

THE HALL SIGNAL.

FIG. 9.

should for any cause assume the danger position, the circuit of the cautionary signal would be broken and that signal would also go to danger. The obvious reason for this is that as the home signal is the controlling signal, when it indicates "Danger, stop!" the indication given by the other signal must, of course, be the same, or there would be at the entrance of the block two signals, one indicating "Danger, stop!" and the other "Safety, go ahead!" Breaking the signal circuit at this point does not cause both of the signals operated by the main battery of Block 3 to assume the danger position, as the two magnets operated by this current are in parallel and not in series; the current flowing from the battery through the contact points of the track-circuit relay, after which it is divided, one-half flowing through the magnet of the home signal, and the other half to the magnet of the cautionary signal. The circuit from each signal back to the battery is completed, either by a common return wire or by connections made with the ground, as is represented in the cut.

The signals at the entrance of Block 3 are shown at safety, indicating that not only is Block 3 clear, but that Block 4 is clear also.

If we suppose the train to have moved up into Block 3, both signals governing the entrance of that block would go to danger, the home signal at the entrance of Block 2 and the cautionary signal of Block 1 changing to safety, while the cautionary signal of Block 2 would remain at danger.

From this description it is seen that a train is at all times protected by a stop signal immediately behind it, and a cautionary signal which is the distance of an entire block behind that one, to give warning to any following trains that a train is in the next succeeding block. This system has been in successful operation for a number of years, and is at present in use, to a greater or less extent, on the Pennsylvania, the Central of New Jersey, the Boston & Maine, the Chicago & Northwestern and other roads. Criticisms that have been made against the system are that the cost of installation is large, and that there is a possibility of the signal giving a wrong indication, from water freezing around the air valve in winter, due to a condensation of moisture upon the valve and in the passages when air was released from the cylinder. The manufacturers claim that this latter difficulty has been overcome, by providing better means of drying the air at the pumping station, by draining the reservoirs regularly of water, and by putting the cylinder inside of an iron pipe, which pipe is made to answer for the signal pole, so that the parts are protected and will not become clogged with snow or ice.

Passing on now to the Hall electric signal, we find, as has been previously stated, that it differs very widely from the ordinary semaphore signal, in that the indications are made by different colors and not by the position of a signal blade. The form and general appearance of this signal is shown in Fig. 8, the signal being represented as indicating safety. The view shown is one taken on the Chicago & Northwestern, the signal being put in between the two tracks, wherever possible, as the trains of that road run on the left-hand track. As will be seen by reference to the figure, the working parts are inclosed in a large box placed on the top of an iron pole, a large glass-covered opening being made in the box, behind which a colored disk is raised or lowered to give the different indications. A white glass exposed in the back of the case whenever the disk is raised, does away with the necessity of bringing a white disk in front of the opening for the safety indication, and serves also to illuminate the disk when the same is brought in front of the opening. The case is painted black for the purpose of making a strong contrast with the red of the disk or the white of the background, and in this way make the indication more distinct and visible at a much greater distance than it would be otherwise. To distinguish a cautionary signal from a home signal, the case of the former is painted white, instead of black, so as to form a strong contrast with the disk, which is painted green in place of red, green being the color used to indicate caution, from its use as such for a night signal. Cautionary signals of this pattern are used in the same manner as with the semaphore signal, the two cases being arranged as shown in Fig. 9, the home signal being the one placed on top, or above the cautionary signal.

Two interior views of the signal case are shown in Fig. 10, the signal being represented in one case as at danger, and in the other at safety. It will be seen that the construction of this signal is exceedingly simple, consisting of a magnet supported on a suitable frame, which also acts as a bearing plate for the armature; of an armature made of special design, which, it is claimed, will lift a heavier weight with the same current than will any other form of armature; the two aluminum wire frames

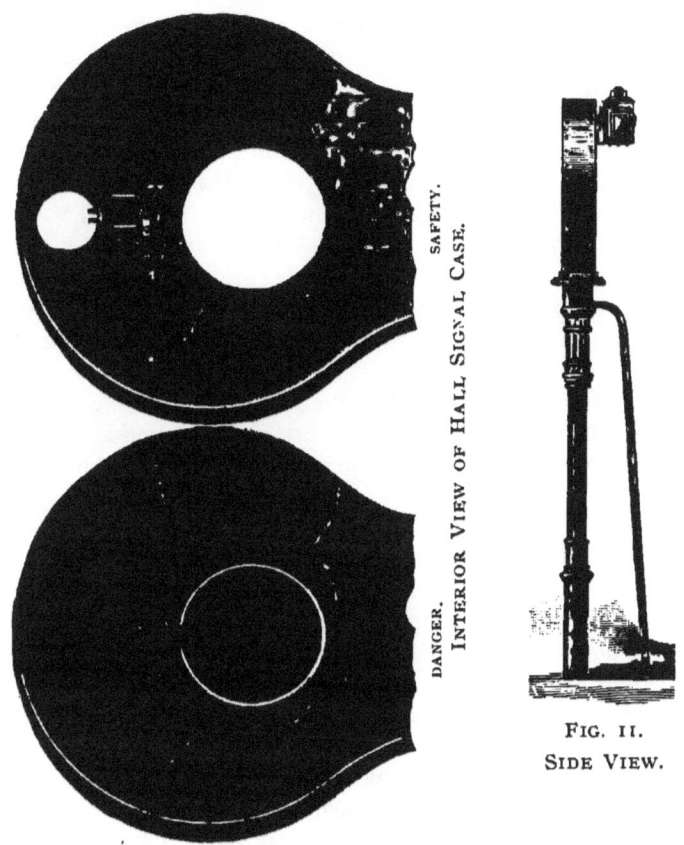

INTERIOR VIEW OF HALL SIGNAL CASE.

SAFETY.

DANGER.

FIG. 11.
SIDE VIEW.

fastened to the armature, over the larger of which colored silk is stretched to give the danger indication, a piece of colored glass being put in the other, which is brought in front of a lamp to give the same indication at night. The large disk being heavier than the small one, the signal moves to danger by the force of gravity. When, however, the magnet is energized, the disks are withdrawn from before the openings by the rotary movement of the armature, and a safety indication is given. The indications at night are made by a lamp placed behind the opening provided in the upper part of the case, as is shown in Fig. 11, the clear white light showing through if the signal is in the safety position, and red or green if it is at danger.

The circuits that are used with the pneumatic system can be used to operate this signal also, as the signal is held in the safety position by the signal circuit, the same as with the pneumatic. For, when there is a train the block and the track relay is short-circuited, the armature will fall, breaking the signal circuit flowing through the signal magnet, and allowing the signal to go to danger by the force of gravity. The cautionary signal being connected with the track-circuit relay of the next succeeding block, in the same way as was shown with the pneumatic system, it will indicate to an approaching train whether that block is occupied or not.

The Hall system is in use on the Illinois Central, the Boston & Albany, the Chicago & Northwestern and many other railroads, the total number of signals in use being in the neighborhood of 1,500.

Very decided objections have been raised against this form of signal by many experienced railroad men, owing to its depending entirely on color, instead of position, for the different indications, they claiming that the impression made on trainmen is not a very decided one, and that the signal is not visible at a sufficiently great distance, except under the best conditions of weather, to allow an engineer to stop before passing the signal, should it be at danger. However, these are questions about which almost everyone will have a different opinion, and it must be left for the management of each road to settle in the way they think best. Another objection is that wet snow will stick to the glass, and, by obscuring the signal, practically put it out of service just when a signal is most needed.

Of all the automatic signals, the Hall is the surest in its workings and the easiest to keep in order, the times when it has been known to indicate "Clear" when such was not the fact being few and far between. This has occurred where the case has been defective, allowing water to leak in and saturate the cloth of the large disk. The electro-magnet is, then, not strong enough, when energized, to raise the disk, unless the counterbalance weight is adjusted further out on the arm of the small disk. Should the cloth dry out and the counter-weight not be readjusted, the large disk will be overbalanced and the signal will be held at safety by gravity when the signal circuit is broken, thus giving a wrong indication.

Certain it is that one can hardly imagine anything simpler and less likely to get out of order than is this signal, for there is nothing touching the disk to catch or get out of adjustment, the power being applied direct by means of magnetic lines of force; there is no friction in the parts other than from one small shaft, and, by being inclosed in a case, the moving parts are protected from interference from any outside agency.

CHAPTER VI.

CONSTRUCTION—THE AUTOMATIC ELEC-
TRIC SYSTEMS.—Continued.

An automatic electric signal, with which, no doubt, the most of us are familiar, is the banner or clock-work signal shown in Figs. 1 and 2, it being the signal brought out by the Union

FIG. I.

Switch & Signal Co. to do away with the objections urged against a disk signal, and before the invention of the pneumatic signal.

It will be seen that the signal is made up of two disks—one being circular and painted red for the danger signal, the other oval in shape and painted white for the safety indication. A square plate placed behind the disk and painted black, to make a good background, brings out very strongly by contrast the difference in the form of the two disks. The framework surrounding the disks is painted white, and also helps to bring out,

FIG. 2.

in a way that is very effectual, both the form and color of the disk that is seen by an aproaching train.

The two disks are fastened to a shaft turned by a weight and clock-work mechanism, the latter being placed in the box seen underneath the disk. The mechanism is alternately released and held by a magnet operated by the signal circuit, or the circuit controlled by the track relay, the disks being turned through a quarter of a circle for each change in the condition of the magnet, thus alternately presenting one disk and then the other in the direction from which a train would approach. If the block is clear, the circuit is closed and the oval disk is displayed, thus giving a safety indication; when the signal circuit is broken, the armature drops, releasing the mechanism which turns the shaft through a quarter of a circle, and the round disk or danger signal is displayed. An ordinary switch lamp, placed on top of the

shaft, is used at night to give indications to correspond with those given by the disks.

The clock-work mechanism is shown in Fig. 3, the weight used for turning the signal being attached to a chain wound around the lower shaft, the shafts carrying the disks being placed on the spindle shown at the top of the figure. It will be seen that the armature of the magnet holds, at all times, one or the other of the two flops, which, when they are released, raise a catch holding one of the cross-arms of a shaft geared to the spindle, allowing this shaft to turn through a quarter of a circle, when it is caught by the other catch, the flop being held up by the armature. The weight is wound up by a handle made to fit on the square end of the shaft, seen in the cut, a threaded nut with a projecting pin being fitted to the shaft, and so made as to separate the contact points of two springs through which the signal circuit is run, and set the signal at danger if the weight is permitted to very nearly run down. This is done so that the signal will be left standing at danger when run down, as otherwise the signal might stop at safety and cause an accident by giving an "All Clear" indication when such was not the state of the block. The signal will give some some 600 indications for one winding, or, in other words, it will indicate correctly the condition of the block for 300 trains passing it.

This signal is in use on a large number of roads, the Cincinnati Southern, the C., M. & St. P., and the Providence & Worcester having quite a number in service. However, it will, in all probability, never come into very general use, from the fact that there is too great a chance of its getting out of order and giving a wrong safety indication; not that it will very often fail to work, but that when it does so fail, it is almost as liable to give a safety indication as one indicating danger.

An automatic signal to be worth anything must be made so that it will very seldom get out of order, as trainmen will lose faith in it if they have to disregard its indications very often. But while everything will get out of order occasionally, particularly if not properly looked after, it does not follow that when a signal does get out of order it should ever show safety. Although the mechanism of this signal seems very simple and well put together, it can very easily become disarranged or get out of adjustment, and show safety when it should not; for if any one of the following things should happen to the mechanism, the signal is just as likely to stop at safety as at danger.

Sticking of the armature, from polarization, or the armature binding in the trunions.

Jamming of the chain between the weight and the walls of the surrounding pipe.

Breakage of the chain, sticking of any of the parts, due to a lack of oil, accumulation of dust, etc.

There is one thing about the signal shown in the cut which

is quite an improvement over some other signals of the same pattern made by this company, and that is in providing a disk to give the safety indication and making the signal one of form as well as of color. Many of the signals have only the one disk, that for indicating danger, in which case it becomes a color signal only; for when the signal is at safety, the edge of the disk is presented, and the background—with this pattern painted white—would be the only thing visible. If the background against which the signal was seen happened to be one presenting little contrast with the white of the signal—the sky, for instance—it is almost impossible to distinguish it until quite close, and while a danger signal would be plainly visible, the safety indication would be very hard to make out.

With the signal shown in the cut, the safety indication can be plainly seen, irrespective of the surrounding objects, as the disk, being oval-shaped, would show very plainly, against the black background surrounded by a white ring.

An automatic signal that is very interesting, as showing a new development in the application of electricity to the operation of a semaphore signal, by means of a motor, is shown in Fig. 4, the apparatus being the invention of Mr. J. W. Lattig, superintendent of telegraph of the Lehigh Valley Railroad. The semaphore being recognized as the best form of day signal, and practically the standard signal of all the roads in this country, it is the hope of almost everyone that some cheap and efficient method of automatically operating a semaphore signal will be found, to place it within the reach of all; so that, looked at from this standpoint, this signal has much to commend it, and while the number that are in use is small, it is to be hoped that the results obtained will be such as to warrant a more extensive trial. As will be seen by reference to Fig. 5, the motor is mounted on the pole below the signal, the signal being cleared by winding up a wire rope attached to the balance lever, the signal blade being pushed by means of an up and down rod into the position indicating safety. The wire rope is made of phosphor bronze, and is wound upon a drum connected to the large gear wheel. This wheel is geared to the armature of the motor, to increase the leverage, and while it takes a longer time to do the work, it increases very greatly the lifting power.

To lock the motor after the signal has once been pulled to safety, and thus economize in the use of electricity, an ingeniously arranged worm gear is made to shunt the electric current from the armature of the motor to a magnet, Fig. 6, placed at one end of the armature shaft, a small circular armature being provided on the end of the shaft, so that when the magnet is energized it

will be attracted and held, thus locking the gear wheels and holding the signal in the safety position.

Normally, the position of this signal is at danger, the idea being to use the current only when a train is approaching—a method of operating an automatic signal known as the "Normal Danger" plan, the several circuits of which will be spoken of later on. When a train approaches the signal, the track circuit relay closes the signal circuit, starting the motor and winding up the wire rope by means of the geared wheel and drum. When the signal has been brought to the safety position, the signal circuit is shunted to the magnet, shown in Fig. 5 above the large gear

DETAIL OF LATTIG SIGNAL.

wheel, energizing it and attracting the circular armature, locking the armature and drum so that the rope cannot unwind, and
holding the signal in the safety position. As soon as the train

passes the signal, the signal circuit flowing through the magnet is broken, and the signal allowed to return to the danger position by gravity, the gearing and the motor revolving backwards as the rope unwinds from the drum.

The signal has been in service on the Central Railroad of New Jersey for over a year, and is reported as giving satisfactory results. As the motor is well boxed, there seems to be little chance

MOTOR FOR LATTIG SIGNAL.

of anything going wrong with it and causing it to give a safety indication when the block is not clear. The chance of this happening from snow or ice clogging the blade is very small, as the signal being normally at danger, it would be held in that position and not at safety, should sufficient ice collect upon it to prevent its working.

The battery, however, required is large, being eight to twelve cells of the Edison Leland type, to each signal, a fact that will

most likely prevent the signal coming into any very general use.
These cells are intended to be used on open circuit work, or inter-
mittently, and would soon run down if the current was used continuously. They give a much more powerful current than the
ordinary gravity cell, and are about the best cells to be had for
this purpose on the market.

The Kinsman block signal system is one that it would be
well to speak of, not so much for what has been done by the
system, as from the several discussions that have taken place
and the very generally expressed desire to have some definite
information in regard to it. This is really not a signal system
in any sense of the word, but one designed to stop a train by
shutting off the steam and applying the air brakes without the

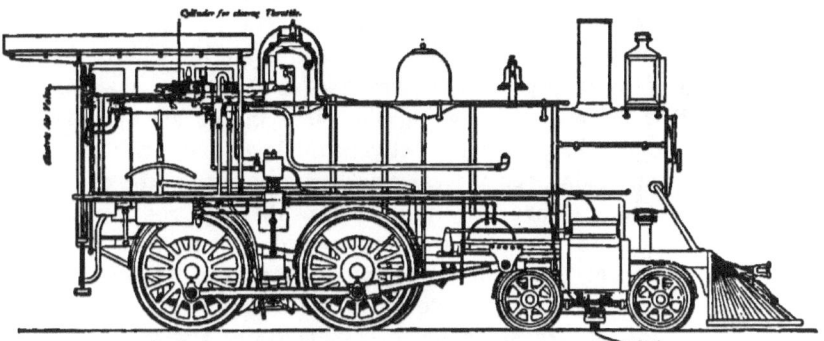

Fig 7—LOCOMOTIVE EQUIPMENT OF THE KINSMAN BLOCK SYSTEM CO.

help of the engineer, if there is a train in the next succeeding
block, or the second block ahead of the engine. It is, of course,
perfectly possible to work a signal in connection with the electric
circuits used, but this is not put forward as being in any way a
necessary part of the system.

The circuits are the same as those already spoken of in connection with the Westinghouse pneumatic signals, but with this
difference, that the signal circuit instead of opening a valve in
the signal cylinder, it trips a handle on the engine, opening an
air valve and admitting air to a cylinder which shuts off the
throttle and applies the brakes on the train.

A general view of the arrangement, as applied to an engine,
is shown in Fig. 7, the special parts belonging to the system

being the cylinder for closing the throttle, the magnet for opening the air valve when energized by a current of electricity, and
the wire brushes attached to the equalizer of the engine truck, to
pick up the current from a pair of guard rails placed on each
side of the track, they being connected to the signal circuit
battery, when the track circuit relay is demagnetized.

The circuits are arranged the same as for a home and distant
signal, except that the current, in each case, is conducted to the
guard rails instead of to the signals. As there were two signals,
so will there be two sets of guard rails that are energized behind
a train and which will stop a following train, should it pass over
either of them.

When an application of air has been made, the engineer does
not lose control of the train, for the magnet is energized momentarily only, as the engine passes over the guard rails, and the
engineer can pull up the handle, which will again be held by the
armature of the magnet. This will release his air, and, by shutting
the throttle lever home, making the latch in the air cylinder
catch and make the connection between the lever and the throttle
valve, he can again open the valve and admit steam to the cylinders. Of course, when the engineer does this and goes ahead,
he must run with caution, expecting to find a train in the next
block, or possibly a switch wrong, as causing the application of
the air on his train. When doing so, he assumes all responsibility for the proper management of his train, and would be
blamed for any accident that might result from his having gone
ahead.

The track circuit and relays used with this system are arranged the same as with the signal systems, except that the signal
circuit is completed instead of broken, when the track circuit
relay is demagnetized, the armature making a back contact instead of a front one. As the normal condition of the armature
is up, the normal condition of the signal circuit is broken;
so that while the track circuit is continuous, the signal circuit is
an open one, and is completed only when the armature is down
and an engine is passing over the guard rails. This plan of
having the normal condition of the signal circuit an open one is
a very bad arrangement, and is very much like making the safety
indication the normal position of a semaphore signal, for with an

open circuit the danger application is the one that is positive, and not the one indicating safety. In other words, if anything should happen to this circuit and it should fail to give an application, a *safety* indication is made, and not one that will indicate danger; the circuit fails to safety instead of to danger. To be safe, the system should be normally clear and fail to danger—a fault which it is manifestly impossible to overcome, from the fact that the apparatus is placed on the engine, where a continuous current through the magnet cannot be used.

It is to be regretted that in the most extensive application made of this system, the relays used in connection with the track circuit were of a somewhat experimental form and one not well adapted to the work to be performed, or the number of failures, as gathered from the report read before the American Society of Civil Engineers, would not have been so large. In that report, it is stated that no failure of the system had occurred where the system had failed to indicate danger when it should have done so, and while this is probably true, there were several instances where it would have failed in this way had it so happened that one train followed another into the block.

There are many things which may happen to the signal circuit and to the several parts of the apparatus, any one of which will cause the system to fail to make an application, and in this way give a safety indication when danger exists. These are: Sticking of the armature of the track circuit relay, from polarization, or from the armature binding on the trunnions; giving out of the spring of the application valve; breaking of the wires at any part of the circuit, or loosening of the binding screws, breaking the connection; broken jar, allowing the liquid to escape; grounding of the current, the voltage being high; a piece of paper, dust or any non-conducting substance getting between the contact points of the relay; brushes failing to make a contact; waste catching in the teeth of the gear wheel, preventing the air valve from being turned; valve sticking, from lack of proper oiling.

In describing the circuits spoken of in connection with the several automatic electric systems, it has been supposed that the signals have been applied only to roads having double tracks, the trains on a given track all running in the same direction. It has also been taken for granted that the blocks were short

enough to make it desirable to have a distant signal the length
of an entire block away from the home signal. In many cases it
is found that in looking over the ground preparatory to installing
an automatic system, that this latter arrangement, owing to the
length of the block, the consequent expense and the possible slowing up of trains, from their having to run the distance of almost
two blocks apart, is not advisable; in which case it is customary
to do away with a cautionary signal and make use of what is
known as the overlapping section. To use an overlapping section is to practically extend the block past the signal into the
block ahead, the two signals standing at danger so long as a
train remains on the overlapping section—that is, that a signal
shall not return to the safety position until the train has not only
entered the next block ahead, but shall have passed the signal the

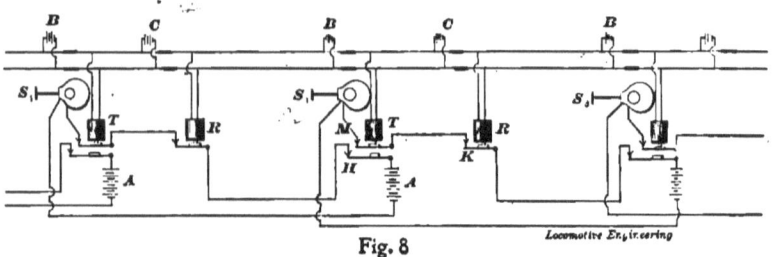

Fig. 8

distance of the overlapping section, the section being of such a
length as will give ample distance in which a following train
could be brought to a stop, should it have approached the home
signal at speed and found it at danger. In Fig. 8 an arrangement
of overlap track circuits is shown, the overlap being of any length
desired. S is the signal placed at the entrance of each block,
R the relay and B the battery for the main track circuit, T being
the relay and C the battery for the overlap section; A is the main
battery operating the signal. It will be noticed that the relay for
the overlap section is a double-point relay, the armature being
provided with two contact points and making and breaking two
separate circuits whenever the armature is attracted and released
by the magnet. By tracing out the several circuits, it is seen
that a train passing the signal and entering the overlap section
puts the signal immediately behind it at danger, and keeps the
signal at the entrance of the block it has just left at danger also.

for if the track circuit relay T is demagnetized, it will break the signal circuit to signal S-1 at H and to signal S-2 at M, and set them both at danger.

When the train passes from the overlap section to the main track circuit, the relay R is demagnetized, breaking the signal circuit at K, keeping signal S-2 at danger, while signal S-1 goes to safety, in consequence of the circuit being restored at the point H, the armature being attracted by the magnet of the relay T, which became energized as soon as the train passed off the overlap section.

Thus, there will always be two signals at danger behind a train as long as it is on the overlapping section, and only one signal

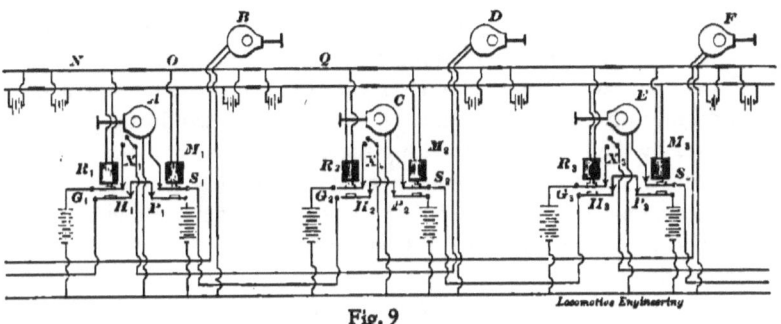

Fig. 9

at danger when it has passed off the circuit on to the main track circuit of the block.

All the circuits that have been considered, so far, are those for use only on a double-track road, but when a single-track road is to be equipped other circuits must be used, as the conditions are found to be more complicated and very different, for not only must a train protect itself by setting the signals in its rear, but it must set the signals ahead of it at danger, also, for trains running in the opposite direction. Such a system of circuits is shown in Fig. 9, being those used by the Hall Signal Co. in several installations which they have made. This arrangement of circuits provides what is called by them "preliminary blocking sections," in which the second opposing signal in advance is set at danger by a train before it passes into the overlap section of the signal. Without this preliminary section it is possible for opposing trains to enter the block at or about the same time, in which case each engineer would suppose that the signal had been set at danger by his train, and a collision would most probably result. With the use of the preliminary section this is impossible, as an engineer passing any signal would know that the track was clear for the block ahead and the preliminary section, also. If a train should enter the preliminary section at the same time that a train running in the opposite direction passed the signal of the block in advance, the signal at the entrance of the block in the face of the train on the preliminary section would be set at danger and that train would be stopped; the train in the block finding the next signal at danger would also come to a stop, and a collision would be prevented. By referring to the figure it will be seen that a train entering the preliminary section N, would put the signal D at danger by breaking the signal circuit at the contact G-1 of the track circuit relay R-1. On the train passing signal A and entering the track circuit O, the signal A would be put at danger by the relay M-1 breaking the circuit at the contact points P-1 and S-1, the signal D being kept at danger by a circuit breaker X worked by the signal A, so that while the contact is made by the relay at G-1, the signal does not return to safety. When the train enters the preliminary section Q, the relay R-2 is demagnetized, breaking the circuit of signal F at G-2 and that of signal A at H-2, keeping the signals A and D at danger, while the signal F, the next one in advance, is put at danger, also.

To show more clearly the effect of the preliminary section, let it be supposed that a train should enter the preliminary section N just after a train running in the opposite direction has passed the signal D; when the train at D passed the signal, it put the signals A and C at danger by short-circuiting the relay, the signal D being set at danger by the circuit breaker worked by signal A. The train having passed signal D at safety, would, of course, proceed on its way, not knowing that a train was running against it in the opposite direction. Not so with the train on the preliminary section, for although it would put the signal B at danger as soon as it entered the section, it would find signal A immediately ahead of it standing at danger and would come to a stop. The train running from signal D to signal B, finding signal B at danger, would also come to a stop, the length of the overlap section, or the distance between the signals A and B, being the distance between the two trains.

An arrangement of circuits that is being extensively advertised by one of the signal companies is one known as the "Normal Danger" plan, the signals being normally at danger until the approach of a train, say, to within 2,000 feet of the signal, when the signal will indicate safety, provided the block is clear. Claims are made for this arrangement that it effects a great saving in battery power, the signal circuit being closed only when the signal is at safety, and that if the signal is at safety it is positive evidence to the engineer that the signal is in good order and that the track is clear, particularly if he has been able to see the signal change from danger to safety. While these arguments are, without doubt, very good ones, there are several objections to the arrangement that with many will considerably outweigh the advantages. These are, that very frequently with the long distances in which the signals would be visible to the engineer, he would be inclined to reduce the speed, not knowing if the signal would be cleared for him to proceed; that if the signal should get out of order in any way, it would very likely not be found out until the approach of a train, thus causing delay, whereas if the signal was normally at clear, track men and others would be able to report the fact immediately the signal was found at danger without apparent cause; that track men and battery cleaners would know at all times, when maintaining the signals, that the circuits and batteries were left in good order, the fact of the signals being left at clear being evidence to that effect. Again, defects are more easily detected and repairs made, the signal going to safety and indicating that everything is all right, immediately the trouble has been remedied.

An arrangement of circuits that is in use on a good many roads, but one that is fast being done away with, owing to the superior advantages of a track circuit, is what is known as a wire circuit system, the signals being set at danger by means of a track instrument placed at the entrance of the block, and being cleared by a similar instrument placed at a certain distance beyond the next succeeding signal. Such an instrument is shown in Fig. 10; the wheels of a passing train striking the end of the lever which projects slightly above the rail, raises the other end and forces upward a piston inside the case, making or breaking the signal circuit, whichever it is intended to do, according to the position of the instrument relative to that of the signal.

This arrangement of circuits is certainly not to be recommended in comparison with a track circuit, since no protection from a following train is afforded should a train break in two, or back up after once passing the clearing instrument. No protection is afforded should a train on a side track not have pulled in far enough to clear the main line. And, again, such an arrangement of circuits would fail to give warning in case of a broken rail—a failure that is liable to occur at almost any time.

In the diagram showing the several circuits, the signal cir-

Fig 10

cuits have been represented as extending the entire length of the block, but in actual practice this arrangement is not always used, owing to the increased resistance of the circuit, due to the length of the wires. By making the line wire into a separate circuit from one signal to the next, and using a relay to make and break the circuit of a local battery, the same results are secured and a saving in battery power effected.

With an automatic electric system, any switch in the block is very easily protected, the signal at the entrance of the block being put at danger when the switch is opened by attaching a circuit breaker to the points of the switch, so that the current through one rail of the track circuit, which is run through the contact points in the box, is not only broken, but the battery end of the broken circuit is connected with the other rail and an effectual short circuit formed. Bringing the wires of the signal circuit down to the switch box, instead of breaking the wires of the track circuit, while a very effective arrangement, is in many cases a more expensive one, and one that is not necessary, the chance of the others failing to act being very slight.

Visible indicators, worked by the signal circuit, should be placed at all switches on the main line, so that if an approaching train has arrived within a certain distance of the signal at the entrance of the block, the indicator will be set at danger, and warn anyone desiring to use the switch that a train is approaching. Automatic signals should be located with reference to the character of the road and the number of trains that are run, the idea being to so space the signals as to make the running time through each block about the same. The plan of putting the signals very close together, if there are curves in the track, and very far apart where the signals can be seen, is a very poor arrangement, as it will often happen, owing to fog, snow or storms, that the signal cannot be seen until quite close to it, in which case trains following each other would be spaced the distance of the longest block apart, and not that of the shortest.

In placing signals at the entrance of a block, it is a very good plan to put the signal a short distance beyond the beginning of the track circuit, so that the signal will go to danger before the engineer passes it, thus letting him see that it is working properly. Where this is done, any engineer stopping because the signal is at danger must be careful not to let his train run into the section controlling the signal, or the signal will not change to safety when the train keeping the signal at danger passes out of the block.

CHAPTER VII

CONSTRUCTION—THE AUTOMATIC MECHANICAL AND THE STAFF SYSTEMS.

With the automatic mechanical systems an attempt is made by mechanical means to automatically put the signal at the entrance of the block at danger, when a train passes it, and to change the signal back to safety when the train passes out of the block. The necessary impulse, or power, to work the signal is obtained from the wheels of the train, an inclined bar placed against the side of the rail being pressed down by the first wheel passing over it, and the small movement thus obtained, being increased by an arrangement of levers, is made to work the apparatus. One of these bars, or trips, as they are called, is placed at the entrance of the block to set the signal at danger, and a second trip, placed at the end of the block and connected with the first trip and the signal by a pipe line, is used to change the apparatus and the signal back to the normal position when a train passes over it.

Two of these systems have come into a limited amount of use —the Rowell-Potter, on the "Alley" Elevated in Chicago, and the Boston, Revere Beach & Lynn in Massachusetts; and the Black system, on the Metropolitan Elevated roads in New York City. The Rowell-Potter system was applied to the Intramural Railway at the World's Fair, but was not a strictly mechanical plant, the release, or restoring of the signal to a normal position, being effected by means of electricity. As applied to the "Alley L," the equipment is nothing more than a station protector, the track for 1,000 feet in front of each station being made into a block, the signal being placed 650 feet from the station. If the blocks were multiplied sufficiently, the entire road would be protected, and trains could then follow each other no closer than the length of a block; as it is now, several trains may be run between two stations, but no train can pass the signal and not be stopped, so long as a train is in the station block. The Rowell-Potter system makes a notable departure from the ordinary signal systems, in that provision is made for stopping a train independently of the engineer, should he be negligent, or, from physical causes, be unable to obey the signal. The system is not only automatic, but obedience to the signal is made compulsory, and all chance of a mistake being made is eliminated.

The principal parts of the system are: the inclined bars or trips, the safety stop and air valve for applying the air if a danger signal is disregarded, and a latching device for holding up a weight and allowing the signal to be kept at danger as long as a train is in the block.

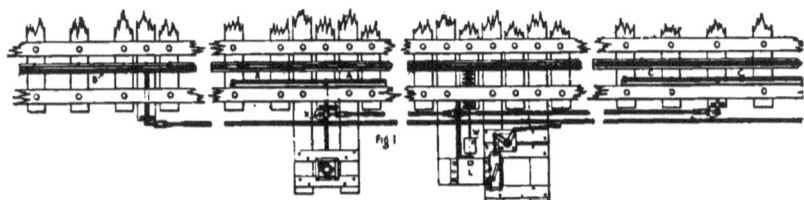

ROWELL-POTTER SAFETY STOP AND SIGNAL SYSTEM.

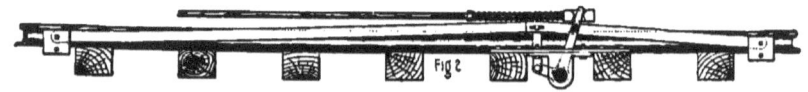

INCLINED BARS OR STRIPS.

The inclined bar, or trip, is shown in Fig. 2, and also at *B* in Fig. 1. One bar is about 6 feet long, the other 4 feet, the point where they are connected being raised 1 inch above the top of the rail. A train passing over the bars will gradually press them down, owing to their being inclined, and the motion so imparted is transmitted by a connecting rod and crank to a pipe line to work the signal or other parts of the apparatus.

The safety stops for applying the air are shown at *A* and *C*, Fig. 1, being placed at such a distance out from the rail that they will, if raised, strike the roller of the air valve on the engine, opening it and applying the air. Practically, the construction is the same as that of a trip, except that the bars are lighter and are raised at the joint by a crank worked from the pipe line. The air valve is shown in Fig. 3, a cross section of the valve, when · open, being shown in Fig. 4. Ordinarily the valve remains . closed; but should an engineer attempt to run by a signal, or should a part of the apparatus get out of order, the safety stop bars (*A* or *C*, Fig. 1) being raised, would strike the roller placed at the bottom of the vertical shaft, pressing it up, which, by means of the cam on the top of the shaft, presses in the valve rod, opening the valve and applying the air, the valve being held open by

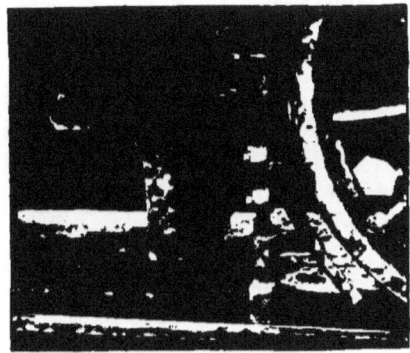

THE AIR VALVE.

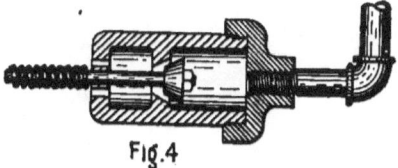

Fig.4

AIR VALVE OPEN.

the latch dropping down in the slot cut in the rod. The wire fastened to the latch extends up through the running board, so that the engineer can, by pulling up the latch, allow the valve to close and release the brakes before the train has been brought to a full stop. A right and left screw on the shaft allows for adjustments to be made to keep the roller the standard height above the top of the rail.

The latching device is shown at L, Fig. 1, and in detail in Figs. 5 and 6. The object of this device is to hold up the weight (seen at W, Fig. 1) after it has been raised by a passing train, allowing the counterweights X and Y, Fig. 1, to carry the signal

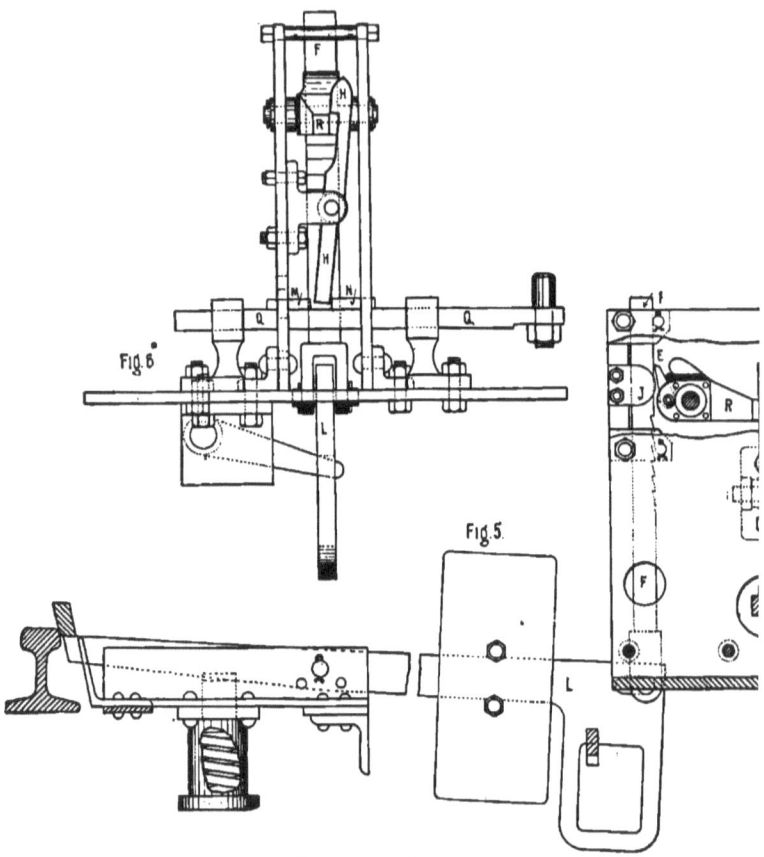

LATCHING DEVICE.

to danger and to drop the weight, thereby raising the two weights X and Y, clearing the signal, and restoring the apparatus to its normal position when a train passes over the releasing trip and out of the block. By reference to Fig. 5, it is seen that the lever L carrying the weight is attached at one end to the inclined bars or trip, and at the other end to the bottom of the rack rod F, which, if raised, will be held up by the pawl piece E, engaging with the teeth cut in the rod F if the rocker R is held by the latch H. If the rocker R is not held by the latch H, the rack will pull the rocker down, bringing the pawl E against the projection J, forcing the pawl piece out and allowing the rack rod F to drop.

The latch H is worked by the two lugs M and N, on the releasing bar Q, Fig. 6, the releasing bar being operated by a motion plate connected by means of a crank and connecting rod to the pipe line operated by the releasing trip. If the bar is drawn out, the latch will hook the end of the rocker, allowing the pawl to engage with the rack and hold it up when it is raised; if the bar is shoved in, the latch will release the rocker, the weight drawing the rocker down, the pawl piece being drawn against the projection and forced out, releasing the rack and allowing it to drop.

The general arrangement of the apparatus is shown in Fig. 1, B being the operating trip placed in front of the signal, where a train will pass over it, and, by pressing it down, raise the releasing trip, and also hook the latch of the latching device over the rocker, setting the instrument to hold the weight up when it is raised. Next to the operating trip, and opposite the signal, is the primary safety stop, which, if the signal is in the clear position, will be depressed, and will allow a train to proceed without stopping it. Next to this the signal trip and latching device is located, the secondary safety stop being placed beyond the primary stop.

The two safety stops are connected by a pipe line worked by counterweights, as shown, so that when one is depressed the other is raised, a crank worked by the lever of the signal trip being used to connect the pipe line with the weight and clear the signal when the weight is dropped.

At the end of the blocked section a trip, called the releasing trip, is placed, to restore the signal to the clear position when a train passes out of the block. It is connected to the operating trip by a pipe line, and so arranged that when the operating trip is down, the releasing trip will be raised. When the releasing trip is pressed down it will raise the operating trip, and thus leave the apparatus ready to be worked by the next train.

The operation of the system is as follows, supposing the apparatus to be in the normal position, with the operating trip raised, the primary safety stopped depressed, and the signal at safety, as is shown in Fig. 7, and that a train is approaching:

When the engine passes over it the operating trip will be depressed, raising the releasing trip and drawing out the releasing bar, latching the rocker of the latching device, so that the weight

ROWELL-POTTER AUTOMATIC MECHANICAL SIGNAL AT "SAFETY."

when raised will be held up. The signal being in the safety position and the primary stop depressed, the engine passes by without the air valve being opened; when the engine reaches the signal trip the bars are depressed, raising the weight which now is held up by the latching device, the crank operating the pipe line to the signal being turned by the lever, changing the signal to danger, raising the bars of the primary stop (as is shown in Fig. 8), and depressing those of the secondary stop, so that the engine passes on into the block without having the air applied.

When the engine has moved beyond the station a distance of 330 feet, it passes over the releasing trip and depresses it, the operating trip in consequence being raised and the releasing bar of the latching device pulled out. This allows the weight to fall and restore the signal to the safety position, the secondary safety stop being raised and the bars of the primary safety stop depressed, the apparatus thus being left in the normal position, to allow a second train to enter the block.

By connecting the two safety stops with the signal trip in the

ROWELL–POTTER AUTOMATIC MECHANICAL SIGNAL AT "DANGER."

manner shown, it insures that the brakes would be applied and the train stopped should the signal not be thrown to danger after the passage of a train. It will also enable the engineer to tell whether he has been stopped by a train in the block, or by some defect of the apparatus, due to breakage or to lack of adjustment. Switches are easily protected with this system, by providing a signal and safety stop to be worked from the points of the switch, at such a distance from the switch as will admit of a train being stopped before reaching the danger point. If all the engines of a road are equipped with the air valve of the system, it is possible to provide the trainmen with a track instrument in the shape of an inclined plane, which can be placed on the end of the ties to open the valve and compel a train to stop, should the engineer not observe the man signaling him. Claims are also made that the stop is an excellent device to be used in connection with any manual system, as it compels obedience on the part of the engineer to the indication of the signal.

As installed on the "Alley L," the system has given good satisfaction. While it has been found necessary to strengthen some of the parts, the wear on the apparatus, as a whole, has been very small. While applications, due to a failure of the apparatus, occasionally happen, there have also been a few failures to apply the brakes, when they should have been applied. This has occurred through water collecting in the valves, or on the outside, and freezing up the vent holes, preventing the air from escaping when the valve was opened.

Should the roller be knocked off, as might easily happen on a surface road, or the inclined bars of the safety stop get broken, no application of the brakes would be made, in which case, should the engineer be depending on the application of the brakes to indicate danger, the consequences might be serious.

Black's automatic mechanical system is in use on portions of the elevated roads of New York City, and is a much simpler system than the Rowell-Potter. It is a signal system only, no attempt being made by mechanical means, or otherwise, to compel an engineer to obey the signal if it is at danger.

The principal parts of the system are the two mechanical trips —one the operating trip at the entrance of the block to set the signal at danger, the other a releasing trip to restore the signal to its normal position—and the motion plate, by which the motion imparted to the pipe line connecting the two trips is made to work a signal. The signal, a photograph of which is shown in Fig. 9, is of the semaphore type, and is supported on an iron post, the top of the post being made in the form of a box or shield, behind which the blade can be hidden when in the safety position (shown in Fig. 10). The post is painted black, so that the safety indication is given by the absence of the signal, rather than by its vertical position.

It will be noticed that three of the jaws on the two up and down rods connecting the "T" crank at the base with the signal, are slotted; this is done to relieve the signal casting of the sudden blows transmitted by the two trips, and allow the signal to be moved to the safety position by the force of gravity. The trips are of the same pattern as those used with the Rowell-Potter system, the wheels of the engine pressing down the inclined bars placed at the side of the rail, thereby turning a shaft connected to the pipe line by a crank, and moving it, the motion being im-

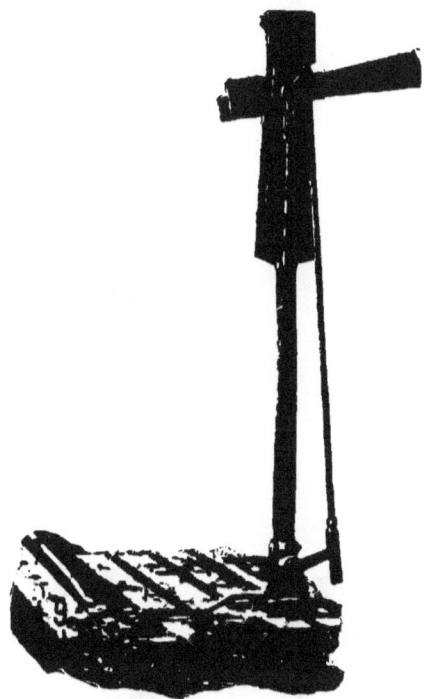

BLACK'S AUTOMATIC MECHANICAL SIGNAL AT "DANGER."

parted through the medium of a spiral spring. The motion plate, by which the motion imparted to the pipe line is transmitted to the "T" crank of the signal, is shown in Fig. 11. The plate P sliding in the frame F, forces the bar A to move from one side to the other, by means of the pin K working in the slot S, the bar A being connected by a rod with the "T" crank at the base of the signal pole. The slot is made somewhat longer than the travel of the pipe line, to allow for changes in the length of the connections, from expansion and contraction, without affecting the movement of the signal.

As installed on the New York Elevated, the blocks are of about 1,700 feet in length, the operating trip being placed a short distance beyond the signal, so that the signal will not go to danger until the locomotive has passed it. The releasing section

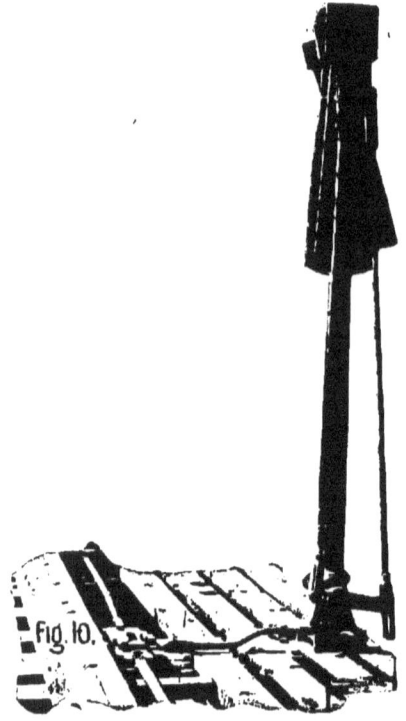

BLACK'S AUTOMATIC MECHANICAL SIGNAL AT "SAFETY."

is carried past the next signal into the next block ahead, thus providing an overlapping section, and insuring that there will always be a signal at danger behind a train. On this road, the blocks are made continuous—that is, the entire track is equipped with the device, and not at stations only, as is the case with the Rowell-Potter system on the "Alley L" road in Chicago.

While the automatic mechanical systems have undoubtedly

been giving satisfaction in the applications that have been made, the argument cannot be made from these installations that such systems would be applicable with any degree of success or durability to the ordinary surface roads of this country. In the equipments spoken of, the length of the blocks is between 1,000 and 1,700 feet, and, judging from the strains put upon the apparatus, this is very nearly the limit at which it is possible to operate the mechanism successfully. This length of block, with the long trains that are being run to-day, would furnish no protection, as the signal would be cleared about the time that the rear car

MOTION PLATE.

passed it. Unless the blocks can be made a mile long, it would be useless to make an application, even if the matter of expense was left out.

Again, since the inclined bars are pressed down by the wheels of the train, it follows that the speed at which the train runs will materially affect the blow given the apparatus; and while, with the present equipment, there has been very little trouble from this cause, the speed has been about 40 miles an hour only, so that one cannot say positively what the effect would be at higher speeds. Any equipment to a surface road would be very hard to maintain during the winter, owing to snow and ice clogging up the parts, which, unless they worked freely, would apply the air and stop trains when they should not be stopped. While the objection to the length of the block would be overcome by using an electrical release with the Rowell-Potter system, it is very probable that such an instrument would require too careful adjustment and have to be of too light a construction to be a practical success, unless the necessary electric current could be obtained from a dynamo instead of an electric battery. Such an arrangement was used with the equipment on the Intramural at the World's Fair, and gave very good results, but as a new design has been gotten out by the signal company, it is evident they do not think the arrangement then used would work successfully on a surface road.

Regarding the applications of the systems that have been made to the elevated roads, criticisms have been made that it is impossible to run the trains on schedule time if the signals are obeyed, and that, in consequence, they are, on the New York Elevated, disconnected the greater part of the time, or the engineers are allowed to run by them when at danger. Any such criticism applies solely to the length of the block, or the distance apart which the signals are placed, and not to defects of the apparatus; for if the signals are further apart than it is desired to run trains, traffic will, of course, be delayed whenever the signals have to be obeyed.

Having now explained the construction of the principal block signal systems used in this country, it would be well to more particularly describe the new Electric Train Staff system, which was spoken of as having been installed and in successful operation on the Chicago, Milwaukee & St. Paul Railway. The instrument used is one invented by Messrs. Webb & Thompson, and has been adopted by the London & Northwestern Railway Co., of England, as their standard apparatus for blocking trains on single-track lines.

The essential feature of this system is that a staff, either of metal or wood, is carried by the engineer as his authority to run his train over a given piece of track, the several staffs provided with this system being locked mechanically in the station instruments, so that but one staff can be removed at the same time from either instrument. Two measurements are provided, one being placed at each end of the block or section of track to be controlled by the staffs. A wire connection is made between the two instruments for electrically unlocking the machines and allowing a staff to be withdrawn. Withdrawing a staff from either instrument locks up both instruments of that section, so that no staff can be taken out until the staff withdrawn is replaced in one or the other instrument. A staff may be withdrawn from either instrument and a train started from either end of the block at any time, provided a staff has not been withdrawn and given to some other train that is in the block.

To allow trains to be run in the block permissively—for it is not always desirable to preserve an absolute block—metal tablets of a different form from the staff are provided in a box attached to the instrument, a special staff, called a permissive staff, being used as a key to unlock the box. Each one of the six tablets which are provided, may be used to forward a train, the last train taking the permissive staff and any remaining tablets.

From this it is seen that when an engineer has a staff with him on his engine, he knows that the block ahead of him is clear, and that no train running in an opposite direction can enter the block. When he has a tablet with him, instead of the usual staff, he knows that there may be other trains in the block running in the same direction that he is, but there can be no train running in the opposite direction.

A general view of the staff instrument is shown in Fig. 12, an ordinary and a permissive staff being shown in Fig. 13. The principle upon which the machine is constructed is, that when a staff is withdrawn, the electric current energizing one of the magnets, which lifts the lock, allowing a staff to be withdrawn, is reversed through the coils of the magnet, neutralizing the effect of the current, and making it impossible to again take out a staff until the currents have been restored to their proper polarity by placing the staff back in one of the instruments.

Details of the instrument are shown in Fig. 14, M being the magnet connected by the line wire with the battery of the other instrument through the key S (Fig. 15), N the magnet energized by a local battery, the circuit being closed by turning the indicator handle H (Fig. 15). T is the armature of the magnets M and N, and is of such a shape as to fit in the slot in the drum D and prevent it from turning, unless the armature is lifted by the magnets when they are raised. The arm carrying the magnet is provided with a tail-piece, which is lifted by a projection on the staff whenever an attempt is made to remove a staff. If the magnets are energized by a current of the proper polarity, the armature is held up when the magnet is raised, and the drum

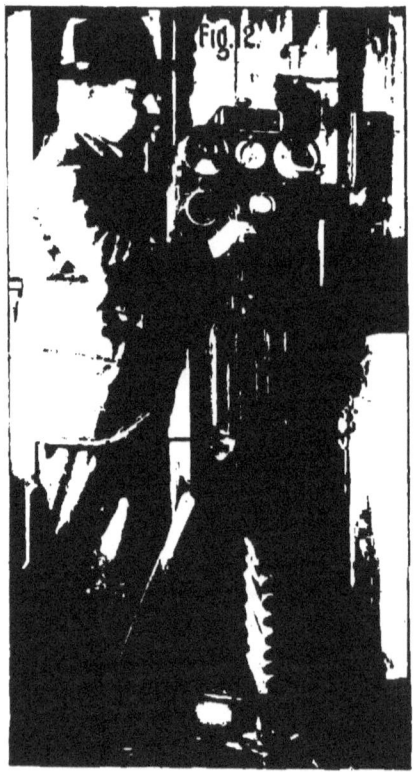

WITHDRAWING STAFF FROM WEBB & THOMPSON STAFF INSTRUMENT.

D is allowed to turn, the staff being drawn through the segmental slot K to the opening O, where it can be withdrawn from the instrument. The levers L, placed on the side of the instrument, are made to reverse the electric currents flowing through the magnet N, by changing the contacts from one end to the other whenever a staff is withdrawn from the instrument, and thus not only prevent a second staff being withdrawn, but to reverse the current sent out to the other instrument when the key S is pressed, and make it impossible for a staff to be taken out of the other instrument also.

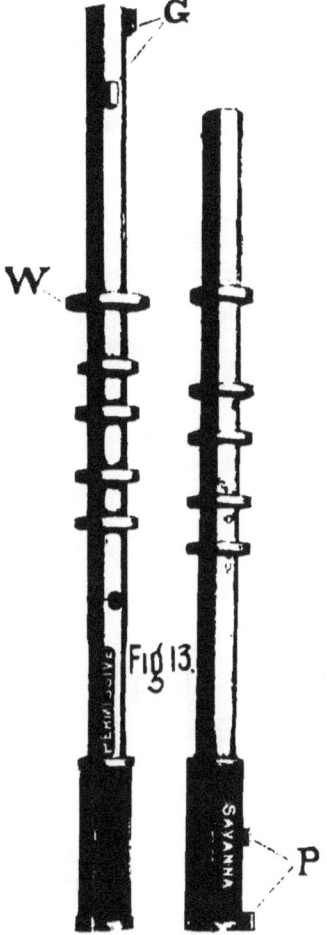

THE STAFF.

To explain more fully the effect of reversing the current through one of the magnets, it must be noticed that the poles of the two magnets are joined together, forming a single pole

piece *P*. If the iron of the two magnets is magnetized, so that
the north pole of one will be opposite the south pole of the other,
there will be a mutual attraction, and each will satisfy the magnetic attraction of the other. If, however, the poles of the two
magnets are of the same polarity, it will have the effect of making
the two magnets act as one magnet, the iron projection *P* between
the two coils now becoming the pole piece, and the armature, in

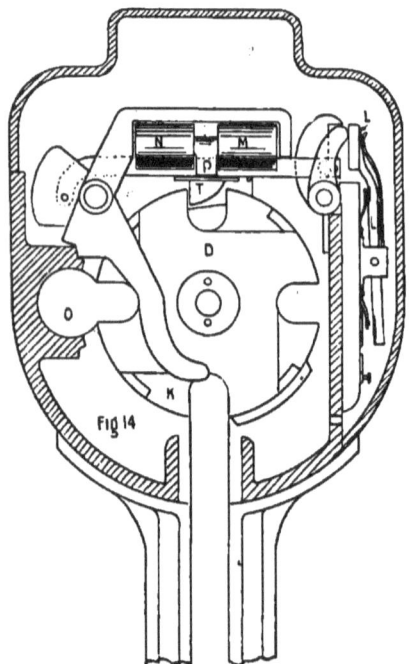

DETAILS OF STAFF INSTRUMENT.

consequence, will be attracted. From this it is seen that there
must be two circuits to work the magnets of each machine—one
from the main line battery of one instrument, closed by pressing
on the key *S;* the other an entirely local circuit, closed by turning
the indicator handle *H* of the other instrument.

A galvanometer *G* (Fig. 15), placed in circuit with the main
line wire, serves to inform the operator, when he wishes to withdraw a staff, when the operator at the other instrument has

pressed down the key S and closed the main line circuit. The indicator J, placed on the left side of the instrument, is used to designate from which instrument a staff has been withdrawn, and also when turned clear around, to break the main line circuit, allowing the galvanometer needle to return to a vertical position, and thus notify the other operator that the staff has been removed and he can release the key. A single-stroke bell, placed on the

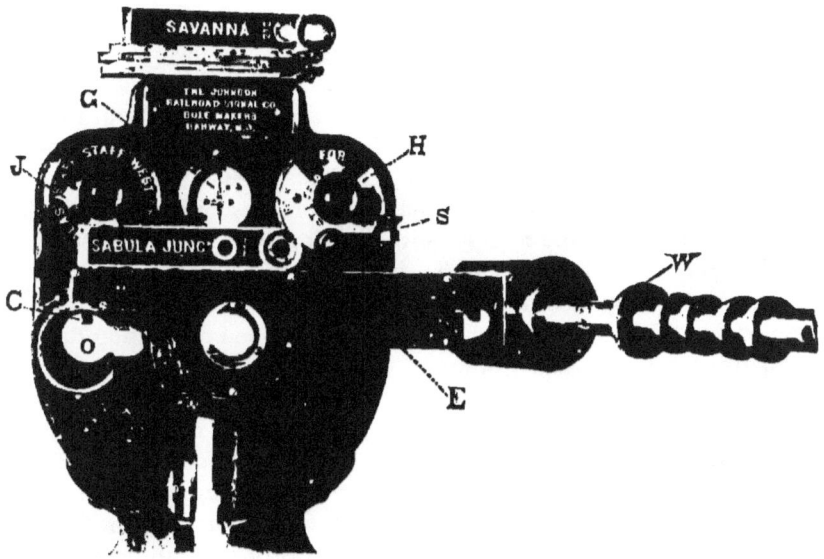

main line circuit, rings each time that the key of the instrument at the other station is pressed.

The staffs (shown in Fig. 13) are made of a piece of iron pipe, name plates of the two stations at the ends of the block being riveted on the end. The rings riveted to the staff serve as projections to fit in between the wings of the drum D (Fig. 14), to raise the several latches, as well as to make it impossible to place a staff taken from the instrument of one block into the instrument belonging to the next block. The number of staffs provided for each instrument is usually ten, but as many may be used as will go into one machine.

The operation of the instrument is as follows, supposing that

A and B represent the stations at the end of the block, and that a train is ready to start from A to B: A asks, by taps of the bell, according to an arranged code of signals, for permission to withdraw a staff. B responds, if there is no train in the block, by pressing on the key S (Fig. 15), sending a current through the magnet M and the galvanometer, the needle of which is immediately deflected. A turns the indicator handle H to "For Staff," thereby closing the local circuit, and lifts the staff to the top of the slot, as shown in Fig. 12. The projection on the staff strikes the tail-piece, as before described, lifting the magnets, which, as as the pole piece is now energized, also lifts the armature and unlocks the drum, allowing the staff to be withdrawn from the instrument. Immediately the staff is withdrawn, the operator turns the indicator J (Fig. 15) to "East" or "West Staff Out," as the case may be, breaking the main line circuit, and allowing the galvanometer needle to assume the vertical position and inform the operator at B that a staff has been withdrawn. Withdrawing the staff automatically causes the indicator H to return to the position "For Bell," breaking the local circuit and preventing the battery from being run down.

The staff is then given to the conductor, who gives it to the engineer, to be kept on the engine. On the arrival of the train at B, the staff is taken to the office and given to the operator, who places it in his staff instrument, and notifies A, by taps on the bell, that the staff has been placed in the instrument. Another staff can then be withdrawn from either instrument, and a train sent in either direction through the block that is desired.

To block trains permissively, six tablets are provided, a projection or lug being provided on the end of the permissive staff (shown at G, Fig. 13), by which the box E (Fig. 15), on the face of the instrument, in which the tablets are placed, may be unlocked and the tablets removed, as shown. As soon as any of the tablets are removed from the box, a catch-piece C is dropped into the opening O, so that the large ring W on the permissive staff will not admit of the staff being put back in the instrument, and as the permissive staff has been withdrawn, both instruments are locked, and no other staff can be withdrawn.

When it is desired to send one or more trains into the block, the permissive staff is withdrawn from the instrument the same as any other staff, and is used to unlock the box containing the six tablets. A tablet is given to each train that it is desired to send forward, the last train being given the staff and any remaining tablets; for, unless all the tablets have been placed in the tablet box of one instrument or the other, it is impossible to put the permissive staff in either instrument, and, until this is done,

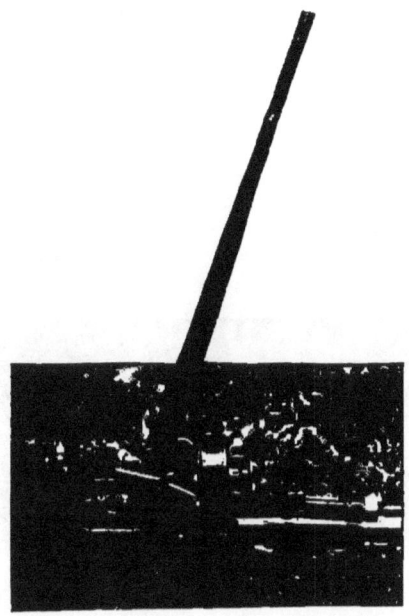

A STAFF LOCK.

the section would be blocked, as no other staff can be withdrawn.

A staff lock, shown in Fig. 16, is provided at all switches in the block. Projections on the staff, seen at P, Fig. 13, serve as a key with which to unlock the switch. To unlock the switch, the end of the staff is placed in the lock and turned, when, if the catch is pressed down, the switch may be thrown by pulling over the lever, as seen in Fig. 17. When the staff is turned in the lock and the switch opened, it is impossible to withdraw the staff, so that a trainman not only has to leave the switch set for the main line, but is compelled to lock it before removing the staff. As no switches can be opened without the staff, and there can be but one staff taken out of the two instruments at the same time, an engineer knows when he has the staff that all the switches in the block are set for the main line and that they are locked.

There have been several staff instruments of different patterns perfected and put in use in England, but the one shown here is very simple and durable, and not likely to get out of order. The battery power required is large, but this is due more to the high resistance to which the magnets are wound than to the particular design of the machine

The system is in use on the C., M. & St. P. Railway, between

SWITCH UNLOCKED AND THROWN.

the stations, Savanna, in Illinois, and Sabula Junction, in Iowa—a section of track that is not only very crooked, but in which there is a very long bridge over the Mississippi River, making it highly important that every precaution be taken against accidents, not only from rear end collisions, but from dispatchers and others making mistakes, and allowing two trains, traveling in opposite directions, to try and use that piece of track at the same time.

The system has given the greatest satisfaction since it has been installed, not only in regard to the safety with which the traffic can be handled, but the facility with which trains can be dispatched. To quote the words of Mr. C. A. Goodnow, superintendent of the C., M. & St. P. Railway, in a paper read before the Western Railway Club:

"I cite these few examples of the many complications that must necessarily arise in the handling of traffic on single track, to illustrate the facility with which the staff system does its train dispatching; its possibilities in connection with the movement of trains on single track, and its especial adaptability to short stretches of track, used by the trains of several divisions or different railways, as compared with the telegraphic movement; the advantage, both as regards safety and facility of handling, being distinctly with the staff system.

"It is not my intention to decry our system of train dispatching. There can be no question but what it is a most economical and satisfactory method of handling traffic, under ordinary conditions, with not too heavy a train movement; but we are obliged to admit that the system is open to objections which particularly relate to safety as well as to facility. The staff system is capable of extended application. It is at once a block signal, a train dispatcher, and a time-table. It is to the movement of trains between stations what the interlocking of switches and signals is at stations and grade crossings."

With the staff instruments in use, the cumbersome method of dispatching trains by orders can be done away with. The dispatcher need keep only his train sheet, informing each operator to which train a staff is to be delivered. There need be no safeguards taken to prevent either he or the operator from making mistakes, as the machines are an absolute check against all such. The time necessary to transmit orders is only that required to send a short message. Orders can be annulled and changed with equal facility, as there is no necessity for doing more than to order the operator not to give a staff to a certain train. Should he disobey orders there would be no accident, and nothing more serious would happen than a delay to the train that the dispatcher wanted to have go forward.

If all the stations of a division were equipped with staff instruments, some means would have to be devised by which a staff could be taken on the engine at speed, as slowing up at all stations would not only be expensive, but would make it impossible to run fast trains.

At present the staffs are taken on at speed by an attachment provided on the tender, similar to a hook on a mail car, but as the arrangement will not work successfully at speeds much above 30 miles per hour, a change of some sort would have to be made before it could be considered suitable for general use.

CHAPTER VIII

INSTALLATION AND CARE OF AUTOMATIC ELECTRIC SIGNALS, WITH A COMPARISON OF THE COST OF THE DIFFERENT BLOCK SIGNAL SYSTEMS.

As automatic electric signals are coming into such general use, and as the number of men employed in looking after them increases, it may be well to give some of the few points learned by me in a somewhat limited experience regarding the installation and care of these signals, in the hope that some of the readers of these articles may be benefited thereby. Automatic electric signals when first installed are generally found to give excellent service, and the officers of the road congratulate themselves on having secured such a "good thing." Very soon, however, reports come from enginemen that certain of the signals were found standing at danger improperly, and upon an investigation being made, it is discovered that the trouble is occasioned by a want of care. The idea that an automatic signal will take care of itself for an indefinite length of time has done much to make such signals unpopular, when it is found that they require to be more carefully looked after than any other kind. Not only must the work be well done and regularly attended to, but the men employed must be intelligent and willing to learn, for there will be many things turning up that will perplex the most experienced.

In the first place, there are so many things that can happen to an electric signal that will throw it out of service that no chances can be taken in the installation, but everything must be of the best that money can buy, and the work must be as nearly perfect for the end in view as it is possible to make it. It will be true economy in the end, and will result in making the signal a success where most probably it would have been a failure had less care been taken.

In installing a track circuit system, one of the most important points to be looked after is the joint or connection that is made between the wires of the circuit and the iron wires joined to the rail. These, as indeed with all of the other joints, must be soldered, but, as one wire is of copper and the other is of iron, particular pains must be taken to make a good joint and to protect it after it is made. A good way in which to make this connection is to strip the copper wire of its insulation for about 12 inches, twisting it separately around the ends of the two iron wires that are joined to the rail, and then soldering each joint thoroughly. In this way two entirely separate joints are made for the one connection, and it is very probable that if one should rust out or break the other would be good and the circuit would be maintained. After soldering, the joints are to be washed and dried to remove all trace of the acid used to solder with, and

GOOD METHOD OF ATTACHING WIRES TO A RAIL.

should then be painted with a good coating of P. & B. compound. Asphalt paint is not so good for this purpose, as it soon cracks, and will not then keep out moisture. The joints should next be taped with insulating material, and wrapped in canvas covered on both sides with P. & B. compound to make the cloth thoroughly water-proof, after which the whole is put in a wooden box or trunking and buried in the ground, the end of the trunking being brought up above the surface, as shown in Fig. 1, to keep the bare wire from coming in contact with the ground.

It will be noticed that the wires, after reaching the rail, extend along it for a foot or more, before being fastened. This is done to prevent the wire from being broken from the jar of the rail caused by a passing train, as making the wires long in this way allows them to spring, instead of being bent, when the rail is deflected.

There are two ways in common use in which the wires may be attached to the rail, each one being controlled by one of the signal companies. That used by the Union Switch & Signal Company is to solder the iron wire to a rivet, which latter is driven in a hole drilled in the base of the rail. The wire leads off at right angles to the rivet, and there is no necessity for bending it, other than to clear the angle bar, when used as a bond wire at rail joints. The other is that controlled by the Hall Signal Company, and is to fasten the wire in a hole drilled in the rail by a tapered plug, having a groove in the side in which the wire is held.

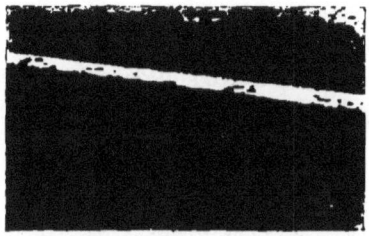

FIG. 2. BOND WIRE AT RAIL JOINT.

With this latter method care must be used in giving the proper set to the wire, or it will be apt to break if a bend is formed at the sharp edge of the hole. To prevent this, the wire must be left straight for about $\frac{1}{4}$ inch above the rail, before bending, to bring it parallel with the base of the rail.

There is quite a difference in the practice in regard to the best way to run the bond wire around the angle bars at a rail joint, but that shown in Fig. 2 will be found to be a very good one. The wire is made longer than the distance between the plugs, to allow for a separation of the ends of the rail from contraction or creeping. Running the wire behind the splice puts it out of the way of trackmen tightening bolts, or shimming rails, and prevents it from bending up and being cut by a passing wheel.

The wooden splices are made of oak, and last a long time if properly put in, otherwise their life is short. As wood, in comparison with iron, is a very soft material, it will very soon become worn if subjected to the blows given a joint by a passing train, so that the only way to make such splices give any kind of service is to support the ends of the rails by a tie placed underneath, or, in other words, make it a "supported joint." The wooden splices are not put in to support the ends of the rails, but to tie them together longitudinally and prevent their spreading.

In laying insulated wires in trunking, they should never be tightly drawn to take out the slack, and whenever a bend is made, or a wire leads off at right angles from the main wire, several inches of slack wire should be left to allow for changes in length due to contraction. In running wires from one signal to the next, it is much the better and cheaper plan to put the wire on the telegraph poles in preference to putting them in the ground. With the former method, while there is the chance of the wire being occasionally broken by storms or from poles falling down, such breakage is easily detected and repaired; while with the latter method it is very hard to locate any break in the wires, particularly if laid in the form of a cable.

On account of the difficulty of detecting breaks and the annoyance occasioned by having a signal fail to work, it is a good plan to use a wire of comparatively large size and covered with good insulation, rather than to use as small a wire as will carry the current without too great a resistance. We are using an insulated wire of No. 12 B. & S. wire gauge with great success, and have never been troubled with its breaking after being once properly put on.

With regard to the relay to be used, a great deal of care should be used in selecting one that is correctly designed, for the uses to which it is to be put; for, while the wiring up may have been poorly done, it will give good service as long as it lasts; whereas with the relay, if not especially adapted to the work it is to perform, it will not work properly during wet weather, and will be continually giving trouble. Where a relay will not work, there is nothing that a repairman can do, except, perhaps, to have a bulletin notice issued that the signal is out of order; for while the circuit is complete, the relay is not sensitive enough to work with the amount of current that flows through it, the greater part generated by the battery leaking across the track and practically short-circuiting the relay.

There are many things, mechanical as well as electrical, that have to be considered in designing a relay for a track circuit, several of which have been overlooked in one lately put upon the market by one of the signal companies, as an instrument embodying all that is required in a well-designed relay.

The most important point to bear in mind is, that the resistance of the magnet should be four ohms and never more than this; for, as the resistance of a single cell is four ohms and the resistance of the external circuit should not be more than the resistance of the battery (to obtain a maximum effect with an electro-magnet), any greater resistance in the relay is a loss rather than a gain, materially increasing the leakage across the track where the resistance between the rails is low.

Electricity will always follow the path of least resistance, the amount of current flowing through two parallel channels being inversely proportional to their resistance. With long track circuits, the resistance between one rail and the other is at times, during wet weather, as low as three ohms, or possibly less, in which case the amount of current that would flow through the relay would be but three-sevenths of that generated by the battery, so that the relay must be constructed to work, not with the whole current of a two-cell battery, but with as small an amount of current as it is possible to make it work.

Having decided on the resistance to which the relay is to be wound, the next point is the length and size of the iron core, for this will affect the amount of magnetic force, or the lifting power of the magnet for a given amount of current.

The value of any current of electricity for producing magnetism in an iron core is proportional to the strength of the current and the number of times it circulates around the core, or, as it is expressed technically, the number of ampere turns. The problem, then, is simply to get the greatest number of turns around the core with an amount of wire that does not exceed the given resistance. This requires that the core be long, so that there will be room on which to wind the wire, and small, so that there will be less wire used in making one turn; but as the number of ampere turns that will magnetize a thin core to any prescribed degree of magnetism, will magnetize a core of any section, whatever, to the same degree of magnetism, it is advisable that the core must also be made as large as possible, commensurate with a given number of turns, the power of a magnet for a given degree of magnetization being proportional to the area of the core.

If the core is made small, the intensity of the magnetism will be greater (the number of turns being larger), and the leakage across from one pole to the other, or the loss of magnetic force, will be much greater. This being the case, there will be a much greater efficiency if the core is made large, and also long enough to furnish space on which to wind the wire, for the wire must be made large to give the greatest number of turns with the given resistance, the magnetic intensity being reduced and the lifting power of the magnet increased. Practice has demonstrated that a core $\frac{5}{8}$ inch in diameter and 4 inches long, wound to 4 ohms resistance, gives a much better and more satisfactory result than will one of $\frac{3}{4}$ inch diameter and $2\frac{1}{2}$ inches long, wound to the same resistance with a smaller wire.

Taking up now the question of the proper construction of the armature, we find that as the piece of iron is not in actual contact with the pole pieces of the magnet, considerable resistance is introduced into the magnetic circuit, the number of magnetic lines of force, and consequently the pull, being decreased in a proportion slightly greater than the square of the distance the armature is away from the poles. This being the case, to obtain a maximum magnetic pull from a given amount of current, the armature should be made to work as close to the poles as it is possible to make it, and all the parts should be made to admit of very careful and accurate adjustment.

To secure a close adjustment of a relay armature, the ends of the shaft to which the iron piece is fastened must be pointed, and the pivot screws or bearings must be cup-shaped, so that perfect freedom of movement without loss of motion may be obtained. Where the pivot screws are turned down and fit in a hole drilled in the armature frame piece, it is impossible to make a close adjustment, as from the nature of the work the pin must 'fit loosely in the hole, and there will be just that amount of lost motion at the armature. If the holes are made almost 1/32 inch large, as will sometimes be found in relays of this construction, it is seen that the armature cannot be adjusted much closer than 1/16 of an inch, as it is necessary, when breaking the signal circuit, to separate the contact point at least 1/32 inch, the spring of the arm carrying the point, allowing the armature piece to make, practically, the same amount of motion. The armature should be arranged so as to allow for positive adjustment at both ends of its stroke; the arms carrying the contact points preferably being made of spring metal, which will bend slightly when the points are brought together, and make a slight rubbing contact, thus tending to keep the surfaces clean and be more certain of making a metallic contact.

In designing the armature, care must be observed to see that the pull of the magnet is applied at a point between the contact points and the center of gravity of the whole piece, or else the pivoted end will be lifted first, the points being brought together only after the whole armature is lifted. With a weak current, such a fault as this will mean that a relay that otherwise would have been able to do its work will fail to lift the armature, and there will be nothing that a repairman can do to fix it, except, perhaps, to tilt the relay and thus lessen the force of gravity—a thing which is sometimes done with the form of relay alluded to, but which should not be so placed, from the possibility that the armature will not fall back and break the signal circuit and put the signal at danger when a train is in the block.

The iron forming the armature should have a piece of paper cemented to the side that is next the pole piece of the magnet, to prevent the two pieces of iron from coming into actual contact with each other. This is done to prevent the armature from sticking on account of polarization, or the residual magnetism that is left in the iron, as iron after once being magnetized will retain sufficient magnetism after the circuit is broken to hold the armature, if the two pieces are in actual contact.

Paper is better than a thin sheet of copper soldered to the armature, as it is lighter, and is also much better than pieces of rubber, brass or other non-magnetic material driven in a hole drilled into the end of the core and left projecting above the surface, as the two surfaces have to be separated much further than with the paper, from a possible tilting of the armature bringing it in contact with the pole piece of the magnet.

To provide the relay with pointed contact pieces is a very poor arrangement, there being a strong probability that the two points will become fused together should a strong current be collected by the circuit during severe storms, in which case the points would then not separate when a train entered the block, and the signal would not be set at danger.

Another objection is that owing to the small area of the point the spark has a greater effect and makes the contact pieces dirty much sooner than when larger surfaces are presented.

Another very important point to be looked after in constructing a relay is the inclosing of the contact points, so that no dust or other substance will be allowed to get between them. Dust, being a non-conductor of electricity, will prevent the points from making a contact, and the signal circuit will not be completed when the armature is lifted by the relay, the signal, in consequence, remaining at danger. With relays of the ordinary pattern, not made with the idea of inclosing the points, a cover that is perfectly dust-proof can be easily made by removing the bottom of a hardwood box and gluing strips of chamois skin on the edges, the box to be placed over the whole relay, and screwed down to make a tight joint with the board supporting the relay by means of screws run through brackets, which must be provided for the purpose on the outside of the box.

Binding posts are another important feature in the construction of a relay, and one which, unless properly made, will give a lot of trouble. There are several designs, only one of which I have found to work well—that is to say, that will not work loose after being once screwed up, and yet will be easy to unscrew. This binding post is shown at A, in Fig. 3. It is turned out of a single piece of brass, two nuts being provided on each of the theaded ends. One end—the longer of the two—is put through the relay base and the nuts tightened; the other is used to hold the wire which is twisted around between the first nut and the body of the pin.

The other points of superiority claimed for this form of post are that it will not cut or kink the wire, making it liable to break; the threads are not easily stripped, and it is cheaply and easily made. To put binding posts in a relay base without providing jam nuts, means that they will have to be tightened every now and then, and that they may at any time work loose sufficiently to break the circuit. Vulcanized fiber washers should not be used to insulate the binding post from the relay base, mica being much preferable, from the fact that it is hard and non-compressible, and will thus keep the binding post from getting loose in the relay base.

To expect that the thumb-screw of a binding post made as is the one shown at B, in Fig. 3, will remain tight after once being "set up" on a wire, is expecting more than it will do, for it will certainly give trouble sooner or later. The objection to this form of screw is that when the post is slotted, as seen in the figure, there is not sufficient strength or spring in the two sides to hold the screw and prevent its working loose from the jar occasioned by passing trains.

To make a binding post of two pieces of metal screwed to-

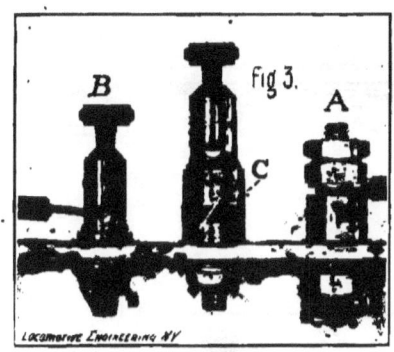

BINDING POSTS.

gether, with a piece of insulating material between, so that a fuse wire can be used to connect the two and thus form a lightning arrester, as is shown at C, in Fig. 3, is certainly not a good plan, as the wire is poorly held, being merely hammered into a groove cut in the outside of the post. If it works loose or rusts through, as will sometimes happen, the trouble will, very likely, be hard to locate, and if, in setting up the thumb-screw, the two pieces should be screwed together a part of a turn, the fuse wire would be broken. A lightning arrester can be easily made by putting a short piece of fuse wire in the circuit, long wood screws provided with three copper washers and screwed into the sides of the relay box being used in place of binding posts, the ends of the wires being placed between the washers and the screw set-up.

As to the care of an electric signal, the part that will require the greatest amount of attention and the one that is most likely to give trouble is the battery. The resistance of the circuits being comparatively low, the consumption of the zincs is rapid, a thick scale of zinc compounds forming which, unless scraped off, will greatly diminish the amount of electricity generated. Again, if the top solution, the sulphate of zinc or the waste product

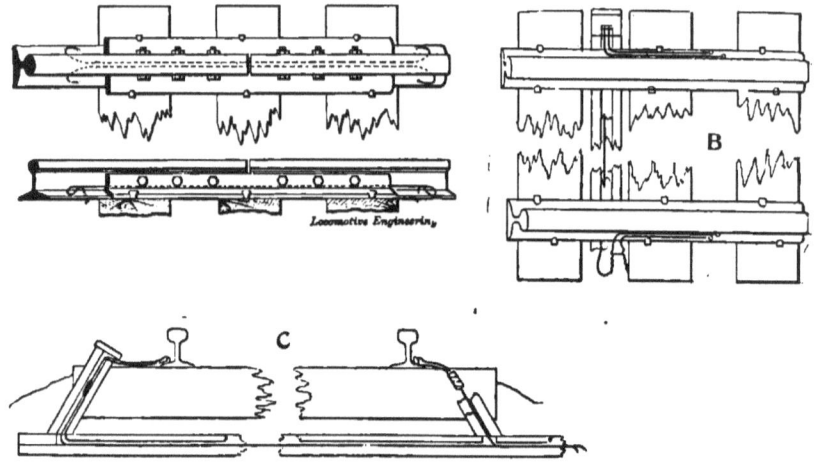

A —C., M. & St. P. Ry. standard track wiring.
B —Wire connections to be made as near the middle of rail as possible. Joints after soldering. to be washed, dried, painted, covered with Okonite tape and wrapped with canvas soaked in P. & B compound.
C —Where two or more Okonite covered wires are in the same piece of trunking, they must be carefully laid so as not to cross one over the other.

of the cell, is not taken out regularly and the cell refilled with water, chemical action will be retarded and the amount of electricity given off will be less. Consequently, to keep the battery up to anywhere near its maximum output, the cells must be constantly looked after and cleaned. If provided with enough sulphate of copper in crystals in the bottom of the jar, the cells will go without touching for a period of three weeks, but by using a larger number than that necessary to do the work when in good condition, the length of time between cleanings may be longer, as there will still be enough electricity given off to work the relays.

As the track-circuit batteries are arranged to give a large amount of current and not a current of high voltage, the area of the zinc exposed to chemical action in each cell will materially affect the amount of electricity given off, and, as with the signal-circuit batteries, the size of the zinc makes a less difference, the cells being in series to increase the voltage, it will be found a very good plan to transfer the zincs from the track-circuit battery, when they are partly used, to the battery of the signal circuit, new zincs being used in that of the track battery.

The glass jars will occasionally, and in some cases frequently, break. Why they do so has not as yet been explained, the cheapest jars lasting as well as the most expensive, or even those which have been annealed. Jars often crack without letting the liquid escape; but when the crack extends below the bottom of the zinc the jar should be replaced by another, as the solution may leak out, and, by getting below the zinc, break the circuit and put the signal at danger. A broken circuit in the track-circuit battery will seldom do this, as the cells being arranged in parallel, the current from the other cell will still work the relay unless the conditions as to weather are bad. If, however, a zinc should fall down and touch the copper, it will short-circuit the track battery, the cells being in parallel; but with the signal-circuit battery, as the cells are in series, it will only reduce the number of cells in service by one.

Care must be used to keep the binding posts and the ends of the wires clean, as well as to see that all screws have been set up securely after the cells have been cleaned. The binding posts removed from used-up zincs, if soldered to wires, serve as very convenient "connectors" by which to join the wire of the copper element and the line wire. It is advisable to run the wires in all battery-well elevators the same, and to make all connections between the cells in the same way, so that a man will not be likely to reverse some of them in connecting up the cells, thus reducing the number of cells available to do work by twice the number that are reversed. This has been done through the carelessness of the battery cleaner, and was not discovered until the signal went to danger, sometime after the man had left, as the current was generated for a short time sufficiently strong to work the signal, and thus led the man to believe that it had been connected up properly.

A new design of battery well that will be found to answer all requirements, and at the same time cost a little less than half of what the ordinary wooden well costs, or only $8 put in complete,

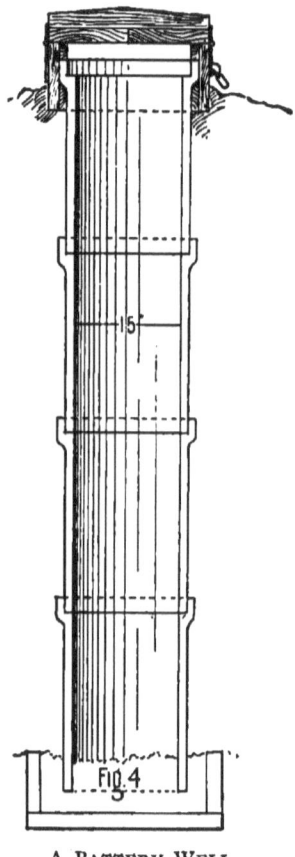

A BATTERY WELL.

is shown in Fig. 4. This well was designed by Mr. H. D. Miles, signal engineer of the Michigan Central Railway, and has been used by him for some time with very good results.

It is made of four lengths of vitrified sewer pipe, the bottom and the joints being made of Portland cement unmixed with

sand. A wooden box, to which the cover is attached, is carefully fitted around the top of the pipe to prevent any loss of heat by radiation during cold weather, and also to keep anyone except the proper persons from getting at the cells.

Battery cleaners should be made to examine the track wires of each circuit every time they clean the battery, so as to repair any wires that may be broken or bent out of place. When a track circuit has been installed, the sectionmen must be cautioned never to break the wires joining the rails; and if necessary to remove a rail or frog, the signal repairman must be sent for in time to get there and make the necessary connections. Trackmen have to be provided with wooden track gauges, or those in which the metal end pieces are separated by a piece of wood or other non-conducting material. Hand and push cars must be provided with wheels having wooden centers, or else they will short-circuit the relay and set the signal at danger. This, perhaps, would not be advisable if it were not that the weight of these cars is not sufficient to make a good contact with the rail when they are running, especially if there is a little sand or dirt on the rail, the result being that the relay is alternately demagnetized and energized, at times with great frequency. With a mechanically-worked signal this will keep the signal turning continuously, running down the weight and subjecting the mechanism to severe strains. With the electric and pneumatically-operated signals, there is no danger of running the signal down, but the frequent operation will, with the pneumatic signal, be a useless waste of power, and with the other may possibly cause it to get out of adjustment.

The question of finding the cause of a signal's failing or giving a wrong indication is one that will occasionally perplex the most experienced, and, what is more, is one that it is very hard to get the average repairman to study up sufficiently to be able to reason out what the cause of the trouble is and how to fix it. A detecting galvanometer will be found a very useful instrument to have in one's outfit of tools when working on electric circuits, as it will not only give approximately the amount of current, but will show the direction in which the current is flowing. If one does not have a galvanometer, an ordinary 4-ohm sounder will answer just as well for testing out and finding a break in any of the wires.

If a signal is found standing at danger improperly, the first thing to do is to examine the relays, as this will show whether the trouble is with the track or the signal circuit. If the relay is energized and the armature held up, the trouble is with the signal circuit; if the armature is down and the signal goes to safety when the armature is pressed up by hand, the trouble is with the track circuit. If the track circuit is at fault it must be tested out with the galvanometer, commencing at the battery and working towards the relay until the trouble is found. If the needle of the galvanometer deflects, as it should do when the wires attached to the instrument are placed on opposite rails, the circuit is good up to that point and the trouble must be looked for further on. By disconnecting the wires from the relay and running a wire from the end of one to the rail joined by the other wire, the wires in the trunking may be tested, as the trouble will sometimes be found to be with these wires where they have broken, or where the soldered joints have rusted out. With the relays, screws may work loose, dirt get between the contact points, or the armature may stick from polarization, any one of which may cause the signal to give a wrong indication, so that a repairman looking for the cause of trouble must carefully examine all the parts to see that everything is working properly and is just as it should be.

Where a signal stands at danger continuously, the cause of the trouble is easily located; but when the trouble is intermittent—that is, when the signal will work for a short time and then will stand at danger without apparent cause—it is much more difficult, and it is sometimes quite a problem to find out just exactly what the trouble is. In this latter connection it may be well to mention that the currents from electric street railways, if any such are near a track circuit, will almost always give trouble unless proper means are taken to make the current from the track-circuit battery flow in the same direction as the induced current, and also to insulate the track circuit as far as possible from such current.

By testing with a galvanometer or volt meter, the direction in which the current is flowing is easily determined and the current from the track battery is made to flow in the same direction, otherwise the induced current, being much the stronger of the two, is apt to reverse or neutralize the other and the relay will not be energized. If this will not overcome the difficulty, the surrounding track should be tested out with a volt meter and the point from which the current emanates, or the place showing the highest voltage, be determined. If one or two rails between this point and the track circuit be cut out as a dead section and well grounded, it will be found to prevent any current from leaking across the track circuit.

Where such currents are known to exist, I give the wooden splice bars and the end posts, before they are put in use, a good coating of asphalt paint to make them waterproof and as good a non-conductor as possible, although I am not prepared to say

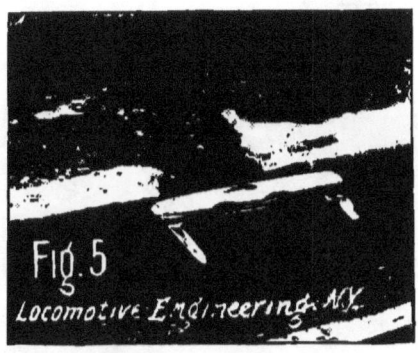

KNIFE MAGNETIZED AND HELD UP BY INDUCED CURRENT FLOWING FROM ONE RAIL TO THE OTHER.

that this is necessary, or that the effect is beneficial for any length of time. Certain it is that the induced currents are at times large, as at one place that I know of the current is large enough to magnetize a four-blade knife sufficiently to make it stick, as shown in Fig. 5, when placed against the vertical side of the head of the rail and across the insulated joint, the signal going to clear with the battery cut off from the circuit. On an insulated section of track, very near the one just spoken of, there is an induced current that will work a relay perfectly without any battery whatever, a battery being used merely as a precaution against a possible cessation of the induced current.

Any track having cinder ballast will be found very hard, if

not impossible, to make work in all conditions of weather, as the cinder when wet becomes a good conductor, allowing the elec-

VIEW SHOWING LOCATION OF SWITCHES WHERE POTENTIAL OF IN-
DUCED CURRENT IS HIGHEST, AND WHERE CURRENT LEAKS ACROSS
THE INSULATED JOINTS TO A GROUNDED DEAD SECTION.

tricity to flow from one rail to the other, short-circuiting the relay and putting the signal at danger. The only way in which the difficulty may be overcome is to remove the cinder, as putting a thick layer of gravel on top of it cannot be relied upon to entirely prevent leakage.

In regard to what it will cost to install and operate the different systems of block signals, it is somwhat difficult to reduce the figures to a common basis by which to make comparisons, from the fact that where operators are employed to work the signals they are given in many cases other duties to perform, so that the entire amount paid them as wages should not be charged to the cost of operating.

For the sake of comparison, let it be assumed that the road to be signaled is 100 miles long, the blocks to be four miles long where the telegraphic and controlled-manual systems are installed, and but two miles long when the automatic is used.

The cost of the telegraphic system would then be as follows:

INSTALLATION.

Equipment complete for 25 stations, each consisting of a two-blade signal and the necessary telegraph instruments at $65 each..$1,625 00
Block wire line at $25 per mile... 2,500 00

Total cost...$4,125 00

OPERATION.

Fifty operators at $40 per month each...$2,000 00

MAINTENANCE.

Wages single repairers and linemen, per month.............................$20 00
Battery supplies and other material for repairs, per month.......... 30 00

Total..$50 00

These figures are applicable to any road, whether single or double track, where the blocks are four miles long, and while this amount will have to be expended if the signals are used, all of it should not be charged against the signals when arriving at the cost of the system. Where the business is such that a road can use its station agents to block trains, there will be no additional expense incurred at these stations, and the $40 paid the agent should be deducted from the estimate. Again, operators are required at all stations where the agents cannot be made use of, at night, as well as in the day, for the purpose of dispatching trains, so that where these are employed it will also not cost any more to operate the signals.

As to the number of operators that will have to be put on in addition to those already employed, when the signals are put in service, it can be stated that with roads doing a business such that the blocks can be four miles long, it will be found, in most instances, that something like ten operators per 100 miles will be required; that number being the average increase required on several divisions of the C., M. & St. P. Ry., when the signals were put in use.

If the estimate of the cost of operating the signals was made on this basis, the amount would be but $400 a month, instead of the $2,000 previously estimated. Taking this figure, interest on the original investment at 6 per cent., and the cost of maintenance, and adding them, we get $5,827.50 as the total amount per 100 miles of road that it will cost most railroads to operate a telegraph block-signal system for a period of one year.

With the controlled-manual systems, the first cost is about $400 per station for the Sykes, and $600 for the Patenall instruments, cost of tower being omitted, though I cannot say that these figures are absolutely correct, having been unable to obtain any definite information. The cost of operation of these systems is practically the same as the telegraphic, but the cost of maintenance is very much more, as will be seen by the following table, which was kindly furnished by Mr. D. B. McCoy, superintendent of the Hudson River Division of the N. Y. C. & H. R. R. R.

Cost of Operating and Maintaining (Electrically) One Tower, One Month.

Controlled-Manual Block Signals—Hudson Division, N. Y. C. & H. R. R. R.

	Patenall System.		Old Sykes System.	
	Tele-graph.	Not Tele-graph.	Tele-graph.	Not Tele-graph.
Operating................	$100 00	$80 00	$100 00	$80 00
MAINTENANCE :				
Wages, batterymen, electricians, linemen, etc....	8 25	8 25	7 50	7 50
Battery supplies........	2 25	2 25	1 75	1 75
Breakage, etc. (including incidentals and tower supplies).............	75	75	25	25
Total.......	$111 25	$91 25	$109 50	$89 50

On this road the signal towers were so located that interlocking machines could be put in and the block operators made to throw switches, and perform other work besides that of blocking trains. On the Erie road the instruments are placed inside many of the stations, where the man employed to work the signals could be given other work.

The cost of the Hall automatic track-circuit system applied to a single-track road, with the blocks two miles long, is about $800 per block, or $40,000 for the 100 miles. For a road having double tracks, the cost will be $60,000, the blocks also being two miles long.

For operation and maintenance, including battery supplies, etc., we have—

```
For single track, per month. .....................l.$400 co
 "  double  "         "       .. ..................... .... 500 00
```

As the total cost of the system for one year we have:

```
For single track—
   Interest on $40.000 at 6%.......... ..............$2.400 00
   Operation and maintenance .. ................... 4.800 co
                                                    _____
   Total.... .......... ............... .......$7,200 00

For double track—
   Interest on $60,000 at 6%...... ... .......... ...$3,600 00
   Operation and maintenance....................... 6,000 00
                                                    _____
   Total................................. ......$9,600 00
```

To equip a road with the Westinghouse pneumatic will cost about $80,000 for single track and $100,000 for double track. This allows for three power stations at a cost of $2,500 each, and a 2-inch supply pipe for carrying compressed air, the pipe being run on stakes and not buried in the ground. Operation and maintenance will be the same as with the Hall system, with the cost of running the power stations added. These figures are based on the cost of several installations that have been made by the signal company, but which are of only a few miles in length. The company, for some reason, are unwilling to furnish an estimate for publication, but the figures given will be found very nearly correct. It is possible, however, that with the reduction that has been made of late in the cost of most signal material, the figures may be reduced somewhat.

The cost of the staff system will be:

25 sets instruments, at $400	$10,000 00
Line wire, at $25 per mile	2,500 00
25 cranes for holding staffs, at $15	375 00
Total	$12,875 00

To this must be added the cost of equipping all the engines of the road, which will be at least $10 an engine.

Signals of some kind, preferably of the semaphore pattern, should be provided to indicate to an engineer whether the staff is ready for him or not. These might be of cheap construction, and need cost but $45 per station. Operation and maintenance will be about the same as with the telegraphic system.

For a single track road, the telegraphic is undoubtedly much the cheapest system that can be used; while for double track the cost of the automatic and the telegraphic systems will be about the same, it being possible to do away with a great many night operators where the former system is used. Where there are more than two tracks, or where men have to be employed solely for the purpose of blocking trains, the automatic will be much the cheaper, as the services of these men can be dispensed with, and the amount paid them for wages, to a great extent, saved.

In making these estimates, depreciation has not been taken into account, for the reason that, from the short time that most of the systems have been in use, it is impossible to say exactly what this will be. With the data available at the present time, any estimate that might be made would have too large an element of guess-work about it to make the results arrived at of any value.

CHAPTER IX

WHAT THEY ARE FOR AND HOW THEY ARE OPERATED.

Interlocking signals, while they give authority for a train to proceed in the same manner as a block signal, differ from the latter in that they indicate the condition of the track, and not the state of the block—whether it is or is not occupied by other trains. If the switches are properly set and the signals cleared, a train has the right to proceed—not regardless of where other trains may be, but solely with respect to the condition of the switches on the route indicated.

Interlocking signals insure safety to a train using the track, by having the different levers and the switches and signals so interlocked that it is impossible to set the switches and clear the signals of any two routes at the same time, that would lead to a collision; by making it impossible for a signalman to clear a signal for a train to proceed until all the switches are in the proper position, and that after having so cleared the signal he is unable to change any of the switches leading to or connected with the track designated.

By the use of such a system it is possible to operate complicated crossings, important junction points or conflicting switches, so that trains can proceed without stopping and without danger of colliding with other trains. That their use is conducive to safety, and at the same time to handling the largest possible amount of business over a given set of tracks, can be easily seen, as no train is delayed to which the signals have been given, and any train not having the signals, although delayed, would not be delayed any more than if the interlocking was not in use—a delay to one train or the other being absolutely necessary, as is shown by the principle of physics, which has been so often demonstrated, that two pieces of matter cannot occupy the same space at the same time.

Practice in regard to the form of fixed signal used at interlock-

ing plants does not vary as is the case with block signals, the semaphore having been adopted as a standard for this purpose very
soon after it was designed. While the semaphore is the standard
form, practice differs, however, in the different countries, in the
blade used to govern a given track. In this country, the blade
projecting to the right, as viewed from an approaching train, is
the one that governs; while in England, where the trains run on
the left-hand track when there are two tracks, it is the one projecting to the left. The use of a fixed signal, to indicate to the
engineer the position of switches, having become standardized,
the necessity of providing some means by which the signal could
be worked from a distance very soon became manifest. With the
growth of the railroads, and the consequent increase in the number of switches and signals, the levers used to operate them were,
for reasons of safety and economy, concentrated at some central
point. It was soon found, however, that this concentration introduced serious difficulties in the proper working of the levers that
had not been thought of. Operators, through mistakes, carelessness, or perhaps by becoming confused, often pulled the wrong
levers, sending trains on the wrong tracks, and occasionally causing serious collisions and very bad accidents.

The first attempt at constructing an interlocking machine was
made by Mr. C. H. Gregory, about the year 1842, and, although
the design was very crude, it was not until 1859 that any decided
improvements were made. In the year 1852 a simple lock was
provided between the signal and a pair of switches, to prevent a
signal being given contrary to the position of the switches. In
1853 an improvement on this was made, in which a notched bar,
connected to the signal wire, was made to cross another notched
bar, working in connection with the points of the switch—an
arrangement that is the standard practice to-day.

Patents were taken out in 1860 by Mr. Austin Chambers, and
also by Mr. Saxby, for an interlocking lever frame, the levers being
interlocked so that no signal could be given contrary to the position of the switch. The interlocking of the switch and signal
levers, as found in the present interlocking machines, was not
arrived at until the year 1867, when Messrs. Saxby & Farmer took
out a patent for a form of spindle-lever locking, and Messrs.
Stevens & Sons a patent for their tappet or crossbar locking.

In both of these forms the locking is accomplished by attachments made directly to the main levers, but owing to the great strain it was possible to put upon the parts, and the consequent necessity for making them large and strong, an improvement was made the fall of the same year, by which the locking was connected to and operated by the latch instead of the lever, the movement of the locking bars taking place before and after the movement of the lever. This form of locking is what is known as "preliminary," or latch locking, and is the one used in all the better class of machines. The locking of the one manufactured by the Union Switch & Signal Company is an improvement of the Saxby & Farmer machine, those made by the Johnson and the National Switch & Signal companies being a modification of the Stevens & Sons patent or "tappet" locking.

With the improvement of the interlocking machine, the design and construction of the several parts used in connecting the levers of the machine with the switches and signals has advanced with equal rapidity. Not only have safeguards been provided by which it is impossible to give a clear signal until the switches are properly thrown, but it is now made impossible to throw or change any switch under a moving train. All the parts are made to move with the least possible friction, and, while of comparatively light construction, the skillful distribution of metal to withstand the strains given the apparatus has resulted in the making of a very safe machine.

Although the principles of construction are fairly well defined, almost every installation of an interlocking plant calls for some expert opinion as to the proper arrangement to be used in connecting up the switches and in deciding on what signals are necessary to control the trains using them. It is in doing this work that the true province of the signal engineer lies, for not only is there a large chance for the unnecessary use of material, but unless the different routes have been properly signaled, trainmen will make mistakes in reading the indications, and accidents will result.

In point of fact, so great is the leeway—not only in deciding what switches shall be connected, what signals shall be used and what locking of the levers is necessary—that many States have given their Railroad Commissioners power to devise rules covering there points, and to see by a personal inspection that all plants are safe and conform to their views. The Board of Trade of England is a very noted example of this, for its jurisdiction extends to the particular form of block-signal appliances and methods to be used in controlling the movement of trains, as well as to a supervision of the interlocking plants used at crossings, drawbridges, junction points and sidings.

That such is necessary or advisable is, in this country at least, a debatable question, as very rarely is it that these bodies are composed of men who understand the requirements of signaling, and if a mechanical expert is employed by them, he will often advise a construction that is not only expensive, but is practically of little benefit.

Laws that require all trains to stop at crossings unless protected by an interlocking, or that a railroad desiring to cross another shall not be allowed to do so without installing an interlocking plant, are but right and just, in view of the danger to which the traveling public would be exposed if such measures were not taken.

That laws should be enacted that all trains should stop at crossings, drawbridges and at important junction points is indeed wise and for the public good, judging from the numerous accidents that have happened whenever this precaution has not been taken; but to go to the extent of passing laws, as has been done by the Legislatures of some of our States, that all trains must stop at crossings, etc., without recognizing the protection afforded by an interlocking plant, is merely retarding the advance of the railroads and increasing the cost of running trains in those States.

To consider, first, the protection of a simple crossing of two single-track roads by interlocking signals, it will be found that the principles involved are much the same for all plants, no matter how complicated the crossing, the fundamental idea being to have everything safe for the train to proceed, after giving a clear signal, and that if it cannot be made safe, the signal must remain at danger and the engineer be compelled to obey the indication and stop. With roads doing a light business, or where the vision is not obscured, very often no protection of any kind is provided, as it is much less expensive to have all trains stop before going over the crossing. Where business is heavy, or because of the locality it is desirable to indicate to or signal a train that it can have the right to the crossing, some form of fixed signal is necessary, as signals given by hand may be misconstrued. There are

A SIMPLE CROSSING SIGNAL.

many varieties of signals used for this purpose, that shown in Fig. 1 consisting of a blade or arm, made to extend over the track which it is intended to block, leaving the other road free for trains to pass. The lantern seen on the top of the pole is provided with red glasses, which are lowered in front of the lamp, to change the white light to red for the danger signal, in the direction in which it is desired that trains shall be held. This method of showing a red light is particularly objectionable, as was clearly demonstrated during the switchmen's strike, as there is no interlocking between the slides, each one being independent of the other, and it is, therefore, very easy to show a white light in all directions at the same time. A much better arrangement is to provide a lan-

tern having two red and two white lenses, to be turned through a quarter of a circle, as there can then be no chance of such a mistake being made.

Another form is that shown in Fig. 2, in which the arm seen above the lamps is used to designate which road may and which may not use the crossing, the crossing in this instance being at a very acute angle. Of the six lamps, three have red lenses and three green, the green lamps being on the side opposite from the arm, and designate at night which road has the right of crossing.

Still another form, and one that is very common in the West,
is that of the two gates shown in Fig. 3, a gate being provided
for each road, and both roads being normally blocked until the
approach of a train, when the gate on that road is turned one
side.

With all signals such as these, while it may be impossible with
the majority of them to make a mistake and give a clear signal
to both roads at the same time, there is nothing to compel the

CROSSING GATES.

engineer to obey the signal or to stop, in case he should disregard
it or, through accidental causes, be unable to stop. That there
is great danger of this happening, is evidenced by the large number of crossing accidents that are reported from time to time.

With the modern interlocking appliances, obedience to the
signal is made compulsory by means of a derailing switch, which,
unless it is properly closed, will derail the train, running the
wheels off the rails on to the ties. Such a device is shown in Fig.
4. It consists of a single switch point, put in one side of the
track, so that, unless it is closed, it will catch on the inside of the

wheel, causing both wheels to leave the rails. It is usually placed on the engineer's side, unless, owing to the location, it is desirable to have the train derailed, when such a thing does happen, off on the other side. A guard rail place about 12 inches inside of the other rail, and extending to within about 100 feet of the crossing, is often used to keep the train on the ties, thus making it not only easy to get the train back on the rails, but to prevent any serious accidents, as might easily happen should the engine

DERAILING SWITCH AND GUARD RAIL.

run off the ties on the ground. This practice, in the light of present experience, is not to be recommended, unless the location is such that it would be almost as bad to derail a train as to have a collision on the crossing, for it has so happened with several derailments that the engine and, at times, part of the train have run clear over the crossing and blocked the other line, simply because the train was kept on the ties by the guard rails. With the simple crossing under consideration, as trains will approach it on each track and from each direction, it is necessary to provide four signals, one on each side, to govern trains intending to cross. These signals, from the fact that they are stop signals, and must not be passed unless at clear, are called, as in block signaling, "Home" signals. These have blades with square ends, and are usually painted red. As there are four signals, there must be four derails—one for each direction in which it is possible for a train to approach the crossing.

Ordinarily, the derails are placed 300 feet from the crossing, although a greater distance than this, or about 500 feet, is advisable, if it is desired to stop every train that is derailed before it reaches the crossing and obstructs the other line; 300 feet, however, is the minimum distance used at any high-speed crossing. If there is a descending grade towards the crossing, the derail should be located further away so as to give the same measure of safety as for a rack having level grade. The signals, where practicable, should be located on the engineer's side of the track, and not less than 50 feet nor more than 200 feet ahead of the derail or switch which it governs. The object of this is to allow an engineer a little leeway in making the stop; for while he is expected to stop at the signal, and not pass it, he may run by it, in which case he would not run off the derail until he had gone past the signal further than he ought, the fact of his getting off demonstrating beyond all doubt that he did not approach the signal at proper speed.

To make it impossible to clear a signal unless the switches which would derail the train are properly closed, a bolt lock is connected to the points of the switch, which prevents the signals being moved from the danger position until the switch point is closed, and, when the signal is cleared, locks the points of the switch so that it is impossible to open them. The bolt lock is formed of two notched bars which are made to cross each other in a suitable frame, and is shown in Fig. 5. One bar is connected to the signal, and the other to the points of the switch, and it is impossible to move either one unless the other is in the position in which it should be.

Distant signals should be provided in all cases where trains are permitted to run at high speed, to give warning to the engineer of the position the home signal may be found in, so that he can, if necessary, be prepared to stop at the home signal. They are usually placed 1,200 feet in advance of the home signal, although this distance, with the high speeds and the heavy trains which are being run to-day, is not sufficient in which to bring every train to a stop should it pass the distant signal at speed, so that a greater distance than this is preferable for even ordinary locations.

If, now, the derails, the home and the distant signals are connected to the levers of an interlocking machine placed in a tower, which should occupy a central position, it will be seen that we

A PIPE-CONNECTED BOLT LOCK.

are in a position to control the movements of all trains wishing to use the crossing. For the sake of distinguishing them, the levers of the machine are all numbered, commencing with those on the left, the signals and derails being known by the number of the lever to which they are connected. For the same reason they are painted different colors; the switch levers black, lock levers blue, home-signal levers red and distant-signal levers green. As a further aid, it is usual to group the signal levers for trains going in one direction, at one end of the machine, the signals for the opposite direction being connected to the levers at the other end, the derails and switches being connected to the remaining levers grouped in the center. It is usual in installing a plant to put in a machine having spaces for one or two levers more than the number actually needed, so that in case it is desired to connect other switches or derails, it would be a very easy matter to put in the necessary levers. These spaces are designated as "spare," the numbers left out being equally divided on each side of the group of switch levers, thus separating the groups as much as possible. A "frame" of the machine is made to hold eight levers, but as the manufacturers furnish what is known as a "half frame," it is usual to put in a machine capable of holding the number of levers divisible by four that is next above the required number.

A plan of this crossing, as outlined, is shown in Fig. 6. By observing the numbering shown, it will be seen that only ten levers are required, as from its not being necessary at any time to close one derail without the other, it is possible to work the two derails by one lever. This will leave Nos. 5 and 8 vacant or "spare," a twelve-lever frame being the smallest size that would hold the number of levers required. If the levers working the derails and signals are now interlocked mechanically, so that it is impossible for the signalman to close the derails on but one track at a time, and to clear a signal for a train to pass over the crossing on that track in but one direction at a time, the interlocking will be complete, and it will be perfectly safe for any train for which the signals have been cleared to proceed, without reducing speed beyond that necessary in going over the crossing frogs.

The mechanical construction of the locking will be explained later on, as it will suffice for the present to say that the locking is arranged in as simple a manner as possible, each lever locking only those levers which, if pulled, would change the route indicated by the signal, or allow two trains to come together on the same track. Each lever, when reversed, is not made to lock every other lever controlling any part of the route, but only such levers as have not already been locked by some lever that is locked by the one reversed. For instance, if lever 2, when reversed, locks lever 6 reversed, and No. 1 reversed locks lever 2 reversed, there is no need of making lever 1 also lock lever 6 reversed, as one lock is sufficient to prevent the lever from being moved.

As the derails on but one track should be closed at any one time, the lever of one set, when reversed, must lock that of the other; or lever 6, when reversed, must lock lever 7 in its normal position. If lever 7 is reversed, it will be impossible to reverse

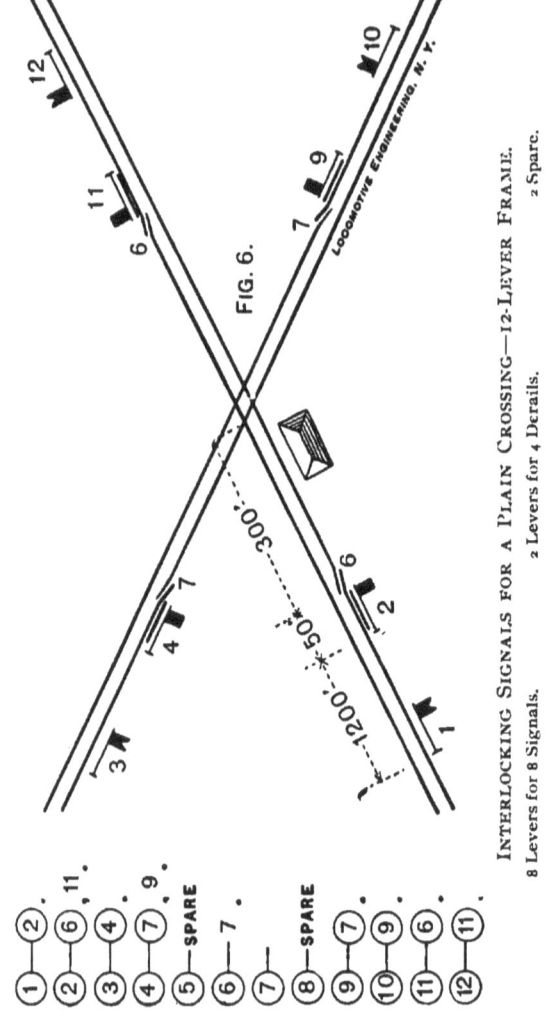

FIG. 6.

INTERLOCKING SIGNALS FOR A PLAIN CROSSING—12-LEVER FRAME.

8 Levers for 8 Signals. 2 Levers for 4 Derails. 2 Spare.

lever 6, as the locking will allow of lever 6 being pulled only when lever 7 is normal. The two levers are thus interlocked, and a signalman cannot make a mistake and reverse both of them at the same time. They both can be in the normal position, but only one can be reversed at any given time. As the signals governing any route must lock the levers controlling the switches of that route, lever 2, when reversed, must lock lever 6 reversed. So, also, must lever 11 lock lever 6 reversed. But as lever 2 and lever 11 are signals governing the same track, but in opposite directions, one of the levers, when reversed, must lock the other lever in the normal position, or else it will be possible to clear the signals at the same time for trains going in opposite directions—a movement, it is evident, that it should be impossible to make. To make the route safe, then, lever 2, when reversed, is made to lock lever 11 normal, besides locking lever 6 reversed.

As the distant signals must never be cleared until after the home signal has been cleared, the lever of the distant signal, when reversed, must lock the lever of the home signal reversed, in which case all the levers for that route will be locked reversed, and all the other levers of the machine locked in the normal position. For if lever 1, when reversed, locks lever 2 reversed, then lever 6 must be reversed, and lever 11 will be locked in the normal or danger position, and a train approaching from the direction of signal 1 will be the only train for which the derails are closed and the signals cleared for it to pass over the crossing.

For the sake of convenience and clearness, the locking performed by each lever, when reversed, is arranged in the form of a diagram or sheet, as is shown in the figure, the circle put around the figures indicating that that lever is reversed—otherwise the lever is supposed to be in the normal or danger position.

When two double-track roads cross each other, the same number of levers can be used, the numbering and locking being the same, except that the signals, when reversed, must not lock the home signal governing trains running in the opposite direction, in the normal position, as there are two tracks, and it must therefore be possible to clear both signals at the same time.

From this it is seen that interlocking signals for the protection of a plain crossing are very simple and are easily arranged. Where switches have to be connected to levers in the machine, and signals provided to govern all the movements that will be made in using the different tracks, the locking of the levers becomes somewhat complicated.

In Fig. 7 is shown a crossing of two single-track roads, one of them having a junction switch or branch line leading off from the main line, as shown. This switch being located less than 300 feet from the crossing, must be connected to the interlocking machine, so that the lever controlling it can be locked with the signals governing the route, or else it would be possible to give a clear signal with the switch open.

As it is possible for a train to approach the crossing from the branch line, it also must be provided with a signal and derail. With trains approaching the crossing on the single track, two signals must also be provided, as it is necessary to indicate to the engineer which of the two possible directions his train is to take. As there should be but one signal pole for a given track, to enable the engineer to know which signal is the one governing his train, and as it is necessary in this instance to have two signals, the two are put upon the one pole, as seen in Fig. 8—the upper blade being used to govern the high-speed or main-line route; the lower, the secondary or branch line.

This, however, is not the practice on all roads, English roads being a notable exception; for instead of the upper blade being used to govern the high-speed route it is made to govern the track leading to the right or left from the switch. In this country it is the right hand, and in England the left. This practice is not to be recommended, as it requires the engineer to locate each side track and decide whether he wants the upper or lower blade, a thing which is apt to be confusing when one is traveling on an engine at a high rate of speed, and has to take the lower blade on one pole and the upper on a pole a few hundred feet beyond it.

Where two or more signals are used to govern several tracks leading from or to a single track—in which case but one signal should ever be cleared at the same time—it is customary to connect all the signals so situated to the same lever in the machine, a selector working in connection with the switches governed by the signals being used to automatically connect the signal which governs the route for which the switches are set with the lever in the tower. Practice in this regard has been carried too far, and the tendency at present is to use a separate lever for each signal, or, at any rate, never for more than two. As a separate lever for each signal is a very expensive arrangement, and as a selector

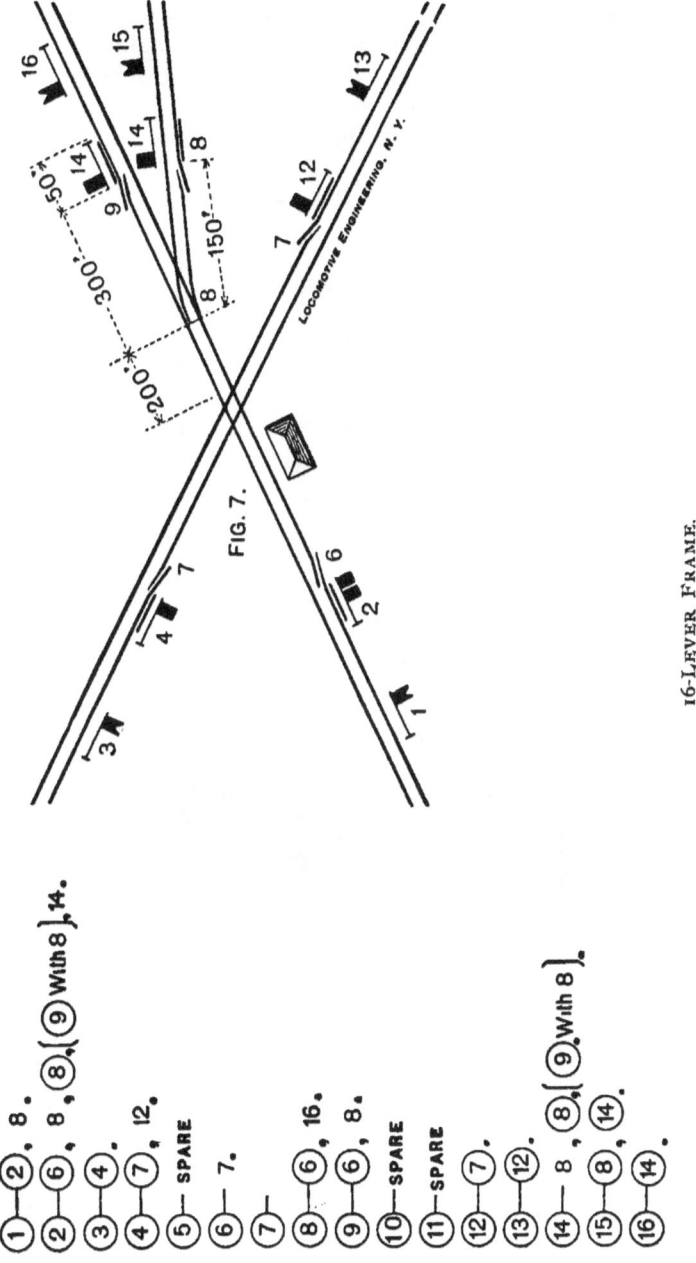

FIG. 7.

16-LEVER FRAME.

4 Levers for 5 Derails and 1 Switch.   3 Spare.

9 Levers for 11 Signals.

for two signals can be made to work well with a little care and attention, it would seem to be good practice to continue the use of this arrangement. Selectors for more than two signals, however, are not to be recommended.

By looking at Fig. 7 it will be seen that thirteen levers are

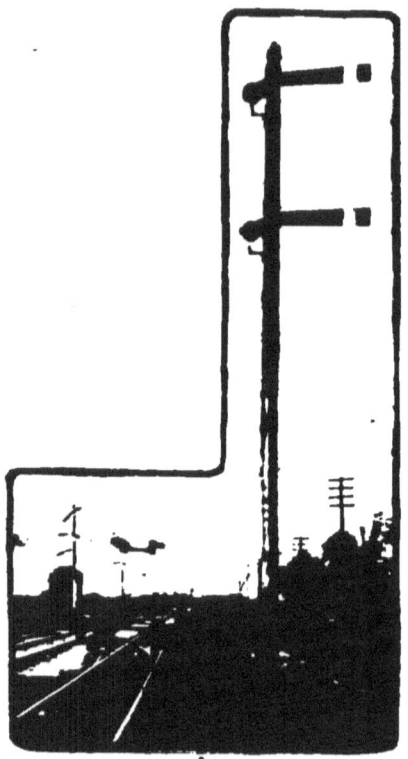

A TWO-ARMED SIGNAL POLE.

required to work the switch, the derails and the necessary signals, and that while the switch and derail on the secondary track are worked by the same lever, the two derails on the main line are worked by separate levers. The reason for this is, that while it must not be possible to close the two derails 8 and 9 at the same time, for fear of two trains running together, at the switch, it must be possible to close derail 6 on the other side of the crossing for either route—the one on the branch or the one on the main line.

The locking required to make the operation of the crossing safe, made necessary by switch 8 being connected to the machine, is also more complicated than that required for a simple crossing. By an examination of the locking sheet shown in the figure, it will be seen that, before any signal can be given to a train, the derails and switch will have to be set for the route it is to take, and that the signal governing the opposing route is also locked. For instance, lever 2 reversed locks derail 6 reversed, locks switch and derail 8 normal or reversed, because the switch is used in one or the other positions each time the signal is cleared; locks derail 9 reversed when switch 8 is normal and the route is set for the main line, and, last of all, locks lever 14 in the normal position, preventing either of the opposing signals from being cleared.

To make it impossible for both roads to use the crossing at the same time, lever 6, when reversed, is made to lock lever 7 in the normal position. As levers 8 and 9, when reversed, both lock lever 6 reversed, the reversing of any one of these will lock lever 7 in the normal position, so that the derails cannot be closed. It will be noticed that lever 8, when reversed, locks lever 6 reversed and lever 16 in the normal position, the object of locking lever 16 normal being that, as lever 14 can be reversed if either lever 8 or 9 is reversed, it would be possible, when 14 is reversed, to reverse lever 16 and clear the distant signal when switch and derail 8 were closed, and thus a wrong signal would be given. By this arrangement it is possible to reverse lever 16 only when lever 14 is reversed, locking derail 9 reversed, with switch 8 in the normal position.

Should switch 8 lead to a side track instead of to a branch line, the signal on side track governing the movements made from the side track to the main line would be made a dwarf or low signal, as shown in Fig. 9, and no distant signal would be provided. The object of this is to lessen the chance of an engineer mistaking the indication of the signal on the side track for the one on the main line, and also to effect a saving in the original cost of the plant. As movements on a side track have

to be made at slow speed, there is no necessity for putting the
signal on a high pole, where it can be seen at a distance, the low
or dwarf signal answering perfectly well for this purpose.

Dwarf signals are used to control all "back-up" movements,
or those made against the normal direction of traffic, the reasons
being the same as in the case of movements made from side
tracks.

When a cross-over between two double tracks at a crossing
has been connected up, it should be signaled as shown in Fig.

A DWARF SIGNAL.

10, the locking performed by each lever, when reversed, being
also given. It will be noticed that back-up derails have been
provided on one track, dwarf signals governing the back-up
movement being connected to and moved by the same levers, so
that whenever the derail is closed, the signal will indicate safety.
Back-up derails are generally not provided, unless the arrangement of the tracks or the traffic is such that movements against
the direction of traffic are frequently made. As the commissioners of several of the States require these to be put in at all
plants under their jurisdiction, they have in such cases to be put

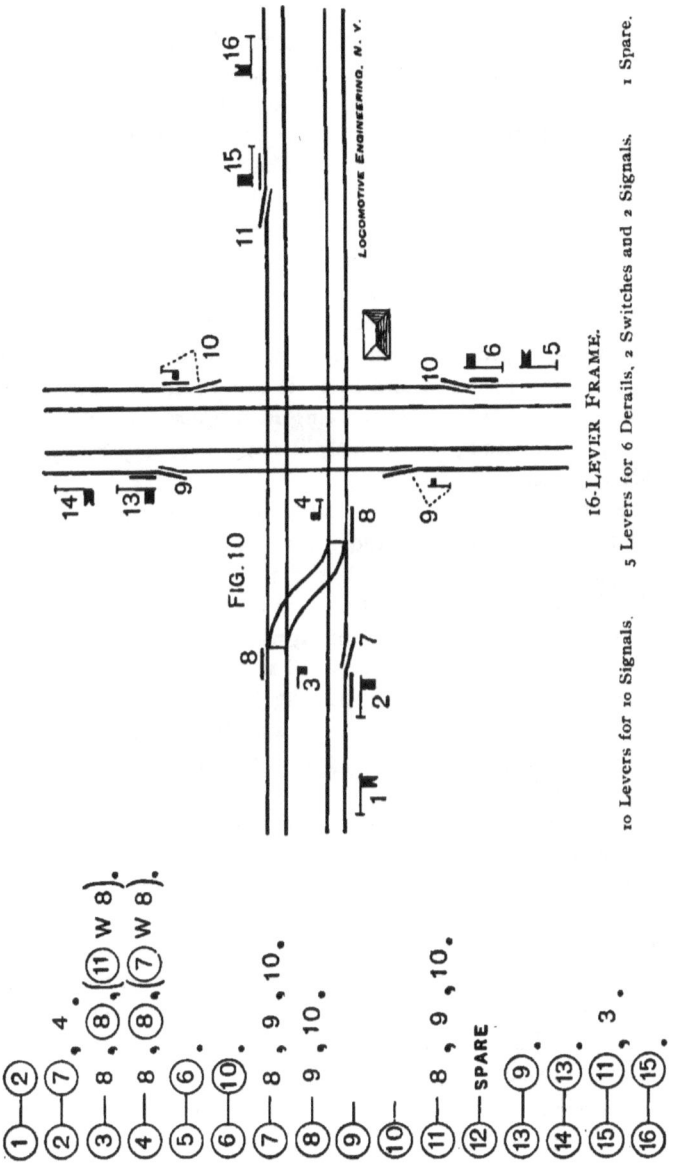

FIG.10

16-LEVER FRAME.

10 Levers for 10 Signals.   5 Levers for 6 Derails, 2 Switches and 2 Signals.   1 Spare.

in whether there is or is not a probability that they will ever be needed.

It is to be noticed that dwarf signal No. 3, while governing back-up movements in two directions, either on the main line or on the cross-over, is a single-blade signal, and does not indicate to trainmen the route they are to take, but only that the route is clear for them to back up. The reason for this being that in practice it has been found to be the best plan, as the movements are made slowly, and the towerman has, in any event, to know the movement it is desired to make before throwing the levers, for the matter to be left entirely in his hands for him to throw the proper switches before clearing the signal.

Again, a single-blade dwarf signal can be put in between tracks in many places where there is not room in which to put one having two blades. The saving in original cost of the plant is also quite an item, particularly if there are very many dwarf signals required.

The combinations of the levers by which the derails are closed and the signals cleared for a train to proceed over the crossing, are very simple with the plant under consideration, the derails of any one track being first closed, the home signal next, and, last of all, the distant signal. When it is desired to use the cross-over, the engineer will run by sufficiently to clear signal 4, when the towerman, putting levers 1, 2 and 6 back to normal, will reverse lever 8 and pull 4. Reversing lever 4 clears the signal, and the switch being thrown, the train is switched over to the other main line.

With plants having any more levers than those necessary to operate a simple crossing, it is necessary to provide in the tower, for the guidance of the signalman, a "combination sheet," showing the order in which the different levers should be pulled to clear the different routes. This order is made necessary by the locking of the levers, those which are free to move being first reversed, then those which are released by the reversal of the first lever, and so on, until all the signals for the route desired have been closed.

Although it would appear to anyone a very easy matter to find out which are the proper levers to reverse to give a clear route, such is not the case, as has been shown in many instances, where, from some cause or other, it has become necessary to put new men in the tower who do not know the proper levers, or when, as in case of accident to the signalman, the trainmen have had to work the levers to let their train over the crossing.

A large size map, with the switches and derails plainly numbered, as well as a combination sheet in which the levers to be pulled to set the different movements are shown in large type, should be framed and hung up in every tower. The wisdom of so doing will be evident to anyone who has ever tried, unaided, to clear the signals for a train at even a small crossing.

CHAPTER X

FOR JUNCTION POINTS AND DRAWBRIDGES
—CONSTRUCTION OF THE IMPROVED
SAXBY & FARMER INTERLOCK-
ING MACHINE.

Junction points, like crossings, unless protected, are dangerous places for trains to run by without first making a stop, not only because the switch may be wrong, but because a train may be approaching on the other track that will also want to use the junction switch. By interlocking the switches, providing signals to govern the different routes, and by putting in derails to enforce obedience on the part of the trainmen to the indications of the signals, there will be no necessity for any train's stopping, unless it be to register or to get orders, as it is practically impossible for the signalman to make a mistake and set the switches and clear the signals, so as to permit two trains to come into collision with each other.

In the preceding chapter the signals necessary to govern a simple switch or junction point of two tracks were shown, and while the same general plan of signaling is followed in all such installations, the particular arrangement of the signals will vary with each location.

In Fig. 1 a junction of a single with a double track road is shown, cross-over switches being provided to allow trains to run on to the single track from either of the other two. It will be noticed that two signals are provided for all facing-point switches, or those where it is possible for a train running in the normal direction of traffic, either to keep to the main line or to take the switch. In these cases the upper blade governs the high-speed route, or is the one that is "cleared" when the switch

166

12-LEVER FRAME.

7 Levers for 9 Signals.   3 Levers for 2 Derails and 3 Switches.   2 Levers Spare.

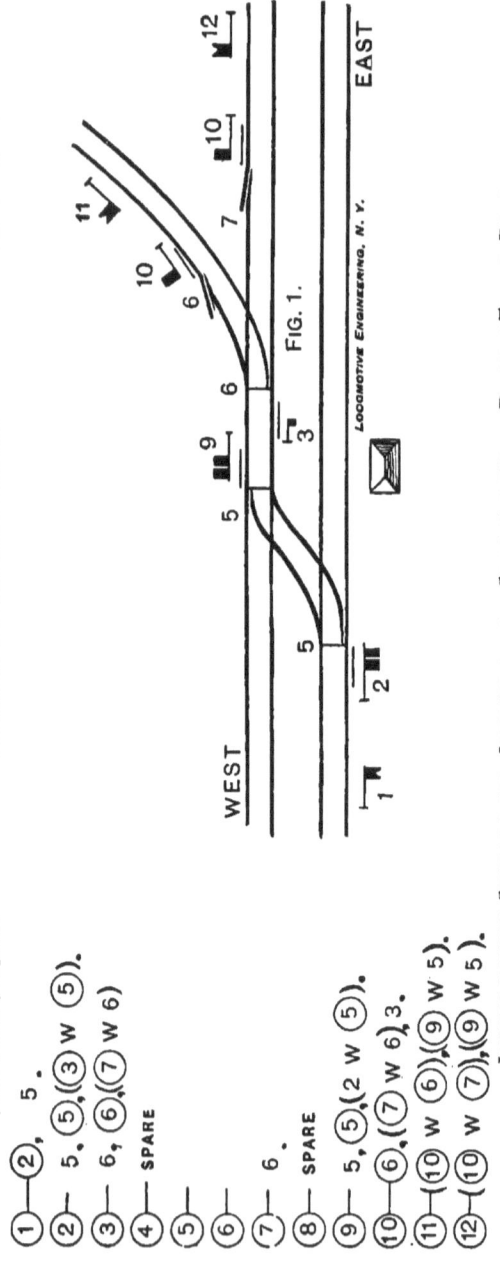

FIG. 1.

LOCOMOTIVE ENGINEERING, N. Y.

INTERLOCKING SIGNALS FOR JUNCTION OF A SINGLE WITH A DOUBLE-TRACK ROAD.

is set for the main line; when the switch is set for the cross-over, the lower blade is the one that governs. The junction switch, or the one numbered 6, is used both as a facing and a trailing point; but as it is normally a trailing point, it must be so signaled, a single-blade dwarf signal being used to govern trains going on to the branch line, while the two signals numbered 10, which govern the switch in the normal direction of traffic, are of the standard semaphore pattern.

As the two signals which govern the switch in the normal direction of traffic should never be cleared at the same time, they can both be connected to and worked by the same lever in the machine, a selector being used to connect the proper signal with the lever, the same as if they were both on the same pole. It is for this reason that they both are numbered 10. The only derails necessary are those on the branch and on the main line, just before reaching the junction switch, where, if a train should run by the signal, it might run into another train, should it happen to be using the switch at that time. Derails are not necessary at any other point, as there are no other switches upon which a train might come into collision with some other train, should the signal be run by when at danger. Any train running by signals Nos. 2 or 7 when at danger would only be going in the normal direction of traffic, so that no collision, which the inter-locking was designed to prevent, could happen. Interlocking signals are not intended to prevent collisions between two trains running in the same direction, as that is the province of a block signal, and not an interlocking plant.

The locking required to make the operation of the plant safe is somewhat more complicated than any of those which have been given, as there are a greater number of levers that have to be locked when the signals governing the different routes have been cleared.

For instance, lever 2, when reversed, must lock lever 5 both ways, normal or reversed, as lever 2 clears the signals for either route. It must also lock signal 3 reversed when cross-over switch 5 is reversed, to make it safe for a train to run on the other track. For, as lever 3, when reversed, locks the lever controlling the route on the main or the branch line in the proper position for a train to proceed in either direction, lever 2, when reversed, practically locks all the levers of the route indicated, making it safe for a train to proceed through the limits of the interlocking.

The distant-signal lever No. 1, when reversed, locks lever 2 reversed with lever 5 normal. This prevents the clearing of the distant signal when signal 2 is cleared for the cross-over or the slow-speed route.

The combinations of levers to be reversed to give clear signals for the principal routes, or the "Combination Sheet," as it is called, are as follows:

Main track, east bound, 2, 1.
Main track, west bound, 7, 9, 10, 12.
East bound, main to branch, 6, 5, 3, 2.
Branch line to west bound main, 6, 9, 10, 11.

The signals and derails necessary to make the use of a junction of two double-track lines safe, so that trains need not stop unless the signals have been cleared for some other train, are shown in Fig. 2. The signals required are much the same as those shown in Fig. 1, but it is necessary to use one more derail, so as to protect trains that use the cross-over and back over on to the west bound main line. A dwarf signal (No. 14) has also to be put in to govern trains making this movement.

In working out the locking of the levers necessary to make the operation of this plant safe, there are several points to which attention should be called. As it would be unsafe for a train to use the cross-over switch if it were possible for the signalman at the same time to close any one of the derails, lever 9, when reversed, must lock levers 6, 8 and 10 in the normal position. Lever 6, when reversed, must lock lever 7, either in the normal or the reversed positions, to prevent that lever being thrown after 6 is reversed. Lever 6 must also lock lever 10 normal, when lever 7 is reversed to make it impossible for two trains to come together where the two tracks cross each other.

It is also to be noticed that the signal levers in all cases, when reversed, lock the levers of the signals governing the opposing route in the normal position, so that it is impossible for the operator to give clear signals to trains running in opposite directions, that would come into collision with each other.

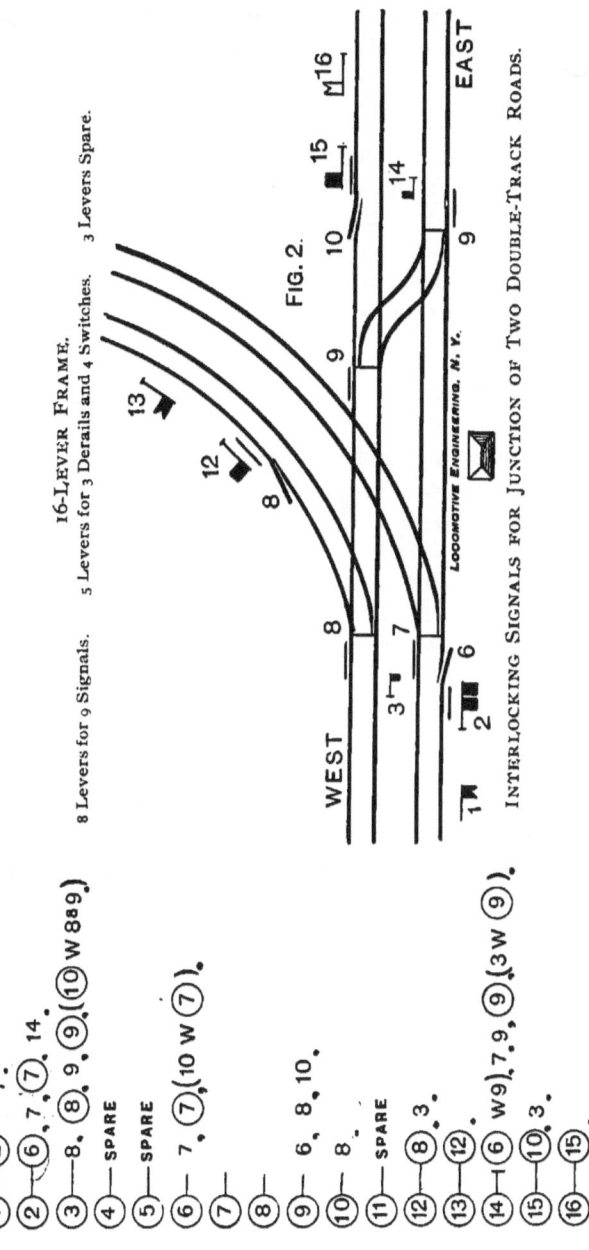

FIG. 2.

16-LEVER FRAME.

8 Levers for 9 Signals.   5 Levers for 3 Derails and 4 Switches.   3 Levers Spare.

LOCOMOTIVE ENGINEERING, N. Y.

INTERLOCKING SIGNALS FOR JUNCTION OF TWO DOUBLE-TRACK ROADS.

(1) (2) 7.
(2) (6) 6, 7, (7) 14.
(3) 8, (8) 9, (9) (10 W 889).
(4) SPARE
(5) SPARE
(6) 7, (7) (10 W 7).
(7)
(8)
(9) 6, 8, 10.
(10) 8.
(11) SPARE
(12) (8) 3.
(13) (12)
(14) (6 W 9), 7, 9, (9) (9) (3 W 9).
(15) (10) 3.
(16) (15) .

The "combinations" of the levers for every movement provided for by the signals are as follows:

East bound main, 6, 2, 1.

West bound main, 10, 15, 16.

East bound main and branch, 7, 6, 2.

Branch to west bound main, 8, 12, 13.

East bound to west bound main, 9, 14.

West bound main to branch, 8, 3.

West bound main to east bound main, 9, 3.

West bound main against normal direction of traffic, 10, 3.

At drawbridges it is just as necessary, or even more essential, that all trains be brought to a stop before passing over the bridge, than it is at a crossing, from the fact that the draw might be open, or opened when the train was too near to make a stop, in which case a worse accident than a collision would be very likely to happen.

Protection and safety in the operation of drawbridges, without requiring trains to make a stop, are afforded by the use of interlocking signals in the same manner as with a crossing of two tracks at grade, and in most cases this is a very simple matter. Each approach to the bridge is provided with a home and, where necessary, a distant signal; derails being put in to throw a train off the track if the indications of the signal are disregarded. The distances these are placed from the ends of the draw should in all cases, except for a very slow-speed route, be at least 500 feet, owing to the distance it is possible for a train to run on the ties after being derailed, should it be running at even a moderate rate of speed. All switches that are between the home signals and the bridge must be connected up and properly signalled, to prevent a signal from being cleared when it was not safe for a train to proceed. The numbering and arrangement of the levers would be the same as that used in the plan of a simple crossing.

It is usual to put the interlocking machine on the draw itself, so that the levers operating the locks of the bridge may be interlocked with the other levers, making it impossible to unlock and turn the bridge while the couplers at the end of the bridge, which make the connection between the levers of the machine and the switches and signals, are closed. As these can be uncoupled only when the signals are at danger and the derails open, it is impossible to make a mistake and allow a train to run into the open draw.

Where the machine is not placed on the bridge, a separate lock has to be provided, which will make it impossible to close the derails on the track leading to the bridge, unless the bridge is in its proper position. This lock is shown in Fig. 3. The end cap, which prevents the plunger from being shoved out when the bridge is open, being moved one side by a lug on the socket casting when the bridge is closed, allows the signalman to reverse the lever and lock the bridge, when the other levers may be reversed. Where the approach to a drawbridge is such that a

A BRIDGE LOCK.

derail cannot be used, owing to the fact that there is no place in which a train can be derailed without entailing great damage, interlocking the bridge and providing the necessary signals do not make it safe for trains to use the bridge without first making a stop, as there is nothing to bring the train to a stop should the engineer run by the signal.

In signaling complicated crossings, terminals, or sets of switches, the method pursued is, in the main, the same as that followed in protecting the simple locations that have been described. As each plan will differ somewhat from that of the other, no rules can be laid down that will cover all cases, and it is only by giving in a general way what can be considered as the best practice that any idea can be given of what should be used. Where the switches are close together, it is often impossible to provide separate signals for each switch, in which case the signal at the limits of the interlocking must be used to govern all the movements that can be made from any one track. This is usually made a double-bladed signal—the upper blade being used to govern the high-speed or main-line route, and the lower blade all other routes. Very often, from the location of the tracks, it is impossible to put the signal next the track which it is intended to govern, one or more tracks intervening between the signal pole and the track to be governed. In cases where there is but one track intervening, it is customary to use a bracket pole, a mast being provided to represent each track, with the signal blade placed on the one corresponding to the track to be governed. Such a pole is shown in Fig. 4, it being made somewhat higher than the ordinary pole, to allow of the signals being easily seen over the top of a train passing on the intervening track. Such an arrangement is objectionable, as the force of the signal is very much lessened by being placed so far away from the track which it is intended to govern; but as in most cases there is no cheap way of providing sufficient space in which the ordinary signal can be placed, the bracket pole will have to be used. The practice on the Pennsylvania road, however, is to separate the tracks, wherever possible, and place each signal next the track it governs—a practice to be recommended if the matter of expense is not to be considered.

It is claimed by some that a bracket pole is a useless expense, and that an ordinary pole will answer in most places where a bracket pole is now used, for the reason that a high-speed route only would be governed by a high semaphore signal, and that there would be no other high signal for an engineer to see, no matter how many tracks intervened between the high-speed track and the governing signal.

Where but one track intervenes, and traffic is in the opposite direction to the way the signal reads, there seems to be no valid objection to such practice, as at night it is practically impossible to tell at any great distance whether the signal is on a bracket or an ordinary straight pole.

Where more than three parallel tracks have to be signaled, a bridge on which the signals can be placed is almost a necessity. This is an expensive arrangement, but an ideal one, as each

FIG. 4.

LOCOMOTIVE ENGINEERING, N. Y.

A BRACKET POLE.

signal can then be placed immediately over the track which it is intended to govern. Such an arrangement is clearly shown in Fig. 5, which is a photograph of one used at Stewart avenue, Chicago—one of the most complicated crossings in America.

In signaling terminals, a plan that is often followed, where the tracks are close together, is to use dwarf signals in all cases, whether for the main line or for a siding. As all movements are made at slow speed, these answer the purpose just as well as the high semaphore, and are much cheaper. Another advantage to be gained by their use is that they may be always put in their correct position—that is, on the right-hand side of the track which they are to govern—for where there are many tracks to be signaled, it is very easy to see how confusing it would be, if not impossible, to tell which was the proper signal, if some systematic arrangement such as this were not followed in locating the signals.

At terminals or yards where movements are made at comparatively slow speed, it is not customary to provide derails to prevent trains coming into collision with each other, but reliance is placed upon the trainmen that they will obey the signal. Experience has demonstrated that this is a safe arrangement, much more so than where no interlocking is used, and switchmen are employed to work the switches and to signal trains.

Where trains run on the left-hand track, as is the case on several roads in this country, the signals, to be next the track they govern, have to be placed on the left-hand side. This running of trains on the left-hand track is a very bad arrangement, if consistency is to be observed in the location of the signals, as the practice regarding which signal is to be used to govern a given track will vary on different roads.

In England, where all trains run on the left-hand track, the signal blades project to the left, as seen from an approaching train, and are placed on the left side, so that the signals governing any one track are as easily picked out as are those where the signals projecting to the right govern trains running on the right-hand track.

Generally, in signaling yards or at crossings, the signal engineer, instead of being consulted as to a good and economical arrangement of tracks while yet there is time to suggest any improvements or a better location, with a view to putting in an interlocking machine, is given a plan of the tracks and asked to signal it, no matter how bad the arrangement may be, after once being made safe, for the movements that are to be made over them.

As the signals that will be required for any given arrangement of tracks, to make the use of the same safe for all trains, is governed by the location of switches and crossings, it follows

FiG.5

that it is exceedingly important that these be placed so that the different routes will be separated as much as possible, the switches and signals being located so that movements covering more than one route can be quickly made, allowing one of the tracks to be cleared for other trains. If the arrangement be carefully worked out with this end in view, fewer switches and also fewer signals will be needed, the first cost and the cost of maintenance being much reduced.

Having outlined the manner in which different arrangements of tracks are signaled, and shown what locking of the levers is necessary to make it impossible for a signalman to make a mistake and pull a wrong lever, it will be best, before describing the different parts used in connecting up the switches and signals, to explain in detail the construction of the different interlocking machines, and show how the locking of the levers is accomplished.

As has been previously stated, the levers of the earlier machines were interlocked by connections made directly to the levers themselves. This resulted in severe strains being put upon the locking, as a signalman would not know, in case the lever pulled hard, whether it was being held by the locking or by the outside connections. The improvement made in the modern machine consists in attaching the locking mechanism to the latching device or latch rod, so that, unless the locking is set for the lever to be reversed, the latch cannot be lifted, and the lever, of course, cannot be pulled over. By this means, raising the latch to unlock the lever, locks the levers of all conflicting routes, and the levers to be released by the reversal of this lever are not unlocked until the lever has been entirely pulled over and latched. This method of locking is known as "preliminary" or "latch locking," and is the one generally used in this country for any machine requiring eight or more levers, although in England the older form is still in general use—a machine of 400 levers having lever locking, probably the largest in the world, having been but very lately put in service.

Of the different machines in use in this country there are three different patterns—that of Messrs. Saxby & Farmer, as made by the Union Switch & Signal Co., and that of Messrs. Stevens & Sons, made by the National and the Johnson Signal Companies. In the main, the different machines are constructed in the same manner and of the same general design; the only practical differences being found in the manner in which the locking is accomplished and the attachment is made to the latch rod. The machines are made so that the levers are centrally pivoted on a main frame; a quadrant being fastened to the top of the frame, by which the lever can be latched in either the normal or the reversed positions. The lower end of the lever is bent out at right angles, to form an arm to which the vertical connection can be bolted. If the connections are of wire, it is necessary that the lever be provided with an arm projecting on the opposite side of the center, to which the back pull wire can be attached. The arm is called a tail piece, and is usually bolted to the lever shoe or center casting of the lever.

The machine made by the Union Switch & Signal Co., and known as the improved Saxby & Farmer machine, is shown in Fig. 6, the locking bars and dogs being carried in a suitable frame, supported by brackets bolted to the main frame. A rocker,

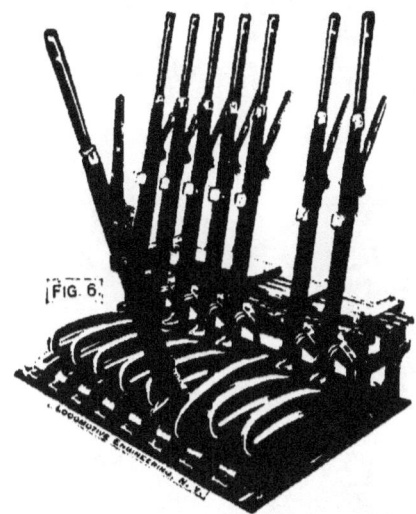

THE IMPROVED SAXBY & FARMER INTERLOCKING MACHINE.

centrally pivoted, and having a slot in which a projection on the latch may be made to slide, is provided for each lever. Raising the latch to release the lever causes one end of the rocker to be raised; but when the lever is pulled over, no further movement of the rocker is made, as the slot is of the same radius as the top of the quadrant. Releasing the latch at the end of the stroke causes it to drop by the power stored in the spring, when that end of the rocker is depressed and the other end still further raised.

This motion is the one made use of in most of the preliminary latch-locking devices, by which the lock rods or tappets can be driven. Motion is imparted to the lock rods by means of a link, used to connect one end of the rocker with a square shaft, which

178

revolves in turned bearings underneath the lock rods, and drives them whenever the latch handle is raised or released. The lock rods are carried in brackets, which are also made to hold the locking dogs, the latter moving on top of and at right angles with the lock rods. Lugs with a beveled end are riveted to the lock

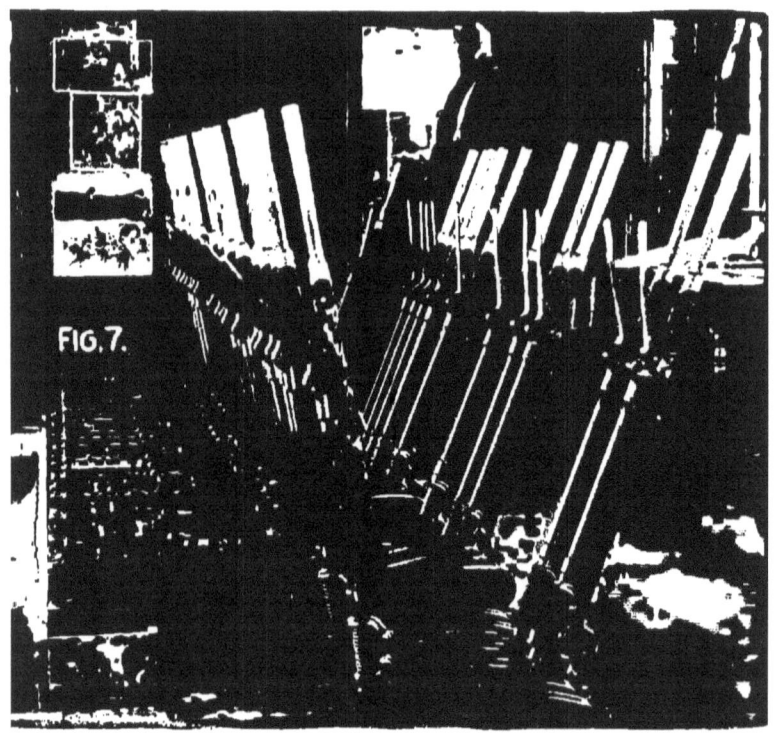

SAXBY & FARMER MACHINE—SIDE VIEW.

rods, so as to engage with the dogs in such a way that, unless the dog is free to be moved, the lock rod cannot be moved, and the latch, and with it the lever, will be locked. When one lever, in a reversed position, is to lock another lever, lugs are riveted on each lock rod, and a dog or cross-piece, shorter by the thickness of one lug than the distance they are apart, and having its ends beveled same as the lugs, is placed in the locking bracket between the two lugs. Making the dog shorter in this way allows one of the bars to be moved, as the dog can be shoved over against the lug on the other bar, thereby locking it, which is just what it was intended that it should do.

This action will perhaps be more clearly understood if reference is had to the diagram (Fig. 10), in which the locking is drawn out as it is arranged on the machine. This diagram is called a "Dog Sheet," and is the working drawing by which the locking,

ARRANGEMENT OF LOCKING, SAXBY & FARMER MACHINE.

as called for on the locking sheet, is worked out. The long lines which represent the lock rods are numbered, not to correspond with the levers with which they are connected, but in the order in which they are placed, commencing with the one next to the levers. A small circle drawn on this line shows by which lever the rod is worked and where the connection is made. The locking brackets are numbered to correspond with the levers, the locking dogs being stamped with the number of the bracket in which they are to be placed, and also at each end with the number of the lock rod under that end. This is done to make it easy to replace the bars and dogs, if for any cause they are removed from the machine.

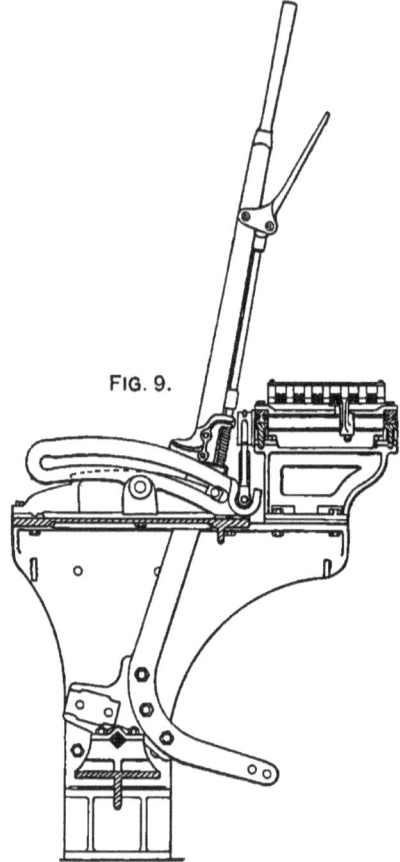

FIG. 9.

DETAILS OF IMPROVED SAXBY & FARMER INTERLOCKING MACHINE.

It will be noticed that in drawing the dogs they are represented as being placed close up to the lug by which the locking is performed, the clearance necessary to allow one of the lugs to be moved being left next to the other lug. The object of this is to make the reading of the dog sheet easy by showing which lever does the locking, and permit of the work being checked up with the locking sheet. Where one lever has to lock two or more levers,

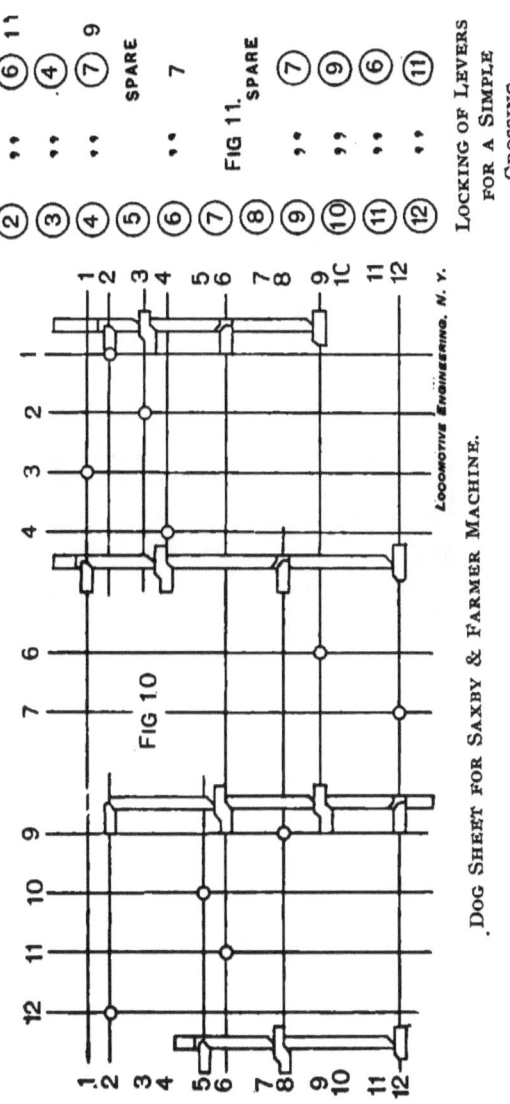

LOCKING OF LEVERS FOR A SIMPLE CROSSING.

FIG 11.

FIG 10

DOG SHEET FOR SAXBY & FARMER MACHINE.

LOCOMOTIVE ENGINEERING. N. Y.

the dog is notched for as many lugs as there are levers to be locked, a reversal of the locking lever forcing the dog over against the lugs of the other levers and locking them. If one of the other levers has been reversed, the dog will strike against the lug of that lever, and prevent the lever that locks all the others from being reversed.

The locking represented by the dog sheet is the same as that which was given by the levers controlling a simple crossing, or as is shown in Fig. 11.

"Special" locking, or the locking which is to be made by one lever only, when another lever is in a certain position, is shown in Fig. 12. As shown, it consists of a lug of special form, pivoted on the locking bar in such a way that it can be moved sidewise by the two dogs, between the edges of which it projects, and also be moved lengthwise with the lock rod, to which it is attached.

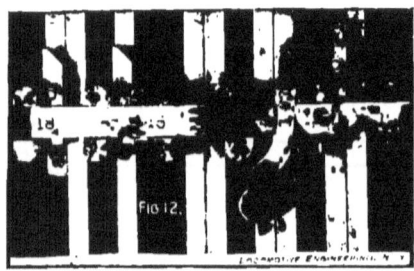

A Special Locking.

In the position shown the two dogs act as one, as the clearance space between the lugs is taken up, while if the special lug is withdrawn, it will allow either of the two dogs to be moved and the levers reversed.

Claims are made for this style of locking that "the arrangement of the bars permits of the greatest amount of locking in the smallest space, and since only the dogs, which are short, are driven by impact, the wear is reduced to a minimum; that, by being placed in a single tier, any required changes may be easily made and the bars easily gotten at;" and, also, that as all the bars are in a horizontal position, any wear that may take place, due to the weight of the bar, does not in any way affect the locking. Objections are made to it that, from the locking being arranged in a horizontal plane, the towers have to be made much larger than where it is arranged vertically, and that in places where there is not much room to be had, this objection is quite a serious one.

CHAPTER XI

THE STEVENS MACHINE AND HOW A SWITCH IS MOVED AND LOCKED.

The machine constructed by Messrs. Stevens & Sons has been much improved since the first one was made, and while the general plan is very much the same, the arrangement of the small parts differs considerably. The improvements have been made, principally, in the arrangement of the latch connection, by which the preliminary locking feature is obtained, and in the design of the special locking.

Two forms of the machine are manufactured and have been quite extensively introduced. That made by the National Switch & Signal Co. is shown in general view in Fig. 1, a drawing of the machine being shown in Fig. 2. As will be seen, all of the parts by which the locking is accomplished are carried on the main frame beneath the flooring, where it is out of the way, nothing being put above the top of the frame but the levers which the signalman has to pull. This gives the machine a very neat appearance, and makes it very easy to keep the tower clean.

The detail parts of the levers are much the same as in other machines, but the rocker (R, Fig. 2), instead of being placed on top of the frame alongside of the quadrant, is suspended underneath, the latch rod P being brought down to engage with and move it whenever the latch is raised or released. A link S connects the rocker with a "tappet" bar T, and prevents the rocker, and therefore the latch and lever, from being moved unless the locking dogs, carried in the frame behind the tappet bar, are in such a position as will allow of the tappet bars being moved. This arrangement is a very simple and strong one, and admits of the power being applied in a very direct manner.

The arrangement of tappet bars and locking dogs, by which the locking of the levers is accomplished, is shown in Fig. 3, tap-

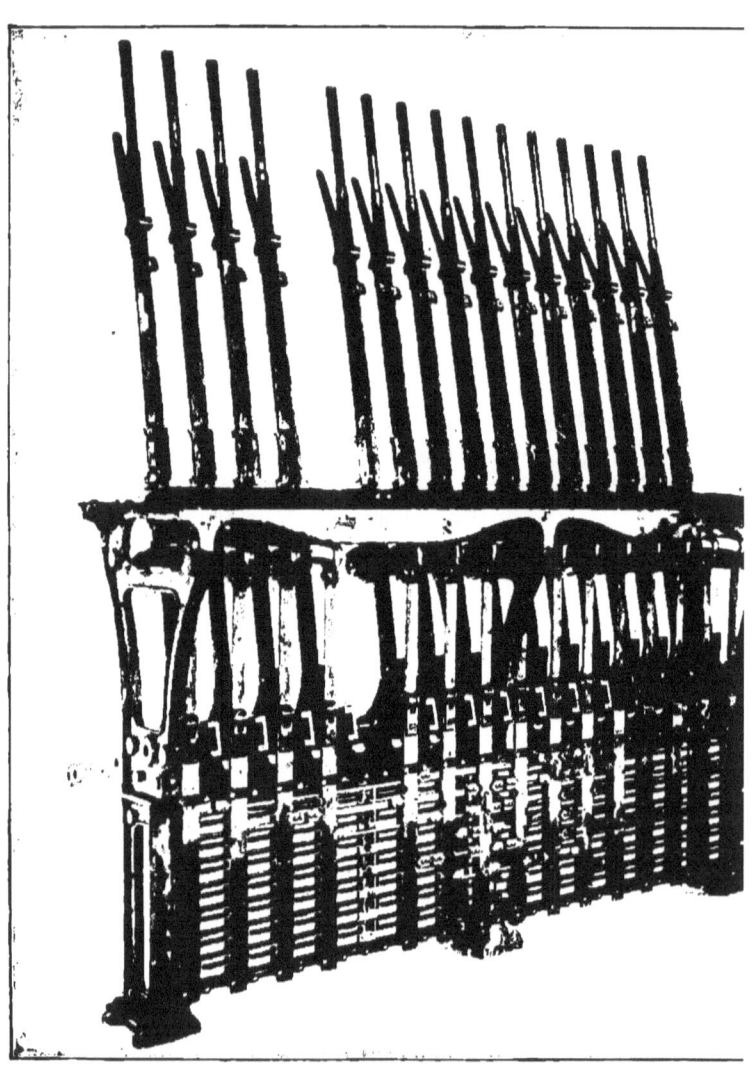

FIG. 1.—THE NATIONAL INTERLOCKING MACHINE.

pets being numbered the same as the levers to which they are connected. The locking sheet from which this arrangement of locking is made, being the locking required for the levers controlling a plain crossing, such as was shown in a previous article.

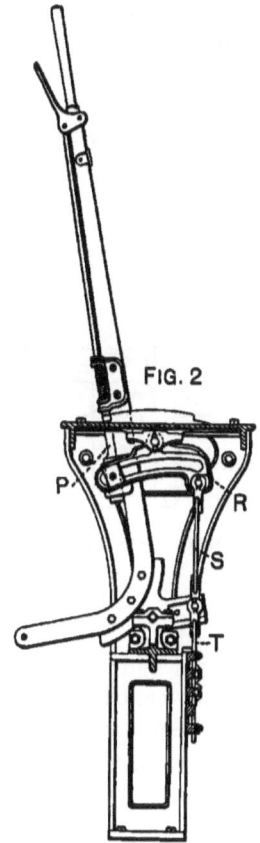

FIG. 2

DETAILS OF NATIONAL MACHINE.

The mechanical construction of the locking is simply that of a bar or tappet locked by a dog moving at right angles to it, and fitting in a notch cut in the edge of the tappet bar. This dog is made longer than the distance between any two tappet bars, the levers of which it is desired to lock, so that one bar will be free to move only when the dog slides into the notch cut in the other bar. Unless the notch in the other bar is in a position to allow the dog to be forced over, the bar is locked and the lever cannot be moved.

Any locking required is very easily arranged in the machine, as the dogs are made by screwing tapered pieces of the proper form to small bars of the length required to fit in the notches which are cut in the tappet bars. As the width of the dog is three times that of the small connecting bar, three dogs may be made to work in the same space in the frame by fastening the dogs to the top, middle or bottom bars. In this way a great deal of lock-

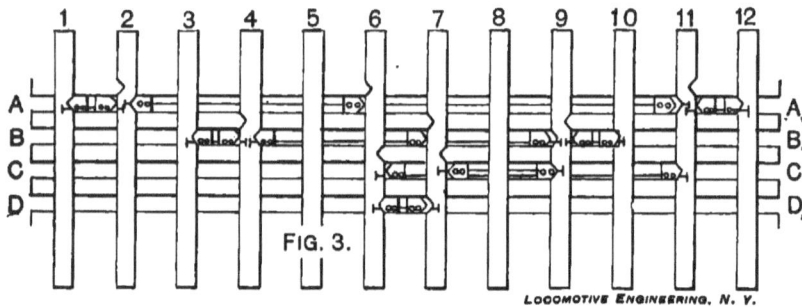

FIG. 3.

LOCOMOTIVE ENGINEERING. N. Y.

DOG SHEET, NATIONAL MACHINE.

ing may be arranged in a very small frame space, and at the same time may be gotten at easily.

The special locking used by the National Company is a very simple and easily arranged contrivance, consisting simply of a square block held by a frame or "cage," fastened on the outside of the tappet, as shown in Fig. 4, special dogs being used, which not only fit in the tappet in the ordinary manner, but project over the bar and bear against the block. If the tappet is in a position where the block is held in between the two they will practically act as one, while if the block is withdrawn, both dogs will be free to move. In this way one lever is made to lock another lever only when a third lever is in a certain position, normal or reversed, whichever is desired. By making cages to hold several blocks, and by using dogs of special form, any special locking, no matter how complicated, can be easily arranged.

The claims made for this style of machine are "that as the rocker is made with either single or double tappet connections, single or double locking can be used, placed on either side of the frame with equal convenience and accessibility, thus doubling the capacity, the symmetrical construction of which secures the greatest economy of room and minimum cost of maintenance, for the reason that more locking can be carried in less space and with less cost than in any other machine—a feature of special importance in all installations; that the locking frame is so designed that the locking is open to the unobstructed view of every part, and thus

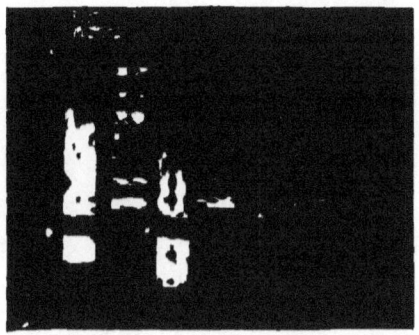

FIG. 4. SPECIAL LOCKING.

not only facilitates free inspection but permits the placing of new locking (for additional levers), or the introduction of special locking, with the greatest convenience and economy."

Few or no objections can be brought against this style of machine, save in the construction of the locking, as the tappet bars are connected in a very simple and direct manner. It will be noticed that with this kind of locking the dogs extend from one end of the machine to the other, instead of across the locking bars, as is the case with the improved Saxby & Farmer locking. Making the bar long in this way means that it will require more force to drive it, and as the bar is driven by sliding friction between the end of the dog and the notch cut in the tappet, it is very apt to cause wear. Again, as the dogs all lie in a vertical plane, any wear will take place on one side only, and will in time affect the locking, possibly necessitating its renewal much sooner than with the other style.

188

The Johnson machine is illustrated in Fig. 5, a detail drawing having been shown in the article on Controlled-Manual Block Systems, the Patenall lock instruments having been applied to one of these machines. This machine differs from the one made by

Fig. 5.—The Johnson Interlocking Machine.

the National Co., in placing the rocker on a bracket fastened to and moving with the lever, instead of suspending it from the main frame. Practically the results are the same, as motion is imparted to the tappet both before and after the movement of the lever, as in the other machine.

Special locking is provided for by a loose dog fastened to the tappet, which acts in the same manner as the block used with the National machine. Instead, however, of fastening this to the surface of the tappet, the bar is cut away to allow the dog to work in the same plane with the other locking dogs, a tie-piece being used to join the two parts of the tappet bar together.

This construction is objectionable and is not as good as the National arrangement, owing to the chance of the bar becoming disconnected and throwing the locking out of service.

With a machine having the rocker situated as it is on this one, the locking can be placed only on the front part of the frame, where it will be behind the pipe connections to the levers, and very hard to get at to make any changes or repairs.

While the improved Saxby & Farmer locking may take up more room than the Stevens locking, there is little doubt that it can be repaired more easily, owing to its being in a horizontal position, or that it will last longer, there being less friction between the locking bars and the dogs. However, both types of machines are strongly made, and will need but little repairs or attention beyond an occasional oiling, and whatever cleaning is necessary to keep every part clean and free from gum, for if the locking is not kept clean it is apt to stick and give trouble.

Next to the machine, the most important part used in the construction of an interlocking plant are the movements by which the switch points are opened and closed and also locked, whenever the lever to which they are connected is moved.

By far the simplest arrangement that can be used is to make a direct connection from the lever to the head rod of the switch, the same as if the connection was made from an ordinary switch-stand. This would provide for throwing the switch, but would not lock it, and as there is considerable spring in pipe lines used to make the connection to the lever, some form of lock with all facing-point switches is absolutely necessary to prevent the points from moving under a passing train.

Locks are easily made by attaching a rod to the points of the switch and providing a plunger or lock pin which can be entered into holes drilled in the rod, thus locking it, and with it the points of the switch. There are two forms of these locks which, as they are generally used at facing switches, are called "facing-point locks," one being placed inside of the line of rails, and shown in Figs. 6 and 7, and the other placed outside of the rails and shown in Fig. 8.

As will be noticed in the one shown in Figs. 6 and 7, the two points of the switch are connected together by a front rod, which answers for a lock rod by passing it through the plunger casting bolted to the tie, holes being drilled in the rod for the plunger to enter and lock the switch, either for the main line or for the side track.

With the form shown in Fig. 8, the lock rod is attached to

INSIDE–CONNECTED FACING–POINT LOCK.

the front rod midway between the two points, and is made long enough to pass through the plunger casting which is placed outside of the rails, holes being drilled in the bar to lock the rod and with it the points of the switch.

Of the two methods, the second is the one ordinarily used and is much the best, as the casting is out of the way and not liable to be caught and torn out by any loose brake beam, or other defective part, on a passing train.

However, the inside lock is the only one in use in England, the claim being made for it that it is the strongest, and that by the lock being made a part of the switch it has got to be kept in working order.

Using locks such as are here shown to lock the switch, necessitates using a separate lever to work the lock, which, in a great many instances, is a very expensive arrangement. Where such

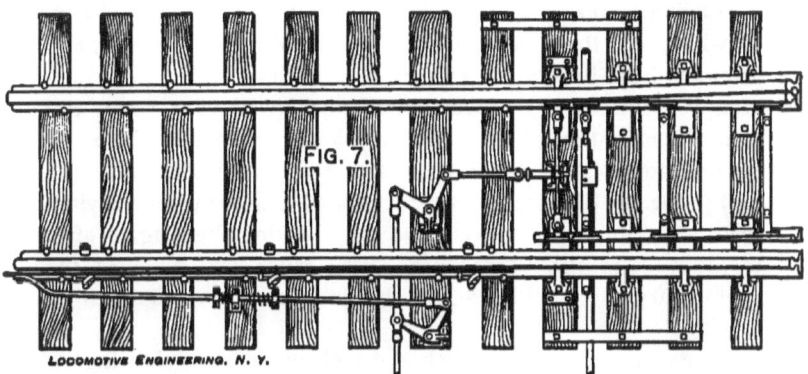

CONNECTIONS TO INSIDE-CONNECTED FACING-POINT LOCK.

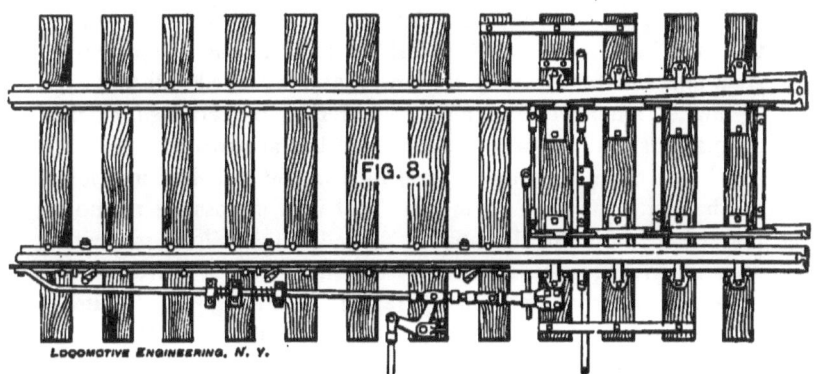

OUTSIDE-CONNECTED FACING-POINT LOCK.

are used, the general plan followed in numbering the levers and arranging the locking is the same as that which has already been described, except that the levers of the signals, when reversed, must lock the lever of the switch lock reversed in all cases, whether the switch is in the normal or the reversed position, for the reason that a switch should always be locked before it is used by a train, irrespective of the way the switch is set—the order in which the levers would have to be reversed to set up any route for a train being: First, the switch or derail lever; second, the locking lever; third, the home-signal lever, and, last of all, the lever of the distant signal.

Owing to the cost of providing two levers to move and lock a switch, and the time required to pull the second lever, many attempts have been made to perfect a machine which would accomplish this by the movement of one lever. The result has been the invention of the switch-and-lock movement, which can be said to be a practical success, the principal feature of the design being the preliminary action of unlocking the switch before the points are moved, and then locking them again after the movement has taken place, very much the same as the preliminary latch locking acts with the levers of the interlocking machine.

A general plan of a switch-and-lock movement, showing its construction and the connections to the switch, is shown in Fig. 9, a detail drawing of the movement being shown in Fig 10. A is the base casting, having a guide at one end, through which the lock bar L is made to pass. A slide bar R is connected by a pipe line to a lever in the tower, and is moved a distance of $8\frac{3}{4}$ inches whenever the lever is reversed or returned to the normal position. Riveted to the slide bar are two lock pins P, which are made to enter holes drilled in the lock bar, and lock the bar with the base casting, so that it is impossible to move the switch until the slide bar is moved and the lock pin withdrawn. Working on one side of the slide bar is a switch crank C, which bears against an operating or driving pin D, fitted between the upper and lower bars of the slide bar R, and is connected to the switch rod by a short connecting rod.

The switch being shown in the normal position, if, now, the man in the tower should reverse the lever, the movements that would be made would be as follows: The slide bar would be moved, withdrawing the lock pin from lock bar, leaving the switch points free to be moved, the operating pin sliding along the straight surface of the switch crank. After the switch had been unlocked, the operating pin would strike the arm of the

switch crank *C*, causing it to revolve and carry with it the
switch and lock bar, the throw of the crank being regulated so

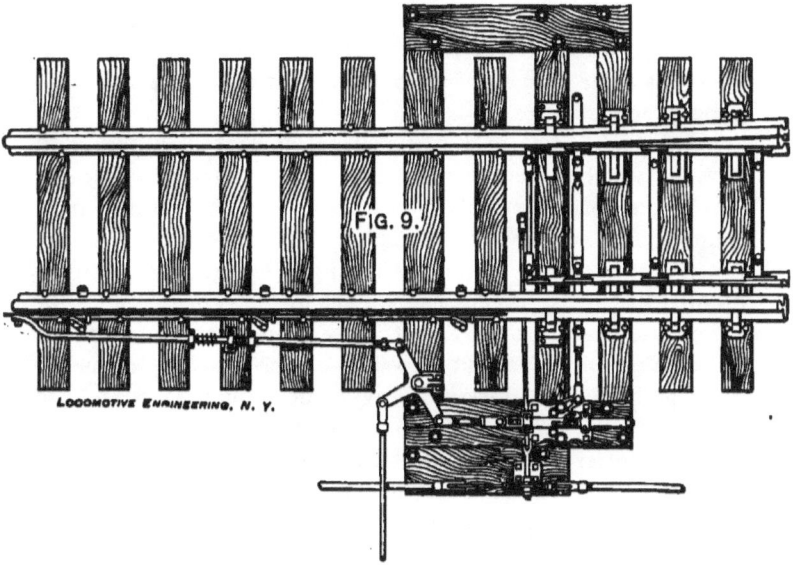

SWITCH-AND-LOCK MOVEMENT AND CONNECTIONS TO SWITCH.

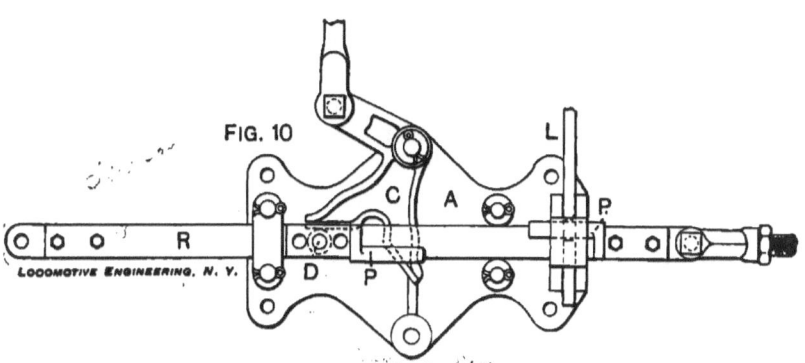

DETAILS OF SWITCH-AND-LOCK MOVEMENT.

that when the switch had completed its movement the operating
pin would slide along the other arm of the crank, entering the

lock pin in the other hole in the lock bar, locking the bar and the switch in its new position.

Theoretically the results obtained are the same as when separate levers are used to work and lock the switch, but in practice it is found that the use of the switch-and-lock movement has some limitations beyond which it cannot be said to be good practice to go.

The weak point in the movement is that with the short motion available there is not travel enough in which to make the locking of the switch certain, owing to the spring in the connections when the switch is any great distance from the tower. As with the locking of the levers in the tower, it is taken for granted that if the lever is pulled over for its entire distance the switch has been thrown, and it is therefore possible to reverse other levers which depend for safety on the fact that the switch is properly set and locked. Any plant cannot be considered safe where the switch-and-lock movement is such a distance from the tower that it would be possible to reverse and latch the lever, owing to the spring in the connections when the lock pin had not entered the lock bar, as would be the case if something should get in between the points of the switch and prevent it from closing.

If a bolt lock was put in the connection to the signal, it would be impossible to clear the signal if the switch was not properly closed; but as it is not practicable to put a lock on the signal for every switch which the signal may be used to govern, dependence must be placed upon the switch being closed properly when the lever is pulled over.

No definite distance can be laid down beyond which it would be unsafe to go, as the number of cranks and any curves which may be in the pipe line will materially affect the amount of spring and lost motion in the connections. Then, again, the number of movements that are placed on a lever will also make a difference in the chances of failure, owing to the greater power required to work the switches.

My experience has been that a switch-and-lock movement for distances up to 500 feet is a safe and easy method of working a switch, but beyond that I would advise a facing-point lock, although the latter cannot be said to be a perfectly safe arrangement. Instances can be named where serious wrecks have occurred from a failure of a facing-point lock, owing to a break in the switch connection allowing the lever to be reversed without closing the switch, the plunger entering the same hole in the lock bar when its lever was reversed, and locking the switch in the same or open position. On the Pennsylvania a staggered lock is being tried to prevent an accident of this kind happening, the staggered lock being made with two lock bars and two plungers of different shapes, which fit in different-shaped holes cut in the bars; so that unless the switch has been moved, the plunger cannot enter the hole in the lock bar and the lever cannot be reversed, and so the signal cannot be cleared.

More than two switch-and-lock movements should not be put on one lever, as the power required to work them would be more than it is safe to put upon a pipe line. While it may work well for a time, the wear upon the parts would be so great that very soon there would not be throw enough at the movement to cause the plunger to enter the hole in the lock bar and lock the switch. Again, the power required to work three movements is often more than one man is able to exert, and by getting another man to help pull over the lever there is great danger of doubling up the pipe should anything prevent one of the movements from closing, the lever being reversed while the switches would be open. More especially is this likely to happen in winter, when the cranks, the movements and the switch points are apt to be clogged with snow and ice.

A very important part of the apparatus that is designed to work in connection with a switch-and-lock movement or a facing-point lock, and which, as yet, has not been spoken of, is a detector bar or slide, which prevents any movement of a switch or lock being made so long as any wheel of a train may be on the bar. The necessity of providing some such arrangement as this is apparent, as without it, it would be possible for a signalman to throw a switch under a moving train—not that he may do so intentionally, but to prevent his pulling the lever by mistake, thinking, perhaps, that the train had cleared the switch.

The construction of a detector bar is shown in Fig. 11, and the arrangement by which connection is made to the crank that moves the switch can be seen in Fig. 9. *A* is the bar which is held against the side of the rail by the link K, the link being pivoted on a casting C or fulcrum point called a clip, which is fastened to the rail as shown. Lugs B are provided on the clip, which limit the movement of the bar and prevent it from ever being allowed to get too much out of adjustment.

When an attempt is made to throw the switch, the first movement of the crank moves the connecting or driving rod of the detector bar and causes the bar to move through the arc of a circle, with the pin of the clip as a center and the link as a radius. This brings the bar to the top of the rail, raising it to about one inch above when the bar is in the center, or has been moved through one-half of its stroke. If a wheel was on the rail at the

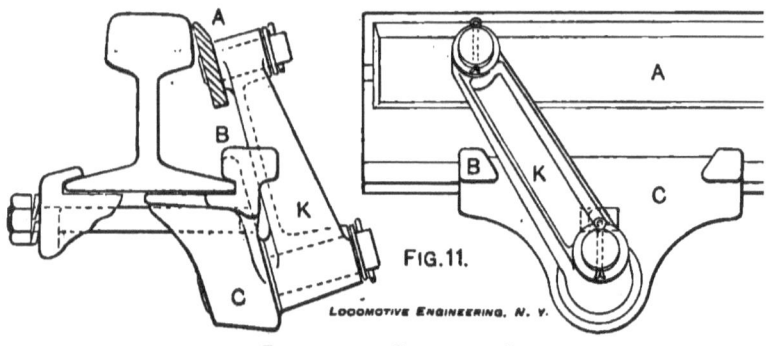

FIG. 11.

LOCOMOTIVE ENGINEERING. N. Y.

DETAILS OF DETECTOR BAR.

time the attempt was made to change the switch, the bar would be raised, striking against the outer edge of the tread of the wheel, which projects about an inch over the side of the rail, and no movement of the switch and lock movement could be made, and therefore the switch could not be changed. As the bars are made 45 feet long, and are placed alongside or ahead of the switch, so that the wheels should first pass over the bar before getting to the switch, it is impossible to change the switch under any part of the train, as this length is greater than the distance between any two pairs of wheels of any car or engine, or of any two cars that may be coupled together.

The general arrangement of a switch-and-lock movement and the connection to the detector bar are shown in Fig. 12, the photograph helping to make the drawing more easily understood. When a facing-point lock is used, in place of a switch-and-lock

GENERAL ARRANGEMENT OF SWITCH-AND-LOCK MOVEMENT AND CONNECTIONS TO DETECTOR BAR.

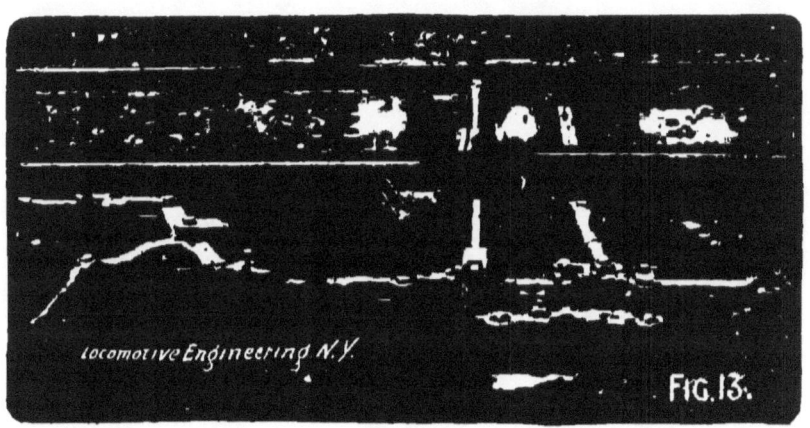

SIDE VIEW OF SWITCH-AND-LOCK MOVEMENT AND CONNECTIONS TO SWITCH.

movement, the detector bar is connected to the lever that works the lock, to make it impossible to unlock the switch while a train is passing over it. If there is no room in which the bar may be placed ahead of the switch, it is usual to use two bars, one on each outer rail, thereby insuring that it will be impossible to change the switch under a train when either track is in use. As the detector bar makes it impossible to change the switch so long as a pair of wheels are on the rails over the bar, it is necessary for an engineer to run by the switch sufficiently to clear the bar, if he wishes the switch to be changed before going in the opposite direction. To have to do this seems to trainmen a useless precaution, and they often blame the signalman for making them run further than is apparently necessary, whereas the man is powerless to make any change until the bar is cleared. Trainmen should never stop their trains with any of the wheels over the bar, for if they do so, they have not cleared the interlocking, and until they do so clear it the switches cannot be changed or a route set for any other train.

CHAPTER XII

DETAILS OF CONSTRUCTION.

There are many points regarding the form and particular arrangement of the several parts used in working the switches and signals at an interlocking plant, all of which are of great interest to signal engineers, or to those whose duties require them to keep such parts in repair, but to the average railroad man, who perhaps will never have occasion to use any knowledge that he may have gained relative to the "details of construction," a discussion of these questions cannot be expected to be so interesting or as useful.

With those, however, who are daily required to read and act upon the indications of the signals, a knowledge of the construction will help them to put greater faith in the indications and to better understand the precautions taken to insure that a signal will not give a wrong indication.

The construction of the different machines and the method of moving and locking a switch having been explained, the parts next to be considered are those used in making the connections, or the means whereby the motion of the levers is transmitted to the switches and signals. Those for the switches and locks are made of 1-inch iron pipe, while for connections to signals they are generally made of No. 9 galvanized steel wire. Pipe is used, as giving for its weight and section the greatest stiffness, this quality being of the first importance from the fact that but a single connection is used between the lever and a switch, the power being applied as a pull for motion in one direction and a push in the other. If the pipe was used in tension only, but few supports would be needed, but to transmit any force by compression, it must be kept in a straight line, and to do this it must be firmly supported at short and regular intervals. These supports are called "pipe carriers," and are made of several different patterns, those of the anti-friction type being the best and the ones now used in all new work. They are made as may be seen in Fig. 1, so as to allow the wheel which carries the pipe to roll on a center pin in a slot cast in the frame, all friction being done away with when the pipe is moved, except that due to rolling, which is very small. There being no rubbing friction, no oil is required with this style of carrier, and it is possible to box them in, no covers being needed.

The tendency of the pipe being to bend in any direction

ANTI-FRICTION PIPE CARRIER.

when power is applied, a small roller is fixed in the top part of the frame of the carrier, to hold the pipe in the groove in the lower wheel. As the lower wheel has to carry the weight of the pipe, the bearing seldom comes against the upper wheel, so that the latter is usually made in the form of a sleeve slipped over a bolt, which answers for a shaft upon which it may turn. With the Evans carrier (seen in Fig. 2), the bearings of this upper wheel are also made anti-frictional, a rod being slipped through the top part of the frame to tie the several parts together, which, in this pattern, have to be made in separate pieces, to allow the wheels to be put in their proper places. The carrier, for this reason, is somewhat more troublesome to put in, two lag screws being needed for each section of the frame, and it is also more troublesome to work with, owing to the difficulty of removing any of the wheels, as is so often desirable in repairing or putting in any new parts, while the advantages gained by using the anti-friction roller on top seem to be very slight.

Pipe carriers are usually spaced 8 feet apart and are fastened to foundations which are buried in the ground. On some roads this distance is reduced to 7 feet, but for ordinary straight work there does not seem to be any need of going to the extra expense involved in putting them closer together. For 500 feet of pipe

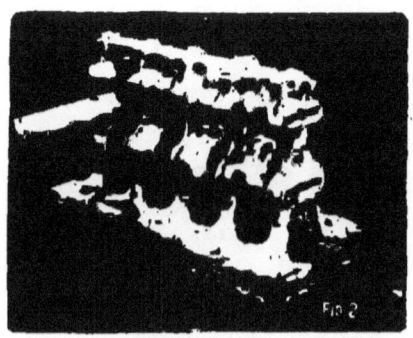

THE EVANS DOUBLE ANTI-FRICTION PIPE CARRIER.

line, the spring of the pipe under a load of two switch-and-lock movements will be nearly one inch, or for 9 inches travel at the lever there will be but 8 inches at the movement. This spring has to be provided for in putting in the work, by making one of the crank arms at the movement longer than the other, so that the 8¾ inches of travel required for the full stroke of the movement will be obtained. In running the pipe lines, they should always be made as straight as possible, and never curved if it can be avoided. Where this has been done, owing to curves in the track, the carriers should be put closer together, to prevent the pipe from springing or bending when the load is put upon it.

In curving out to run around a side track, when the angle is not sharp enough to require the ordinary form of crank, radial or ordinary cranks should be used, as shown in Fig. 3, the pipe all being run in straight lines. In joining the several lengths of pipe

202

to make a long line, they are screwed together with an ordinary screw coupling such as is furnished with the pipe, an iron plug about 4 inches long, having holes for rivets drilled in each end, being put inside and riveted to each pipe, as shown in Fig. 4. Riveting the pipe in this way takes a great deal of the strain from the threads, and will even hold the pipe together should the threads work loose. Jaws for making the connections to cranks or switch-and-lock movements are fastened to the pipe by an ordinary coupling, the threaded end being turned down to go inside the pipe and be riveted to it in the same manner as a plug.

As this method is patented and controlled by one of the signal companies, other ways of accomplishing the same end are to be found in use, but none that are on the market at the present time can be said to be satisfactory, except to weld the pipe to the solid end of the jaw.

The connection between the lever and the switch being practically a solid connection, expansion and contraction have to be provided for to keep it of the same length, or else the movement might not be completed when the lever was reversed. The simplest way of doing this is to put a rocker in the middle of the pipe line, so that the motion or direction of travel in one half will be in the opposite direction from what it is in the other. When one half of the pipe line expanded with an increase of temperature, the other would have expanded the same, the rocker being turned on its center to a new position, while the total length of the connection from the lever to the movement would not be changed.

Putting a rocker in the pipe line to reverse the motion is a very awkward and expensive arrangement, on account of the space required and the difficulty of running the pipe where there are more than two lines to be compensated.

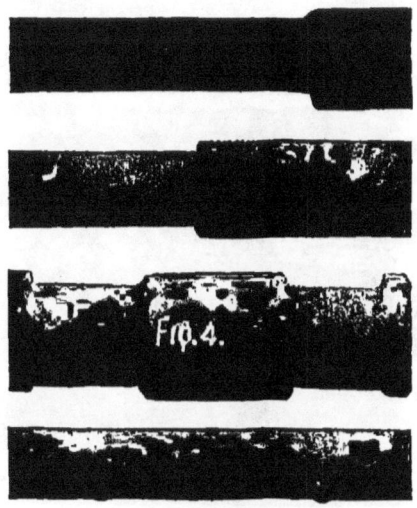

A PLUGGED PIPE JOINT.

A device that accomplishes all that is required in this direction—and in a very neat way, too—is shown in Fig. 5, it being what is known as a "lazy jack" or compensator. As will be seen, it is made by arranging two cranks with a short connecting rod between them, on a base casting, one of the cranks being of a very obtuse angle and practically a rocker, and the other of a very acute angle, to change the direction of the thrust of the pipe line and make it as near a right angle as possible. In this way the pipe is continued in a straight line, while its motion is reversed and expansion and contraction provided for. But owing to the angles at which the two cranks are set with each other, the throw or travel of the pipe line is limited, the cranks, if turned too far, getting too near the dead center when it would not be possible to move them either way. For this reason one compensator is usually provided for every 500 feet of pipe, although distances of 700 feet are not uncommon. For distances less than 100 feet no compensator is needed.

Where the pipe line is under 500 feet in length, the com-

A "LAZY JACK" COMPENSATOR.

pensator is put in the middle of this distance, or 250 feet from either end, and so, when two or more are used, they are each put in the middle of the length of pipe which they are to compensate. This appears simple enough, but workmen, unless watched, will divide the distance, spacing the compensators evenly between the levers and the movements, thus leaving a certain part of the line unprovided for. For example, if the distance to be compensated is 900 feet, the compensators should be put one-quarter of this distance, or 225 feet from each end, instead of 300 feet, as would seem at first sight to be the proper distance.

If it should be necessary to place two cranks quite close together in any pipe line, they may be connected up so as to
reverse the motion, and thus take the place of a compensator. To
arrange them in this way will be found very convenient in running
pipe lines around side tracks that have been put in after a plant
is in operation, and when it is desired, on account of the connections to the switches, to keep them in the same relative position with reference to the track. This arrangement is clearly
shown in Fig. 6, where the cranks are arranged to compensate

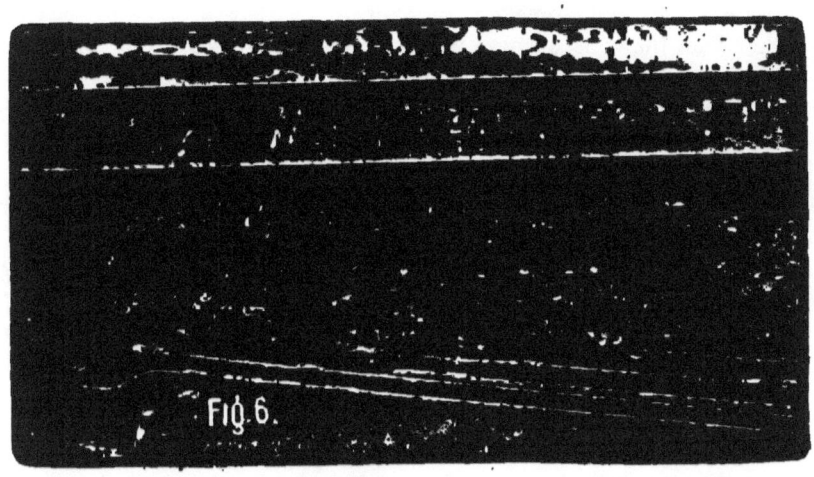

Fig. 6.

and the lines outside of the side track are brought under and extend on parallel with the main line in the same numerical order.

The foundations for the cranks, compensators and other parts
of the apparatus subjected to very heavy strain are made of heavy
oak lumber, dovetailed and braced, the whole being buried in the
ground to the proper depth, tamped and finally concreted, this
being made of one part cement to two of sand and three parts of
crushed stone, such as will go through a 2-inch mesh. The con-
crete should be put in at least 12 inches deep, and for 12 inches
around each side of the foundation. The cement used should
be of the best quality, on account of the strains that are put upon
the foundation, and while it is not necessary to go to the expense

of getting the imported article, none but the best of domestic manufacture should be used.

At the present day the standard practice of connecting the home signal with the lever in the tower is to use two lines of wire, bolt locks, to prevent the signals being cleared unless the switch is closed, being connected to the down-pull wire, or the one that pulls the signal to clear. On several roads, however, a decided step in advance has been taken by making this connection of pipe instead of wire, thereby doing away with the necessity of constant adjustment, and the possibility of giving a wrong signal from this cause or from the breakage of a wire.

That the consequences would be serious were a wrong indication to be given by the home signal, no one will doubt, and while the cost of making the connection of pipe is considerably more than where two lines of wire are used, the additional safety secured in the operation of the plant most certainly warrants its use.

When the home signals are wire-connected, a bolt lock should be put in the connection to the distant signal as well as to the home signal. This is to make it impossible to clear the distant signal, as well as the home signal, unless the switch or derail has been properly closed, for if a bolt lock is not used, there is nothing to prevent the signals being cleared if the wire to the home signal should break between the bolt lock and the lever, the operator being then able to reverse the home-signal lever and pull over the lever of the distant signal. Should the wires to the home signal be caught, or should the derail not be closed and the bolt lock hold the wire, it is possible, from the spring in the wire, for an operator to reverse the home-signal lever and then give a clear distant signal when the home signal had not been cleared.

Connecting the home signal with pipe admits of the use of a strong and well-designed selector, and one that will act as a bolt lock as well as a selector. This selector is shown in Fig. 7, and, as will be seen, consists of two slide bars working in grooves in a cast base piece, and which are connected to the two signals to be operated, a third slide being provided which is connected to the signal lever, and so arranged by means of a crossbar that it may be made to slide in either of the grooves occupied by the other two bars, and, by shoving them out, clear the signals to which they are connected. The crossbar usually is connected to the lock bar of the switch, the operating slide being brought behind the slide which will clear the proper signal, to govern the switch the way it is set. Where not convenient to connect the selector directly to the lock bar of the switch, the crossbar may be worked by a motion plate operated by the pipe line working the switch, or else a direct connection, consisting of a crank and short connection, may be used. When the crossbar is attached directly to the lock rod, the selector is made to act as a bolt lock, for, as the operating slide works in a notch cut in the crossbar when

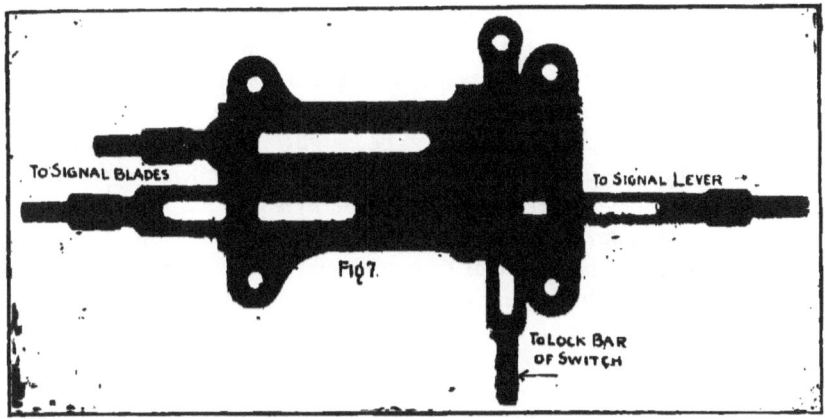

SELECTOR FOR PIPE CONNECTIONS.

the slide has been pushed ahead to clear the signal, the crossbar will be locked, and with it the switch.

Where the connections are of wire there are several different forms of selectors that may be used, the design of each being made upon the same general plan. The connections being of wire, the signals must all be cleared by a pull instead of a push, each signal being connected to a long hook which can be caught by a sliding plate connected to the lever in the tower, and drawn back when the lever is reversed, instead of being pushed forward, as is the case with the pipe-connected selector.

Differences in design are found in the several devices, whereby the movement of the pipe lines to operate the switch is automatically made to select the hook connected to the proper signal. Of these the one in most common use is where selection is made by means of a driving bar carrying dogs, which are set to throw every hook out of engagment with the sliding plate except the one to be operated, the driving bar being driven by means of a motion plate worked by the pipe line connected to the switch. Another way, and one that is more certain in its action, is to make the switch connection turn a shaft by means of an escapement crank, cam lugs on the shaft being provided to raise all but the proper hook to be operated.

With all of these forms of selectors, dependence is placed for their proper operation upon the assumption that the proper hook will drop and be caught by the sliding plate when the dogs or cams are set by the movement of the switch connection, and that the adjustment of the wire will be such as to bring the point of the hook in the proper position to be caught. As the adjustment of the hooks is often bad, owing to changes in the length of the wire—and they can easily be prevented, by snow, ice, dirt, or by a poor adjustment of the dogs on the driving bar, from being caught—it will be seen that the arrangement is not a very good one. To be relied upon, it should be positive in its action, and this can only be obtained by using pipe connections instead of wire.

A device that is sometimes used in place of a derailing switch at short sidings, or where it is desirable to allow cars to stand as near the main line as safety will permit, is shown in Fig. 8, and is known as a "scotch block." It is connected to a lever in the machine, so that it can be raised on top of the rail in the position shown when it is desired to block the line, or else lowered out of the way when the track is to be used. As may be supposed, it answers the purpose very well, derailing any car or engine that attempts to pass it, but as in so doing it is apt to cause some damage to the trucks or brake gear, the device should not be used, unless there are very good reasons for not putting in the ordinary form of derail.

In the design of the tower, simplicity and cheapness, as well as adaptability for the purpose for which it is constructed, are the principal points to which attention may be called.

As will be seen by Fig. 9, the tower is made two stories in

A "SCOTCH" BLOCK.

C. M. & ST. P. TOWER.

height, to allow the operator to have an unobstructed view, as far as possible, of the tracks protected by the interlocking, the stairs to give access to the operating room being put on the outside of the building.   A substantial frame work is put in, on which to place the machine, and heavy oak "lead-out" timbers are placed on top of the foundation on which to bolt the rocker shafts, or the

Fig.10.

ROCKER SHAFT LEAD-OUT.

cranks used to run the different connections out from the tower. The arrangement for this purpose which is the easiest to put in but the most expensive to use, is a rocker shaft lead-out as shown in Fig. 10.   These should be made with the arms welded on instead of being fitted on a hexagonal shaft and fastened by a set screw, as is the case with the one shown, for the reason that the cranks are not accurately fitted as they should be and cannot be held tight by the set screw.   As a little lost motion at the center is very much increased at the end of the crank, the travel of the pipe line being reduced by just that amount, it will be seen that this arrangement is not as good as when the arms are welded on, for, owing to the levers being interlocked, all lost motion in the connection is to be avoided.

By a judicious use of ordinary and box cranks, many lead-

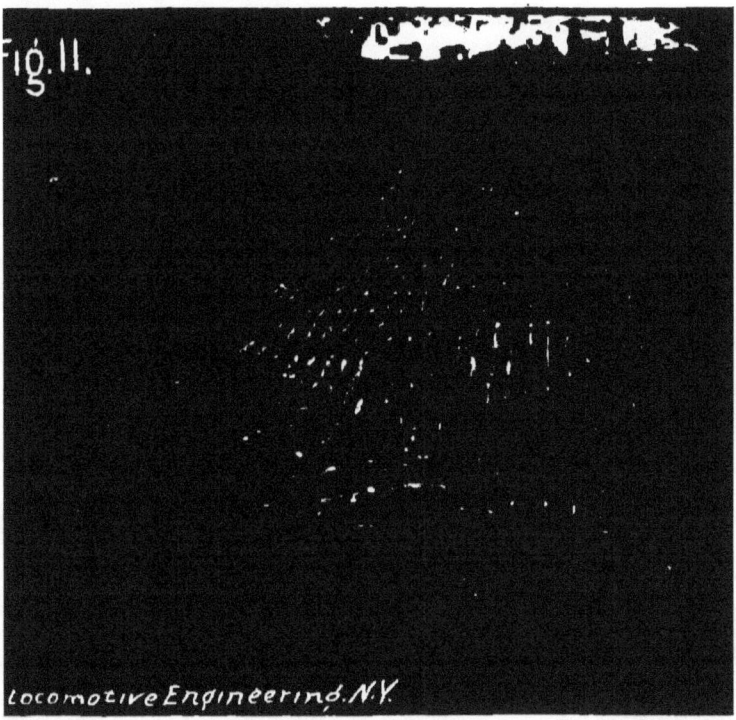

A BOX CRANK LEAD-OUT.

outs put in with rocker shafts could have been put in much more cheaply and yet with practically the same results. A box crank is shown in Fig. 11, and consists of an arrangement whereby any number of cranks are made to work on a single base, and make it possible to turn at a right angle, and in a very small space, a large number of pipe lines.

Towers should always be made somewhat larger than is neces-

sary to hold the machine to be used, to allow for possible additions
to the plant, the expense of so doing being very little in comparison with what it will cost to enlarge one already built.

One very prominent road builds its smallest towers large
enough to take a 24-lever machine, thereby providing for the

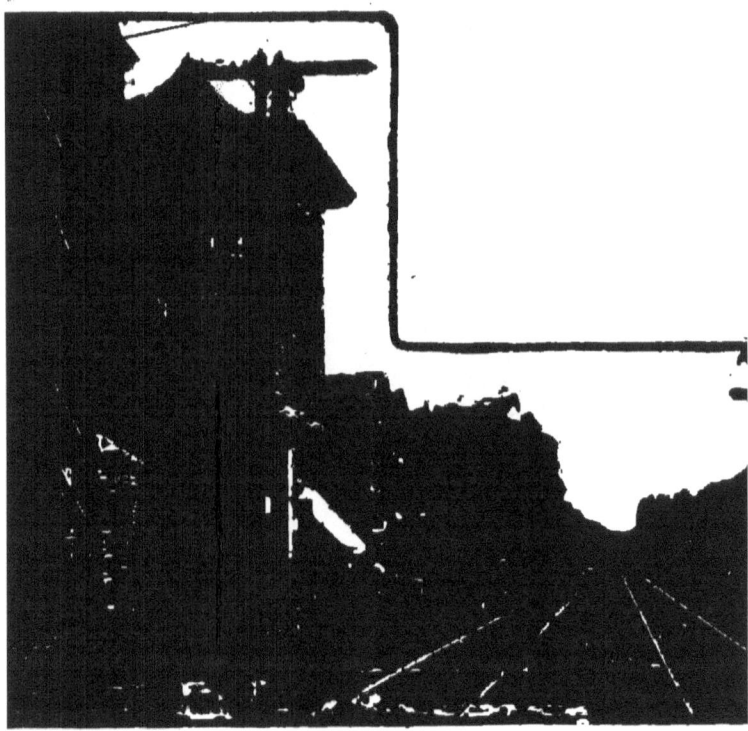

A SPECIAL TOWER FOR USE IN CITIES.

future and also give ample room in which to get at all the parts.
For towers that have to be located in places where there is but
little room—between tracks, for instance—or where, as with the
new electric street railway interlocking in cities, the tower has to
be put upon the sidewalk, some form of iron framework has to be
used, as shown in Fig. 12, the pipe connections being boxed in

(Fig. 13) to prevent anyone except the proper persons from getting at or tampering with them.

The location of the tower is an important point and should be carefully considered before a decision regarding it is made. In a general way it may be said that it should be placed at some

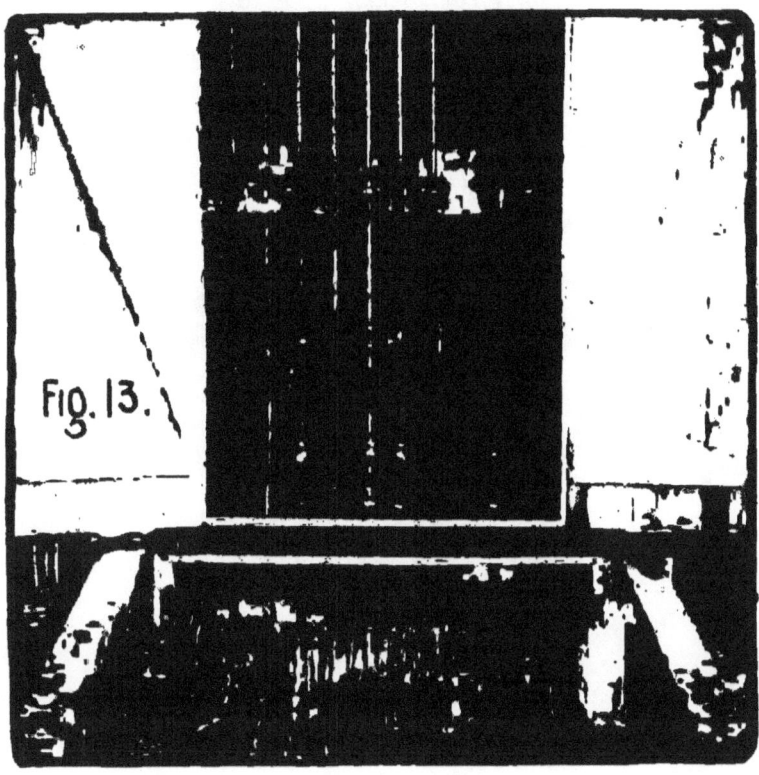

LEAD–OUT CONNECTIONS FOR SPECIAL TOWER.

central point, where the best view of the tracks is to be had, this point being almost always on the outside of the curve. If there is but little choice in this respect, the tower should be located where the straightest, and therefore the simplest, connections can be made to the switches and signals.

Among recent additions and improvements to the tower may

be mentioned a ladder, to allow of easy access to the roof in case of fire, as is shown in Fig. 9, and the casing surrounding the stove,

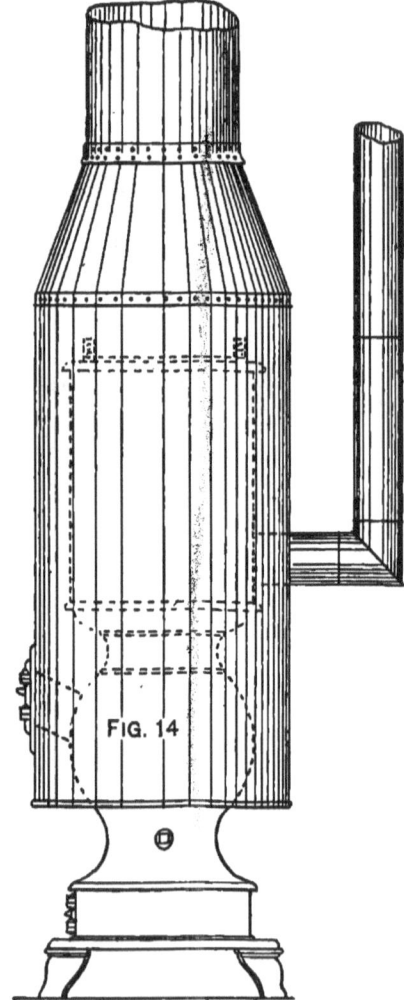

FIG. 14

SIGNAL TOWER STOVE AND CASING.

shown in Fig. 14, which has proved itself to be just what was wanted, as nearly all the heat is carried to the operating room, which is kept warm, while no coal is wasted heating the lower one.

It is customary in climates where there is much snow or ice in winter to box the pipe lines, as well as the switch-and-lock movements, to prevent their being clogged by ice forming on the pipe and carriers. The boxing should be made of 2-inch material, the side pieces being 16 feet long, to bring the joints over the pipe-carrier foundations. Where the wire lines to the distant signals are run in cities, or in yards where people are likely to be tripped up by them, they also should be boxed. This boxing should also be made of 2-inch material, pieces 6 inches wide being used for the sides and 8 inches for the top. This is not the usual practice, 1-inch stuff being most generally used; but as the 2-inch will outlast the other almost double and will need but little attention or repairs, there can be no question but that it is true economy to use it.

In the operation of an interlocking plant, a safety device known as "electric locking" of the levers is now being introduced more than ever before, as the advantages to be had by its use are becoming more generally known. With it the levers of the machine are electrically locked, so that the operator, after once clearing the signal for a train to proceed, is unable to move the levers controlling the derails and switches until the train has cleared the limits of the interlocking. The lock itself is a very simple contrivance, consisting of an electro magnet, supported on a suitable frame and bolted to the locking brackets of the interlocking machine, as shown in Fig. 15, so that the armature when down will engage with a lug on the locking bar and prevent it from moving, and when raised by the attraction of the magnet will leave the bar free. A heavy casing is provided to inclose the magnet, so that when locked by the padlock provided for the purpose, the operator will be prevented from getting at the armature and releasing the lever before the train has cleared the interlocking.

To drop the locks and lock up the machine, a circuit breaker is attached to all the signal levers, so that whenever a signal is cleared, the circuit through the lock is broken, de-energizing the magnets and dropping the armatures. To prevent the circuit from being restored when the signal is returned to the normal position, which should be done by the time that the last car of a train has passed it, a track circuit is made use of to energize a relay, the armature of which, when down, breaks the circuit through the locks in the same manner as the circuit breaker on the signal lever.

The circuits made use of, and the manner of connecting them up, are shown in Fig. 16,, T being the track circuit through the rails and energizing the magnet E; F, the locking circuit through

ELECTRIC LOCKS FOR INTERLOCKING MACHINES.

the locks L, the circuit breakers B, the contact points D of the track relay E, the magnet M and the contact points P of that magnet; R, the releasing circuits energizing the magnets N, the armatures of which make a back contact when the magnets are de-energized, and complete the circuit F through the magnet M (but not through the locks), if the track-circuit relay is energized and the circuit breakers closed. The operation of these locks,

217

and the effect on the circuits when a train passes through the interlocking, is as follows: The locks being normally held up, the switches are set and signals cleared for the train to proceed. Clearing any of the signals breaks the circuit F at the point B, dropping the locks and locking the derail lever reversed, so that it cannot be changed, at the same time dropping the armature of the magnet M, breaking the circuit at the point P, and preventing the locks from being raised when the signal is returned to the normal position. When the train passes on to the track circuit, it de-energizes the magnet, breaking the circuit F at the point

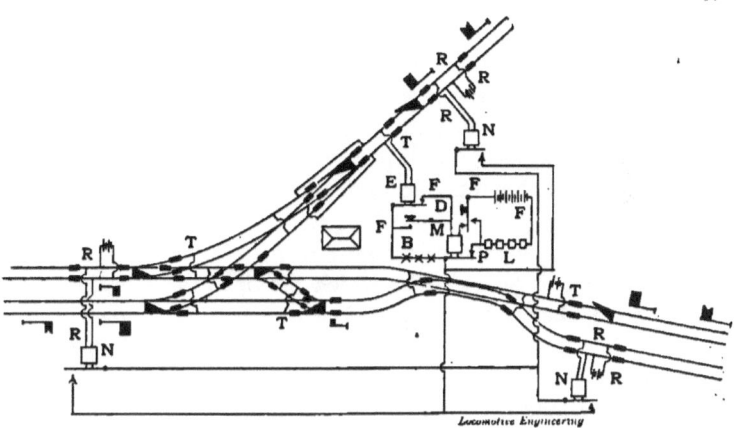

FIG. 16. ELECTRIC LOCKING CIRCUITS.

D, so that the circuit cannot be restored and the locks lifted, if all the wheels of the train have not passed out of the interlocking. When the train reaches the releasing section, the magnet N is de-energized, the armature falling and completing the circuit F through the magnet M as soon as the circuit is restored at the point D and circuit breakers X. Energizing the magnet M raises the armature and completes the circuit through the point P, so that when the train passes off the releasing section, although the circuit F is broken at the contact point of the magnet N, it is maintained through the contact point P. The locks, however, are not raised until the circuit is broken at the magnet N, for although the circuit was completed through the locks and the point P

when the magnet M was energized, it was also complete through the contact points of the magnet N, and as there is less resistance through these than through the locks, most of the current would flow that way, and the locks would not be raised until the contact at that point was broken.

If the signals have not been restored to danger before the train pases off the releasing section, the circuit F will not be completed through the magnet M and the machine will remain locked up.

An arrangement of circuits applicable to a simple crossing, in which the locking circuit is done away with, is shown in Fig. 17. With this arrangement the track circuit inside the derails is made the releasing section and no locking circuit is used, the action being the same as in the previous arrangement, with the magnet E left out. The cost of putting on this arrangement, complete, is not more than $150, and if proper care be used in the installation, it will cost but little to maintain and will seldom get out of order.

In case of accidents, or a failure of the circuits to release the locks, a switch is provided by which the operator can close and release the locks, by breaking a glass inserted in the cover of the box in which the switch is placed. Inclosing the switch in this way is done to put a check upon the operator, to prevent him from throwing the locking out of service without good and sufficient reasons.

The circuits here shown are the simplest and best for this purpose that have ever been designed, and have given most excellent results since they were put in service. They are much superior to the mechanical or interlocked relays that are used by the signal companies, as the action is positive, there being no trouble with sticking of the armatures, as with the latter, nor is it possible for the operator at any time to release the locks by jarring the relays.

The advantages to be derived from locking the levers in this way are: That the operator must return the signal to danger after the passage of every train, before it leaves the limit of the interlocking, thus compelling him to keep the signals at danger and not clear any one of them until on the approach of a train; that as long as any part of a train is within the interlocking, no change can be made in any of the switches that would lead to a collision or derailment—an advantage that is very great, considering the number of times that switches are run through by operators throwing the switch in front of a train, thinking

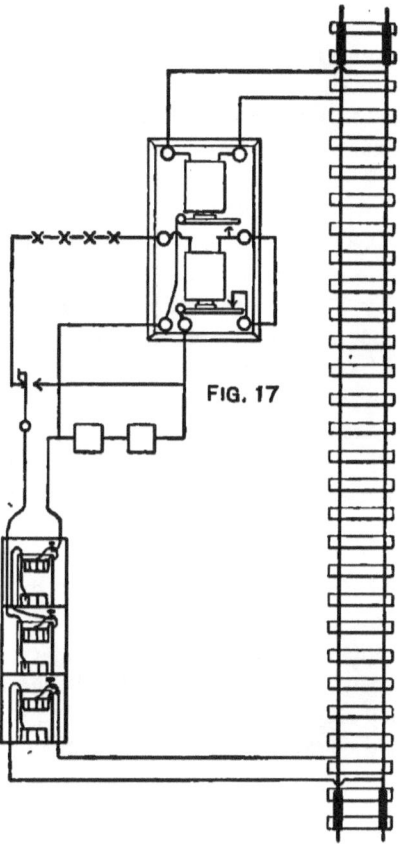

FIG. 17

ELECTRIC LOCKING CIRCUITS APPLICABLE TO A SIMPLE CROSSING.

that it has passed out of the interlocking; that having once cleared the signal for a train, it is impossible for the operator to open the derail or change switches so as to cause a derailment, although he is perfectly free to return the signal to danger at any time.

That this latter is a very desirable feature, is shown by the large number of accidents that have happened by operators taking away the signals from one train and giving them to another, the train from which the signals were taken being derailed, owing to their having approached the crossing expecting to be allowed to proceed. One instance can be named where the operator cleared the signal for an approaching freight and then went to sleep. Hearing the whistle of a train on the other road, and forgetting that he had just cleared the signals for a freight, he changed the levers, opening the derails just in front of the engine. The engineer of the freight having observed the signal at clear, was approaching the crossing at a fair rate of speed, which, as the train was a heavy one, was sufficient to shove the engine and four cars completely over the crossing, entirely blocking it. Had the train for which the signals had been changed not been a passenger, and a light one at that, a collision would have happened, it having come to a stop within a car length only of the other train.

Then, again, with the electrical locking, there can be no question as to which train the signal had been given, and the claim so often made by engineers when they get into trouble, that the signals were taken away from them, will not hold with a plant so equipped. To those who fail to see the advantage of this and the great help that it gives in enforcing discipline, I would refer them to the superintendents who are able to send their engineers to plants so equipped, with the request that they come back and tell them if they were able to change the signals and switches, as they claim was done to them, and that if they could do so they would be given full pay for the time they were off.

CHAPTER XIII

THE WESTINGHOUSE ELECTRO-PNEUMATIC AND THE GIBBS ELECTRIC STREET RAILWAY SYSTEMS.

Many attempts have been and are now being made to operate the switches and signals of an interlocking plant by some power other than that of a human being, invention having passed successively from the first pneumatic machine put in service in 1876, to a hydraulic machine used in 1880, to a combination of these or a hydro-pneumatic machine in 1884 and to the electro-pneumatic in 1891. Of these, the electro-pneumatic is the only one that can be considered a success, the few plants in this country that are now operated by means of air, water or electricity having as yet not been in service long enough to demonstrate that they are anything more than an experiment.

As the several inventions along the lines named have been made principally by Mr. Geo. Westinghouse, Jr., the system that is in use to-day is one that bears his name. With the electro-pneumatic system the power to move a switch or clear a signal is obtained by the use of compressed air, the action of this power being controlled by a valve worked by an electro-magnet, the electric current to energize the magnet being in turn controlled by an interlocking machine having switches by which the circuits through the several electro-magnets can be completed.

As the connections to the switch and the signal instruments are of pipe for carrying the compressed air, and insulated wire for conducting the electric current, there is no complication of parts, as with a mechanical plant, the only apparatus used outside of the tower being such as is required at the switch or signal. For the same reason there is no limit to the distance that the different movements can be placed from the tower, other than what it would be safe for a man in the tower to operate. A description of the valve and cylinder for operating a semaphore signal has already been given in the article on "Automatic Electric Block Signals," that appeared in the May issue of "Locomotive Engineering," the same arrangement being used for an interlocking plant.

To briefly describe the action of the valve: When the lever of the interlocking machine which works the electric switch is turned, the circuit through the magnet of the signal instrument is closed, energizing the magnet, causing it to attract the armature and open the valve admitting air to the cylinder, at the same time closing the exhaust passage by which the compressed air is permitted to escape. As soon as the compressed air is admitted to the cylinder, the piston is forced through the length of its stroke, the movement being transmitted by means of a balance lever and connecting rod to the signal, which is moved to the position indicating safety. When the operating lever is returned to its normal position, and the circuit broken, the magnet loses its power, allowing the valve to be pressed up by the force of a spring, the passage by which air is admitted to the cylinder being closed and the one releasing the air being opened, the piston in consequence being pressed up and the signal returned to danger by the force of gravity.

The arrangement used for operating a switch is shown in Fig. 1, and consists of the switch-and-lock movement used with a mechanical plant and a cylinder, the piston of which is made to work the movement the same as if it were connected to the lever of an interlocking machine. The connections to the switch points, the lock bar and the detector bar being made in the same way as with a mechanically operated plant, the same certainty of action and protection is afforded as if it were operated by mechanical connections instead of by compressed air.

The construction of the valve and cylinder by which the necessary movement of the piston is obtained, is shown in Fig. 2. The valve used is of the ordinary slide-valve pattern, passages to the cylinder and to the exhaust being arranged in the same way as on a locomotive. To work the valve, two small pistons are fastened to each end of a yoke, which is made to fit over the valve, the small cylinders in which these pistons work being known as valve cylinders. Admission of air to the valve cylinder to move the piston, and with it the valve, is controlled by a magnet of the same construction as the signal magnet, air being admitted behind the piston when the magnet is energized by the electric current sent out from the interlocking machine.

As a check upon the performance of the admission valve, a lock pin is provided which fits in a socket in the back of the valve and locks it in either of the two positions it should occupy. This locking pin is riveted to a piston which is held down by means of a coiled spring placed on the opposite side

ELECTRO-PNEUMATIC SWITCH AND LOCK MOVEMENT.

from the valve. To lift the lock pin and release the valve so that it can be moved, a magnet is provided, the armature of which, when attracted, is made to open an exhaust passage to the atmosphere and allow the air on top of the lock piston to escape. The pressure of the air on the other side of the piston overcomes the pressure of the spring, raising the piston and with it the lock pin, thus leaving the valve free to be moved. When the current through the lock magnet ceases, the armature is released, closing the exhaust passage and allowing air to accumulate on that side of the piston, once more restoring the equilibrium, when the pressure of the spring will force the piston back to its normal position and lock the valve.

The operation of the valve admitting air to the cylinder, by which motion is imparted to the piston in the cylinder and the switch-and-lock movement worked, is as follows, the lever of the interlocking machine being in the normal position with the circuit closed through one of the valve magnets: With the first

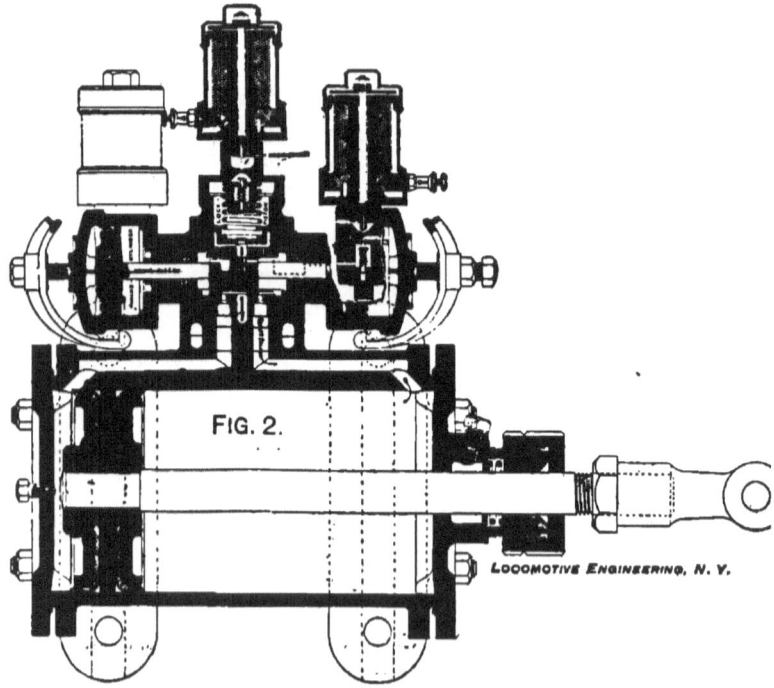

FIG. 2.

Locomotive Engineering, N. Y.

DETAIL OF VALVE AND CYLINDER.

movement of the lever, an electric circuit is formed through the lock magnet, which, when energized, opens the lock exhaust and permits the pressure of the air to raise the piston, and with it the lock pin from its seat. A further movement of the lever breaks the circuit through one of the valve magnets, permitting the air to escape from the cylinder controlled by that valve, and energizes the other valve magnet, admitting air to the valve cylinder. This forces the valve piston, and with it the valve, to the other position in which air is admitted to one end of the cylinder and opened to the exhaust at the other, the compressed air forcing the piston through the cylinder and performing the movements desired.

When the movement of the lever is completed, the circuit through the lock magnet is broken and the magnet de-energized; the armature, being released, closes the exhaust passage, allowing the coiled spring to force the piston back, seating the pin upon the other side of the valve and locking it, until the whole process is repeated in the other direction. In this way the valve is locked open, to one end of the cylinder or the other, at all times, the pressure being kept upon the piston to prevent any accidental movement of the switch.

The construction of the interlocking machine is very different from that of the machines used in operating a mechanical plant, as the levers, instead of transmitting the mechanical force necessary to work the different parts, have only to change the several electric switches controlling the movement that it is desired to make. The general appearance of the machine is shown in Fig. 3, the upper row of levers, called the switch levers, being used to make and break the circuits that connect the main battery with the switch valves, the lower levers being called signal levers, as they are used to make and break the circuits to the signal valves. Each of these levers is attached to a shaft carrying a rubber roller, on which are fastened small brass strips with which the connections are made between the two springs bearing against the roller, when the roller is turned to the proper position, the circuit between the two springs— which are the two poles of the circuit—being thus completed. By arranging these strips so that the several circuits are completed in the proper order, the movement desired is made by merely turning the lever. So also, if all the levers are not in the proper position to safely perform the movement, contacts would not be made on the roller of the lever improperly set and no current would be sent out from the machine, the levers being thus electrically interlocked.

To prevent the levers controlling conflicting routes from being reversed (if such it may be called) at the same time, locking bars driven by mitre gears on the shaft are arranged, by which it is made impossible to turn the levers that clear any two routes that may lead to a collision. The locking is of the improved Saxby & Farmer type, arranged in a manner similar to that shown with the mechanical machine.

As a still further check, there is placed at each signal and switch movement a circuit breaker, from which wires are run to magnets placed on the machine, the armatures of which are

ELECTRO-PNEUMATIC INTERLOCKING MACHINE.

made to operate latches controlling the levers, so as to delay the completion of the movement until after the signal or switch has completed its movement, the object of this being to prevent any other lever from being moved until the switch or signal that is being operated has completed its movement; for until the lever has been moved to its extreme position, the locking will not permit any other lever to be moved. The electric switch by which the indication is sent to the machine, that the movement of the switch has been completed, is to be seen placed on top of the switch-and-lock movement, a photograph showing its construction being shown in Fig. 4.

It is thus seen that a double check is had upon all the movements of the levers, and that the possibility of a mistake being made by an ignorant or careless operator is well guarded against. And, to quote from a recent technical paper, "the sequence of movements, by virtue of which a clear signal cannot be given

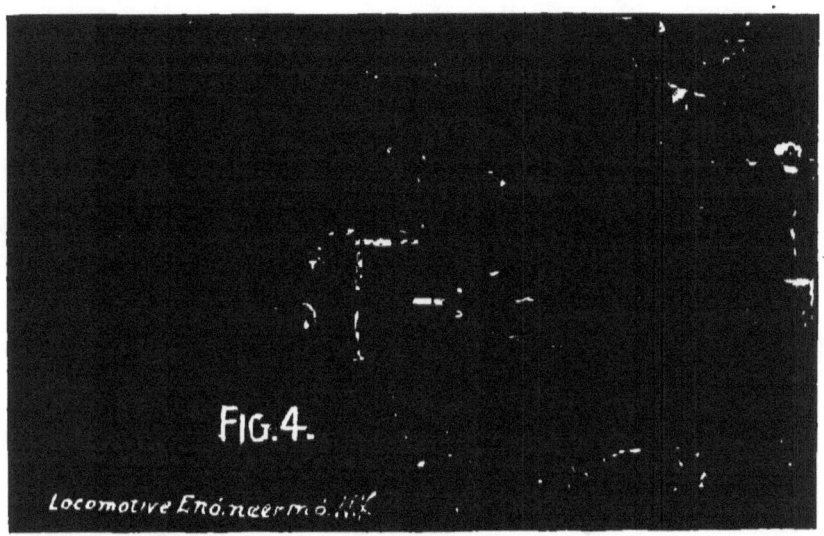

FIG.4.

Locomotive Engineering.

INDICATION SWITCH BOX.

until the route has been prepared for it by setting the switches in their proper position, is absolutely secured by the order in which the several electrical circuits are closed."

With this system, owing to the amount of work the magnet has to perform, the current has to be of a comparatively high voltage, and as the current is used at all times, whether a movement is being made or not, it has been found necessary, or rather more economical, to generate the electricity by means of a dynamo, more especially as a power plant has to be provided to furnish the compressed air. It is also customary to use storage batteries, keeping them charged, so that in case of a shut-down of the dynamo, the batteries will furnish the current to operate the plant. At small plants where the current is generated simply for the interlocking, it is usual to run the dynamo only during the day—the storage batteries that were charged when the dynamo was running, furnishing the necessary current at night.

In the operation of an electro-pneumatic plant, the facility with which the different movements are made reduces, to a great extent, the number of men required to do the work. While in most cases one man is· required to move the levers, another as a train director, and other men have to be employed to run the engine, the number required at a mechanical plant having one hundred or more levers, is so large that the cost of operation of the electro-pneumatic is not any greater and, in many cases, is much less. More especially is this the case where, as at terminals, a plant for generating electricity has been put in for other purposes, the only expense then being the cost of the additional power expended to provide the current used to work the plant and for furnishing compressed air.

Owing to there being no mechanical connections from the machine in the tower to each of the different movements, this system lends itself most readily to all applications where there are many and complicated sets of switches, sharp curves, or to places where it would be almost impossible to operate a mechanically connected plant. The connections from the tower being of wire only, the tower can always be placed in the most advantageous position for controlling the movements of trains, the arrangement shown in Fig. 5 being a good example of what it is possible to accomplish in this direction.

At locations such as are found at large terminals or freight yards, where the number of movements to be made is large and the number of switches and signals to be worked is very great, the dispatch and safety with which every movement can be made warrants the use of such a system, even if the first cost is greater. At all such locations it is usual to equip the tower with such electrical devices as will aid the train director in his work, enabling him to keep himself informed as to the movements of trains, the condition of the tracks and the position

of the signals. The view shown in Fig. 6 well illustrates this, being a photograph of the instruments in a tower on the Pennsylvania road, and kindly furnished by the Union Switch & Signal Co.

The several instruments shown comprise train describers, by which information is signaled as to what train is coming;

TOWER HOUSE FOR ELECTRO-PNEUMATIC INTERLOCKING MACHINE.

disk and semaphore indicators to inform the operator when a track is occupied; drop annunciators to give information regarding the starting of trains on certain tracks; telegraph instruments, telephones and electric bells. In addition to these a miniature model of the tracks operated is provided as a part of each interlocking machine, the switches being movable and mechanically connected to the levers, so that the model will accurately represent the position of the switches on the ground.

This is a great help in the operation of the machine, as the operator can see at a glance the position of all the switches, and not have to look at each lever to see what position it is in.

Incandescent electric lamps can also be used with great success, instead of oil, at an electro-pneumatic plant; for while

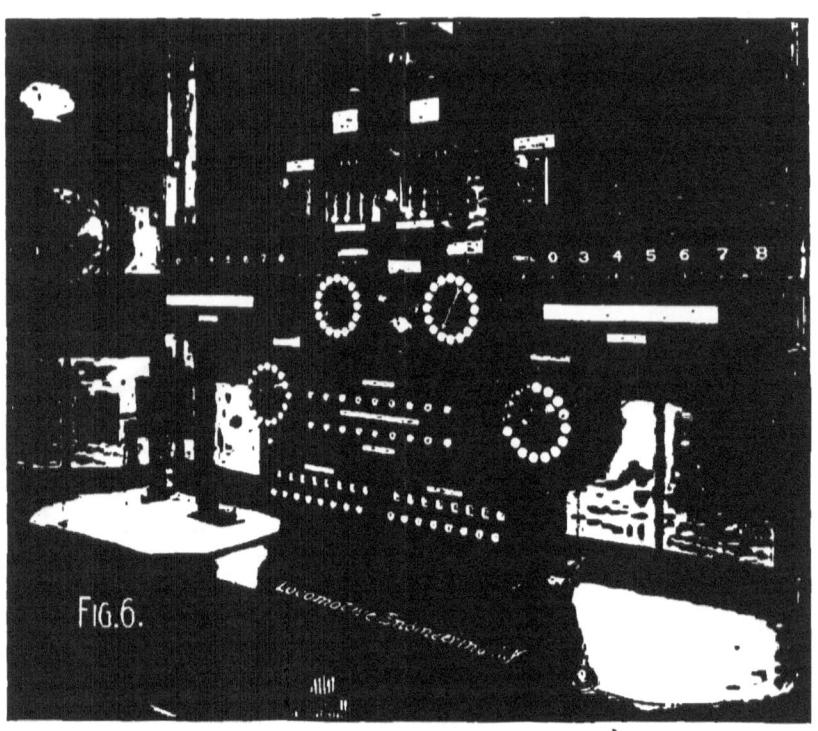

ELECTRICAL ANNUNCIATOR AND INDICATOR INSTRUMENTS IN P. R. R. TOWER.

the cost will be about the same, the service will be very much better.

The cost of an electro-pneumatic plant for small installations is greatly in excess of one mechanically connected, but when the number of levers is large, or the tracks very complicated, the cost will, at most, be the same—and may be somewhat less. As there is hardly any limit to the number of movements that can be put upon a single lever, a very much smaller machine can be used, the cost in consequence being very much reduced.

As an instance of this kind, at the Stewart avenue plant, Chicago, there are but 48 working levers in the machine, occupying a space 5 x 24 feet, to work 84 signals, 37 switches, 22 double slips and 22 movable frogs; while with a mechanical machine, according to American practice, 187 working levers, occupying a space 14 x 77 feet—and to English practice, 243 levers, occupying a space 17 x 93 feet—would be required.

If the plant has been properly installed, the repairs will be no greater than with a mechanical plant and it will be much easier to keep in working order. In winter, trouble will be experienced from freezing up of the valves and pipes, unless proper precautions are taken to get rid of the water of condensation formed in compressing the air. The contacts at the different movements must also be kept free from snow and ice, or else a contact will not be made, and it will not be possible to entirely reverse the lever.

An interlocking device which has come into use in the last two years, for the protection of a crossing of an electric road with a steam or with another electric road, and which promises, with the rapid increase in the use of electricity for street railroads, and their extension consequent upon the same, to be quite extensively introduced, has been patented by Mr. George Gibbs, Mechanical Engineer of the Chicago, Milwaukee & St. Paul Railway.

At any street crossing, when a change is made to electricity as a motive power, the danger of using the crossing is very much enhanced, owing to the increased speed with which the the cars approach the crossing, their great weight and consequent inertia, and the liability of failure of their source of power, due to a shut-down at the power house, blowing out of fuses, or jumping off of the trolley wheel when the car is on the crossing. "There seems to be no good reason," to use the words of Mr. Charles Hansel, C. E., "why the statute of the State of Illinois, which requires all new crossings of steam railroads at the same level to be protected by a suitable system of signals, derails, etc., should not include the crossings at grade of all railroads or railways which carry human freight, for it cannot be regarded as unreasonable that street railways should comply with the requirements of public safety in the same manner and in the same measure as is required of steam roads.

"In cities where such grade crossings occur, the police regulations generally require the railroads to keep a flagman posted at the crossing to signal traffic. This practice gives but a small measure of protection, while the charge to the railroads for operating is the same as if this flagman had physical control of the crossing. Considering the subject from a financial point of view only, it appears that if we can construct a system of signaling to be controlled by a single man in a tower overlooking the crossing, with mechanism so arranged as to make it impossible for trains or cars on the steam railroad and the electric railway to reach the crossing at the same time, we have invested well; for with such a device the danger of crossing is eliminated, and the operation of either line is the same as regards safety as if no such crossing existed, and both roads are relieved of the constant danger to life and property and consequent payment of damages. The saving in rates of insurance to the electric line where such protection is provided, is alone sufficient to pay the fixed charges on the investment."

The principal features of the apparatus used by Mr. Gibbs are the cutting off of the current from an insulated section of the trolley line, making it impossible to move cars when it is desired to block the line, and in the use of a derailing device to be operated in paved streets, to prevent cars from rolling on or over the crossing, when the current is cut off from the trolley. These devices are connected to and operated by any of the usual forms of interlocking machines, the derailing device or "scotch block" being connected to the same lever that works the switch and cuts the current off from the trolley wire.

A general plan of the arrangement, as applied to a double-track crossing of a steam and electric road, is shown in Fig. 7, the trolley lines in which sections about 800 to 1,000 feet, according to grade, are insulated, being shown in the center of the tracks of the electric road. These insulated sections extend to within about 50 feet of the crossing, but never over it, and in this way make it impossible for the current to be taken away from a car at a place where it would be liable to be hit by a train on the other road. A feed wire connects the insulated section with the electric switches on the machine, which, in turn, are connected to the supply wire from the power house, the insulated section, when the switch is closed by the reversal of the lever of the interlocking machine, becoming a "live" wire and delivering current to any car that may be in the section.

The construction of the scotch block is shown in Fig. 8. It

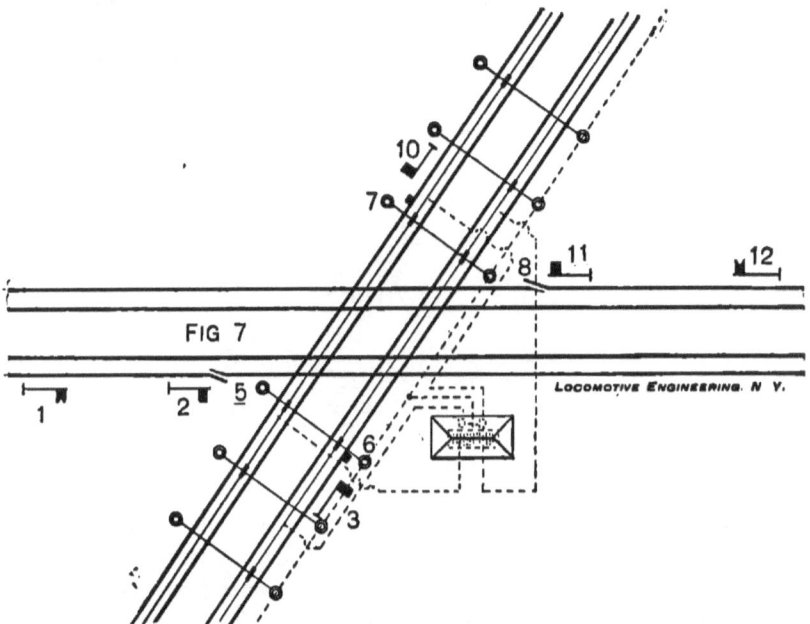

GENERAL PLAN SHOWING WIRING, GIBBS ELECTRIC STREET RAIL-
WAY INTERLOCKING.

consists of a strong cast-iron box, which is placed outside of the rails, a groove being cast in the box in which an iron block 2 x 4 inches in size is raised or lowered whenever the cam lever is moved by the lever of the interlocking machine to which it is connected. When the block is down the top is flush with the top of the box, but when it has been raised, owing to the line of motion being inclined to the axis of the rail, it will project out from the box and over the head of the rail. The block is raised and lowered by means of a roller and pin working in the slot of the cam, but when in either of its extreme positions a solid bearing almost the size of the block is made on the cam and directly in line with the axis of the cam and the cam shaft.   In this way the thrust of a wheel, whether of a car or heavy wagon, will be taken by the shaft and not transmitted to the pipe line and lever.   The block, when raised, projects about 4 inches above the top of the rail, sufficient, it has been found, to either derail the car or to practically bring it to a stop.   The block does not project entirely over the head of the rail, and so does not interfere with wagons or other vehicles which are continually running in the flangeway of the street road.   This is an important feature in its design and one that has a great deal to do with the success of its application.

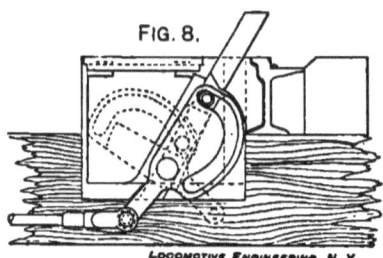

FIG. 8.

LOCOMOTIVE ENGINEERING, N. Y.

DETAILS OF "SCOTCH" BLOCK.

In Fig. 9 are shown the electric switches and the connections to the levers of the machines by which they are worked.   The levers to which they are connected are the ones that work the scotch blocks, the current being always shut off from the insulated section of trolley wire when the block is raised.   Placed on each side of the two electric switches, relays are to be seen through which the current to each insulated trolley section is made to pass.   Either of these relays, when energized by a car in the insulated section, is made to complete a local circuit and work a bell to inform the operator when a car has entered the section.   A small electric switch worked by the signal lever breaks this local circuit and stops the bell as soon as the signal is cleared, the operator's attention, in this way, being more forcibly attracted to the fact that the signal had not been cleared.

It will be noticed, by examining the figure, that a large three-way reversible switch, to which the supply wire is run before being connected to the two cut-out switches, is placed on the frame-work immediately below the switches. This is used to cut out the switches and relays in case any accidental short circuit

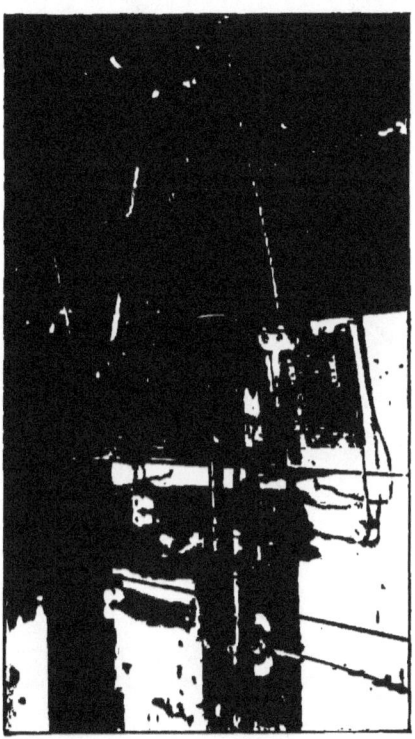

FIG. 9. ELECTRIC CUT-OUT SWITCHES AND CONNECTIONS TO IN-
TERLOCKING MACHINE.

should be made, or any of the parts get broken, the trolley wire being in this way energized so as not to block the electric road.

An additional feature which experience has demonstrated to be of great value in the safe operation of the plant, and one which has also been patented by Mr. Gibbs, is an arrangement of locks and releasing circuits whereby the levers of the machine are locked up after the signal has once been cleared for a car on the

236

electric road until after the car has passed over the crossing. The circuits used are shown in Fig. 10, the locks, relays and circuit breakers being connected in the same manner as was shown in a previous article, where electric locking was applied to the levers controlling a simple crossing, except that when the releasing relay (the upper one shown in the figure) is energized the current is made to pass through the locks, releasing them as soon as the circuit is completed instead of around the locks in the shunt

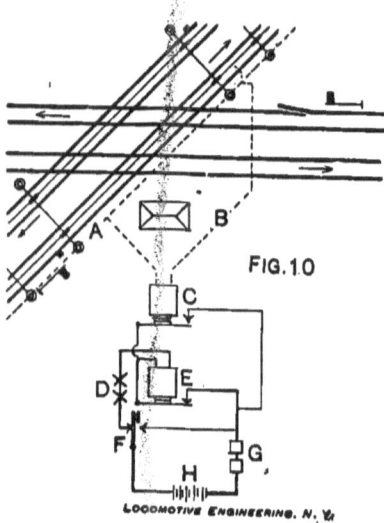

FIG. 10

LOCOMOTIVE ENGINEERING. N. Y.

ELECTRIC LOCKING CIRCUITS FOR ONE TRACK ONLY OF A DOUBLE
TRACK ELECTRIC RAILWAY INTERLOCKING.

A, supply wire ; *B*, wire to insulated section of trolley ; *C*, releasing relay ; *D*, circuit breakers ; *E*, locking relay ; *F*, hand releasing switch ; *G*, locks ; *H*, battery.

circuit, when they would not release the levers until after the releasing circuit had been broken. To obtain a current with which to energize the releasing relay, a short section of the trolley wire on the further end of the crossing is insulated in the same manner as the cut-out section and is connected to the supply wire through the coils of the releasing relay.

When the car has passed over the crossing and the trolley runs on the insulated section, the relay is energized, lifting its armature and completing the circuit through the locks, lifting them and also restoring the circuit through the locking relay, causing the circuit to be maintained and the locks held up after

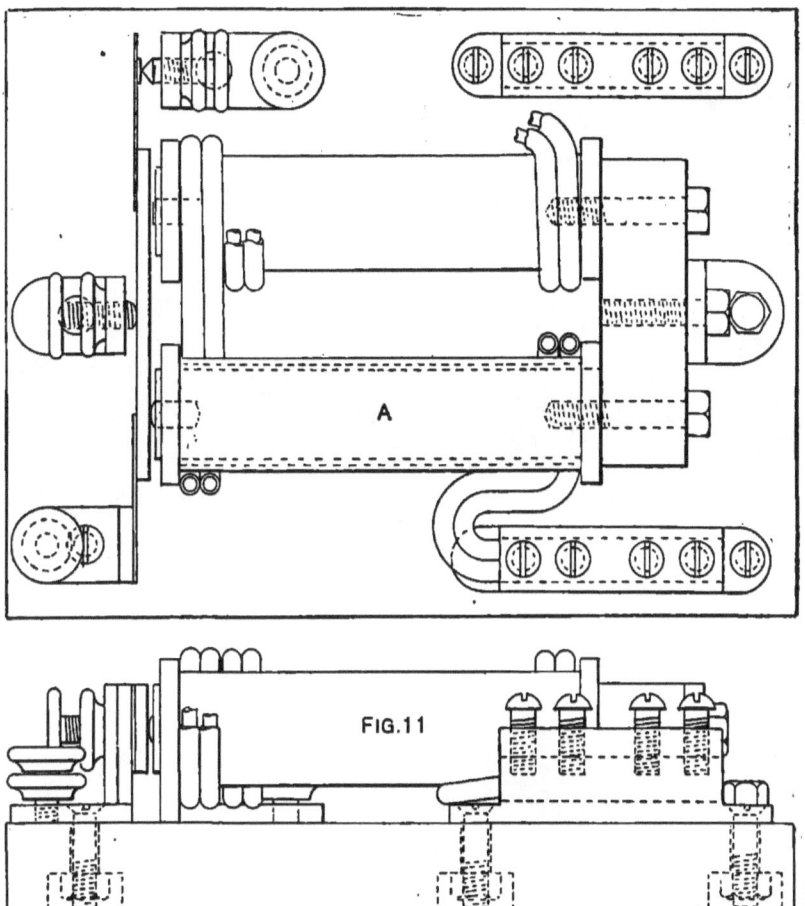

RELAY FOR HEAVY CURRENTS USED BY MOTOR CARS.

A, core wound with two stands No. 6 double cotton-covered magnet wire wrapped with Okonite taping $\frac{1}{16}$ inch thick and paper well shellacked.

the car has passed off the releasing section. As the current which passes through the releasing relay is the one used to propel the car, it is at times a very heavy one, amounting to seventy-five

SIGNALS FOR STREET CARS. GIBBS
ELECTRIC STREET RAILWAY
INTERLOCKING.

SCOTCH BLOCK.

amperes at 500 volts, or about 50 horse-power. A relay to carry such a current as this is constructed of very different proportions from the relays ordinarily used for the currents generated by a battery, and, for this reason, its design may be of interest to those who are not familiar with such things.

This relay is shown in Fig. 11, the core pieces being 1 inch in diameter and 4 inches long, arranged in the usual horseshoe form and wound with a single layer of two No. 6 cotton-covered magnet wires, which are soldered together where they enter the binding posts. The iron core pieces are covered with $\frac{1}{8}$-inch insulating material to prevent the current, the voltage of which is very greatly increased during thunder storms, from breaking through the insulation, and by reaching the locking circuits, burning out the locks and relays. To prevent, if possible, any damage being done in case the insulation should break down, the wires of the locking circuits are connected to the relay with a piece of $\frac{1}{2}$-ampere fuse wire, 6 inches long, which will burn out and prevent the current from grounding through the locks.

This system is now in use at twenty crossings of electric with steam railroads in the city of Chicago and one in the State of New York, and is destined to have a greater number of applications as soon as the benefits to be derived from its use become more generally known. It is practically, in its workings, as safe an appliance as the interlocking used at a crossing of two steam roads, and insures that the cars of the electric road will have the same protection afforded them in using the crossing that is given to the trains on the other road.

CHAPTER XIV

AGREEMENTS, CONTRACTS, SPECIFICA-
TIONS, INSTALLATION AND REPAIRS.

In the early days of railroading, before many roads were built and while the rights of each were in process of development, it appeared a just and reasonable thing for one road to grant any road the privilege of crossing its tracks whenever such a thing was desired—it being understood that the road making the crossing would be responsible for the maintenance of the same. As business increased and the demand for other tracks arose, the question immediately presented itself as to who should pay for the additional crossings made necessary thereby, each road very generously desiring to make the other road stand the entire cost.

This led to the roads interested drawing up an agreement, in which it was clearly stated who should maintain the crossing and what proportion of the cost each road should bear when any new work was to be put in.

The expediency of so doing having been established, any road desiring to cross the tracks of another was forced to sign an agreement whereby they were to put in and forever maintain the crossing at their own expense, and, furthermore, would put in and maintain any crossings made necessary by the laying of new tracks by the road first built.

The protection afforded at a crossing by the use of an interlocking plant having, in comparatively late years only, attracted the attention of railroad officers, no mention was made in the earlier crossing agreements of any appliances to make the use of a crossing safe, a flagman to signal trains being all that was thought necessary at even the busiest crossings. In these cases, when it was desired to install an interlocking plant, a new agreement had to be drawn up, covering the proportion of the original cost which each road should bear, and what proportion each should pay of the cost of operation and maintenance, one road or the other taking charge of the installation, operation and maintenance and billing against the other for their proportion of the cost.

At the present day, when one road desires to cross the tracks of another, the requirement is generally made that an interlocking plant shall be put in and maintained by the road wishing the crossing, as well as putting in and keeping up the crossing frogs, ties, etc., whether or not the business over either of the tracks will be such as to warrant the additional expense. But as laws have been passed in several of the States requiring all new crossings to be protected, and as it is in most cases only a question of a few years before an interlocking would be needed, it is certainly good policy for any road in drawing up an agreement allowing another road to cross its tracks, to include an interlocking plant in its requirements, stating what form of apparatus will be required. Such an agreement should practically be an "iron clad" affair, covering every point, of which the following list comprised the main items called for in an agreement lately made and which are given here for the information of those who may not be familiar with what may be required.

First. That the party of the first part, or the road first built, shall have the use of the tracks now owned and operated by it without any material impairment of their usefulness or safety by the party of the second part, or the road desiring to put in the crossing.

Second. That all crossings which it is the desire of the first party to construct, maintain and operate over the tracks of the second party shall be furnished and properly put in by the party of the second part.

Third. That the second party will furnish all the materials for and construct and put in all crossing frogs, crossing signals, gates, targets and other fixtures, according to plans and specifications furnished by the first party. All parts to be forever maintained and kept in good repair at the sole cost of the second party. And in case of failure to promptly furnish and put in or keep in repair any of these parts, the party of the first part may do the work and bill against the party of the second part for the full amount so expended. Any damages resulting from defective condition of said parts being paid for by the party of the second part, saving the party of the first part harmless therefrom.

Fourth. In the passage of the respective trains of the parties interested over the crossing, the passenger trains of the party of the first part shall have preference over the passenger trains of the party of the second part, and in like manner the freight trains of the party of the first part shall have preference; but in all cases passenger trains shall have preference over freight trains of either road.

Fifth. If at any time a difference of opinion between said parties shall arise, the question in dispute shall be referred to a board of arbitration consisting of three competent disinterested parties, one to be chosen by each of the parties to the agreement, and the two so chosen to choose a third. That written notice shall be given of the time and place of the meeting, and that at the time and place appointed they shall proceed summarily to hear and dispose of the matter in dispute, the determination of such board of arbitration being absolutely final and conclusive upon the parties interested.

Sixth. That within ninety days from the date of these presents the party of the second part will provide said crossing with an interlocking plant, with pipe home signal connections, electric locking, and annunciators, and if at any time a device satisfactory to the chief engineer of the party of the first part be manufactured for the purpose of giving a continuous rail over the crossing on the line having the right of way over the same, it shall be put in and connected with the interlocking plant. The specification, locking, dog-sheet and general plan of the interlocking shall be submitted to and approved by the party of the first part before the contract shall be executed. That the party of the second part shall bear the entire cost of such interlocking plant, operating and maintaining it at their own expense. That any additional tracks laid by either party are to be connected to the interlocking and maintained at the sole cost of the party of the second part, and that the party of the first part may take charge of and maintain and operate the plant, if the operation and maintenance by the party of the second part be not satisfactory to the party of the first part, the party of the second part paying all bills upon presentation for the amount expended in maintaining and operating said interlocking plant.

While the above conditions comprise the most important points generally considered in an agreement between two steam roads, there are several other points which have to be included when the agreement is entered into by parties controlling a steam railroad with those controlling a line operated by electricity. Briefly, these are, that all overhead wires shall be maintained at a height of twenty-three feet above the tracks of the steam road, conductors to be arranged for the return electric current, so as to prevent, as far as possible, leakage from its tracks, that will affect the operation of electricallly controlled railway signals, telegraph or telephone wires. That the overhead electric wires shall be so arranged as not to interfere in any way with the operation of the street gates, which the steam road is compelled by city ordinance to maintain at such points of crossing.

The agreement having been signed by the parties interested, the next step is to prepare the plans and specifications for the interlocking and submit them to the signal companies for their bids. The plans submitted by the railroad company, when drawn up by the signal engineer, usually consist of a plan of the tracks with all the derails, switches and signals required, properly shown and numbered, the location of each and the distance from the crossing being clearly stated. Lines representing the connections to the switches and signals are also drawn, as well as lines to show where any heavy boxing is to be put in and which it is desired to have the signal company include in their bid. Where no signal experts are employed by the railroad company, a plan of the tracks is usually submitted to the signal companies with a request that they draw up a plan showing the proper signals to be used and how the several connections should be run, their bid being made upon the plan so drawn up.

Their bids are usually made upon specifications gotten up by them for the kind of apparatus which they manufacture, it being understood that the work is to be put in to the satisfaction of the railroad company contracting for the same. These specifications usually state the kind of machine, the number of levers and the number of switches and signals to be operated. They also give the size of the tower and of what the signal connections shall be made, practice in this regard being different on the different roads. The switch connections are given in detail, the size of pipe, method of fastening and means of compensation being also given. The distances apart that the pipe carriers and wire pulleys are to be spaced is stated, as well as the sizes of the different foundations and the thickness of lumber to be used in the boxing.

The part of the work that the railroad company is expected to do is plainly stated, comprising, for the most part, the track work in preparing the switches, derails and movable frogs ready to be connected. All preliminary grading necessary to be done and proper drainage wherever required. To furnish broken stone, sand and cement for concreting the heavier foundations, and to provide permits for building the towers and for digging across streets when necessary in cities. Railroad companies having a signal department usually submit with the plans to the signal company for their bid, any specifications in regard to details that they may wish to have followed when the work is put in. These generally relate to standards of the railroad not called for by the specifications of the signal company, or where some apparatus is to be used of a different design from that manufactured and furnished by the company bidding on the work. .

The bids having been submitted and a selection made, the contracts are signed and the work commenced by the signal company, the railroad furnishing the material and doing the work that it was agreed in the contract they should do. The signal expert appointed by the railroad to inspect the work goes over the ground with the signal company's foreman and gives the exact location of the tower, the derails, signals and where the pipe lines shall pass under the tracks. The different ways of doing work are discussed and an understanding arrived at as to what will be considered good work and what the railroad will require, it being specified in the contract that the work shall be done to the satisfaction of the railroad company.

As the work proceeds, points in regard to construction will, from time to time, come up which the signal inspector will be expected to settle, to prevent a possible rejection on his part when the plant has been completed. Inspections will have to be made quite frequently to see that the work is being properly done and that the standards of the railroad are being followed.

When railroads have a regularly organized signal department, they often install a plant with their own men, buying the material from one of the signal companies, as their experience has been that the work will, at least, be better done, even if it should cost no less.

After the plant has been completed and before it is put in service, each lever should be connected to the switch or signal it is to throw, and a trial made to see that every part works properly. To do this without interrupting traffic only one switch, or the switches to be worked by one lever, should be connected at the same time, those to the arm plate casting of the signal being left connected, as until the blade is bolted up no indication is made.

Should the work prove satisfactory, a day is appointed on which the plant will be put in service, this being a day or so before the signal company will have finished the boxing, painting and other work that can be completed after the plant is ready to be connected up and put in service.

Notice of the fact is given to all the railroad companies interested, so that proper bulletins can be issued notifying trainmen that the interlocking will be put in service at such a time and that they must be careful to obey the signals in running over the crossing. In connecting up the plant the signal blades should first be bolted on, this being done so that all the blades will be put up at the time appointed for the plant to go into service. After the time has passed, but not before, the derails may be connected up, the trainmen then being responsible for the consequences should they allow their train to run past a signal when at danger.

With States that require an inspection to be made by the railroad commissioners, or some one appointed by them, before a permit will be granted allowing trains to proceed over a crossing without stopping, an appointment with the Commission must be made, when they will inspect the plant, blue prints of the general plan, locking and dog sheets being sent in for examination and approval before the inspection is made. Should the work have been done as they think it ought to be to make the operation of the plant safe, a day is usually named in which the plant may be put in service, the permit when received reading as having been issued on that day.

Should the locking of the levers not meet their approval, or some part be left undone, in their judgment essential to the safe operation of the plant, a permit is refused, and, when the changes or additions desired have been completed, another inspection has to be made. For this reason, when a Railroad Commission has to approve the plans and inspect the interlocking, it is a very good scheme to submit the plans to them before the work is proceeded with, so that no delay will be caused by any objection on their part.

If some other interlocking plant is already in service on that division, a bulletin notice is all that need be issued to trainmen, informing them that the interlocking will be put in service. But if it is the first plant to be installed, a set of rules should be issued to the men and an examination made to see that they know how to read the signals and understand what the consequences will be if they disregard them. These rules should describe a signal and explain what the different indications mean; they should make it clear as to which signal will be used to govern a given track, and what will be the several duties of the trainmen when using the tracks protected by the interlocking.

After a plant has been accepted by the railroad and put in operation, they are then responsible for its condition and will have to see that it is kept in good working order, repairmen and inspectors being kept for this purpose. The organization of the force differs on almost every road, each one believing that theirs is the best and that the others are either not keeping up the plants as they should be, or else are doing it at a very much greater cost.

Several roads employ men as inspectors who are responsible for the proper condition of the plants within a certain district, other men being employed to do the work and report to them. Each repairman is given so many plants to take care of, he being expected to go and look them over as often as possible, making any adjustments or slight repairs that may be needed. Should there be no repairs to make, he is to put in his time cleaning up the plant, or, at any rate, looking for work.

This way of doing things is, in the long run, a somewhat expensive one, as in most instances there is no work for the repairman to do, or rather, none but what in the majority of cases the signalman can look after. The man's time has to be charged to repairs, whether there is any work to be done or not. In case of any large amount of repairs being needed, additional help has to be employed, as one man is not able to do very much by himself, and while the claim may be made that by keeping a man on the ground almost all the time the plant will not run down sufficiently to need any very general repairs, experience and reason will, I think, prove that this is not so, and that no matter how well this man may attend to his duties, it is not practicable for him to keep the plant in first-class condition, or, in other words, from wearing out.

Another plan is to divide the road into districts, making each one so large that the repairman is able to get around only occasionally, making inspections and light repairs only and having help furnished him when any large amount of work is to be done. At some central point an additional force is employed, which is used in putting in any new work, making general repairs, or any repairs needed in case of accident. These men should all be experienced workmen, one or two of them being capable of taking charge of or putting their hands to any work that may turn up. They should be able to do a good job in pipe fitting, machine work, blacksmithing, carpentry, cleaning batteries and adjusting relays, and while such men are not to be found every day, if the signal engineer will see to it that only good men are employed and that they are given a chance to learn, they will become very efficient and be able to do good work in any of the lines enumerated. Of course, at very large plants, one, or perhaps two repairmen will be needed at all times, their presence being made necessary more as a protection in case of accident, to keep the road from being blocked, than because of the amount of work there is to do.

Another plan, again, is to have practically no regular repair force, but only such men as are needed for new work and general repairs. On the road following this plan, the signal engineer has the hiring of one of the operators, who will be responsible for the maintenance of the plant and must make all necessary repairs and adjustments while attending to his other duties. This man must have had sufficient experience, before being appointed to a position, to enable him to make any ordinary repairs, and being in a position to reap the benefits from keeping the plant in good condition, is very apt to do so, provided he can find the time. And right here is where the greatest objection to the plan can be made, for, if the road at that point is a very busy one, then the man will certainly not be able to leave the tower long enough to do anything more than to change the adjustment of the connections, or to clean and oil the different parts when necessary.

Of the three ways spoken of, the last is much the cheapest, but if the chances of accident and possible delay to trains where this plan is followed be taken into consideration, the conclusion must be arrived at that it is economizing in the matter of labor at the expense of safety. Where a road has in service a number of block signals, interlocking plants and switch signals, sufficient to keep a regular repair force employed, such as is outlined in the second plan, it will be found by far the best and easiest method of having any new work done or repairs quickly made. The cost will be but little, if any, more than with the last plan outlined above, and the equipment will be kept in better condition.

In regard to the railroad employing their own men and putting in their own work, I think that, as a rule, this is not a good plan, for unless the railroad has as good foremen as the signal companies employ, and they seldom have, the work will be more cheaply done by the signal company. The claim that the work will be much better done when put in by the railroad will not count for much, if a competent inspector is appointed to supervise the installation, as the signal companies are certainly willing and try to put in the work to the entire satisfaction of the parties having the work done. Their reputation is at stake, and while they may not do as good work when no one is sent to supervise the installation, they can hardly be blamed for this, as they have not to take care of a plant after it is finished, and by doing new work only, do not find out the weak points in their work.

Unless a railroad will employ the services of a good foreman, it will, I venture to say, cost them more in putting in an interlocking plant than if the work was done by one of the signal companies. The chances of a man's doing the work wrong and having to go over it a second time are so great, and the work is so often done in the country, where the men have of necessity to be left very much to themselves, that unless the man in charge not only knows how to do the work, but is capable of properly handling men, the work will cost very much more than was expected. As a matter of protection, in case of accident or breakage of the apparatus, every signalman should be taught how to disconnect and spike a derail or switch, to make adjustments, or any repairs that may be needed to make it safe for trains to pass through the interlocking. A catalogue of the apparatus manufactured by the signal company installing the plant will be found an excellent book to put in each tower, as the signalmen will then be able to make themselves familiar with the correct name of each

FIG. I.

part, and, in case of accident, to give page and order number of any new pieces that may be wanted, in this way insuring that the right parts will be sent him.

To enable the signalman to make temporary repairs, he must be provided with a set of tools, of which the following is a list of those commonly furnished, the articles needed in furnishing a tower when first put in service being also given: One machinist's hammer, one spike maul, one hand axe, one hand saw, one claw-bar, one 12-inch combination monkey wrench (Fig. 1), one socket wrench for ¾-inch bolts, one pair 10-inch Button's pliers, two cold chisels, one fine file, six sheets emery cloth, one long-neck oil can, one short-neck oil can, one squirt can, one white hand lantern, one red hand lantern, two red flags, one telegraph table with drawer, one office chair and cushion, one bracket lamp, one corrugated rubber mat the length of the machine, one Seth Thomas

eight-day clock, six fire buckets, six hand grenades, one water
bucket, one tin drinking cup, one broom, one mop, one coal hod,
shovel and poker.

The number of fire buckets and hand grenades in this list may
be surprising, as one would hardly think there would be much
danger of a tower catching fire when as isolated as they usually
are. But the fact is they catch fire very easily, from matches care-

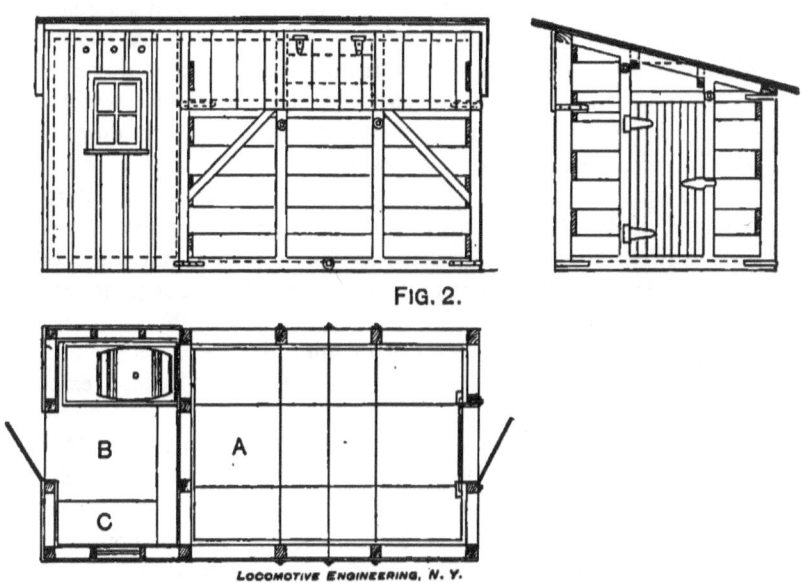

FIG. 2.

LOCOMOTIVE ENGINEERING, N. Y.

COAL AND OIL HOUSE, C., M. & ST. P. RY.

A, Coal-room, floor plank laid on cinders ; *B*, Oil-room, earth floor ; *C*, Zinc-lined shelf.

lessly thrown away, from blazing grass and from many other
causes, and, from the fact of their being isolated, generally burn
down entirely after once catching fire, the interlocking machine
being destroyed, causing delay and great inconvenience in the
handling of trains. To reduce the chance of fire no lamps should
be allowed in the tower, nor should any greasy waste be allowed to
lie around or accumulate. The lamps should be cleaned in the
day time, in a house provided for the purpose—the design shown
in Fig. 2 being that of the coal and oil house supplied to all of
the interlocking plants of the Chicago, Milwaukee & St. Paul

railway—the house being placed not less than one hundred feet from the tower.

For the guidance of the signalman, the following set of rules, signed by the general superintendents of the roads interested, is framed and put in all the towers of the St. Paul Company, the man in charge being held strictly accountable for the proper observance of every one of them:

1 Trainmen are instructed to obey the directions and signals of the signalman; you will, therefore, see that trains are passed without delay or stoppage when it is known to be safe to do so.

2. Precedence on conflicting routes will be determined by time cards. A delayed train must not be given the line running on the time of an opposing regular train.

3. The normal position of signals is at *danger;* of derailing switches, open; of levers, thrown *ahead,* where they must always remain when no train movements are being made. Each signal in succession *must be* thrown to its normal position as soon as rear of train has passed it.

4. When train gives notice of its approach, set switches and signals for the desired route; but be sure that no obstacles exist on route before setting signal for it.

5. When a signal has once been given for any train, should it be necessary to change the position of signals or switches, the signal may be changed to *danger,* but the switches must not be changed nor the signal given to another train on an opposing route until the train which first had the signals has come to a full stop.

6. No switching which requires blocking the main track must be allowed within five minutes of the time of any regular train.

7. Levers used in switching must be returned to their normal position as soon as switching is completed.

8. In case of derailment at switch, disconnect switch and take detector bar off by removing clips from rail. Take great care to protect interlocking from unnecessary damage while replacing cars or locomotives. Report all cases of failure of trainmen or others to observe proper precautions to prevent unnecessary damage, as you will be held accountable for the same. Pass no trains after the derailment until all parts liable to damage have been examined and steps taken to protect trains. Be sure that track is safe before allowing trains to pass over.

9. In case of accident, notify division superintendent and mechanical engineer at once by telegraph and call section foreman.

10. In case of accident to switch, disconnect it, set it for the main line and spike it.ˑ Use a flagman to protect all disconnected switches.

11. Should it be impossible from derangement to throw signals when switches are closed train must come to full stop; signalman may then flag it past *home* signal after protecting all conflicting routes by placing their signals at *danger*.

12. Never move a switch lever when a train covers the switch or detector bar.

13. During freezing weather move all levers frequently and keep apparatus free from snow and ice.

14. *You* are not allowed to and must see that *no one* but an authorized workman makes any change in the apparatus or locking, except under written order from the division superintendent or mechanical engineer.

15. Do not handle the apparatus roughly; pull the levers with a steady movement, being especially careful to move the signals without injurious jerk.

16. Keep all switches, locks and detector bars clear of cinders, ballast, sand, etc., and keep apparatus oiled.

17. Report at once any disregard of rule forbidding use of sand by engines with number of engine, train, etc.

18. Inspect all switches, signals and lighted lamps carefully as often as the weather or other indications may require, reporting every case of trouble.

19. Lamps must be handled carefully; keep them clean and in order, as per special circular of instructions; light and place them in position at the proper time.

20. Daily reports must be filled out according to instructions and sent regularly to division superintendent and mechanical engineer. These reports must be full and intelligible, giving exact character and location of trouble or defects in plant and pattern number or correct number of broken part.

21. Allow no one to enter tower whose duties do not require him there, without a written permit from the division superintendent or mechanical engineer.

The daily reports alluded to are made on manifold paper of

the form as given herewith, a copy being made out each day by each of the signalmen and sent to the proper officers.

Form S—1.

CHICAGO, MILWAUKEE & ST. PAUL RAILWAY CO.

DAILY SIGNAL REPORT.

....Tower.

Time ....M.......... ....189..

To....................................... ....

Is apparatus in good working order ? ....

What trains have been delayed ?..................................... .....

....

Note carefully any defects, looseness or breakage of apparatus or trouble with lamps, and state what steps you have taken to repair. Give train and engine numbers in cases of disobedience of signal rules.

Remarks................... ....

....

(Thirteen blank lines.)

....*Signalman.*

These reports are of great assistance in keeping track of the workings of the different plants and of any accidents or delays which may have happened. It also permits of a record being kept of almost everything that takes place at each of the towers, and by summarizing them comparisons can be made of the performance of each.

The following list is a somewhat condensed summary of these reports for forty-one interlocking plants for the month of July, 1895, from which some idea can be formed of what has occurred during the month, and has been mentioned in the reports:

Damage by accident, 2.

Failure through neglect of operator, 5.

Train off track at derail, 1.

Ran through open derail, trailing point, 1.

Defects of apparatus; lack of adjustment, 6.

Other defects, 2.

Track relays out of adjustment, 1.

Failures of circuits from other causes, 2.

Large repairs completed, 8.

Number of times at work making repairs, 88.

Inspections made by repairmen, 147.
Trains delayed; defects of apparatus, 1.
Trains delayed by other trains, 32.

EAST BOTTOMS INTERLOCKING,

C., M. & ST. P. RY., AND K. C., O. & S. RY.

CROSSING

MO. P. RY. AND C. & A. RY.

Machine.
Saxby & Farmer,
8 Signal Levers.
9 Switch Levers.
1 F. P. L.
2 Spare.
20 Lever Frame.

Agreement of Expenses.
Date of, 5-28-92.

Construction and Maintenance.
C. & A. Ry., 25 per cent.
Mo. P. Ry., 25 "
K. C., O. & S. Ry., 25 per cent.
C., M. & St.P. Ry., 25 "

Operation.
K. C., O. & S. Ry., 50 per cent.
C., M. & St. P. Ry., 50 "

Contract.
Date of, 1-26-94.
Cost of, $4,791.
Tower, 800.
Built by U. S. & S. Co.
Maintained by
C. M. & St. P. Ry.

A general plan of each interlocking, with a sheet giving the agreement as to division of expenses and other information, as shown above, if made on a sheet 4 x 7½ inches in size and all fastened together, will be found a very convenient form in which to keep any information pertaining to interlockings, which has to be referred to so frequently by the superintendents, the auditor and the men in the signal department.

By making the originals on tracing cloth, copies can be cheaply and easily made and furnished to each officer desiring a set.

CHAPTER XV

SWITCH SIGNALS.

Of the fixed signals, the first to come into use in the early days of railroading were the ones intended to indicate to engineers the position of the switch, a target of simple form placed upon a revolving stand being the device used, very much as is the common practice of to-day. Naturally, each road adopted a form they thought the best, a proceeding which resulted in almost every road using a different pattern, the clear signal on one road in many instances being used on other roads to indicate danger.

As the switch signals are used solely to indicate the position of the switch, whether it is open or shut, it cannot be said that much confusion would result from their being used in opposite ways on different roads, and no doubt this is the true reason why—up to the present time—there has been no change in the practice, and a standard for all roads seems to be as far off as ever. Practice has demonstrated that the best signal is one of position and not of form or color; but as there is no simple means by which the indication can be given in this way, practice has almost entirely resolved itself into one of form, colors being also made use of, particularly where forms to give two separate indications are used, one for safety and the other for danger.

Outside of the form of the signal, of which the best is certainly the most distinct, there are three different methods in use of indicating by means of a target the position of a switch, the first being when the target is visible and an indication made for the danger; the second where the target is made to show for safety but not for danger, and the third where with two targets on the same shaft, one is used to indicate safety and the other danger. As illustrating this, figures 1, 2 and 3 plainly show the three ways spoken of. Of the three the last is certainly the only one that meets the requirements of one of the first principles of signaling, which is that an indication must be given for safety as well as for danger. As between the other two, the first is by

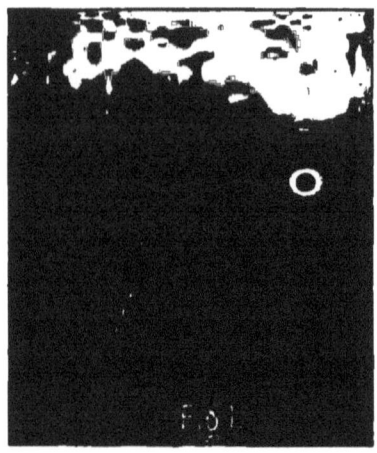

SWITCH TARGET USED TO INDICATE DANGER.

TARGET USED TO INDICATE SAFETY.

far the better, the presence of a signal being a much more forcible indication and more likely to be noticed than is the absence of one, and as it is much more important to have the danger signal seen and acted upon than it is with the one indicating safety, the first is the one that should be adopted. Again,

SWITCH TARGET GIVING INDICATION FOR MAIN LINE OR FOR THE SIDE TRACK.

with the signal showing for safety, one signal will often be obscured by another signal, so that if it should be left at danger, it would be almost impossible for the engineer to notice the fact until quite close to the switch. For this reason, and because of the difficulty met with in obtaining two forms that are distinguishable at any great distance, the plan of using a signal that will give a danger indication only, is believed by many to be the best.

Practice in regard to the usefulness of a switch signal would be much improved if the target was elevated, as is shown in Fig. 4, the top of the stand being about twelve feet above the top of the rail. As will be noticed, this stand is provided with targets to give the two indications, one a form composed of circular disks joined together, and the other a straight piece of sheet-iron with pointed ends and fastened to the shaft in an inclined position.

The difference between the two forms with this signal, which has been quite extensively introduced, is not distinguishable at so great a distance as one would suppose at first sight, owing to the vertical height of the inclined piece being but little more than that of the circular disks. Should the upper and lower ends of these pieces be left on making the outer edges vertical lines intersecting the two inclined sides, as shown by the dotted lines in the figure, the difference in the form of the two targets would be much more noticeable and be distinguishable at a much greater distance.

While the target ordinarily used on a switch-stand answers the purpose of a signal fairly well when the track is straight and the target can be seen, there are a number of places on almost every road where it is desirable to have a signal placed at some distance away from the switch, to be worked in connection with the switch to give warning to an approaching train of the position that the switch is in. The conditions to be met are that any signal so used should be of the semaphore pattern, and placed on a high pole as in the case of a block or interlocking signal, the indication of this form of signal—as has already been pointed out—being more positive and distinguishable at a much greater distance than any other. As the switch is the danger point, and is provided with a signal—a red target in the day time and a red light at night— the signal placed at a distance becomes in reality a distant signal and should be so used, the blade being painted green and the end notched, while at night the light should show green when the signal stands at danger.

In connecting the signal with the switch, it should be so arranged that the signal would have to be put at danger before any

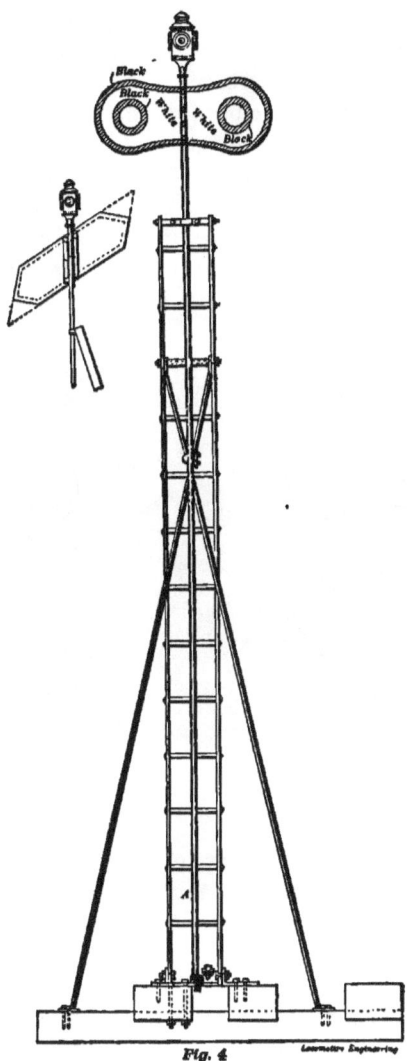

Fig. 4

HIGH TARGET STAND GIVING TWO INDICATIONS.

movement of the switch could be made, and that in closing the switch and clearing the signal the switch would have to be completely closed before any movement of the signal could take place

—or, in other words, the levers operating the switch and signal should be interlocked. And in the manner of accomplishing this are to be found the only differences that exist between the many devices that are used or have been designed for this purpose.

The simplest construction is that of a two-levered stand, such as was shown in a previous article for working a distant signal in connection with a home block signal, locking bars with a movable dog to work between being attached to each lever, so that the lever working the signal could be pulled over only when the lever working the switch had been reversed.

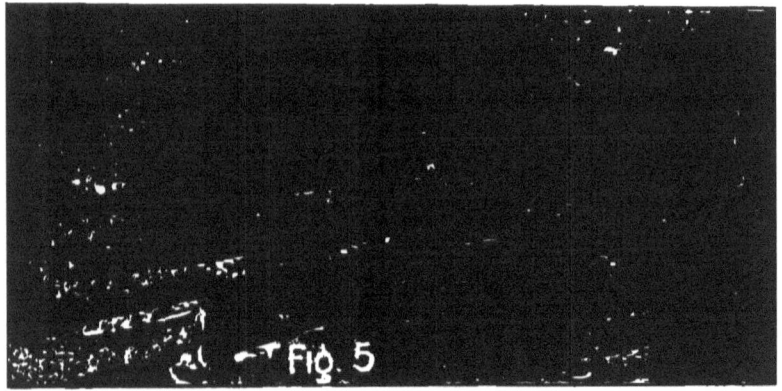

U. S. & S. Co. INTERLOCKED SWITCH STAND.

Although simple, this arrangement is comparatively an expensive one, the levers and locking parts being made of many small pieces carefully fitted, and for this reason has not come into use as much as have some of the less expensive designs.

The design shown in Figs. 5 and 6 is one made by the Union Switch & Signal Co., the levers being interlocked in a very simple manner. As an additional safeguard, the lever working the signal is locked with the switch by means of a lock-rod (seen in Fig. 6), so that it is impossible to move the lever to clear the signal unless the switch has been properly closed.

As will be seen, the arrangement consists of two levers, fulcrumed on a base casting, one of the levers being provided with a wheel around which the connection to a distant signal is made to pass, and the other with a crank-pin placed at the proper radius, to which the connecting-rod to the switch may be fastened and the switch thrown when the lever is pulled over from one side to the other. By passing the connections to the signal around the wheel in the manner shown, the proper movement of the wires is obtained for working the signal, one wire being pulled in and the other unwound. Both movements of the signal are thus made positive,

VIEW SHOWING LOCK ROD.

and the possibility of a wrong indication being given is very much lessened.

The locking of the levers to prevent their both being moved over at the same time, and thus giving a wrong indication while the movement was being made, is accomplished by means of two pins (seen in Fig. 5), which work at right angles with the levers and fit into holes drilled into the center castings, lugs being provided on each lever, which forces one of the pins into the hole in the other lever, until the lever that is being moved is pulled entirely over. With the switch closed and the signal at safety, the switch-lever is locked until the signal-lever is moved to its ex-treme position, when the signal will have been changed to danger; with the signal at danger and the switch open, the signal-lever can-not be moved until the switch-lever is pulled over to its extreme position and the switch closed. There is nothing, however, to make the switchman throw the signal-lever back and clear the signal before locking the switch (unless the lock is fastened to the handle), so that it sometimes happens that the signal is left at danger with the switch set for the main line. The arrangement, though, works very well, and has been well designed to overcome the objection that can generally be made to any arrangements using two levers, in that there is always a possibility of the locking or other parts being removed in making repairs to the switch or stand, and by a failure of the section men to properly replace them, the signal might be left at clear with the switch open.

As this has happened in several instances where two-levered arrangements have been used, very bad accidents being the result, it would seem desirable to have an arrangement with which it would not be possible for this to occur. Such a one has been de-signed and patented by Mr. George Gibbs, and is shown in Fig. 7, a drawing of the motion-plate being shown in Fig. 8.

As will be noticed, the body of the stand is cast in one piece, the crank-shaft for moving the switch to which the target is fas-tened being made to turn in bearings in the center of the casting. In place of a direct connection being made from the crank to the head-rod, the connecting-rod is attached to a sliding-bar work-ing in grooves cast in the bottom of the stand, a pin being pro-vided on the bar which fits in the slot of the motion-plate or cam attached to the lower end of the shaft and moves the bar whenever the cam is turned. This movement provides for the opening and closing of the switch; to work the signal, a gear-wheel having a groove around which a chain may be passed is fastened to the sliding-bar in such a way that when the cam is in a certain posi-tion teeth cast on its outer circumference will engage with the teeth of the gear-wheel and turn it, the chain to which the wire to the signal is attached being wound up.

In this way, by turning the shaft, the cam is made to do two things: one to work the sliding-bar to open and close the switch, and the other to turn the wheel pivoted on the bar to wind or

unwind the chain and work the signal. To make these two operations take place at different times during the turning of the switch-

GIBBS' INTERLOCKING SWITCH STAND AT "DANGER."

lever, and thus make the arrangement safe, as the signal should
be changed only after the switch is closed or before it has been
opened, the teeth are put on that side of the cam which will cause

them to engage with the gear-wheel only when the slide has been moved to close the switch, the wheel at other times being free and not moved by the movement of the cam. As the signal is weighted to stand at danger, unless held at safety by a pull on the wire, and the first motion of the lever made to open the switch turns the gear-wheel unwinding the chain, the signal is allowed

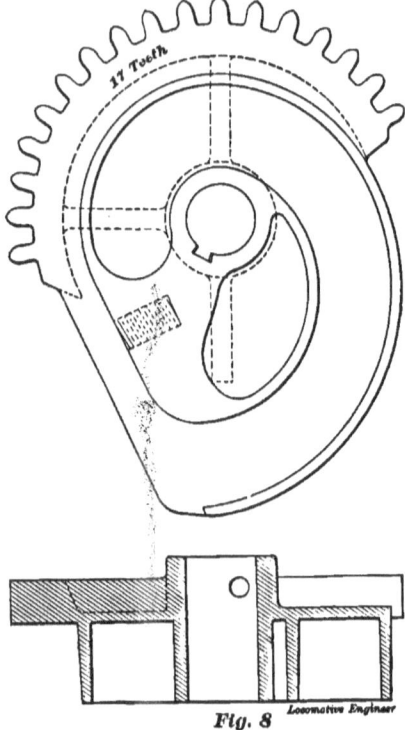

Fig. 8

MOTION PLATE OR CAM OF GIBBS' STAND.

to go to danger before the switch-points have moved, the pin on the slide-bar being brought into contact with the spiral groove of the cam to move the switch only after the chain has been unwound from the wheel.   In turning the lever to close the switch and clear the signal, the first movement turns the cam and moves the sliding-bar only, thereby closing the switch, a further move-

ment bringing the gear-wheel back, causing the teeth to engage with those on the cam, turning the wheel and clearing the signal without any further movement of the bar.

Should it be desired to connect up two switches to one signal, so that when either or both switches are opened the signal will stand at danger, a device known as a controller is made use of, which is shown in Fig. 9. This device accomplishes the purpose for which it was designed, by taking up the slack in the wire, when the switch nearest the signal is closed, and allowing the signal to be worked in the usual manner by

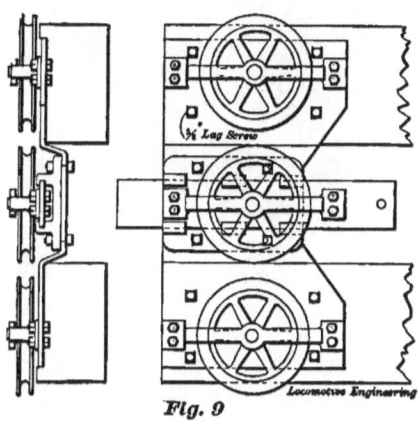

Fig. 9

SIGNAL CONTROLLER.

the stand that is farthest away. The wire from the stand nearest the signal being attached to the slide of the controller, when that switch is opened the middle wheel of the controller is allowed to be drawn in between two other wheels, the wire to the signal being slackened up sufficiently to allow the signal to go to danger. When both switches are closed, the wire is drawn in the same as if only one stand was used and the signal is pulled to clear. In service this stand has given very good results, and but one objection, that of having but one wire to work the signal, has been found with it, dependence being placed upon gravity to make the signal go to danger when the switch was open. While this would seem to be a very serious objection,

268

owing to the danger of wires or chain freezing up in winter, in practice this has not proved to be the case, if care be used in the installation to secure proper drainage. As there is but one wire the signal will work with a much lighter pull, the extra work of moving the other wire being ,dispensed with and the signal, therefore, being much easier to keep adjusted.

An interlocking switch-stand and signal, which possesses several novel features, is one made by the Allentown Rolling

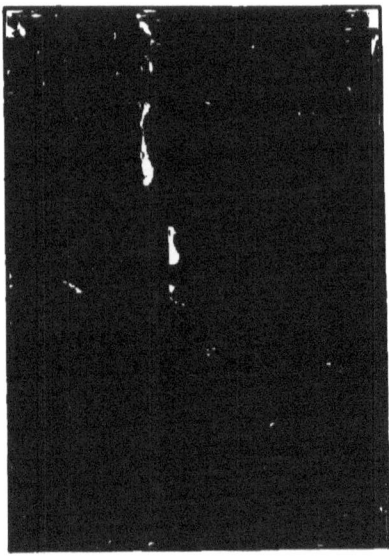

ALLENTOWN ROLLING MILL CO. INTERLOCKED SWITCH STAND.

Mill Co., and shown in Figs. 10 and 11, the signal blades—which are of the usual semaphore pattern—not being shown. As will be seen by reference to Fig. 10, which is a view of the stand, two levers are used: one to work the distant signal, and the other the home signal and the switch. Two wires are run from the operating lever to the distant signal, the lever being made in the form of a T-crank with the wires attached to the two arms, so that when one is pulled by a movement of the lever the other is slacked up. Working above the top of the T-crank, in grooves cast in the frame of the stand, is a slide to which is attached the cable used to pull the signal to danger, the blade being made of cast-iron, which considerably overbalances the weight of the spectacle arm on the opposite end. The slide when in its normal position, or raised as shown in the figure, fits in a groove cut in the head of the switch-shaft and locks it, preventing the switch from being opened until the slide is pulled down. This is done by raising the switch-lever handle, an arm

COMPENSATING ARRANGEMENT ON DISTANT SIGNAL CONNECTIONS.

projecting through the yoke and engaging with a lug on the slide, pulling it down, and with it the signal to the danger position, when the switch can be thrown.

To interlock the T-crank operating the distant with the home signal, the upper arm of the crank is made to work in a plane immediately below the slide, the latter striking on the arm so that it cannot be pulled down unless the crank has been turned to a position causing the distant signal to indicate danger. With the slide down the crank is of course locked, so that the distant signal cannot be cleared until after the slide has been raised, which occurs only when the home signal goes to the safety position after the switch has been closed.

The ingenious arrangement used at the distant signal for automatically compensating the expansion and contraction of the wire, so as to always bring the signal down to the same angle with the vertical, is shown in Fig. 11. The two lines of wire from the interlocked stand are attached to a loose lever hung on two pins fastened in the opposite arms of a T-crank, the middle arm having attached to it the pipe connection to the signal casting, this signal being of the usual construction and weighted to go to danger when any part becomes disconnected or breaks. Should a wire break, the tension of the other wire would pull the loose lever off from the T-crank and leave it free for the signal to go to danger by gravity.

To take up expansion and contraction of the wire lines, the T-crank, instead of being bolted to a rigid foundation, is fastened to one end of a crank, the other or longer arm being weighted to put a tension on the two levers, and as the weight is very much in excess of any pull required to work the signal, the crank is made to act the same as if fastened to a rigid body instead of to a movable support.

Mechanically this stand is well designed, and the arrangement for compensating the wires is a very good one; but on the whole the arrangement cannot be said to be a very reliable one, owing to the short travel of the wire and to the fact that the normal position of the home signal is at safety. From the short travel and the spring in the wires it is possible to unlock the stand without changing the distant signal to danger should the cranks or wires become in any way fastened, and from the other objection that it is certain that the signal would indicate safety if certain parts should break, or be left disconnected by a malicious or careless workman. In point of fact, there seems to be at the present day no mechanical switch-signal which does not possess some objectionable features; so that if a reliable device is desired that can be made to work with but few failures, and these only on the side of safety, recourse must be had to some form of automatic electric signal. They are expensive, it is true; but is it not better to use such a

device if by its action almost perfect protection can be secured?
In very dangerous places the matter of expense should not be

ELLIOTT'S ELECTRICALLY-LOCKED SWITCH STAND.

allowed to enter into the question, as a device that can be
relied on is worth all that it costs.

Experience has demonstrated that the automatic electric
signal can be made to work with certainty at any distance from
the switch, to show to an approaching train the position the

switch is in, and by putting a visible indicator at the switch, a warning can also be given to anyone desiring to use the switch that a train is approaching.

Taken in connection with this subject, an electrically-locked switch stand has been recently patented by the writer, by which

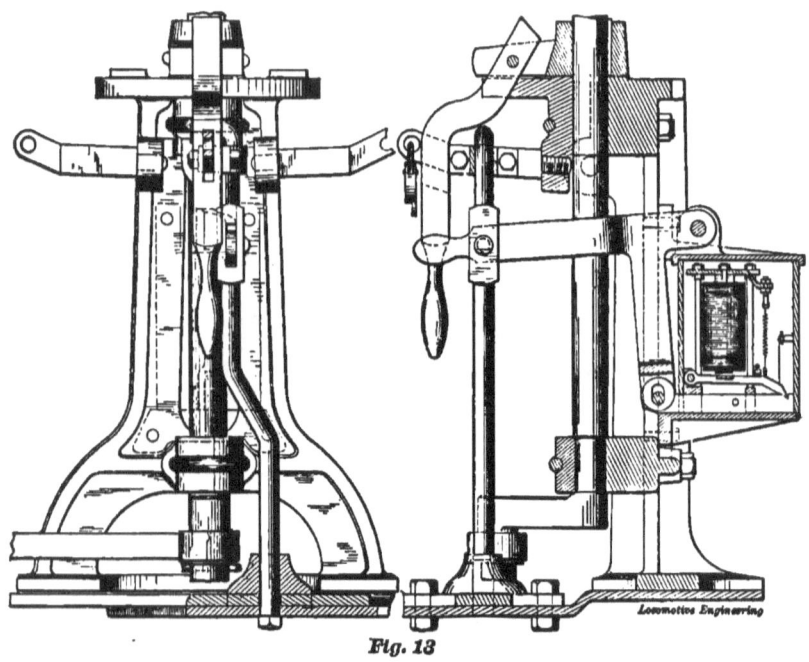

Fig. 13

DETAILS OF ELECTRICALLY-LOCKED SWITCH STAND.

control of a switch may be put in the hands of an operator at any distance away, enabling him to prevent a train from leaving a siding or branch for the main line, unless it was so desired. In this device, of which a general view is shown in Fig. 12 and the details in Fig. 13, an electro-magnet is made to lock a slide controlling a lock-rod or plunger, which passes through a lock-bar attached to the points of the switch, so that unless the magnet is energized the rod cannot be withdrawn and the switch opened. As will be seen, the armature of the magnet is made to drop into a notch cut in the slide controlling the lock-rod, the upper end of the latter being brought under the switch-lever, so that the switch cannot be shut and locked in the usual way without forcing the lock-rod through the lock-bar, and allowing the armature to drop in the notch in the slide and lock the rod until the magnet is again energized.

To work the switch, the two levers are raised together, as shown in Fig. 14, the upper lever allowing the lock-rod to be raised with it if the slide has been unlocked, withdrawing the lock-rod from the hole in the lock-bar before the switch-

UNLOCKING SWITCH.

lever has cleared the slot in the switch-stand and the spring of the switch has been brought to bear on the lock-bar. Immediately the switch-lever has been raised to a horizontal position, the lock-lever can be dropped and the switch turned in the usual manner, as shown in Fig. 15.

To enable anyone desiring to use the switch to know when it has been released, without being put to the labor of trying to raise the lock-lever, a small indicator has been provided, which works behind a thick piece of glass put in the side of the box covering the magnet, which will show when the switch has been unlocked, so that anyone finding it locked need only watch the indicator and take it easy.

A circuit-breaker, provided in the box, is made to break the current through the magnet, as soon as the slide has been part way withdrawn, so that the operator can tell exactly when the switch has been opened, and also if it has been closed after the switch has been used, a disk indicator placed in the tower being put in the circuit for this purpose. Where the switch is placed at any very great distance, bells or a telephone can be

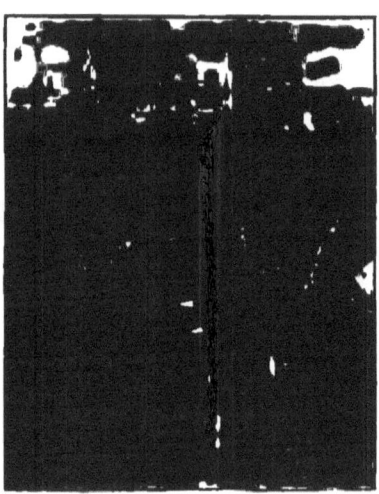

TURNING SWITCH.

put in for purposes of communication, the wires for operating the switch being used for this purpose also and the cost of additional wires saved. This switch has now been used for over a year and has given excellent results. If properly installed few or no failures will occur, and these need not cause more than a few minutes delay or the time required to unscrew and take out but one bolt.

Another device that is used in connection with the ordinary switch-stand as a protection for main-line trains, and which has of late been quite extensively introduced, is the one designed by Mr. Pennington, of the "Soo Line," and now known as the Pettibone-Mulliken Derailing Switch. This derailing switch, while in reality an interlocking device, is intended for use at all storage or passing tracks, where the conditions are such that a car might accidentally roll out on the main line and block it; so that in taking up the subject under the head of switch-signals, one is not departing very far from the spirit of the title, even if there is no signal used in connection with the device. As will be seen by reference to Fig. 16, which is a general plan of the arrangement, connections are made from an ordinary switch-stand to a derailing-switch placed in the side-track at such a distance from the main-line switch that a car being derailed would not foul the main line. To work the derail, a small T-

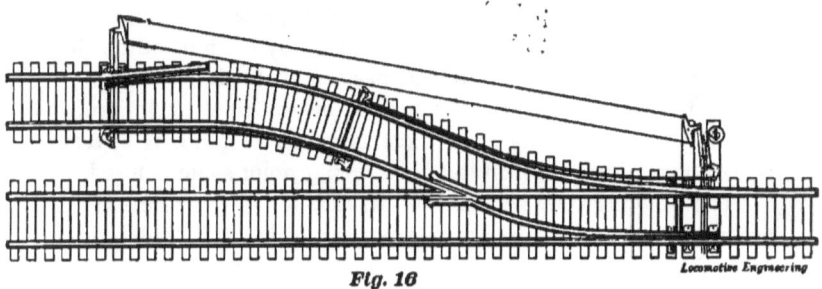

Fig. 16

Locomotive Engineering

PETTIBONE-MULLIKEN DERAILING SWITCH.

crank and connecting-rod is bolted to the ties at the switch and at the derail, the connecting-rod being attached to the end of the head-rod in each instance. The two arms of the T-crank being connected together by wire, it follows that when the switch is opened and the T-crank turned, the crank at the derail is moved a corresponding amount, the derail being moved at the same time as the switch. By arranging the connections so that when the switch is set for the main line the derail will be open, it will be seen that if the switch is kept closed, as it should be, ample protection is afforded against cars accidentally running out and blocking the main line. This device has one very great recommendation, and that is its cheapness, for the field of its usefulness is large, the need for some device of this kind being made evident on any road almost every day. Beyond its cheapness the construction used has but little to recommend it, and the wonder is, from the large chance of accident due to the lightness of its parts, that no case for which it was responsible has as yet been reported. Judging by what has been found best in all other kinds of track work the parts are all made too light, and while there would appear to be no necessity for making any part stronger than the wire, which is the weakest part, the fact that the device is generally put in and has to be cared for by section men, calls for a construction sufficiently durable to stand the treatment it will receive.

By using wire instead of a more solid connection, there are possibilities of accidents happening from any one of the following causes:

That, if the wire pulling the derail point closed should break, the point would most likely be pulled open by the tension on the other wire, especially if a train was passing at the time.

That a wire which may be broken at any time by trainmen stepping on it, a thing they most certainly will do, is a very weak connection by which to hold a facing point switch closed.

That, having only section men to care for it, the connections are apt to get out of adjustment from expansion and contraction, and in so doing allow the point to open sufficiently to be caught by a sharp flange.

Should the parts be made stronger and pipe used in place of wire, an arrangement safe enough for every purpose would be had and one that would need little or no repairs. The manner of running the pipe and making the connections is also shown in Fig. 16, the pipe being run on carriers screwed to the ties, where it will be out of the way of trainmen working around the switch. To arrange for compensation two cranks are made use of, as shown in the figure, it not being possible to put in the usual "lazy-jack" compensator, on account of the large foundation needed.

To this arrangement the only criticism that can be made is its cost, which is more than double that of the wire connection and if taken in comparison amounts to a great deal when there are many of them to be used. However, this is a matter for each one to decide, whether the additional safety secured by the use of the pipe connection is worth the increased cost. Undoubtedly, the subject is one well worth looking into by those interested.

In closing this, the last article of the series, which I hope have proved interesting to the many readers of "Locomotive Engineering," let me acknowledge my indebtedness to Mr. Geo. Gibbs for the very valuable suggestions and able criticisms made by him while these articles were being written. While some may criticise the frankness with which opinions concerning the different devices have been expressed, I will say they are such as have been formed by me for the greater part from a personal experience with the several devices mentioned, and that in thus publicly expressing my views it has been done with the hope that they may be of some benefit to others situated as I am and aid them in their work.

www.ingramcontent.com/pod-product-compliance
Lightning Source LLC
Chambersburg PA
CBHW060606030726

47498CB00005B/1564